The Wingman

THE VANCOUVER STORM SERIES

STEPHANIE ARCHER

The Wingman

Stephanie Archer

ORION

Stephanie Archer writes spicy laugh-out-loud romance. She believes in the power of best friends, stubborn women, a fresh haircut, and love. She lives in Vancouver with a man and a dog.

For spicy bonus scenes, news about upcoming books, and book recs, sign up for her newsletter at: https://www.stephaniearcherauthor.com/newsletter

Instagram: @stephaniearcherauthor
Tiktok: @stephaniearcherbooks

To check content warnings for any of Stephanie's books, visit www.stephaniearcherauthor.com/content-warnings

For Aimee Cox, who didn't waste her second chance

An Orion paperback

This edition first published in Great Britain in 2024 by Orion Fiction
an imprint of The Orion Publishing Group Ltd
Carmelite House, 50 Victoria Embankment
London EC4Y 0DZ

An Hachette UK company

The authorised representative in the EEA is Hachette Ireland, 8 Castlecourt
Centre, Dublin 15, D15 XTP3, Ireland (email: info@hbgi.ie)

5 7 9 10 8 6

A CIP catalogue record for this book is
available from the British Library.

ISBN (Mass Market Paperback) 978 1 3987 2431 0

Printed in UK Clays Ltd, Elcograf, S.p.A.

MIX
Paper | Supporting
responsible forestry
FSC® C104740

www.orionbooks.co.uk

"STOP STARING AT DARCY," Jordan says as she trades my empty glass for a new beer.

I pull my attention from three tables away, where my friend and roommate is on a date with some guy whose gaze keeps straying to her tits.

"I'm not staring."

My eyes return to Darcy's hair, pale-blond and gleaming in the low dive bar lighting. It's her first date after a broken engagement with my best friend, Kit. Her back is to me, so I can't see her expression.

"What's your read on him?" I ask Jordan. "I don't think she's laughed once."

Darcy's date is doing most of the talking.

Jordan rolls her eyes. "She's fine."

"I know she's fine."

As the late-twenties bartender and owner of the Filthy Flamingo, the dive bar we frequent after Vancouver Storm games, Jordan's had plenty of experience watching train-wreck dates.

On a date, though, Darcy should be more than fine. This

guy should be falling at her feet, doing whatever he can for her attention. Darcy Andersen's the full package. Smart, hilarious, and gorgeous, with pretty, pale-blond hair, sea-green eyes, and an adorable nose that turns up at the tip. And she's the biggest fan of the fantasy romance series *The Northern Sword*, which is how we met eight years ago—when I took the seat beside her in first-year university English, wearing a t-shirt from the book series.

She's going to get snapped up in a heartbeat.

Not that I care. It's nice having her all to myself after she's been living in Calgary with Kit for four years, is all.

Jordan arches a brow. "So why are you sitting here like her overprotective dad?"

Knots tighten in my chest, but I give her a lazy, confident grin. "What, I can't have a drink by myself?"

"You're never by yourself, party animal."

I huff a tight laugh. I knew we should have gone somewhere else.

On the Vancouver Storm hockey team, I'm the life of the party. The fun one who rallies everyone to go to the Filthy Flamingo after games. The crappy little dive bar with band posters, cheap beer, and string lights across the ceiling is where we prefer to hang out. It's rare that we're recognized here, and if the other patrons do recognize us, they'd never dare say anything in front of Jordan.

Darcy wanted to come here, though.

"I told Kit I'd look out for her after they broke up." I rub the back of my neck. After playing hockey together since we were teenagers, the guy's my closest friend, even if we do play for different NHL teams now. "And she was nervous about tonight, so I volunteered to sit a few tables away for support."

"For support."

"Yeah. In case anything happens." I sound defensive, so I

throw on another one of those cocky smiles. "I can be very intimidating."

As a defenseman, I'm a big guy. I work with some of the best athletic trainers, dieticians, and coaches in professional sports, and it shows.

"Yeah." She snorts with a flat look. "You're terrifying, alright."

I give her a charming grin, but my gaze swings back to Darcy. "Go see what they're talking about."

"Owens, leave her alone."

I put my hands up in surrender. "I promise not to interfere unless she sends me the signal."

Flick your drink coaster onto the floor, I told Darcy earlier, making her laugh, *and I'll call you with a fake emergency*.

Jordan shakes her head, but her mouth twists up with wry amusement. "You two are ridiculous."

She heads back to the bar, and my gaze slides over to Darcy again.

She tugs at her sleeve. Shifts in her seat. Glances over her shoulder.

I pause with my beer halfway to my mouth.

He says something that makes her shoulders hitch up with tension. I'm back on high alert, wishing I could read lips, when her paper coaster flies off the table and hits the floor. My mouth slides into a grin, and I press my phone to my ear as it rings.

"Hello?" she answers, sounding worried.

"Something, something excuse."

She gasps, and I grin wider at the back of her head. "Oh my god. What? Are you okay?"

"I have half a percent of battery left and chose to call you instead of 911." My chest expands, sparks cracking and popping behind my sternum. I'm smiling like a fool. "I could climb down the side of the building, but this *is* the penthouse, and I *am* naked."

"You got hit by a car?" I can hear her trying not to laugh.

"Yes. Naked. I was flexing and the driver got distracted. I caused a ten-car pileup."

"And you're in the hospital?"

"Yep, and they keep staring at all my muscles." I sigh. "It's making me feel objectified, like a piece of meat. I don't know how I'm going to get through this without you."

From three booths away, I can sense her eye roll. A shy wallflower, I am not. She covers a laugh with a quick cough.

"You poor thing. That sounds scary. I'll be right there. And Hayden?"

"Yeah, Darce?"

"Don't cry. It's going to be okay."

She hangs up, and I chuckle.

See, *that's* the kind of stuff we should be doing. Not her on some date with a guy who can't stop drooling over her tits.

———

"Naked on the patio?" Darcy drops into the booth across from me about thirty seconds after she walked by with the guy. "Really?"

My flirtatious grin widens. "There's a reason I keep a key out there."

She rolls her eyes, but she's smiling.

"Guess he's not your Prince Charming if we needed the emergency call."

"Not even close." She leans her forehead on her hands. "That was a disaster."

I shouldn't be so happy to hear this. "I'm sorry."

"He said *I'm from a big family, and we have big babies, with big heads*." She catches sight of me doubled over, laughing, and gives me a hard look, although her mouth is twitching. "Stop laughing."

"What? He's warning you ahead of time."

She groans. "He kept talking about *his* future wedding and how his mom had everything planned." Her pretty face pulls into a cringe. "And then he wanted to kiss me outside."

My smile drops. "Did you?"

She's Kit's ex. She's off-limits, and she's her own person who can make her own decisions, but I think about some guy's hands all over her, and I want to break something.

"Of course not." Her expression turns horrified. "I lied and said I had a cold sore, and that it was a form of herpes, so we shouldn't."

Relieved, I laugh into my drink. "I'll have to remember that one."

"Like you'd ever need it, with the parade of supermodels you date."

I make a face. "Three. Not a parade."

She makes an unhappy noise. Her eyes linger on the floor, mouth turned down at the corners.

"What's wrong?"

She shakes her head, blinking. "Nothing."

"Darce," I drawl.

Her eyes meet mine, and she pulls that plush bottom lip between her teeth. "I thought going on a date would be fun, but it was horrible. He wanted all the things I don't want."

My fucking heart. I can't stand seeing her like this. "What's the rush, you know? It's only been a month."

"The rush is that I wasted—" She cuts herself off, eyes turning wary.

"Wasted what?" Time? Wasted time? They were together for eight years.

"Nothing." She shakes her head. "I'm making a fresh start here in Vancouver. New city, new team at work, new apartment as soon as I find one."

"New apartment?" I send her a *what gives?* expression. "You're living with me."

"No, I'm *crashing* with you. I can't stay there."

"Sure, you can."

She gives me a flat look. "Hayden. I can't afford that place."

"We didn't say a word about rent." And I'm not accepting a dime from her. She has a good job, but with how much I have and how fun it is finally living together, I feel like she's doing me the favor.

She drops her head back in exasperation. "Do not start."

"I'm just saying; I make millions of dollars per year." I flash her a cocky grin. "I don't need your sad little actuary money."

She shakes her head, but she's laughing. "God, your ego. Maybe you do need me around to keep it in check."

"I'd love that."

"Anyway." She waves me off. "On top of all that, new relationship status. Single." She falters on the last word, rubbing a hand over her stomach like she's nervous.

Her and Kit's breakup is none of my business, but when she called to tell me the news, she was still so fucking upset, and I just—

I couldn't do nothing. It's Darcy. She's my friend, too. Cheering her up, distracting her, is my job.

"You don't have to jump back into dating." I grip my glass harder. She should just hang out with me instead. "Just have fun."

"Yes." Her eyes light up, and she gestures at me. "Fun. Exactly. I've sat on the couch moping about the breakup for a month, and"— she swallows—"I was ready to break up with him a long time ago."

I force myself not to react. "I didn't know that."

I don't even know the full extent of why they broke up. She hasn't wanted to talk about it, so I haven't pushed it. When she's ready, she'll tell me.

I'm curious as hell, though. Did he do something? They always seemed so happy together.

"The guy tonight was ready to introduce me to his extended family," she continues. "He wanted swans at the wedding, Hayden." She stares at me, and I shake with laughter. "Swans *and* horses. He had everything planned out. He just wanted to slot someone in there." She makes a grossed-out expression. "I just want a fun distraction. Where are those guys?"

I wink at her. "Right here, babe."

She snorts. "My god. You're like their leader. Bring me to them."

I should be used to it, but the label stings, especially coming from her.

I never meant to get this reputation. I've just never met a woman I'm interested in something long term with. If I detect any interest in commitment, I don't ask her out. I don't lead anyone on, and I don't feed them lines, but I always make sure everyone has a good time.

I'm a pretty face, a nice set of abs, and a really, really good fuck, and I don't pretend to be anything more.

"Wait." Her eyes narrow. "You date, but you never get attached."

Over the rim of my glass, I give her a quizzical look. "Okay?"

"You *always* have fun. You're amazing at the whole dating thing and have had years of practice. You've probably been on hundreds of dates."

"Where are you going with this?" Wherever it is, I don't like it.

Her lips tip up, and her eyes glow with interest. "I want to be like you."

"Devastatingly handsome?"

She grins wider. "No, a player. Hayden, I want you to teach me to be a player."

HAYDEN'S GRIN dissolves like it's the last thing he expected me to say.

"You can be my wingman."

I don't know why I didn't see it before. Hayden Owens—otherworldly handsome, rich hockey star, life of the party, all-around incredibly lovable person, and the biggest player I know. Every week, he's going out with a new girl.

Hayden has the life I want—pure fun and no commitment—and he's always in control. No one steamrolls him. No one makes the decisions for him.

After Kit, I am so *sick* of being an accessory to some guy's life.

I smile wider at Hayden, and he looks scared.

"In all the years we were together, Kit and I never went on a real date. We went to a party, and then we were together. The hockey party." It was the Friday during the first week of university, the first week Hayden and I met in English class.

He blinks, frowns, looks away. "Yeah, um. I remember."

"Right. You were there."

After chatting all week before class, I thought Hayden was

going to ask me out... Now is not the time to think about that, so I swat the thought away.

He's miles out of my league. He dates supermodels, actresses, and influencers, and every single one of them is tall, with dark hair and huge boobs. Nothing like me, with my short stature, pale hair and eyes, and complete lack of curves.

Not that I care. We're friends.

"I've never flirted with a guy," I continue. "I've never asked a guy out. I've never even gone out for Valentine's Day or gotten flowers."

I'm trying to get over it, to move on and not think about Kit, but the farther I get from the breakup, the angrier I become. After trying to break up with him in December, Kit asked that we wait until after the holidays. He had important games to focus on, he said.

On New Year's Eve, though, in front of all his Calgary teammates and Hayden's Vancouver teammates, Kit proposed.

Who *does* that?

I froze. I didn't want to embarrass him, so I said yes, and the next morning, I broke it off for real.

Concern flickers in Hayden's gaze. "He never took you out on a real date?"

I tap my tongue on my upper lip, holding back the truth. They're best friends, and I don't want to make Hayden feel like he has to choose between us, so I'm glossing over the details of the breakup.

Across the table, he watches me carefully.

"I mean—we were in school, so we were broke and busy with studying and hockey. If we got dressed up, it was for hockey events."

His pretty blue eyes linger on me, and his jaw flexes. "Why didn't you say anything?"

"It doesn't matter now." I wave him off.

I don't want to linger on the past. I'm twenty-six years old—it's time for me to make up for lost time and have all those fun dating experiences I missed out on.

His mouth slides into a lazy, flirty smile. "You want flowers, Darcy? I'll buy you flowers."

I huff a laugh. I can always count on Hayden to lighten the mood. "You know what I mean. I want to get all dressed up, go to a nice restaurant, be told I look pretty, and then go home and have sex against a wall."

He chokes on his beer, coughing.

"Or, like, in the shower." I shrug with a baffled expression. "I don't know. Wherever people have super passionate hookups. And then I never want to see that guy again."

He's still coughing, and his cheekbones are going pink.

"Are you okay?"

"Yep," he croaks, not looking at me.

"You said it yourself. I need to have fun."

"Fun with *me*. Going out after games and watching *The Northern Sword*." Our favorite book series is now a TV show. His smile dims a notch. "Not with some guy who talks over you and looks like he's trying to guess your bra size."

A thrill shoots through me at the edge to his voice. It's so unusual for him. He's just protective because we're friends, though. "He was staring at my hips to see how big of a baby I could push out."

Hayden grits his teeth and takes another long sip of beer.

"You always know what to do or say. You've slept with hundreds of women."

He groans. "Not hundreds."

"A lot. If we gathered them together, they probably couldn't fit in this bar—"

"Okay." His expression turns flat. "I get it."

"I'm not sex shaming you. I want to *be* like you. How do

you get better at something? Do what the pros are doing. Learn from the best. I don't even know where to start. I don't know how to approach a guy."

He watches me for a long moment, running his hand through his messy golden-blond hair. He looks like he's about to say no, but a guy walks past our table, and Hayden's gaze hardens before his eyes meet mine.

"Alright."

"Really?"

"On one condition." He leans toward me, eyes sparking. "Move in with me permanently. There's no point in you finding your own place when I have the spare room. Besides, I don't like living alone."

This again? Hayden lives in the penthouse, and his apartment is gorgeous. Two-story windows overlooking the city, a massive kitchen and living room, a sprawling patio with a hot tub and garden. Even the guest bedroom is nicer than any hotel room I've ever stayed in.

When I called him last week from Calgary to break the news about Kit and me, he insisted I come out to Vancouver. He didn't even hesitate. He must have heard something in my voice—something frustrated, disappointed, and broken—and he convinced me that a new city was exactly what I needed.

Without him, I'd be back in Calgary, probably wallowing, not having fun at a bar.

"You've already done so much for me." I give him a half smile. "I don't want to take advantage."

After four years away, Hayden's the only friend I have left in Vancouver. Most of my Calgary friends were actually *Kit*'s friends, and I've lost touch with a lot of people from university.

Hayden's kind of all I have right now. I can't mess that up.

"Vancouver's a nightmare for rentals," he says, and I sense he's trying to keep his tone casual. "You don't want to end up living with some weirdo who sneaks into your room and sniffs your panties."

A horrified laugh bubbles out of me. "Gross."

"And if you find me in your room," he adds with a cheeky smile, "I'm just making sure they fit."

"Ew." I sputter with laughter. "Don't try on my panties. You'll stretch them out."

"Yeah, I will." His eyebrows bob and he sends a pointed look down at his crotch. "In the front."

My face is going warm, but I can feel the remnants of disappointment from my date fading away.

"Your stuff's already at my place." He shrugs his broad, toned shoulders. "And I love your parents, but I know you don't want to live with them." They live in a quiet suburb an hour from Vancouver. "You'll have to drive back and forth every home game, and then it'll be late, and you'll just end up crashing at my place."

He gives me a *whatcha gonna do?* look, like it's settled.

I hide a smile. "You're so confident I'll be going to all your games."

"You will."

My stomach flips over at the cocky way he says it and at his knowing, confident smile.

Hayden always gets what he wants in life. He's the perfect wingman, the perfect guy to teach me how to date.

"What about when you have dates over?" I toy with the paper coaster on the table. "Having a female roommate is going to cramp your style."

This past week, he hasn't gone out on a date or had anyone over. It's probably a record for him.

He clears his throat, looking away. "Don't worry about that. It's the deal I'm offering, Darce. Take it or leave it."

Not much choice, is there? Besides, living with Hayden over the last week has been easy and fun.

"Deal."

His big hand surrounds mine as we shake, and a zing of electricity runs through my blood at the contact of his warm palm against mine. Our eyes meet, and my breath catches.

Whatever charisma Hayden has, I want some of it.

"This is going to be so much fun," I tell him. "And I'm a fast learner."

He wears a tight smile that doesn't reach his eyes. "Can't wait."

HAYDEN AND A PLAYER from the opposing team slam into the boards in front of us, and the glass rattles. His gaze lifts to mine in the front row, and he shoots me a boyish, playful grin.

I grin back, shaking my head as he skates off after the puck, a little thrill in my chest.

It shouldn't be so hot, watching my friend play hockey, especially since I'm freshly single.

It is, though. There's something about Hayden playing this brutal contact sport that has me captivated.

Around us in the arena, the fans cheer and holler, yelling at the refs for missing calls. It's a sea of Storm jerseys from over the decades, and I feel a little out of place in just my winter coat.

"We're so glad you joined us," Pippa Hartley says with a shy but friendly smile, leaning past her sister, Hazel, to look at me. Both are clad in their own Storm jerseys. I met them last year through Hayden. "It's so much more fun sitting down here than up in the box."

The whistle blows and play stops. Jamie Streicher, the surly, serious Storm goalie, turns at the net in front of us to grab a drink of water. His eyes go straight to Pippa, his fiancée, and even through the goalie mask, the way his expression softens is obvious.

Every time I see them together, he can't take his eyes—or hands, if she's close enough—off her. Hayden said they went to high school together and reconnected when she was hired as his assistant last season. She's a singer-songwriter now and released her first album last year. Celebrities are supposed to have huge egos and be rude and demanding, but it seems like fame hasn't changed Pippa one bit.

"Yeah, you know that's your seat now, right?" Hazel smiles with raised eyebrows. "You sit with us now, down here where the action is."

I bite back on my grin. "If you insist."

"We do. You're ours now." Hazel turns back to the game, gaze going to her fiancé, Rory Miller, the cocky, teasing team captain. He also went to high school with her, Jamie, and Pippa, although Hazel seemed to hate his guts until they started dating at the beginning of this season.

This winter, Hayden whispered to me that he suspected they were just pretending to date to make her awful ex jealous, but there's nothing fake about the way she looks at him or the sparkling diamond ring on her finger.

Besides working as a physiotherapist for the team, Hazel teaches yoga and recently opened her own body-positive inclusive fitness studio here in Vancouver. She's gone down to physio work one day a week for the team while she gets the studio off the ground.

"Are you doing okay?" She studies me openly. I have a feeling that I could tell her anything right now and she wouldn't judge. "With the breakup and all?"

"Hazel," Pippa says patiently. "She might not want to talk about it."

Hazel shrugs. "It's fine if you don't. But I'd be a bad friend if I didn't ask and offer my support. Fuck that guy, by the way."

I laugh silently. "No, Kit's not a bad guy."

"I don't care. Most hockey players are trash, except for Streicher and Rory." Her mouth tips up. "Hayden's pretty great, too. He made sure Rory got home that night he drank too much and got a tattoo. It seems like he always takes care of his friends." She slides a sidelong glance at me.

"He does." I swallow. "Hayden's the best."

"So," Hazel says quietly, "like I asked, are you okay?"

"I think so?" A light, uncertain laugh slips out of me. "I have no idea. I feel like I'm holding it together, given the circumstances."

"I do, too." Her mouth tugs up into a wry smile. "I think you're doing great."

"Enough about me. How's the studio?"

"It's a ton of work, but," she beams, eyes sparkling, "it's pretty great. It doesn't feel like work when I'm there, you know?"

She tells me about creating the class schedule, hiring teachers and front-desk staff, and the interest she's already gotten from locals.

"It feels almost too good to be true, that I get to do it every day. That it's my *job* now," she says. "I'd do it for free."

Her words cause a tug in my chest, a sense that Hazel has something I want. It's not jealousy—I want her to have her dream job. It's envy, because women like Hazel and Pippa go for their dreams.

I wish I could be more like them, but I've been burned before. My actuarial job may be boring, but it's safe. No one gets hurt.

"And whenever I doubt myself," she adds, glancing over at

Rory, who's lining up for a face-off, "Miller is right behind me, telling me I can do anything."

The ring on Hazel's left hand catches the light, sparkling and glinting. My mind flicks to the ring I handed back to Kit a month ago, and an ache throbs through my chest. When I glance up at Hazel, though, she's staring at her hand with a dreamy expression.

"Your ring is beautiful." A pale-blue stone with shades of gray, surrounded by tiny, delicate diamonds on a rose-gold band.

"Thank you." Her mouth curves into a smile. "I'm surprised at how much I love it. I never put much stock into jewelry or engagement rings, but..." She bites her lip. "It has meaning. Rory could give me a ring pop and I'd probably love it."

There's a funny feeling in my chest—a whisper of something I've never had. A complete and utter infatuation with someone.

"Pippa, you're on break from your tour for a bit?" I ask.

She nods, tucking a lock of honey-blond hair behind her ear. "Until the wedding in April. I'm writing another album until then, between wedding planning and taking Daisy out on lots of forest walks." She shoots me a hesitant expression. "Is it safe to assume Kit isn't coming to the wedding?"

"Does that screw things up? I can find a date if you need the numbers to even out or whatever."

"No, I figured you'd go with Hayden."

"What?" My eyes go wide. *Like a date?* "Why? Did he say that?"

"No," she says slowly, glancing at Hazel. "But you're roommates now, right? Isn't that what he said?"

The air whooshes out of my lungs. "Yes. Roommates.

Right. That makes sense. And we're friends. He's probably already bringing a date."

Someone tall, with long dark hair and huge boobs, like the women he always dates.

Pippa and Hazel glance at each other. "He isn't," Pippa says.

"Oh. That's good." My eyes go wide. "I mean, not *good*. I just mean I'm relieved. No!" I shake my head. "This is coming out all wrong. I like hanging out with Hayden, and that's it."

And the thought of having to watch his date laugh at his jokes and touch him all night makes me feel weird.

They exchange a weighted look.

"What?" My eyes dart between them. I'm being so weird. They probably regret asking me to hang out with them.

Hazel sucks in a breath. "We suspect—"

"Nothing," Pippa interrupts her. "We suspect nothing. It's great. Living together seems like a good thing."

"It is..." Eyes narrowed, I bite my lip.

Hazel raises an eyebrow. "Say it."

"He won't let me pay rent."

Pippa presses her lips into a line, trying not to smile, and Hazel grins openly.

"Really?" Hazel asks like it's the best thing she's ever heard. "He won't let you pay rent? Interesting. Because he's such a good friend?"

Pippa elbows her. "Stop it."

I blow out a long breath, thinking about how I cornered him in the kitchen this morning. "He's so frustrating. Every time I bring it up, he changes the subject, and when I pressed him on it, he said not to worry about it. That he's not exactly hurting for money."

The e-transfers keep timing out when he conveniently

forgets to accept them or pretends to lose the notifications in his email.

Hazel laughs. "These guys are so fucking cocky."

"I don't want to take advantage of him."

"You're not." She rolls her eyes. "He loves having you there. And I'm sure you can find ways to make it up to him that have nothing to do with money."

My eyebrows shoot up as heat races through me. "Uh..."

"That sounded more suggestive than I meant. I just mean, these guys can buy anything, so give him what money can't buy." She shrugs. "Just be his friend. Watch his games and cheer for him. Drag him to my yoga classes so I can kick his ass. Watch that weird fantasy show with him."

"*The Northern Sword*? Uh, it's not weird. It's only the best fantasy romance series I've ever read."

Hazel wrinkles her nose. "Not you, too."

"It's so good. You can borrow my copies, but you have to give them back."

Hazel rolls her eyes, but she's smiling. "He said the same thing to me. You and Hayden are a match made in heaven."

Warmth bubbles in my stomach at her words, and I can't help but smile. My gaze goes to him on the ice—fast, strong, and determined—and a thrill shoots through me.

Nothing would ever happen with Hayden, I know that. Kit was kind of soft-spoken, a little passive, and more on my level, but Hayden? He's larger than life, both in looks and personality. He could have anyone.

And tonight? I'm going to start learning his ways.

WITH TWENTY SECONDS left in the third period, we're tied with Chicago.

Blood rushes in my ears as Volkov and I chase the other team's forwards down the ice. As defensemen, we have one job: keep the puck away from our goalie.

My gaze back cuts to Darcy, where she's sitting with Hazel and Pippa behind the net, and a rush of determination hits me.

Miller rears back for a slapshot, and as the puck sails toward the net, I hold my breath. There's that feeling in my chest again, the one I haven't been able to shake lately. Like something isn't quite right.

The puck hurtles past the goalie, and the crowd explodes, roaring with noise.

"That was a beautiful play, boys," Miller crows, wrapping me in a bulky, back-slapping hug as the goal horn bellows and lights flash around us.

I grin, laughing as Miller jostles me, but it feels forced, and then I feel like a fucking asshole for it. My team scored; I should be over the moon. We do one last face-off that lasts three seconds, the game ends, and we shuffle off the ice.

Darcy catches my eye, giving me a shy grin and wave. Pride

expands through me and I wink at her through the glass. It's nice having her here at games, watching me play and chatting with Hazel and Pippa.

The other night replays in my head, when she asked me to be her wingman. I've been trying not to think about it, hoping she'd forget about her request.

"Owens," Coach Ward calls as we skate off the ice. "No postgame press for you. Meet me in my office."

A weight thunks in my gut. If the coach wants to see you after a game? It's not good.

———

"I'm putting you on offense," Ward says, leaning back in his desk chair to regard me in that calm, quiet way of his.

I stare at him, wondering if I heard right.

Tate Ward is in his late thirties, young for an NHL coach and probably too good-looking, too, if you read the comments on Storm social media posts. A decade ago, the guy was a player for Vancouver, breaking records left and right, but after a knee injury ended his career, he went into coaching.

After a season and a half with the Vancouver Storm, he's becoming known for taking big swings based on his instincts. With only two and a half months left in the season and a decent shot at playoffs, though, moving a player to a new position is the biggest swing he's taken so far.

I stare at Ward for a long moment. "Until Kerrington's back?"

One of our forwards, Kerrington, was injured in a game a couple of weeks ago.

A subtle shake of his head. "Permanently. Kerrington's out for the rest of the season. I'm letting the team know at practice tomorrow."

I blow a long breath out. No one likes to hear that their friend and teammate is done.

That doesn't explain why I'm here, though. Even with Kerrington out, Ward has thirteen forwards to choose from, and I'm one of the best defensemen in the league. My brows knit together.

I'm the support guy. I'm the guy who plays well with others and thrives with Volkov, the grumpiest asshole on the team. I'm the backup muscle, not the star.

"I've only ever played defense," I tell Ward.

His smile hooks higher. "Now, that just isn't true, Owens."

I think back to a month ago. The exhibition game we played against Calgary at an outdoor rink in Whistler. Miller suggested I play a shift as a forward as a last resort.

"The League Classic."

He nods once. "Yep."

"That wasn't a real game." It didn't count toward our regular season. "It was just for fun."

His eyes narrow as he studies me in silence, and discomfort twists in my chest.

"I'm not the star."

Ward makes a thoughtful face. "What if you are?"

I fold my arms over my chest, trying to summon my affable, good-natured grin, but I can't find it.

"It's your choice," he adds, still watching me, "but I think it's the right move, and I'd like you to consider it."

Playoffs are in three months, at the end of April, and we have a decent shot. Ward's always pushing us to play our role, focus on our positions to serve the team. Defense is the position I know and thrive in.

Am I thriving, though? Or am I just making it work? The game replays in my head, and the weird feeling in my chest when Miller scored resurfaces. Something's changed, and I can't put my finger on it, but I have an ugly suspicion that it's only going to get worse.

Across from me, Ward waits with his usual knowing patience. When he became coach, the Vancouver Storm changed for the better. Unlike the previous coach, he doesn't have an ego, and he works one-on-one with every player on the team, from first-line stars to fourth-line rookies. He knows every member of the Storm organization by name, even the people he doesn't interact with, like cleaning staff, accountants, and Zamboni drivers. For fuck's sake, he knows the people working the concession.

One team, he always says. I admire that about the guy, that he treats everyone with respect, makes everyone feel included and valued.

I rake my hand back through my hair. The trade deadline is in March, and I'm not interested in leaving. Volkov, Miller, Streicher, Hazel, Pippa—these people are my family. Darcy's here in Vancouver now, too, and the thought of having to move away from her again sends a streak of resolve through me.

I don't want to give Ward any reason to trade me, and even more, I want to make him proud.

"Okay." My chest is tight as I give him a firm nod. "I'm in."

"I was hoping you'd say that." A pleased smile breaks out across his features. "You start training with the other forwards tomorrow morning."

CHAPTER 5
DARCY

"YOU SURE YOU'RE NOT TIRED?" Hayden asks when we slide into a booth at the Filthy Flamingo after the game. The narrow, dingy dive bar in Gastown has band posters framed all over the wood-paneled walls and twinkling lights strung across the ceiling. "We don't have to stay long."

I've been here a few times when visiting Hayden, and it's my favorite bar in Vancouver. With its hidden entrance in a dark, quiet alley, it's the secret hangout of the Vancouver Storm, especially after games. Jordan, the pretty, surly bartender with long dark hair, slings drinks behind the counter, and behind her, Polaroids of the regulars, including the team, are tacked up.

I give him a shocked look. "No way. I want to go out."

Kit always wanted to go right home after games. I would have to drag him out with his team, or with Hayden when we were in town. The rage in my blood continues to simmer.

Hayden grins. "Good girl."

I scrunch my face at him and he chuckles. Hazel, Rory, Jamie, Pippa, and Hayden's defensive partner, Alexei, are all here, as well as other players and partners. Everyone's spirits are up after the win, and the bar is lively with laughter and conversation.

Jordan drops our drinks off, and Hayden and I clink our glasses together.

"Cheers." He makes pointed eye contact with me.

I stare back, widening my eyes. "Cheers."

"What are you doing?" Hazel asks, glancing between us with an amused smile.

"You have to make eye contact when you toast," Hayden explains, like it's obvious.

I nod. "Or you have seven years of bad sex."

Hayden adopts a stricken expression. "We can't take the risk."

Hazel laughs.

I especially can't risk it, with how dull my sex life has been in recent years.

Beside me, Hayden rests his arm on the top of the booth, accidentally brushing my shoulder, and tingles run down my spine. "There's something very important that we need to talk about, Darce."

"What?" My eyes widen.

His expression is so serious. "Your birthday."

A laugh slips out of me. "Oh. That."

"Yeah. That." His eyes spark with interest. "What are we doing?"

My birthday isn't until April, months away. "Nothing. Playoffs start around then; I don't want to do a big thing when you'll need to focus."

"We might not make playoffs."

I roll my eyes, thinking about his speed and agility on the ice earlier tonight. "With the way you play? You will."

His grin hitches a little higher. "Don't try to distract me.

We need to have a party. It's the first year since school that we'll spend it together."

I make a noncommittal noise. Back in university, my birthday coincided with the end of exams, and we'd have big raging parties and invite everyone we knew. Since we graduated, though, my birthdays have become a much quieter occasion. At the idea of turning a year older, my stomach knots with dread.

Right. This feeling. This is why I don't have big parties anymore. I hate turning a year older when my life feels so stagnant and misaligned. Like I'm on the wrong train track, going in the wrong direction.

Things are changing, though. Hayden's going to teach me how to be a player, and I'm going to have all those fun dating experiences I missed out on.

"What did Ward want to talk about after the game?" I ask, changing the subject.

He hesitates. "He's putting me on offense."

The guys look over at this, interested.

"Really." Rory watches Hayden with curiosity, his mouth tipping up by the second. "Interesting."

Hayden shrugs and glances at Alexei. "Yeah. He's letting the team know tomorrow."

Alexei makes a low noise of acknowledgment, folding his arms over his chest and frowning at the table. The media has speculated about his impending retirement for years. He's still a strong player, but the sport is brutal on these guys' bodies. He took a hard hit tonight, and just walking to the bar, he favored his left side.

"I think it's a smart move." Rory's usual roguish, playful grin is replaced with something thoughtful and supportive. The captain, I realize. Rory Miller pretends to be cocky and showy, but he loves his team and he wants the best for his players.

"He brought up the League Classic," Hayden adds.

"That's exactly what I was thinking of." Rory nods, leaning in. "It worked, Owens, and I think Ward noticed, too."

Hayden just shrugs, and I take a moment to picture him in the new position.

He's easy-going, friendly, and relaxed. He wants everyone to feel included; he's always been like that, even back in university when he'd invite everyone on our floor to parties, even the weird kid who never came out of his room. It's what I love about him, that he's so open-hearted and loving. He never pushes his way to the front like some guys. Maybe that's why he's done so well in defense.

Sometimes I wonder, though, if he thinks he doesn't deserve to be the star, and what it would be like if he pushed his way to the front. Defensemen protect the goalie, but forwards score goals and get the glory. I picture Hayden on the ice, going after what he wants with predatory focus. My mind switches the scenario, and he's pursuing a woman, his gaze steady on her with that handsome, confident grin of his, caging her in with his body and making her heart beat faster.

Making it clear he wants her.

A shiver rolls through me, landing between my legs, and I clear my throat.

"You okay?" Hayden smiles and arches a curious brow. The others have returned to their conversation, not paying attention to us.

"Fine." My voice sounds high and weird, so I clear my throat again. "I can see it, you playing offense."

He gives me a strange look. "Really?"

"Mhm."

Hayden's a big guy like the other defensemen, but there's something about the way he plays—fluid and easy, like he's filling in the gaps on the ice—that makes me think he's holding back. Like he's playing for others but not himself.

My thoughts go to the analytical models I have saved on my laptop at home. A couple of years ago, I found a hockey analytics conference on YouTube. I watched video after video of people discussing how they use data and statistical analysis to find patterns and predict outcomes. This data helped the teams play better, recover from injuries faster, and score more goals.

I built my own models, just to see if I could. Unlike my boring day job, it was everything I loved about math in university: how it helps the world make sense, how you can practically predict the future by understanding the past.

I haven't opened them in forever, but maybe I could use them to help Hayden.

I wave the thought away fast.

The Vancouver Storm have a whole coaching and training staff to help the players be their best. They don't need some woman who likes to plug numbers into a program as a hobby getting involved.

There are consequences that come along with being wrong with this stuff. Shame aches behind my sternum. My mistakes can affect other people.

"Darcy?" Hayden studies my face with concern. "What are you thinking about?"

"Nothing." I force a laugh, shoving away the memories from my first job out of school, the memories I thought I'd buried so well. I pull out my phone. "I've been reading about being a player."

He gives me a wry smile, eyes twinkling under the bar lights. "Research? You did research?"

"Of course." I give him a *duh* look. "Do you even know me?"

He shakes his head, still smiling. "Okay, Andersen, what did you find?"

I pull up the bookmarked site. "How to Be a Player 101."

CHAPTER 6

"NO." Hayden laughs, peering over my shoulder at my phone screen. "This isn't real."

"It is. Just wait." His fresh-out-of-the-shower scent washes over me, clean and sharp, and my stomach dips. "Rule number one: A player is always confident and chill." I give a pointed look to Hayden beside me—stretched out with his toned arm across the top of the booth—and match his body language. He moves his arm away to give me space. I'm shorter than him, so I have to stretch to reach the top of the booth. It looks neither confident nor chill, but it makes Hayden laugh.

I tip my chin, give him a sleazy smile, and wink. "Hey, baby, how you doin'?"

He snorts. "You're a natural."

"Thank you." I chuckle and turn back to my list. "Rule number two: Have a player-worthy pad. Leather couches and a big-screen TV will make women feel at home." My expression turns dubious. "I don't know if that's true, but your apartment is nice."

He wasn't lying during his emergency phone call—he does live in the penthouse of his building in the Gastown neighborhood. It's a loft-style apartment with brick accents, two-story windows with a view of the North Shore, a sprawling kitchen, and a huge patio with a hot tub, covered seating area, and tons of greenery. It's perfect for entertaining and hosting parties, and I'm sure it would impress any guy I go out with.

I picture bringing guys there after dates, though, and get a weird twinge in my stomach. Hayden's my friend, and I dated Kit in front of him for years, so it shouldn't matter, but putting the moves on a guy while Hayden's in his bedroom, or worse, *watching*? That gives me the *no* feeling.

"*Our* apartment," he says.

I give him a curious look. "Hmm?"

"You said 'your apartment,' but you live there now, too." His mouth tips up. "That was the deal. You promised."

Warmth settles in the middle of my chest. "You own it, though. And I don't pay rent."

He shrugs me off. "Details."

"Hayden."

He meets my eyes, and the corner of his mouth slides up in a boyish grin. "Darcy." I open my mouth to protest, but he cuts me off. "I like having you as a roommate. You like living there, right?"

"Of course." He's a hell of a lot tidier than Kit, and he does all his own laundry. I use the main bathroom, and he has his own attached to his bedroom, so we're not fighting over the shower. I like coming home after work to see him when he's in town and not playing a game. "It feels like we're back in university, living in dorms."

"Good." He leans in and lowers his voice. "So stop arguing."

I laugh, and my heart squeezes with affection for this guy. No matter how famous he gets, regardless of how much money he makes or his status as one of the best players in the league, he's kind.

"Any changes you want to make to the place," he adds, "I'm fine with."

"*Any* changes?" I narrow my eyes, trying not to smile and give away the surprise I have waiting for him when we get home. "So if I wanted to hang a giant disco ball in the middle of the living room and paint the floors neon orange, you'd be cool with that?"

He grins. "Sounds fun."

"You're just the most agreeable guy in the world, aren't you? Or maybe you just really want me to get laid."

Mid-sip of his drink, he coughs. Once he recovers, he nods at my phone. "What's number three?"

"Rule number three," I read. "Look like a player, not a square. Show those ladies you're here for a good time, not a long time. You don't want anyone thinking you're husband material, so your hairstyle, clothing, and car should reflect your true player nature. Peacocking will give your game a boost of rocket fuel, lubricating conversation." I grimace. "Gross." My expression changes as the words sink in, and I look down at my wool sweater. A sweater identical to the one I wore the other night but in a different color.

This sweater is warm and durable. It looks nice with jeans, but I can also pair it with low heels and wear it to the office. The price was reasonable. For an item of clothing, it's as responsible as it gets, and yet I don't *love* it. It's fine. I don't get excited about wearing it, and I don't think it looks that good on me.

In university, I used to wear a *The Northern Sword* t-shirt all the time. That's how Hayden and I met—he recognized it, and we started talking before class.

Why don't I wear stuff like that anymore?

Isn't it a little, uh, loud? Kit asked once when I brought home a new bright orange dress. Something about the vibrant tangerine color had made me so happy. *You really want to stick out like that?*

I make a face at Hayden. "I look like marriage material."

"Come on," Hayden says, giving me a look of disbelief.

"It's true." I gesture at myself. "I look responsible, like I always do my taxes on time and get oil changes when I'm supposed to and take a vitamin D supplement."

He arches an eyebrow, eyes twinkling. "You do all those things."

"Exactly." I flap my hand at him and he laughs. "Don't you see? I need to dress and look like someone you *don't* bring home to mom. That's what rule number three is trying to say. *You're here for a good time, not a long time.*"

"Wait." Rory leans forward with a curious grin. "What are you reading?"

"It's a list on how to be a player." I hold up my phone. "I found it on the internet." Everyone pauses their conversation to listen in, confused. "Hayden's my new wingman."

There's a long beat of silence at the table before Hazel's lips part in surprise, eyes lit up with interest. "Really?"

My cheeks feel warm, but I force myself to sit up straighter. "Yep. I just got out of an eight-year relationship and I'm not going to waste another second."

Hazel and Pippa exchange another one of those weighted glances. Rory looks at Hayden, and there's something in *his* eyes that I can't read either. Jamie just stares at Pippa like she's a snack he wants to eat.

"What?" I look from one face to another, worry rising in my throat. "You think it's dumb. You think it's a bad idea."

"No!" Pippa perks up. "You just got out of a long relationship and you deserve to have fun. And Hayden's the perfect person for this."

Hazel wiggles her eyebrows at Hayden. "Exactly. You two get along *very* well."

Hayden looks away before he gestures at my list. "You don't need to change your appearance, Darce."

"I know I don't *need* to, but what if I want to?" Something urgent flows through me. "I'm making a fresh start. Why am I dressing like the version of myself I left back in Calgary?" I look down at myself. "I should buy new clothes."

"What's wrong with your clothes?" Pippa asks, looking heartbroken. "I love that sweater."

"I wore this sweater on a date, and the guy practically introduced me to his mother on the spot," I tell her and Hazel, making them grin. "It's responsible. I don't want to look responsible, I want to look hot. I want to look like someone you have fun with, not someone you spend forever with. And I want to wear clothes I love, not clothes I feel neutral about."

Hazel gives me an appraising nod. "I can get on board with this, but don't look at me for fashion advice." She gestures at her yoga leggings. "Everything I wear is made of Lycra. Easy to move in."

Rory's eyes flicker with interest. "I'm not complaining."

"Don't be gross," she says to him, but she's smiling, and my heart does a funny thump.

"You know who would be good to go shopping with?" Pippa says to her sister. "Georgia."

Hazel's eyes go wide with enthusiasm. "*Yes.*"

At the end of the table, Alexei makes a noise of disgust. "If you want Darcy to drain her savings, maybe. The doctor's a bad influence."

"Excuse me." Hazel gives him a hard look. "Just because *you* don't get along with her doesn't mean she's a bad influence. What is this, second grade?"

"She's one of the team doctors, and you'll love her," Pippa confides to me. "She wears the best shoes."

Happy, light feelings bubble through me, and I bite back a grin so I don't seem too eager. "I'm in. Just say when."

"Great." Pippa smiles. "I'll arrange something."

Hayden's looking down at me with a wary expression, so I give him a playful nudge. "What's peacocking?"

"Wearing something bold that people comment on."

My gaze rakes over him—he's wearing a black soft-shell jacket that brightens the color of his blue eyes, a crisp white t-shirt, and jeans. Nothing bright or bold. "You don't do that."

His flirty grin appears. "I don't need to."

I snort. "Well, obviously I do."

He tugs on a lock of my hair, and it makes my scalp tingle in a pleasant way. "Buzz cut?"

I chuckle. "It's a great look, but I'm not sure I can pull it off."

A memory of a conversation I had with Kit floats into my head. *I've always wanted to dye my hair purple,* I told him. *Since I was a little girl. A pale purple, like lavender.*

He made a face. *You don't really want to do that to your hair, do you?* he asked. *It would look childish. Your hair is nice as it is.*

God, he was annoying. He had this specific image of the ideal woman, and now that I've had some distance from the relationship and time to stack all these memories side by side, I see that I never fit that image.

I showed him glimpses of who I really am, and he discouraged it. What does that say about me?

Maybe he was right about the hair, though. It would be a lot. I doubt pale-purple hair would go over well in my stuffy corporate insurance office.

Hayden nudges me with his elbow, watching my face. "What else is on that list?"

"Rule number four: always have a plan. That's where you come in, of course. I've got everything else covered."

Hayden doesn't say anything, so I read the last one on the list.

"Rule number five: never get attached." My mouth tugs up into a crooked smile, but it feels forced. "No chance of that, obviously."

Hayden watches me for a long time. "Are you sure you want to do this?"

There's something serious in the way he's looking at me, like he's worried I'm making a big mistake.

It doesn't feel like a mistake, though. It feels like my only option. I can't go back to who I was before, letting someone take the reins on my life. Even now—hanging out at the bar with everyone, talking and laughing and not worrying that we're staying out too late for Kit, who liked to go to bed early—I'm starting to feel like myself again.

Hayden's worried I'll get my heart broken, I bet. If I were to fall for someone, I'd lose myself all over again. I just know it. I'm not like Hazel or Pippa, who both have a strong sense of self. I'm still figuring myself out.

"Absolutely," I tell him. "The probability of me falling for someone is zero. I'm not looking for anything serious." I smile to show him I'm totally fine. "So when do we start? Now?"

He rubs the back of his neck. "Not here, with everyone watching. Let's go out tomorrow, just you and me."

"And you'll show me how to hit on guys?"

He taps his tongue to his top lip, features tight. "Yep."

Excitement and nerves flutter through me. "Tomorrow, it is."

CHAPTER 7

DARCY

"WE COULD HAVE it at the Filthy Flamingo." Hayden holds the front door open for me when we get home later.

I walk inside the apartment and my shoulder brushes his chest; he takes a sudden step back away from me, and I frown.

The first couple of times, I thought I was imagining things. Hayden's a touchy-feely guy. Countless times over the years, he's thrown his arm around me. He gives piggyback rides and ruffles my hair and never hesitates to wrap me in a big, warm bear hug.

But since I moved in, he doesn't touch me. No more hugs, no throwing his arm around me. Tonight at the bar, he moved his arm before I could accidentally brush against him. And now, he's backing away to give me space.

"Darce?"

He acts like my skin is made of spiders or something.

"Hmm?" I kick my shoes off.

"Your birthday, which I haven't forgotten about, even though you changed the subject earlier."

I sigh, but I'm smiling.

"What's the hesitation?" He takes my jacket and hangs it for me. "The league is giving us a week off between the season and the playoffs this year. It's a new thing Ward pushed for."

My lips part in surprise. "Wow. That's awesome." Players are usually exhausted by the time the season is over, and they head into playoffs tired and injured, not playing their best.

"We could do the party then, a few days after your birthday, once the regular season is over. And I don't know about you," Hayden says over his shoulder, striding into the open kitchen, "but I love any excuse for a party."

"I'm well aware." I twist my mouth into a grin.

"I've been called a party animal." He pulls his water bottle out of the fridge and drains half, the strong line of his throat bobbing.

Maybe a big birthday party is exactly what I need. It'll be like a deadline. I'll have everything figured out by then.

Urgency and excitement spark inside me.

"Fine, what the hell?" I shoot him an indulgent smile. "Let's do it."

My eyes flick to the patio door and a laugh threatens to bubble up. I hid something out there earlier and I've been waiting all day for Hayden to get home and stumble upon it.

"Is the patio door locked?" I ask, feigning innocence. "I always get nervous about that kind of stuff."

He snorts. "We're on the twentieth floor. You think someone's going to scale the building?" He makes a sympathetic teasing noise. "I'll keep you safe from intruders, Darce."

I bite down on my grin and pretend to look worried. "Can you check anyway? Please?"

His expression softens. "Of course."

Hayden walks through the living room to the patio doors, sees the garden gnome peering in the window, and nearly jumps out of his skin.

"Jesus fuck! No!" He shudders.

I'm doubled over laughing.

"Where did that come from?"

"Oh my god, it's Daniel!" I put on a huge, welcoming smile and wave at the creepy porcelain gnome I bought earlier today. Tears sting my eyes, I'm laughing so hard. "He finally found where you live. He said he's been searching for you."

"Darcy." Hayden rubs a hand down his face, staring at the garden ornament with disgust and disdain.

Daniel the Garden Gnome has been following Hayden since his grandmother gifted him to me back when we visited her for lunch one day during our third year at university. The biggest mistake Hayden ever made was telling me how much he hates garden gnomes and how creepy he finds them.

"And he got a new hat." I walk over to the glass and wave at the gnome. "Nice to see you again, Daniel. What's that?" I bend down and cup my hand to my ear, pretending to listen. "You want to sleep in Hayden's bed?"

Hayden cringes. "Keep that fucking creepy thing outside where it belongs. Or better yet, get rid of it."

"You said I could make any change I wanted."

"Not that change. Anything but that."

He backtracks through the living room, grabs his water bottle, and heads toward the hallway that leads to our bedrooms. "Maybe we'll get lucky and a bird will carry it away and drop it in the ocean."

My chest shakes with laughter. "Good night, Hayden."

At the entrance to the hallway, he pauses, smiling back at me. "Good night, Darce."

Maybe he refuses to touch me for some reason, but I'm starting to see how fun living with Hayden will be.

"OWENS, we're not at the driving range," Miller calls the next morning during practice. "Don't rear back so far."

I huff a laugh and adjust my swing, sending the puck hurtling toward Streicher in the net.

"Nice." Miller watches while I work through the rest of the pucks.

By the boards, Ward makes notes. It's one of our lighter practices of the week. We're focusing on detailed work like wrist shots and snap shots, but I can't tell whether I'm living up to his expectations.

Eventually, Ward blows his whistle.

"That's good for today," he calls to us, gesturing to the bench. The third-line forwards hit the ice and we skate away.

My gaze strays to the other end of the ice, where Volkov's working with the assistant coach and the second-line defenseman they moved into my old spot on the first line. It feels strange not playing with him anymore, like I'm wearing new shoes that need breaking in.

"So what's this shit about teaching Darcy to be a player?" Miller asks with a smirk as we head to the dressing room.

I bite back a groan. I was hoping he'd forget, but knowing

Rory Miller, there was no fucking way. I adopt my own cheeky smirk.

"Why? Do you want in on those lessons?"

He laughs. "Those days are long gone for me, buddy. I'm locked down for life." A proud grin stretches across his face, and there's a weird pang in my chest.

In the dressing room, I pull my practice jersey off and sit to unlace my skates while Miller drinks water.

"She feels like she missed out on things while she was with Kit, and she wants to date again. Who better to teach her than the master?" I puff my chest out and give him a cocky grin.

In this moment, it doesn't feel like something to be proud of. So I've dated a lot. So what?

"Why doesn't she just practice with you?" He tips his chin at me, smiling.

"We're friends."

He stares at me for a long beat. Back in December, we went to a bar, and the night ended with me dropping a very drunk Miller off at his apartment to Hazel with a brand-new tattoo he got for her. He probably doesn't remember the talk we had about Darcy and Kit or how I was feeling weird about Kit hinting at them getting engaged.

I hope he doesn't remember, at least.

"You're friends," he echoes. "And that's why you insisted she live with you?"

"Yep."

"And that's why you're going to teach her how to fuck other guys?"

Sharp, hot jealousy races through me, and my molars grit. I pick a point on the opposite wall and burn a hole through it with my gaze. "It's not like that."

"Sure, it is," Miller says. "You're going to teach her everything you know and then send her off to live happily ever after with another guy."

I suck a deep breath in through my nose, trying to get a hold of the anger surging through me.

I fucking hate that image.

At the bar that night, a guy walked past our table, his eyes all over Darcy. If I weren't there, he'd stop to talk to her. He'd buy her a drink, maybe two or three. Darcy's smart—the smartest person I know—but she's a lightweight. Maybe he'd make some dumb, transparent excuse to get her to his place. Maybe she doesn't want to but doesn't know how to say no. Maybe she's had too much to drink to get home on her own.

The nightmare sends a cold streak through me, chilling my blood.

Thanks for keeping an eye on her, Kit texted when he found out she was staying at my place.

Eating gravel sounds better than watching Darcy learn to hit on guys, but at least this way, I can watch out for her.

"She wants my help." I pull my skates off. "She's my roommate and my friend, and she's fresh out of a relationship. I'm not going to be some fucking creep, hitting on her and making it weird when she clearly doesn't want that."

She chose Kit over me, after all. If she wanted me, wouldn't she have made a move at some point in the last eight years?

I'm not the guy women settle down with. I'm the guy they get things out of their system with. Jessica Haley made that clear in eleventh grade when we lost our virginity to each other and then she dumped me. I put so much effort into making sure our first time was good for her, that she felt comfortable and safe and got enjoyment out of it, that she told her friends. She told *everyone.* After we broke up, her friend Keeley found me at a party, pulled me into a closet, and informed me that she wanted to experience my skills firsthand.

It happened at a party the next weekend with another girl. And the next weekend. I didn't brag about these encounters, but the girls talked, and I earned myself a reputation for being a player.

Mr. Right Now, I was voted in high school. I still remember the way Kit laughed until he was red in the face, doubled over with his yearbook open.

Women don't pick a guy like me, not long term. I'm fine with it, and I accepted it a long time ago.

"I told Driedger I'd look out for her," I admit, rubbing the back of my neck. "She wants to learn how to date, so I'll show her how to date." I stand and adopt a casual expression that conveys how little I care about this, how indifferent I am. "Darcy and I have fun together, and it makes no difference to me who she dates."

Besides, I don't have those feelings for her anymore.

I shoot him a confident grin. "And you're forgetting one thing, Miller."

"Yeah?" He arches a brow, mouth tilted in that fucking annoying knowing way of his. "What's that?"

"She's not my type," I lie. "I like tall, dark hair, and curvy."

That's the type of woman I date, but it's not *my* type.

My type is Darcy Andersen.

Hayden's the biggest player you'll ever meet, Kit told her at the party, grinning at me.

He said it like it was a good thing, when really, it crushed my chances with the first girl I'd ever really connected with.

She shot me a knowing grin. *I can see it. He's too good-looking to be monogamous.*

So much for thinking I could start fresh.

My jaw works, and something flickers in Miller's eyes that I don't like. Compassion, I think.

"I'm not buying it," he says.

I rack my brain for something funny and irreverent to say, but I'm coming up blank. I hate that he's smarter than he looks and acts, and I really hate that I'm not smart enough to fool him.

He claps me on the shoulder as he passes, and I tense.

"That's okay," he says, walking to the showers. "I'll be here when you're ready for advice."

"SO, if I want to show a guy I'm interested, how do I start?" Darcy asks that evening in the Yaletown bar I chose so we could do this without the risk of my teammates seeing.

And that's why you're going to teach her how to fuck other guys? Miller's words from after practice send a fresh round of tension through me.

"Hayden?"

"Yeah." I clear my throat, focusing on Darcy. "Okay. Flirting. Uh, it's easy. You're going to find someone you're interested in, then make eye contact."

She hums, absorbing this. She looks pretty tonight, with her hair loose and a little wavy around her shoulders. She always looks pretty, though, with her small, sloped nose, high cheekbones, and heart-shaped mouth.

My eyes drop to her lap. She's wringing her hands, and protectiveness surges through me.

"Hey." My voice goes soft as I tilt my chin at her hands. "What's the deal?"

She makes an uncertain face, shrugging.

"Nervous?"

"A little. I've never done this before."

I resist the instinct to put my arm around her. "This is going to be a walk in the park for you, I promise. Give any guy attention, and he's going to have his tongue on the floor. You're gorgeous."

Her eyebrows go up and her smile turns teasing. "I'm *gorgeous*?"

I didn't mean to say that. I shrug like I say that to women every day. "You knew that."

"I mean," she makes a face, "not necessarily. You've never told me that."

Because I've always kept a tight leash on thoughts like that. I put on a wry grin. "Don't get a big head over it. That's my thing."

She chuckles. "Sorry, I won't threaten your ego. So I stare deep into a guy's eyes from across the bar. Got it." She makes her eyes go as wide as possible, unblinking gaze boring into me, irises sparkling with suppressed laughter. "Am I seducing you, Hayden?" she whispers in a creepy voice.

"No." I stare back, wearing my own weird, creepy expression, holding back a laugh. "You forgot to smile."

She puts on a blank, soulless smile, still not blinking, and we both start laughing.

I let out an exaggerated sigh. "This is going to be more work than I thought."

"I promise to behave and not act like a possessed doll from a horror movie until at least the third date." She sips her drink and licks the salt off the rim, and I have to pull my gaze away. "Okay, eye contact with a guy for a couple seconds, small smile. Then what?"

"Then, if he's smart, he'll show up like a dog looking for a treat."

"What if he doesn't, though? What if he's shy or something?"

"If a guy's interested, he'll let you know." The words come out with more force than I mean. "Don't settle for anything less than a guy who worships the ground you walk on."

Like me, the voice in my head says, but I ignore it.

She makes a thoughtful humming noise, nodding to herself, digesting this.

"Wasn't that on your player list? Be confident and chill? You're a catch, so act like it."

She smiles, and every shade of green in her eyes sparkles. "You're a catch, too."

Our gazes rest on each other, and it's one of those perfect moments where it's just the two of us and I think, *maybe*. Maybe if things were different. If I'd gotten my shit together that first week and asked her out before Kit swooped in.

Even if we did get together, it would only be a matter of time until Darcy sees what everyone else does, and then it'd all fall apart.

"Alright." She takes a deep breath. "Let's do this."

The bad feeling I've been carrying all day gets bigger and louder, but we're doing this so she can feel confident, so she can be in control while dating, and so she can make up for lost time. We're friends, and she needs my help.

"First, find someone you like."

Darcy's gaze moves around the bar. Her eyes linger on a person behind me before she jerks her gaze back to mine.

"See someone?" My voice is tight and I grip my glass harder.

A tiny nod. "He looked at me."

"Good."

Not good. I hate this. Every protective, possessive instinct in my body pounds like a drum. It's taking all of my control to not turn around to look at the guy.

"Next time he looks, do the smile. Not the creepy one."

She snorts, shifts and crosses her legs, glances behind me, and a moment later, her mouth curves up into the cutest shy smile I've ever seen.

It's a knife to my gut.

"Like that?" she whispers, looking back at me.

I swallow. "Exactly like that."

"Now we wait?" She sips her drink again, searching my eyes.

"If you were with one of your female friends, I'd say yes, but because you're with me," I gesture at myself, "he's not going to approach. On account of me being so big and strong." I flex a bicep and she laughs into her drink. A smile stretches across my face, and some of the tightness in my chest eases.

"You can be very intimidating. What do you suggest?" Her smile falls, and her features flood with worry. "Please don't leave."

Damn if my heart doesn't do whirly loops through my chest at that. "I'm not going anywhere."

An idea occurs to me, and I glance over my shoulder at the group of guys. It'll probably work—one of them is wearing a Storm hat.

"Which one?" I murmur to Darcy.

"Green plaid," she says quietly.

The man in the green plaid shirt leans in while his friend talks. His eyes move to Darcy and then back to his friend. I scan over the group of them, scrutinizing for any red flags, but they look like a regular group of guys.

Darcy's target glances at her again and smiles, pretending to listen to his friend while clocking Darcy's every move.

I catch the bartender's attention, and she comes over. I can't believe I'm about to do this.

"Can we get a round of drinks for that group at the end of

the bar, please?" Darcy watches with curiosity, and I give her a flat smile. "Just watch."

―――

"Owens." Storm Hat nods at me with interest. "Who do you like playing with the best?"

Not sixty seconds after we sent the drinks over, the guys dropped by to thank us and tell me what huge fans they were. I'm a great wingman, so I introduced Darcy as my roommate and invited them to have a drink with us at the bar.

"Volkov, no question." I'm only half listening, straining to hear Darcy and Green Plaid's conversation.

My knee bounces with restless energy. Watching Darcy talk to another man while he stares at her with stars in his eyes feels so fucking wrong. Every muscle in my body is tense, and my chest is tight with a weird, protective urge to grab her hand and pull her out of here.

Confidence-wise, she seems to be doing okay. She's biting her lip a lot the way she does when she's nervous, but I don't get the stranger danger vibe from her.

"...don't know if you have plans for the rest of the night," Green Plaid says to Darcy, wearing a hopeful expression, "but we were going back to my place—"

"We can't," I blurt out, standing. "We have to go."

Darcy gives me a strange smile, and I scramble for an explanation so I don't look like her overbearing bodyguard. If I were wing-manning anyone else, Volkov or one of the other guys on the team, I'd be happy to tag along and keep the party going.

I don't like the idea of Darcy in this guy's apartment, though. Anything that gets us closer to his bedroom, which is what he's trying to do—because anyone with eyes would want Darcy in their bed—makes me pissed off and nauseous.

"We've got that thing tomorrow morning." I lift my brows at her before catching the bartender's eye for the bill. "With Streicher and Pippa and Daisy. So we should get going."

I'm bullshitting through my teeth. Sometimes, Pippa and Hazel organize hikes on the North Shore of Vancouver with Pippa and Streicher's dog, and I tag along, but there's nothing going on tomorrow, and Darcy knows that.

"Right." She smiles, and the mischievous sparkle in her eye feels private, just for us. Our little secret. "The hike."

"Streicher?" Green Plaid asks. "Like Jamie Streicher?"

Darcy smiles and nods at him. "Yep."

He's making moon eyes at her. "I love hikes."

I fight an eye roll in response to him shamelessly trying to get an invite. "That's great."

The bartender swings by with our bill, and I pay, gently pushing Darcy's hand aside when she tries to hand over her card. Sparks zing up my arm and I pull my hand back.

"Lots of great hikes in Vancouver," I add.

I step between them to help Darcy into her coat while the guy backs up to give us space. I'm being a territorial asshole, and the exact opposite of a wingman, but I can't seem to stop myself.

My expression is tight but friendly as I put a hand to Darcy's lower back, forgetting my rule about not touching her. "Nice chatting with you, guys. Have a great night."

"Wait." Green Plaid's eyes flare with surprise at Darcy. "Can I, uh—" He laughs lightly, pulling his phone out. "Can I get your number?"

She looks at me, her gaze full of uncertainty.

"She lost her phone," I lie, hauling her out of there without looking back. "Maybe next time."

A moment later, we're outside in the cold night air, and I can breathe again.

"THAT WAS A TOTAL DISASTER," I tell Hayden as we walk down the street, back to the apartment.

His brows shoot up in alarm. "What do you mean?" His eyes flash. "Did he make you uncomfortable? What did he say?" He glances behind us, at the bar, jaw tightening.

"No. Oh my god, relax. He was perfectly nice. I'm the one who was weird and awkward. We had nothing to talk about. *Nothing*. At one point, I actually asked him if he 'came here often,' like some sleazy dude in a hotel bar." I cringe at the memory.

Hayden's face breaks into a grin. "You *are* sleazy; what can I say?"

I laugh. "How will I ever be a player if I'm so sleazy?"

"You'll manage." His features tighten. "I'm sure Green Plaid thought it was cute."

I give him a sidelong look. He doesn't seem as happy-go-lucky and boisterous tonight as he usually is. "Are you okay?"

"Yeah." He arches an eyebrow. "Why?"

"You wanted to go home early." I reach up and rest the back of my hand against his forehead, pretending to check for fever. "You must be deathly ill."

He huffs a laugh, looking away. "I'm just tired."

"Oh." I nod. "That makes sense."

It doesn't really, though. Hayden's a night owl. He loves staying up late, and he's an extrovert. Being around people energizes him. He *loves* to move the party to a second, third, or fourth location.

If I think about the situation from his perspective, though, maybe watching his best friend's ex hit on guys isn't his idea of a fun time. I broke his best friend's heart, and now I'm moving on. He probably thinks I'm heartless. Maybe he resents me for it.

My stomach clenches at the thought of Hayden harboring frustrations with me. He's so kind; he'd never say anything to upset me.

It still doesn't sit well with me, though.

"Thanks for tonight." I give him a grateful smile. "I know it probably felt like teaching a baby to walk. I'm lucky to have you as a friend." Without thinking, I loop my arm around his waist like I've done a hundred times.

"You, too, Darce." He gives my shoulder a quick, friendly squeeze before stepping away, and a stab of embarrassment hits me.

He's definitely avoiding touching me. He's mad that I dumped Kit and broke his best friend's heart.

I can't list all the reasons Kit and I are wrong for each other without making it weird between them, so I keep my mouth shut, but none of it sits right with me.

———

"I love that your apartment is so close to bars and restaurants," I tell Hayden as he unlocks his front door.

His eyes narrow, but they spark with teasing. "Our apartment."

"Right. Our apartment." I'm about to set my shoes inside the front hall closet when I pause, frowning. "Where'd all your gear go?"

Yesterday, the closet was filled with hockey stuff. Today, it's half-empty.

Hayden shrugs his big shoulders. "Moved some to my closet, some to the storage locker downstairs."

"Why? It wasn't in the way."

"It *was* in the way. There was barely room for your coat." He makes a face. "And it smells like sweat. I know it stinks, even if you didn't say anything."

"I didn't notice anything. You always smell good."

"I want you to have enough room for your stuff. Like I said, *our* place."

My face feels warm with pleasure. Sometimes I forget how considerate Hayden can be, how he's always thinking about the well-being of others. "Thank you."

"Don't mention it," he says over his shoulder, walking into the kitchen. "Water?"

I nod, and he pours two glasses before heading to the living room, and I follow.

"Well, that was a waste of an evening." I flop down on the sofa beside him. "Sorry about that."

He shakes his head, smiling. "You did fine. Sorry, I, uh"—he glances at me—"pulled you out of there before you could get his number."

"I was already trying to think of an exit strategy after I told him he smelled weird."

Mid-sip, Hayden starts laughing and coughing on his water.

I give him a few firm slaps on his back. His t-shirt is so

warm under my fingers, and the planes of his back are shock-ingly toned.

He clears his throat, still laughing. "I have to hear this."

"He smelled like pencils, but worse? Like rotten pencils?"

Hayden's shoulders shake, and I pinch his ribs, which only makes him laugh harder.

"I read a study where the researchers believed that it's part of our evolutionary system, when we think members of the opposite sex stink. They thought it meant—" I groan, burying my face in my hands. "I don't want to repeat it. This is exactly why I need lessons on how to be smooth like you."

He grasps my hands and pries them away from my face, grinning. "Come on."

I'm wincing so hard, I'm going to strain a muscle. "I told him our DNA isn't compatible and that we might be distantly related. I blabbed on for about five minutes about the study and then explained in very clear terms that he didn't smell good to me."

Throwing his head back, he lets out a booming belly laugh. My heart flops around in my chest, delighted at entertaining him.

"He didn't seem to mind if he still wanted your number," he says once he's composed himself.

"Yeah." Nerves and hesitation tumble in my stomach.

He frowns, watching me. "What's that face?"

I suck in a deep breath and try to put my feelings into words, something I've never been good at. Equations and patterns, I can do all day, but sifting through the swirling tension and worry doesn't come so easily.

"Tonight was stressful and scary," I admit, letting out a shaky breath. "I didn't feel like a player." Instead of being in control, I felt like things were happening *to* me.

Hayden makes a low, sympathetic humming noise. "Shit, Darce. I'm sorry."

"No, it wasn't you. You were great. I needed you there."

His mouth tips up at that, and I return his smile.

"I feel like I'm diving in too fast, but I don't want to sit around and wait." Impatience races through me. "Rule number four is *always have a plan*, and I jumped into the flirting deep end without knowing the next steps." The idea takes shape in my head, sharpening. "If Green Plaid didn't smell like moldy pencils, and maybe I did like him, how would I show him I want to move things back to his place?"

On the sofa beside me, Hayden's quiet for a long moment. "You could practice with me."

My eyebrows pull together. "I am practicing with you."

He runs a hand over his hair. "No, like, practice *on* me."

"Oh." I blink, staring into his eyes. Hayden has these crushing blue eyes, light in the center with dark rings. "Like, use you."

My pulse picks up. Why does that sound so dirty? He doesn't mean it like *that*.

"Yeah." He swallows, interlacing his fingers and resting them on his flat stomach. "If it would make you more comfortable."

Nerves rush through me, but they're not shaky and heavy like they were earlier in the night when I had to talk to that guy. These are lighter, sitting higher in my chest, fluttering and buzzing and fizzing through me. The excited kind of nerves.

This isn't what I had in mind when I wanted Hayden to teach me to be a player, but my brain snags on this idea, wondering what it would be like. I'll probably never get another chance to experience flirting with Hayden Owens.

Besides, he's the expert. He's done this tons of times.

Do it, an impulsive, devilish feeling whispers.

"I do love to be prepared." My heart's beating faster and I'm suddenly aware of how *male* Hayden is. How much space he takes up and how big his hands are. How good he smells.

"And I'm still your wingman." His eyes drop to my mouth.

"Exactly."

He's not going to get attached—that's not who he is—and this isn't anything more than him helping out his friend.

I shift my legs under me on the couch, facing him. "So I'm at a bar, chatting with a guy, and want to, uh, progress things. What do I do?"

Hayden's jaw clenches for a brief moment. "You want to hook up."

"Right." I can't even imagine feeling ready for that, but I'm supposed to be practicing and preparing. "How do I make that clear?"

The long line of his throat works, and his gaze drops to my mouth again. "Touch him."

My expression turns alarmed as images race through my mind.

He cracks a smile. "Not like, grab his package, Darce. Touch his arm, make up an excuse to touch his hands. Say you want to compare hand sizes."

I arch an eyebrow. "That old trick? That can't actually work."

He gives me a knowing smile, and I get a weird stab of unease picturing him trying it on other girls.

"My, what tiny hands you have." I hold my palm out. "I bet my hands are twice the size of yours."

He snorts and begrudgingly gives me his hand, pressing our palms together.

Oh.

That's interesting.

Awareness rolls through me at the sensation of his calloused palm against mine. Every nerve on my hand lights up, tingling, snagging all my attention. It's not even funny how much bigger his hand is than mine, and my mind immediately goes to dirty places.

He must be proportional. I mean, he has to be. He's a big guy; of course he has big hands, and... Hayden's dick is probably huge. My mouth goes dry. I've heard the rumors.

He pulls his hand back, and my palm feels cold.

"I'll add that one to my toolbox, even if it feels a little high school." I give him a teasing grin. "What other tricks do you have?"

"Just find other ways to touch him." His brows bob. "He won't mind, trust me."

"Like this?" I rest my hand on his arm. It feels a little awkward, but his skin is warm. He's not pulling away like I'm burning him, so that's something.

He smiles down at me, nodding, features relaxing. "Mhm."

"Or like this?" I reach up, pretending to see something in his hair. "Oh, I think you have something in your hair."

He chuckles, but when I sink my fingers into his thick hair, he lets out a deep sigh, eyelids falling halfway closed.

Delight flutters in my chest. He *likes* me playing with his hair. I wonder what else he likes.

"Your hair is really soft." I run my fingers over his scalp, dragging them through the luxurious strands, and his jaw ticks. "I'm going to start stealing your conditioner."

"Yeah." His voice is rough. "That's perfect."

Reluctantly, I pull my hand away. Tension hangs in the air as Hayden watches me, waiting for my next move, and that impulsive urge strikes again.

"Or..." My hand comes to his thigh. He's so warm through

the fabric of his black jeans, and under my hand, his muscles tighten.

Hayden has the thighs of a professional athlete—strong, thick, muscular. From beach vacations and pool parties over the years, I know that, under his jeans, they're dusted with golden-blond hair.

Having my hand on his thigh isn't quite the same as noticing the way his swim shorts stretch over his body from behind my sunglasses, though. A pulse of heat moves through me, and my skin prickles.

"Like this?" I look up into his eyes.

"Yeah." He nods, nostrils flaring and breathing uneven. "Exactly like that. You're doing great."

Some weird impulse has me stroking my thumb across his thigh, lightly pressing into the thick, tight muscle.

Hayden has a nice mouth, I realize, staring at it. For such a strong face, his lips are a surprisingly delicate shape, and my fingers itch to trace them.

"That's good." He snatches my wrist up and drops it in my lap like it's on fire, turning away from me. "You've got the hang of it. You're a natural."

Embarrassment rockets through me. I probably had my jaw unhinged while furiously rubbing his thigh.

A player watches for signs that his advances are unwanted, the list said. *Don't be a creep.*

"Great." I tuck my hair behind my ear, pretending I didn't make it weird. "That was easy."

"I'm going to go to bed." He jerks to his feet, not looking at me, and moves to the hallway, shoulders and back tense. "I need to take a shower. Good night."

"Oh. Okay." My pride stings at the way he's scrambling to get away from me. "Good night. Thanks for your help," I call after him.

His bedroom door slams, and a moment later, I hear his shower running. I sit there, cringing. He couldn't get away fast enough.

Let that be a reminder to me. He's my wingman and nothing more.

"HEY," Hayden says behind me as I wait inside the arena entrance a few days later. He approaches with a puzzled expression on his face, looking around. "I heard there was a cute girl waiting down here..." His gaze finds me and his face falls in an exaggerated, comical way. "Oh."

I shake with laughter. "Very funny. Hi."

"Hi. Are you waiting for Georgia?"

I smile and nod. We're going shopping. "She should be down any minute."

Our gazes hold for a long moment, and I think back to a few nights ago, when I had my hand on his thigh. All night, I tossed and turned, worrying I'd made a fatal friendship error and ruined everything, but the next morning, Hayden acted like it never happened at all.

I keep thinking about it, though.

"Excuse us," someone says, working with another person to carry a giant teddy bear through the lobby.

"Hey, guys." Hayden gives them a friendly smile, and my gaze lingers on the giant heart on the teddy's chest.

Be my Valentine? is stitched on the heart. I can feel my mouth turning down.

"We're going to the children's hospital tomorrow," Hayden explains.

A noise of acknowledgment comes out of my throat. Since the decorations started going up in stores a few weeks ago, I've been dreading Valentine's Day. Kit and I never celebrated it. He was always traveling for work, or we'd make some excuse about how busy restaurants were, which I was fine with. It was never a big deal to me.

The idea of seeing happy couples everywhere tomorrow sends a streak of cold dread through me, though.

Hayden's expression shifts, looking weirdly serious. "Hey, Darce? There was something I wanted to ask you—"

"You must be Darcy," a woman with thick auburn hair and a broad smile calls as she strides through the lobby on her heels. "Owens said you looked like the love child of a fairy sprite and a cupcake, and I see exactly what he means."

She beams at me, and her whiskey-colored eyes are so shockingly pretty—everything about her is—that I'm stunned.

"Hi. I'm Georgia."

I shake her manicured hand. With Hayden, I'm used to his charisma. I've had eight years to adjust, but with this woman? I feel like I just met a celebrity.

So this is one of the team doctors. Georgia can't be more than thirty, but she carries herself with confidence I'll never have. Her hair cascades around her shoulders in long curls. Her makeup's impeccable and her freckles are adorable. Her brown tweed coat is professional yet stylish, and it's an unexpectedly perfect match to her emerald-green velvet heels. Her dress slacks end just above a voluminous green velvet bow on each ankle strap. I bet she had these pants hemmed especially for these shoes.

"Wow." I blink at her, and she and Hayden chuckle. "Hi." I arch an eyebrow at Hayden. "Fairy sprite cupcake?"

He just shrugs and smiles.

Georgia gives him a wry look. "You should hear the things he says about you. When we go for lunch, he's like, Darcy this, and Darcy that—"

"She's exaggerating," Hayden interrupts, and the tips of his ears go pink.

Delight spreads through me, and I bite back a smile. I'm about to tease him, but the elevator dings, the doors open, and Alexei steps out with his bag and jacket on, probably heading to the parking garage. Our eyes meet and he gives me an approving nod.

"Darcy," he says as a greeting before glancing at Georgia with a grumpy expression. "Got your claws in her already, Dr. Evil?"

She stiffens. "Who let you out of the care home, Grandfather?"

His features harden and his gaze drops to her feet, lingering. "Those aren't office appropriate."

"That's rich from someone with four teeth."

She gives him a cool smile, undeterred by his intimidating presence. His nostrils flare, and Hayden and I watch them like a tennis match. I'm in awe; she's my new icon.

"I have all my teeth," Alexei says in a low, deadly voice.

"For now. You've broken every other bone, so it's only a matter of time until you're spitting Chiclets. I'm shocked you don't have a reserved parking spot at the hospital."

I make a curious expression at Hayden, and his eyebrows bob once, eyes lit up with amusement.

Alexei towers over her, staring down at her with a hard set to his jaw. "You're not my doctor anymore. Don't waste valuable energy on me that you can be using to find a rich husband."

Georgia just sighs like she's tired of him. "That's enough

male energy for today." She makes a shooing motion at the guys before looping her arm through mine. "We're going to go spend money now."

"What you do best," Alexei mutters under his breath, walking away.

Hayden snorts. "I'll see you at home, Darce. Have fun. Bye, Georgia."

"Wait." I take a step toward him, and Alexei pauses, waiting for Hayden. "You wanted to ask me something."

Hayden's brows snap together, and he glances between the other two. "I'll just ask you later, at home. It's not important."

As they leave, Alexei gives Georgia a lingering hostile stare over his shoulder. She does a friendly finger wave, but the second his back is turned, her hand flips to a middle finger.

"I'm guessing you and Alexei don't really get along," I say as we leave the lobby.

We step outside and she smiles up at the sky. "Oh, good, it's not raining." Her eyes slide to me. "Let's just say it's a good thing I'm not the Russian's doctor anymore. My scalpel might slip and cut off his favorite part."

I chuckle. "You don't operate on players."

"I know." She gives me an innocent, slightly wild smile, and I laugh harder.

"You don't think he's attractive?"

She makes a horrified face. "Volkov? You're kidding, right?"

An embarrassed laugh bubbles out of me as we walk down the street. "I think he's kind of hot in a scary way. He's got that merciless, mysterious thing going on."

Georgia looks stricken. "He's not actually your type, right?"

"God, no," I rush out. "I like to laugh, and I don't think Alexei actually knows how."

Born in Russia, his family immigrated to Canada when he was a kid. He doesn't have an accent, but there's something serious, watchful, and a little predatory about Alexei that I can see being attractive to the right person.

"And I'd like someone a bit friendlier," I add.

"Like Hayden." Her mouth tips up.

"No, not like Hayden." My face goes red. "We're just friends." What is it about me that makes people jump to that conclusion constantly? "Anyway, don't listen to what Alexei said about your shoes." My eyes linger on the pretty bows, so feminine and flouncy. "They're beautiful."

She kicks her foot out, admiring them with a happy sigh as we wait for the light to change. "Bright shoes cheer me up, especially when it's raining every day. The winters here can be such a bummer."

I look down at my responsible work loafers. They're not ugly or anything. They have a little gold buckle, and they're comfortable. They match the rest of my corporate wardrobe. When they wear out, I buy a new identical pair.

They're not exactly inspiring, though, and they definitely don't cheer me up. My gaze moves to Georgia's shoes.

When I look up again, she arches a brow. "Do you need to be alone with my feet?"

I give her a quick, slightly self-conscious smile. "No, I want to buy shoes like yours. I don't have anywhere to wear them and they wouldn't match anything else I own, but—"

"If you wait for the opportunity to wear the fun things you have, you'll be waiting a while," she says softly. "Wear what you love whether it's out on a date or to the grocery store." Her mouth curls up. "You should have seen the looks I got in medical school from the male students. Profs, too. I think a pair like these would suit you," she says as the light changes and we cross. "We'll get you a pair tonight. A new pair of shoes is like an omega-3 for your soul." Her smile turns coy and playful. "I'm a doctor, so I know what I'm talking about."

I bite back a big smile, hesitating. With her tailored clothes, shiny hair, and impractical shoes, Georgia has the put-together, polished vibe of old money. "I don't know if I can afford the places you shop."

She waves me off. "I usually buy on consignment. I hate spending money." She glances behind us, at the arena still visible from a few blocks away. "Don't tell that to the Russian, though. He thinks I'm a spoiled little rich-girl princess."

My eyes narrow, and under my studying gaze, she shifts like she's uncomfortable.

"Why does he think that?"

"Just easier, I guess." She stops in front of a storefront and gives me a broad, excited smile. "Here we are. Let's get you some beautiful clothes."

"NOW, THIS IS INTERESTING."

Half an hour later, Georgia has a pile of clothes gathered for me to try on. Her head tilts as she studies a bright floral minidress that looks like something from the seventies.

My eyebrows go way up. "That looks like my grandmother's Chesterfield."

"Then your grandmother has great taste. You don't know if you like things until you try them on, Darce."

I smile at her use of my nickname.

"Is it okay that I call you Darce?" she asks. "That's what Hayden calls you."

My heart warms. "Of course." When my gaze swings back to the dress, uncertainty rises up my throat. It's so bright, like the tangerine dress I donated when I moved out of the place I shared with Kit.

"I don't know. It's really bright. I wear a lot of gray and white and black." I shrug at her. "You know, easy colors."

Loud, I hear him say. Like seeking attention or standing out is a bad thing.

I look down at the tan dress clutched in my hand—something I grabbed because I can wear it to work. It's boring, and it inspires nothing inside me.

When I look at the dress Georgia's holding up, though, something sparks in my chest. That's a dress that a really fun, confident woman would wear—a woman like Georgia.

"Please?" Georgia asks in a pleading voice, giving me innocent doe eyes.

My mouth twists into an amused smile. "Are you manipulating me?"

"It's only manipulation if it works." She puts the dress back on the rack with a shrug. "Besides, you just got out of a relationship, right?"

My muscles tense. "Did Hayden tell you that?"

"No, but he used to say 'my friends Darcy and Kit,' and now he just says 'my friend Darcy.' And you two are living together, so..." She shrugs, studies a jacket, glances at me, and brings it with her.

"So I have to wear the dress that the '70s threw up on because I just broke up with my boyfriend?" I ask with a smile.

Georgia nods with enthusiasm. "Yes. Thank you. You get it. This is the start of a new phase of your life. You moved cities, and you're single now. Why not buy a new dress? Get a new haircut. Sign up for a running club and then only go to the first session because the people are too hardcore. Get your nails done in gold glitter and then be stuck with them for three weeks."

Kit would *love* the tan dress.

What do I want, though? My brain prickles. What kind of colors do I like to wear?

"This is the perfect time to reinvent yourself, Darcy. Madonna reinvents herself every decade, and if you shit on her *Ray of Light* era, we're no longer friends."

"I would never." I chuckle.

"Good. You know, when I'm having a totally shit day and I start to feel down, I just look at my shoes and I think, *oh yeah, I'm Dr. Georgia fucking Greene.*" She grins. "Confidence comes from within, but it's okay to jump-start it with something external."

Oh god—there's that feeling rising inside me again, like I'm going to say something weird. Like when I said that stupid stuff about the guy at the bar not smelling right.

"When I was a kid, I had a mermaid doll with purple hair," I blurt out. "And I thought it was so pretty," I add, trailing off, feeling weird, like I just tripped in public or something.

Instead of laughing, her eyes illuminate. "You would look amazing with purple hair."

"Like a pale lavender," I elaborate.

She nods harder, gaze fixed on me but slightly unfocused, like she's imagining it. "Totally. It would look lovely with your green eyes."

I picture my hair in soft-purple tones, all loose around my shoulders like something out of a fairy tale.

Isn't that kind of unprofessional? Kit asked about my purple hair idea.

Hair's a big step and a lot of commitment, but a dress? My gaze slides to the bold dress that Georgia put back on the rack.

A player dresses with confidence and style.

I grab the dress, and Georgia yelps with excitement, clapping her hands.

———

Half an hour later, I have a decent selection of items in my "yes" pile.

"I haven't seen the dress with the flowers yet," Georgia calls.

Behind the curtain, I stand in my bra and underwear, staring at the dress on the hanger.

I've been avoiding it. I'm not sure why. It's a chaotic mess of soft pink and melon orange and pastel purple, with shards of teal.

"I don't think I have the right shoes for this," I call back to her.

"Put. The. Dress. On."

This is stupid. I don't know why I'm hesitating. I shove past the weird feelings, unzip the dress, and pull it on.

Oh.

Oh.

There's no mirror in the dressing room, but when I get the hidden side zipper up, the dress feels amazing. The lining is smooth against my skin, and there's a comforting weight to the fabric. It's not too tight or too baggy, and it's the perfect length. I'm petite, so dresses are normally too long on me, but this dress hits at what feels like the right mid-thigh length.

I pull the curtain back, and Georgia's jaw drops. Then she crows in victory. When I'm standing in front of the mirror, *my* jaw drops.

She smiles at our reflections with smug pleasure. "The universe sent us here tonight so we could find you *that dress*."

It doesn't look like I'm wearing my grandmother's couch. It doesn't look like a kindergarten art project gone wrong. The dress is flirty and whimsical, and very, very seventies, but in a fun way. "I thought the print would be too much."

She throws her hands in the air, pleased as punch. "What did I say?"

"You have a gift."

She bows. "Thank you, thank you. Honor me by actually wearing it and not just letting it sit in your closet."

"Deal." I grin, still admiring my appearance.

Excitement dances in my chest, and I stand an inch taller. *This* is the special magic Georgia was talking about—a new haircut, fun shoes that cheer you up, a new nail polish color. And even though I've never worn something so bright, it doesn't feel like I'm forcing myself to change.

Maybe this is who I was the whole time, and I think I like her.

THE FRONT DOOR opens that evening while I'm making dinner, and Darcy carries in a handful of bags from her shopping trip with Georgia.

"Hi," she calls, smiling and setting them in the closet.

"Hey." I pull the roasted veggies out of the oven. "Just in time. Did you eat?"

"No, Georgia had to get to a clinic she volunteers at." She comes to stand beside me, and when her arm brushes mine, I take a step toward the sink to put some space between us.

"Is there enough?" She rubs her arm absently where we touched. "You eat so much."

I chuckle, dishing her out a plate. "I made extra for you." I was hoping she'd be home in time. My chin tilts toward the island chairs. "Go sit."

She gives me a grateful smile. "Thank you."

"Don't mention it." I follow her and set a plate down in front of her before taking a seat on the stool beside her. "Looks like a successful shopping trip."

"Georgia forced me to buy a bunch of stuff and we made a plan to go again in a few weeks." She takes a bite and her eyes close as she chews. "Oh my god," she mutters, and her sigh of happiness and satisfaction goes straight to my groin. "This is so good. Beets and goat cheese are a match made in heaven."

I swallow, staring at her mouth. A weird, masculine sense of pride expands in my chest as she enjoys the dinner I made for her.

My gaze lifts to hers, and our eyes hold. I'm thinking about the other night, when she sifted her delicate fingers through my hair and touched my thigh. It felt so fucking good I could hardly stand it. Within seconds, I was painfully hard, and I almost pulled her into my lap right there so she could feel how well her flirting had worked. Instead, I made myself come in the shower, muffling my groan into my hand as I pictured that sweet little mouth wrapped around my cock, swallowing me down.

"Georgia is kind of intense, but I like her. I think we're friends now." She eats another bite of food, and I watch as the mouthful disappears, her lips sliding over the fork.

"Georgia's great." I yank my attention away from things I shouldn't be thinking about. "She doesn't take shit from any of the guys." Especially Volkov, which irritates him to no end. "Are you going to show me what you bought?"

She bites her lip, hesitating, but her eyes glitter with excitement.

I arch an eyebrow at her, starting to smile. "Don't tell me she made you buy a leather catsuit or something."

She laughs. "No. She made me buy a dress that's different from what I'd normally wear, but I love it."

"Show me."

She wrinkles her nose. "I don't know."

Forgetting my vow not to touch her, I nudge her with my elbow. "Come on."

She gives me a long, deliberating look. "Okay, but I'm not trying it on for you." She slides off her stool and heads to the front door, where her shopping bag sits. Then she pulls out a bright orange, pink, and purple dress.

My grin stretches ear to ear. It's so fun and pretty. So Darcy. "I love it, Darce. Great choice." It's short, too, and Darcy has great legs. Smooth and toned and soft-looking.

"Really?" She holds the dress up, studying it with a small smile. "I guess I need something nice if I end up going out on a date."

My lungs tighten, and I picture her wearing this dress that makes her feel pretty and special while she's sitting across from some fucking guy making eyes at her. Hot jealousy wrenches in my gut, and my teeth grind.

She frowns at me. "What's wrong?"

"Nothing." I clear my expression, but her curious gaze lingers on me.

"What did you want to ask me today, in the lobby?"

My nerves jump, but I'm grateful for the change of subject, and now I know exactly where she's going to wear that dress.

"I was thinking we could get dinner."

She shrugs. "Sure."

We get takeout all the time, and I made it sound too casual.

"No, like, uh. Let's go out on a date." I run my hand over my hair. If the guys on the team saw me all nervous like this, I'd never hear the end of it.

Her brow furrows with confusion. "A date."

She thinks I'm hitting on her. She thinks I'm asking her out for real. "Because you said you were nervous to date new people right now, and you like knowing all the next steps," I add quickly. "So let's go out on a practice date. As friends. And as your wingman."

I clear my throat. *Jesus fuck, Owens. Get your shit together*. This is embarrassing. It's like *I'm* the one who needs lessons.

"Right." She seems relieved. "Practice date, as friends."

Her expression is hard to read, but I can see her mind working.

"Unless you've changed your mind."

"No." Her eyes go wide. "I haven't changed my mind. That's a really good idea." She nods to herself. "We should definitely go on a date."

He's my best friend, and I'd never say this out loud, but Kit's so fucking dumb for all the chances he missed with Darcy. Never taking her out on a real date? Unbelievable.

"That date with the guy who kept talking about weddings and babies didn't count," I say for some reason.

She smiles. "You just want to be the first."

Hot, possessive feelings rocket through me, and the primal part of my brain likes the idea of being the first *anything* where Darcy's concerned.

"You got me." I give her a flirty smile. "Come on, Darce, feed my ego."

She rolls her eyes. "Your ego is big enough, but yes, I'm in. When were you thinking?"

"Tomorrow."

There's a long pause between us where her brow wrinkles with adorable confusion, and I wonder if I've gone too far.

"Tomorrow's Valentine's Day."

"Yeah." My pulse beats in my ears like I'm running drills on the ice. "I know. You said you've never been out on Valentine's Day."

"I haven't."

"Well, I'm your wingman, and we're practicing, so it's my job to show you what it should be like."

Her eyebrows go up, but she's smiling. "Taking your role very seriously, I see."

"The most serious." I'm smiling, too. Around her, I can't help it. "You deserve to know your worth."

My words linger in the air, hovering dangerously close to the truth: that I'm disappointed and furious that Kit never spoiled her the way she deserves, and that I'm disappointed and furious that I never noticed.

Kit had her for eight years, and he didn't take her out *once*?

Fuck him for making her feel like that. Fuck him for not treating her well enough.

Maybe I feel a sick sense of territorial pride, too, at being the first guy to take Darcy out on Valentine's Day. She's a knockout. She's smart and funny and beautiful and kind, and she wants to go out on Valentine's Day.

Even if she doesn't want a relationship right now and we're just friends, I want Darcy to have whatever she wants. It's as simple as that.

I fold my arms and lean back against the counter. "What do you say?"

The corner of her mouth curls up in a shy smile, and I want to drag my thumb over her bottom lip, just to see what would happen.

"I'd love to go out with you on Valentine's Day."

"For practice," I add, so she doesn't think I'm getting the wrong idea. "Because I'm your wingman."

"Sure." She nods hard. "Totally."

"Good."

"Yeah. Good."

We stare at each other for a long moment, smiling, and something expands in my chest.

I don't tell her I've never been out on Valentine's Day, either. I've always been careful not to lead women on—no meeting each other's families, no sleeping over at each other's places, and definitely no going out on Valentine's Day. That's a serious relationship kind of thing.

Tomorrow, though, I'm going to show Darcy exactly how she should be treated.

———

Later, I lie on my back, head on my pillow, and stare at the ceiling, listening to the soft sounds from Darcy's room as she gets ready for bed—padding back and forth to the bathroom to brush her teeth, the muffled slide of her dresser drawers, and, maybe I'm imagining it, but the rustle of sheets as she climbs into bed.

Tomorrow needs to be special and memorable. It needs to be the best fucking Valentine's Day she'll *ever* have.

Should I be doing this? Kit thinks I'm watching out for her, taking care of her and making sure she's okay, not changing her life. From his periodic texts asking how she's doing, I suspect he's taking the breakup harder than she is.

And yet I reach for my phone and open my group chat with Miller, Streicher, and Volkov.

I need your help, I text.

THE NEXT EVENING, I put the finishing touches on my makeup while waiting for Hayden.

I look *good*. My hair is smooth, shiny, and cooperative, and I'm wearing my favorite perfume—an orange vanilla scent—and the dress I bought yesterday.

Excitement shivers through me. My first Valentine's Day.

Hayden appears in my bedroom doorway and lets out a long, low whistle.

"Look at you." His eyes rake over me.

The sight of Hayden Owens in a bespoke navy suit makes me forget my own name. I could kiss his tailor for the way the slacks and jacket somehow make him look even taller and broader, and for how the deep, rich navy blue makes his eyes even brighter. It's the perfect shade of navy, setting off his short, golden-blond hair.

"Wow," I say, at a loss for words.

Hockey players are supposed to be greasy, sweaty, and toothless, but Hayden Owens is that old Hollywood, sparkling, breathtaking kind of handsome. In any era, his broad smile, strong jaw, and deadly blue eyes would have people starstruck.

It should be easy to forget how good-looking he is because

we've been friends for so long, but it isn't. I'll never get used to how beautiful he is.

My gaze snags on his thick hair, freshly trimmed and styled with product, and I think about how soft it was when I dragged my fingers through it the other night. How his eyes fell halfway closed. The way his voice took on that gritty, raspy edge that made me clench my thighs.

My skin goes warm, and I clear my throat. "You got a haircut?"

His eyes trail up and down my form—my bare legs, my dress, my neckline, my hair. "Gotta look good for my date tonight," he says absently.

I feel his gaze like he's touching me. A shiver rolls down my spine.

He arches a brow, looking smug. "You know how to make a guy feel special, Andersen."

Warmth blooms in my chest, and we look at each other for a long moment. There's a fizzy feeling behind my ribcage, moving up into my sternum, and my breath catches.

Oh. Oh, no.

I'm developing a crush on Hayden.

I remember the urgent way he jumped up when I touched his thigh, like he couldn't get away fast enough. How he moved away from me in the kitchen last night. How he won't loop his arm around my shoulders or mess up my hair anymore. He's told me a million times how he cuts things off with women the second he senses they're getting attached, because it's the right thing to do when he knows he won't want a relationship.

He was very, *very* clear that tonight is about practice and him wing-manning me, and nothing else. He repeated the word *friends* about twelve times to be extra clear.

If a guy's interested, he'll let you know, he said the other night.

I can't have a crush on Hayden. He's a total player, he's my friend, and, most importantly, he's my *wingman*. He barely endured me touching his leg. He doesn't want this, so I'm not going to get ideas. He's just being kind, because that's who he is.

"We should get going." I look away and slip a pair of earrings on. Silly Darcy, swooning over a friend who's miles out of my league.

We head to the living room, but at the end of the hall, I stop dead in my tracks, jaw dropping.

The kitchen island is covered in bouquets of red roses. Multiple bouquets. I've never seen so many roses in one place.

"For me?" I sputter, heart lifting.

Hayden stands behind me, so close I can feel his body heat. "They're not for *me*." The strong line of his throat works as he swallows, rubbing the back of his neck. "Of course they're for you. You're my date."

I touch one of the blooms, brushing my fingertip over the smooth petal while delight courses through me. I count the vases on the counter.

"Eight." He looks away, folding his arms over his chest. "One for each year we've been friends."

My heart squeezes. "Hayden." The word comes out so soft, and I'm about to melt into a puddle. "You didn't have to do this."

"Darcy, this is what people do when they take someone out on Valentine's Day."

"I don't think they do." I estimate a price. Add 20 percent for Valentine's Day. Multiply by eight. "They definitely don't do *this*."

He shrugs. "This is what you deserve, and I wanted to make it special for you."

My heart flip-flops in my chest. "It already is."

"It's a first for me, too," he admits with a boyish, rueful smile. "I've never bought someone flowers."

I like that too much. "I'm honored."

We smile at each other, and his scent washes over me. God, he smells good. Warm and masculine, clean and fresh from his shower. Arousal twinges between my legs.

It's the week of my cycle where I'm supremely horny, and it's the hormones clouding my thoughts, I tell myself. I'm not going to get turned on by the way my best friend smells.

I'm not going to do something stupid and ruin everything.

I arch an eyebrow at him. "I'm starting to question your judgment when it comes to dating, though."

He laughs a little, but he steps into my space. I freeze as he reaches up to touch my earrings, inspecting them. The way he focuses on them, frowns and narrows his eyes, makes my breath hitch. Or maybe it's the brush of his fingers against my neck as he untangles my hair from them.

He steps back abruptly.

"Pretty," he says, giving me a quick, tight smile, and I don't know whether he's talking about the earrings or me.

The earrings. Probably the earrings.

"Shall we go?" I sound breathless.

He nods, eyes still on me, and my heart does a funny, excited flip.

A warning bell rings in my head, and I wonder if this date was a bad idea.

"THIS RESTAURANT FEELS LIKE A FAIRY GARDEN," I tell Hayden, leaning in and scanning the space.

It's one of the most popular restaurants in Vancouver, with tropical flowers and lush greenery spilling from the ceilings, cozy fireplaces, and warm, romantic lighting splashing a golden glow across the room. In the corner, a band plays ambient music for the sea of tables for two.

Hayden gives me a quick smile. "Glad you like it."

There's a strong couple energy in here, I notice. A lot of hand-holding, a lot of googly heart eyes, and a few people sitting on the same side of the booth.

One couple is actually feeding each other.

I snort, glancing over at Hayden to get his reaction, but his gaze is on the wine list. Under the table, his knee bounces a fast rhythm. I frown at him.

"Are you okay?"

He jerks his gaze up. "Yeah? Why?"

Reflexively, I set my hand on his knee. I skim my hand over the smooth fabric to calm him, but his whole body jolts, and he knocks his water glass over, soaking the white tablecloth.

"Shit." He scrambles for his napkin to mop it up. "Sorry."

I stare at him in amused confusion. I've never seen him like this. "What is *up* with you tonight? You're supposed to be the cool, confident one. I'm the awkward dork."

His smile is sheepish, and a wash of pink spreads across his cheekbones as he swallows. "I'm, uh, a little nervous."

I shake my head, smiling. "It's just me."

"Yeah." His big chest rises and falls with a deep breath, and he nods, although he doesn't look convinced.

"*I* should be nervous. This is probably where you bring all the supermodels you date." I grin at him, teasing. "I have a lot to live up to."

His fingers tense on the wine list, but he gives me a tight smile. Something inside me sinks. The idea of Hayden with other girls never used to bother me, so why now?

"You haven't been dating lately."

He hasn't gone out on one date or had one friend over to the apartment since I moved in.

He shrugs. "It's been busy."

Not more than a normal season. "You've found lots of time to hang out with me."

"Sick of me already?" His mouth tilts up.

I grin. "No. I love living with you."

That sounded weird. I should have said *I like living with you*. Not love. *Jesus, Darcy.*

His throat works, and his smile softens. "I love living with you, too, Darce."

Something thunks in my heart, heavy and pleasant, and I have to pull my gaze away from his deep blue eyes. "I don't want you to tiptoe around me."

"I'm not."

"You're welcome to have women over." A bad taste fills my

mouth, and the thought makes me nauseous, which is totally unfair. Hayden can do what he wants. "I can find someplace to be or wear noise-canceling headphones or go hang out at Hazel and Rory's—"

"Darcy." His gaze flares with intensity. "It's fine."

"We're roommates, so just treat me like any other room-mate. I mean, you had women over when you lived with Josh, right?"

I don't know why I'm pushing this so hard.

His jaw works. "I really don't want to talk about this anymore."

My stomach twists with unease. Okay, so maybe we're not as good of friends as I thought. "Okay. Sorry."

"No, it's fine." He rubs the bridge of his nose. "I'm trying to focus on the season." He looks away for a moment, then meets my eyes again. "And I like hanging out with you."

My heart does a dumb pitter-patter. "I like hanging out with you, too."

He pauses, hesitating, watching my face. "Sometimes, I wonder what it would be like. A relationship," he explains, glancing away. "I see Streicher and Miller making heart eyes at their fiancées and"—he shrugs, and there's that endearing wash of pink across his cheekbones again—"it doesn't look so bad."

I laugh and wrinkle my nose. "I can't even picture you with a girlfriend." For as long as I've known him, he's kept things casual. "Hayden, you'd hate it." Especially after years of free-dom. "Rory and Hazel, and Pippa and Jamie, they're all in the honeymoon phase. Kit and I were there once, too."

Things were so good, until they weren't. Until the shiny newness wore off. Until I started realizing how wrong we were for each other.

"I'm not saying what happened to Kit and me will happen to them," I continue. "I actually think they're all perfect together, but there are a lot of aspects to a relationship that you just don't have to deal with when you keep things casual." I blow a breath out, thinking. "You don't have to go to family dinners with the other person, no birthday or Christmas gifts, and you don't have to listen to them rant about work at the end of the day."

His eyes move over my face, and the corner of his mouth tugs up into a reluctant smile. "Those don't sound so bad."

He only wants it because he's never had it. The novelty appeals to him, not necessarily the commitment part.

"Valentine's Day, for example." I gesture between us. "This year is fun because it's our first time."

His eyes flash with something at those words, but I barrel on.

"But imagine having to do this *every year*?" I make a face. "Flowers, making the dinner reservation, buying gifts? It's a lot."

His gaze is full of an emotion I can't place. "Like I said, it doesn't sound so bad."

I chuckle. "I think this is a 'the grass is always greener' kind of situation. It's totally okay if you're not cut out for monogamy like that. Not everyone is. With your way, no one gets hurt, no one gets disappointed."

He clears his throat and his eyebrows bob once. "Yeah, you're probably right."

Something in his expression gives me pause, though. A quiet vulnerability.

"I'd be doing the women of the world a disservice by taking myself out of the game." His cocky grin is back, but there's a bitter edge to his words.

I don't like the way he says this. My eyes narrow. I'm learning to be a player because Hayden has the perfect life, but now I wonder if I was wrong.

I wonder if Hayden's as happy as he seems.

"Or you'd make one woman really, really happy," I blurt out, because I don't like him talking about himself like this.

He laughs, but there's a humorless sharpness to it, like he doesn't believe me.

"Anyway." He leans forward and glances around the restaurant before his eyes meet mine. "I've never brought a date here. I called the owner first thing this morning and begged for a reservation. I told her I wanted to bring a beautiful girl here so she could eat the best food in the city. We do team dinners here sometimes, so she was happy to help me out."

Our eyes hold, and my throat tightens. *Beautiful*, he said. The word flits around my head like a butterfly.

His eyes skim over the drink menu. "You like merlot, right?" He frowns in concentration, thinking. "We should probably get a bottle."

I nod, giving him a strange smile. The server appears, and Hayden orders with a familiarity that surprises me. The guy I know from university drinks whatever beer is on tap.

"Do you want anything else to drink?" he asks me, and I shake my head, at a loss for words.

The server dashes off, and he gives me a funny smile as I sit there, staring at him.

"Something you want to say?" he prompts, smiling wider.

"You order wine like an expert. I've never seen you drink wine."

"Sure, you have."

"No, I haven't." I'm wearing a goofy smile. He's better at this dating thing than I realized. I don't know why he was so nervous tonight. "I've seen you do a two-story beer bong on one knee. You made five hundred Jell-O shots for a party you were hosting. And you always order beer when we go out."

"Darcy, don't be ridiculous." His expression turns serious. "I already checked, and they don't have Jell-O shots here."

I burst out laughing, and a pleased grin cracks across his handsome features, like he loves to make me laugh.

"And maybe you don't know everything about me," he adds.

My pulse trips. Living together, I've lost count of the things I never took notice of with him—how tidy he is, how he takes his elderly neighbor's recycling out, how he's happy to take a photo or sign something for anyone who stops him on the street.

"Maybe I don't."

He knows how to order wine at a nice restaurant because he's well-practiced at wining and dining women, I realize with a pinch behind my ribs. Maybe he's not dating *right now*, but soon, he'll be back to normal. Bringing girls home. Sleeping with them on the other side of the wall.

Things I should be learning to do. I pull my mind back to the present. I'm not going to think about the future; I need to focus on why we're here—so I can practice.

"So, if you were on a date right now," I ask, "what would you talk about?"

He shrugs. "Just regular things."

He's so likable and flirtatious as a baseline; I bet if he were actually *trying* to get into a girl's pants, they'd melt right off. My knees press together under the table. What's that like, feeling so attracted and turned on by someone that I can't stand it?

"Like what?" *Try it on me*, I secretly beg.

He rakes a hand over the back of his hair. "We'd talk about her job, where she goes on vacation, what she does for fun."

That sounds like the kind of stuff I talked about with that guy the other week at the bar, except the conversation didn't flow at all. "Let's practice."

He regards me with a playful spark in his eyes. My heart jumps. *This* is the Hayden I know, fun and confident and silly.

"So, Darcy." He leans forward and gives me a seductive, arrogant smile. "What made you ask me out?"

I bite back a laugh and clutch my chest dramatically with a faraway look. "You were standing on the table in the middle of the bar, flexing those big muscles—"

His eyebrows bob and he grins wider, entertained.

"—and I thought, *now that's a man.* Then you roared and tore your shirt open, and I fainted."

"And I caught you." His smile is magnificent as he leans back in his chair, watching me. "You woke up in my arms, caught one look at my rippling muscles, and fainted all over again."

Laughter bubbles out of me and he smiles over his wineglass. Behind him, the band begins to move around the restaurant, serenading couples.

"My turn." He wants to play this game? I'll play.

Hayden's teeth flash as he shrugs, playing with the stem of his wineglass. "Go for it. I'm an open book."

He picks up the glass to take a sip, and I'm distracted by how hot he looks like this, drinking red wine in an expensive suit. It fits the lines of his body like a glove, the crisp white shirt making his skin glow.

The game. Right. Making each other uncomfortable with questions.

"So, Hayden." I lower my voice. "What kind of porn do you watch?"

He chokes on his sip of wine, and people around us glance over as he clears his throat.

"That bad, huh?" I wince at him, biting back my laughter. "It must be the really kinky stuff."

He clears his throat again, staring at the table, his glass, the floor. Anywhere but me. "Yep, that's it. The really kinky stuff."

"What are we talking?" I lean forward, lowering my voice another notch. God, this is so fun. A million times better than trying to navigate an awkward conversation with someone new. "Spanking? Pee stuff? People sitting on cakes?"

"All of the above." His ears are pink and his voice is tight, and he won't meet my eyes.

He's lying.

"Seriously." My eyes narrow. Now I need to know. "What kind of porn?"

He fidgets with his shirt collar, glancing around. "Can you stop saying the word *porn*, please?"

Delight bubbles up my throat, but I hold the laugh down. "What, you don't like when I talk about *porn*?" I raise my voice on the last word, and someone at the table beside us drops their fork. Any embarrassment I should feel is wiped away by how fun this is. "What a little prude you are, Hayden."

He lowers his face into his hands. "I can't take you anywhere," he mumbles, but I can see his features tightening in a smile.

"You're hiding something." I toy with the stem of my own wineglass, high on power, and when he lifts his head, his eyes linger on mine.

He looks so fucking guilty.

"It must be *really* good if you don't even want to tell *me*," I gesture at myself, "your best friend in the whole world."

I don't know why I said that. Kit's obviously his best friend. I'm just the roommate.

"Can we talk about something else?"

I want to keep pushing his buttons. It's fun to turn the tables on him and make *him* embarrassed for once, but also, I need to know. It's none of my business and it's crossing a million friendship boundaries, but the idea of Hayden lying on his bed with his hand wrapped around his cock races into my head. I picture his abs rippling, his face tense with pleasure as he watches a video on his phone.

"Sir, would your beautiful date like to be serenaded?" one of the band members interrupts, standing behind me.

My whole body recoils and I wrench around. "No," I blurt out, eyes wide. "No, thank you."

Hayden's grin turns mischievous. "Yes. Yes, she would."

"DON'T LISTEN TO HER," Hayden tells the musician, eyes gleaming. "She's just being modest. She would love a song."

Even as I'm giving him a death glare that promises pain, I'm smiling. The band starts playing, and the song is so sappily romantic, ridiculous, and humiliating that I clamp my mouth shut to avoid laughing. Hayden's eyes are bright, brimming with entertainment, and something happy, warm, and liquid overflows in my chest.

The singer warbles, and Hayden grins and nods at me.

My stomach tenses with restrained laughter, but I refuse to be rude and offend the band. Hayden pulls out his phone and films while I sit there, captive. He gestures to his lips and mouths *smile*, and a laugh bursts out of me. I cover it with a cough, but the musicians aren't convinced.

"I'm so sorry," I tell the band, who are giving us dirty looks. "We're not laughing at you."

They finish up—I think they skipped a few verses on account of our weird reactions—and leave to torture some other couple.

"Wow." I beam at Hayden. "Thanks a lot. Some friend you are."

"Worth it. You looked like you were about to crack a rib."

Even though I'm red-faced and embarrassed, I can't stop smiling. If this is what celebrating Valentine's Day is like, I've been missing out.

———

We're waiting for our bill when a server passes behind Hayden, carrying a giant cake with sparklers on it.

I lean in, thinking about my teasing him about porn earlier, and tilt my chin at the cake. "Does that turn you on?" I whisper, wincing. "Do you need a napkin for your lap?"

He groans, rubbing his forehead. "God, you're weird."

"I know." I smile at him. "And you love me anyway."

Like, I meant to say. And he *likes* me anyway.

I'm about to change the subject when the server appears back at our table, sliding a plate between us.

"I have a tiramisu here." She sets two spoons down with it.

I frown. "We didn't order—"

"On the house." Her eyes glow with excitement before she disappears.

Hayden and I exchange a strange look. "Maybe she's a Storm fan," I muse, although she was looking at me, not Hayden.

Spoons in hand, we both lean forward to dig in.

We see it at the same time.

An engagement ring.

My heart stops. I feel sick. My spoon hovers midair. Hayden's wide eyes are on me, but I can't tear my gaze away from the diamond ring on the plate.

It's placed gently on top of the tiramisu, sitting there inno-cently, sparkling in the warm restaurant lighting. It's similar to the one Kit gave me, with a big center diamond and a white-gold band.

Marry me? is written in chocolate syrup along the rim of the plate, and all the happy feelings and enjoyment I collected throughout the evening scatter like marbles.

In my mind, I'm back in the bar on New Year's Eve while Kit kneels in front of me, and everyone stares, waiting for my answer.

"I'm *so* sorry." The server reappears, looking sheepish as she reaches for the plate. "I got the tables mixed up."

"Can we get our bill, please?" There's an authoritative edge to Hayden's tone I've never heard. "As soon as possible."

"Of course." The server takes one look at my devastated expression and winces again. She probably thinks I'm disappointed the ring *wasn't* for me.

"Are you okay?" Hayden's hand covers mine as the server hurries away.

"Yeah." I try to clear my head and bring myself back to the present. Back to the fun we were having just a few minutes ago. "I'm fine. That was just weird."

His hand is so warm, and without thinking, I flip mine over so we're palm to palm, craving more contact. The light scrape of his callouses against my skin anchors me, and I draw my gaze up, meeting his.

The tension behind my ribs releases, and I exhale. "I'm okay. Honestly."

"I know."

His gaze is so gentle and caring. I know him holding my hand is just because he's worried, and it doesn't mean anything, but the intimacy makes my breath catch. Every nerve in my palm tingles against his. I bet a scan of my brain would show it lighting up like a firecracker.

"I tried to break up with Kit in December." I don't know

why I'm admitting this when I told myself I'd keep my mouth shut about it so it wouldn't affect their friendship.

I want to explain my weird reaction to the engagement ring, though, and I don't want to risk Hayden thinking I was careless with Kit's heart.

Hayden's gaze sharpens and his hand flexes around mine. "What?"

"Remember that charity skate event where you dressed up like an elf?" I rub my free hand over my stomach, over all the knots tightening at the memory. "And he brought up having kids and getting married and stuff?"

Hayden's jaw tightens and he nods once.

"I broke up with him that night." My face falls. "Or, I tried to."

"Tried to?" he repeats in a low, deadly voice.

I blow out a tight breath as the memory of Kit's crushed expression floods my head. "He wanted to focus on hockey for the next month because he had a lot of big games. He said we should talk about it in January."

Hayden's expression is unreadable. "And what did you want to do?"

"I wanted to break up." The words come out with more force than I mean. "I wanted to break up with him back in August, but it was his birthday, and you can't break up with someone around their birthday, and then the season was starting and he was away a lot..."

"So you waited until January." His jaw ticks again, expression hard.

"That's what we agreed on." I swallow past the rocks in my throat, frowning down at the table.

"And then he proposed on New Year's in front of everyone."

I nod, chewing my lip.

"Fuck," he mutters, letting out a heavy breath and tightening his hand around mine. "Fucking hell, Darce."

"I don't want you to blame him." I shake my head, wincing. "I think he thought it would solve things—"

"Don't make excuses for him." His eyes lock on mine, sharp with intensity. "That was a really fucked-up thing for him to do."

"I don't want to come between you guys. I just wanted to explain why I freaked out."

His eyes are soft like velvet, so kind and understanding and affectionate that I want to drop myself into his lap, wrap my arms around him, and bury my face in his neck so I can inhale his warm scent and let him comfort me.

It *was* a really fucked up thing for Kit to do, and the relief that Hayden thinks so too has all the tension in my chest dissolving.

Hayden frowns at our hands, then pulls his away, and the moment's over. "Sorry," he mutters.

I try not to deflate. He's a touchy-feely guy, except with me.

The server comes by with the bill, and Hayden rolls his eyes when I try to pull out my credit card.

"Darcy, no." His voice is firm as he pays it. "Don't even try that."

The server leaves, and I give him a grateful smile. "Thank you." I pick my napkin up off my lap and drop it on the table, putting on a confident smile. "Let's go home. I got you a little something."

"Oh, yeah?" He grins, and there's my Hayden again.

I mean, not *my* Hayden. The old Hayden I know and love. *Like*. Whatever.

"Great." He stands and helps me into my coat. "Because I got you something, too."

"HOW DID I DO TONIGHT?" Darcy asks over her shoulder as I help her out of her coat.

Her eyes move around the apartment, over all the flowers I bought her, and she smiles.

"Andersen, you aced it. This has been the best date of my life." I shoot her a flirty grin to make her think I'm joking. "A-plus."

I can't stop thinking about what Kit did to her, proposing in front of everyone. The shocked expression on her face when he got down on one knee looks so much different in hindsight.

I felt guilty for thinking she didn't seem as excited as she should have been. Now I know how right I was.

She reaches down to take her heels off. "Best date of your *life*? You say that to all the girls."

"Half the things we talk about, I don't say to other girls."

I don't talk about what type of porn I like or give them lessons on how to touch guys. And I sure as shit don't knock water over on the table because I'm sweating like some nervous teenager.

She bites back a smile, glowing with pleasure, and my heart

squeezes in my chest. I've been trying not to stare at her all night, but I can't keep from letting my gaze linger on her.

Fucking hell, she's so beautiful. Smug pride weaves through me, expanding in my chest. Darcy rolls out of bed, makeup-free and hair a mess, and fine, I'll admit it, I'm attracted to her. But tonight, all dressed up?

She's stunning, and she looks like that for *me*.

My gaze drops to the hem of her short dress and the soft, smooth skin of her legs. I wonder what panties she's wearing. Darcy likes things to line up and coordinate, she likes things that make sense, so I'm thinking they match one of the colors on her dress.

My mind goes to the row of panties hanging in the bathroom to dry a couple of days ago. I had to grab something from under the sink when she wasn't home.

The light-pink pair, I bet.

"Best date of your life *so far*," Darcy says, lifting a brow. "I might not put out."

I blanche, hit with the overwhelming urge to haul her over my shoulder and carry her to my bedroom.

Her eyes widen and she claps her hands on her face. "I was kidding," she moans, going red beneath her fingers. "I'm sorry. That was a joke. I was trying to be funny and it came out weird."

"It's fine." A hoarse laugh slips out of me. Is she trying to fucking kill me? "I know you were kidding. I'm going to change out of my suit."

In my room, I change into athletic pants and a t-shirt. Through the wall, I listen to her moving around her room—opening and closing drawers, her light footsteps, and then the click of hangers in her closet. The swish of her taking her dress off is probably in my imagination. The walls aren't *that* thin.

Even so, I imagine her standing ten feet away in just her bra and panties.

My groin tightens. Jesus fuck. The things I would do to Darcy Andersen with my tongue alone. I'd work on her for hours, wringing every drop of pleasure out of her, coaxing her body to limits she didn't know existed.

Lust pulls heavy at the base of my spine and I suck in a deep breath, scrubbing a hand over my face before heading back to the living room. When I see her, my steps falter. She's sitting cross-legged on the sofa in leggings and an oversized black hoodie.

An urgent sense of possessiveness uncoils inside me. "Is that my hoodie?"

Her eyes cut to mine. "Yeah. Is that okay? It was on the couch and all mine are in the wash."

It's so big on her, and it's the cutest thing I've ever seen.

Fuck, I like that. I like that so much.

I can't even picture you with a girlfriend, she said earlier, in disbelief. The memory pinches hard, right behind my ribs.

"It's fine," I mumble.

Still, I imagine her losing the pants, just wearing my hoodie and a pair of panties. No bra. Smooth, soft skin. Maybe she's in my lap. Maybe she has her arms around my neck.

Maybe we're making out.

I turn away, wishing I'd taken a cold shower before changing.

"You still haven't answered me," she says as I take a seat on the sofa and stretch out.

"About what?"

"What kind of porn you watch."

Blood rushes to my cock, and I lean forward with my elbows on my knees and my head in my hands, thinking of the least arousing things I can in order to head off my erection. The smell of hockey equipment. The pain when I broke my collar-bone in high school. The way pickles look, all shriveled and green.

Nope. I'm still picturing her sitting on my lap in my hoodie, moaning into my ear as I slide her underwear out of the way and work my fingers between her legs. Another shock of lust rockets through me.

It would be so easy to tell her about the OnlyFans couple I've been watching for years. They're a young married couple, and their videos don't feel like typical porn. Sometimes they're rushed and desperate and intense, sometimes they're slow and sleepy and lazy, but they always feel real. They never show faces, but she's petite, with long pale-blond hair. He has a similar build and hair color to me.

They look like Darcy and me. I pretend they're us. It's my shameful secret. One that I'll take to the grave. I pretend the videos are ones we made together, for our eyes only, and that it's her bouncing on my cock, gasping and shaking and moan-ing. It's my head between her legs, drawing her orgasm out. It's Darcy's ring finger that sparkles. I pretend that we're married, and that it's my hand clutching hers through our orgasms.

"I don't remember," I mumble into my hands.

She laughs. "Liar."

The second she sees, she'll know. Especially if she finds out they're the only porn I watch. I've lost interest in everything else.

"Okay, presents time." She hands me a small gift bag. "I saw this on Etsy last week and thought of you."

I give her a quick smile. "You shouldn't have." Inside the bag, my fingers meet soft cotton, and I pull the t-shirt out to look at it. The image on the front is an illustration of all the characters from *The Northern Sword*.

"It's by a local Vancouver artist," Darcy adds, a touch of shyness in her voice.

My chest floods with warmth as I stare at the lines of the illustration. "No one's ever bought me clothes except my mom."

Darcy groans. "Great. I'm like your mom?"

I laugh. "No, that's not what I meant. It's nice. I love it."

It feels like she's taking care of me. Like I'm hers.

I stand and whip my shirt off, and her eyes widen in alarm.

"What are you doing?"

"Trying it on."

"Now?"

"I want to make sure it fits." Satisfaction thumps in my chest when I catch Darcy's eyes lingering on my taut stomach.

I work hard. My body is my job, and I know what I look like. From the way she's staring, Darcy does, too.

"Excuse me, ma'am." I snap my fingers, smirking and pointing at my face. "Eyes up here."

She jerks her gaze up, her face turning a fucking adorable shade of pink. "Sorry."

I chuckle, flexing. "It's fine. Go ahead and ogle me, Andersen."

"Oh my god." She turns away as I change positions to show off more muscles. "Stop it, you egomaniac." An embarrassed laugh slips out of her, and I grin harder.

"Am I making you uncomfortable?" I flex my biceps, one at a time, and she cackles with laughter. "Are you getting too warm? Is it hot in here, or is it just me?"

"Does this actually work on women?"

"I don't know. I don't act like this with women. They'd run screaming."

I never laugh or act goofy like this with the women I go out with. I don't laugh like this with anyone but her. Darcy makes a pleased humming noise, and I relent, pulling the t-shirt over my head.

"What do you think?" I hold my arms out for her approval, and she smiles, nodding as her gaze moves over me, snagging on my chest, shoulders, and waist.

"It fits." She meets my eyes, lifting her brows in a question. "Do you like it?"

"I love it." I really fucking do. I like her buying me clothes, and I like her wearing my hoodie. I like going out for dinner and sitting on the couch beside her after in the home where we live together.

"One more." As I take the seat beside her on the couch, the line of her throat works, and she hands me a flat wrapped package about the size of a book.

"Jeez, Andersen, you're spoiling me."

She shifts, pulling her knee up beneath her on the couch. Even though we're not touching, I can feel her body heat. I pull the wrapping paper off, and my heart shoots up into my throat.

It's a framed photo of us in university. Third year, I think. We're dressed in green, wearing cheap plastic hats that we got on the St. Patrick's Day pub crawl. One of my arms is looped around her shoulder, and we're both holding our dyed green hands up to the camera, smiling ear to ear.

"It's too sentimental, isn't it?" She winces. "Sorry. I just love this photo. It's my favorite."

The ache in my chest unfolds, taking up more space. "Hey." I hook my arm around her like in the photo, pulling her against me. My *no touching Darcy* rule fades into the background. "Shut up," I murmur, teasing.

"You don't have to display it or anything," she protests.

I press a hand over her mouth, stifling her laughter. "Just shut your little mouth, okay?" I say gently to make her laugh again, my skin tingling at the way her smile feels under my palm. "I love it." I press a quick, firm kiss to her forehead.

Now I don't feel so weird about my second gift to her. She's going to say I spent way too much, but this framed photo of Darcy and me is priceless.

Besides, she's going to hate my first gift, and I can't wait.

"What are you smiling at?" she asks.

I grin wider. "I can't wait to give you *your* present." I head to my room, slip the small box into my pocket, and then carry the big box back to the living room.

"You really didn't have to get me anything," she says, eyes lighting up with curiosity as I set it on the coffee table. The box is light but big, taking up half the surface of the table. "You already got enough flowers to last a lifetime."

"Oh, wait until you unwrap it to thank me." I try not to grin too hard as I flop back down on the couch.

She pulls the paper off and her curious expression drops into a flat, unamused frown.

"Hayden."

I start shaking with laughter as she stares at the box, repulsed.

"Please tell me this is a joke and that's not actually what's inside."

"Open it and find out." God, this is fun.

She opens the flap of the box and groans. "Are you serious?"

"FOR VALENTINE'S DAY, you got me a pillow shaped like a man's chest?"

Hayden's eyes glitter with amusement. This is Hayden at peak handsome, smiling and relaxed, his long, toned limbs sprawled out across the sofa. "For cuddling. Do you like it?"

I make a strangled noise, but I start laughing. "No!"

On the box, an exuberant woman has the stuffed arm propped around her shoulder.

"Is this a message? Should I practice on inanimate objects first?"

He pretends to look concerned. "Did you want the one with chest hair instead?"

I whirl on him, unable to hold back my curiosity. "Was that an option?"

"Oh, yeah." His eyes sparkle. "I wasn't sure what your preference was." He lifts the stuffed man chest up and props it over his shoulder. "You can sit on the couch and watch TV with it."

I cringe. "It looks so small next to you."

He gives me a knowing, flirty smile, and I roll my eyes.

"Don't be weird."

I pray he doesn't take his shirt off and start flexing again. My skin still feels warm from when he did that earlier.

"Well." He tosses the man chest onto a nearby chair, sighing like he's disappointed. "I'm sorry you hate your present. I'm a terrible wingman." He reaches into his pocket and pulls out a black velvet box. "I didn't have time to wrap this one."

"That's okay." I narrow my eyes at it with suspicion. "Too big to be an engagement ring, so that's good."

His smile falters, and I press my mouth tight. I always say the wrong thing.

"Sorry. Just thinking about earlier, I guess." I open the box, and all the weird feelings fall away.

The bracelet is beautiful. A delicate gold chain with tiny clusters of hexagons and glittering, clear stones. I run the pad of my thumb over them, memorizing the textures.

"Are those honeycombs?"

His gaze is easy and warm on me. "Mhm."

We hold eye contact for a long moment, and I wonder, does he remember? A few years ago, I went down a rabbit hole about bees. It was all I could talk about for weeks. Bees can count. Their hives are built in an organized, methodical, *mathematical* fashion. Even though they're just a tiny insect, bees work together to build strong, stable beehives with these hexagons.

It's what I love about math, the sheer wonder and awe of it. How it's everywhere in nature.

My eyes go to the sparkling gemstones. "Tell me those aren't diamonds, Hayden."

"Sure." A pleased grin spans his handsome features. "They're *not* diamonds."

"Hayden." I was trying to scold him, but it comes out softer than I meant.

"They're lab grown," he adds, watching me. "I know you."

I'm speechless. Lab-grown diamonds, or synthetic diamonds, are the same composition as traditional diamonds—same hardness, structure, and sometimes better clarity—except they're grown using high heat and pressure rather than mined. They're another example of how math and science improve our world.

"I love it," I whisper, smiling up at Hayden, pleasure wrapping around my ribs in tight bands. "It's too much."

Hayden just smiles and shrugs, and my stomach flutters. No one sees me like he does, and I'm not sure what to do with that.

"Thank you." I reach for a hug, and he wraps his arms around me, pulling me into his hard chest.

"Happy to, Darce." His voice is low in my ear, making my skin prickle. Against me, his chest rises and falls with his steady breathing, and my mind flips to earlier, when he took his shirt off.

Muscles. Ridges. Smooth, golden skin. A light smattering of dark blond chest hair trailing from his defined pecs, down his abs, and into the waistband of his pants.

I wanted to count each of his muscles with my tongue. I wanted to press my lips to his collarbone and then skim them down each ab, feel them jump under my mouth as his breath catches.

An image filters into my head, of running my palms over his smooth chest while I'm on top of him, straddling his lean hips, working myself down his thick length. Arousal shocks through me.

My crush is stronger than ever, and I really, really want to fuck my best friend.

Against my fingertips, his t-shirt fabric is soft, and he's so warm. Hayden smells like a fresh, clean forest. I take a deep inhale and my scalp tingles. His scent does something to my brain, making my thoughts sharpen and focus on him and him alone.

The hug should have ended seconds ago, but he's still holding me tight.

I'm about to do something stupid.

"I do miss this part," I murmur against him.

His voice is low, his breath tickling my ear. "Which part?"

"Physical affection." Nerves tumble around me. I should stop talking. "Cuddling. I miss cuddling."

I miss sex, and every brain cell in my head wonders what it would be like with him.

Electricity snaps in the air, tense and sparking like the moments before a thunderstorm. He pulls back a few inches with a serious expression, his breathing uneven, and the hairs on the back of my neck rise. His entire thigh is pressed against mine, so solid and toned. His eyes are such a crushing blue I could fall right into them.

His jaw flexes and he swallows. "Then we should cuddle."

DARCY'S EYES WIDEN, pupils flaring past every shade of green in her irises, and my blood drums in my ears.

Why did I say that?

Because I want her. I want her so fucking badly. Being so close to her is agony, inhaling her scent and feeling the warmth of her skin, watching her pretty, plump lips curve into a pleased smile in response to the present I picked out for her.

At dinner, she claimed buying gifts was one downside of being in a relationship, but shopping for her Valentine's Day gifts was the highlight of my week. Spending money on her gave me an expanding sense of masculine pride. Buying her things could become an addiction if I let it.

And now I'm proposing we cuddle? What the hell am I doing?

My arm is still around her shoulder, and I can't bring myself to move it. She's so warm. Her hair smells so good. My control is shredded.

I'm her wingman, and she isn't interested in anything serious, but I want her too much to think clearly.

"Cuddle." My voice sounds hoarse, so I clear my throat.

Jesus. I'm acting like a teenage boy on prom night. "We should cuddle, since you miss it."

Self-loathing drips into my blood. I'm the fucking worst. Kit thinks I'm looking after her, and instead, I'm finding ways to touch her.

He manipulated her by proposing in front of everyone when he knew she wanted to break up, though, so fuck that guy.

Warning bells ring at the edge of my conscience, but I ignore them. Christ, I want to kiss her. If I were smart, I'd head straight to my room—alone—and release all this pent-up sexual frustration in the shower with my forehead against the tiles, muffling my groan.

I'm not smart, though. Not where Darcy's concerned.

"As friends," I add, my heart pounding. She can see right fucking through me, I'm sure, but I'm flying down a hill with no brakes. "I'm sure there's some science about how it's good for people."

"Oxytocin." She wets her lips. "It's released when people touch. They encourage parents to do it with newborns."

Tension hangs in the air.

"I'll do it." I swallow. "But only if I can be the baby."

She bursts out laughing, and even though my pulse drums in my ears, I grin. A few knots in my chest ease, and I lower down on the sofa, holding my arms open. Like it's the hundredth time we've done this, she tucks herself against me, her back to my front, and just like that, we're cuddling.

It's the best thing I've ever experienced.

Instinct grips me by the throat as I fold myself around her, pulling her closer to me. She's so soft, so warm, such a perfect fit against me. We're lined up against each other, and I wonder if she can feel my heart racing.

What am I doing? Do I care?

"This okay?" I murmur.

"Mhm." She turns, glancing over her shoulder. "Can you breathe like that? My hair is probably suffocating you."

"I'm good." I could die like this. She smells like heaven. It's taking every shred of my control not to press my nose to the back of her neck. Instead, I rest my chin on the top of her head.

Is this what having a girlfriend is like? Is this what I've been missing out on for years?

It would never be like this with anyone else, though. It's not the act of cuddling with a woman, it's cuddling with *Darcy* that's sending my body and mind into overdrive.

You know what? Fuck it.

Driven by my dumb caveman brain, I press my nose to the back of her neck and inhale deep.

All the blood in my body rushes to my dick, and in three seconds, I'm hard as steel. My lips part at the intense urge to thrust against her.

Holy *fuck*.

I read an article once where a porn star said when he's having performance issues on set, he smells the back of his female costar's neck. Something about pheromones. I told everyone this at the bar, and Miller tried it with Hazel. He said it didn't work.

Well, it's fucking working now.

My balls ache with arousal and my cock strains against my pants. If Darcy moves even an inch, she's going to feel it.

Panic threads through me, cutting through my blinding lust. I need a cold shower. I need to jerk off. Fuck. No. I just need to get out of here.

Darcy lets out a content sigh and shifts, and my mind goes blank as her ass presses back into me.

She tenses.

I tense.

Neither of us is breathing.

She opens her mouth to say something, but I almost fly off the sofa, hurrying to my feet and turning away. I saw her reaction to the ring tonight; I can't be doing this. This isn't what she wants.

I'm going to ruin everything.

"I need to go to bed." I'm halfway out of the room. "Thanks for, uh. Yeah. Good night."

Moments later, I'm in the shower, water running down my body. I'm so hard it hurts, and I'm already close to coming. One hand props against the tiles, and the other grips my erection, sliding up and down the length as my mind races with images of Darcy.

Her on her knees at my feet, pretty plush lips wrapped around the width of me, taking me all the way to the back of her mouth while her gaze rises to mine.

Me on my knees in front of her, an arm around her hips to hold her steady, her leg over my shoulder, my tongue deep inside her, feeling her writhe and convulse on me. My face soaked with her arousal. Listening to every gasp and moan.

Pleasure coils around the base of my spine, my balls tighten, and my release hits me with sharp ecstasy. I clench my eyes closed as I come, breathing hard, muffling my groan.

Like always, I hope this release gets rid of the lingering desire for her. The pull toward her, the intense attraction that seems to grow every day.

It's not enough, though. It never is.

THE NEXT MORNING, I'm waiting in the kitchen among the eight bouquets of flowers, breathing in their floral scent and rehearsing what I'm going to say, when Hayden appears, bag strung over his shoulder and ready to leave for a seven-day away game stretch.

My gaze falls to his chest, and I automatically smile. "You're wearing the t-shirt."

He glances down at it, mouth tilting up. "Of course I am."

It doesn't seem weird between us after last night, so that's good.

In the mornings, Hayden's so handsome, blue eyes all sleepy, hair still damp from his shower, and dark-blond stubble coating his sharp jaw. My fingers itch to touch it, scrape through it with my nails.

No. After last night, no more touching. He had the right idea by cutting it short.

My face heats at the memory. God, I'm so embarrassed.

His eyes go to my wrist. "And you're wearing the bracelet."

I find the delicate chain and toy with it like I did all night when I couldn't sleep. It's hard sleeping in the bed alone; I've always slept better with someone beside me. On top of that, I was worrying all night about messing things up with Hayden.

"Of course I am." I give him a quick smile. "I'll drive you to the airport."

He blinks, lips parting, and his expression turns apologetic. "Volkov's picking me up."

"Oh." I was planning to use the time in the car to apologize for last night. "I didn't think of that."

"It's fine. You should be sleeping in, not chauffeuring me around." He drops his bag and heads to the front hall closet to grab his boots. "Go back to bed."

If we don't talk about last night, it'll be weird, and Hayden is pretty much all I have right now. I don't want him to think I'm getting the wrong idea about us.

I can't fuck things up with him. I just can't.

"You can't leave yet." I try not to sound frantic. "You're a zombie without your morning coffee."

I hit the button on the espresso maker and the machine whirs to life. A moment later, a stream of espresso drips into the tiny cup.

His eyes go from the espresso maker to me, a wary expression on his features. "I was going to get a coffee at the airport."

"Airport coffee sucks. Ours is much better."

His eyes warm at the word *ours*. "I guess I have a few minutes." He takes a seat at the kitchen bar and accepts the espresso I hand him. The cup looks comically tiny in his huge hands.

"So, um." I move so I can see him around the flowers and lean on the counter, concentrating on not wringing my hands or fidgeting. "Last night."

He stills, and our eyes meet.

"I'm really sorry." I look at him dead-on while my heart pounds. "We cuddled, and I got horny."

Hayden coughs mid-sip, staring hard at a spot on the floor, and my face flames harder. Pressed against his body, my hormones took over and made me grind back against him.

He was hard. I swallow, remembering how his intimidating erection felt pushing against me.

Just like I suspected, he's proportional. I shiver at the memory.

I know what happened: he got turned on because he's a hot-blooded human in need of regular sex, which he hasn't been getting lately because he spends all his time with me. He's a good friend, so when I basically begged him to cuddle me, he said yes.

I need to show him I'm not reading into his body's response and that nothing has changed between us.

"It's not a big deal." Rule number one: Always be confident and chill. "It took me by surprise because I haven't felt that way in a long time." Uh, I'm losing the plot here. "You're —" I wave my hand at him, and he arches an eyebrow with amusement.

"I'm what?"

"Big. Tall. Broad. Muscles. Good smelling." With each word, his grin hitches higher. My skin is too warm. "Stop smiling."

"What's wrong with smiling?"

"You look smug."

"You just told me I make you horny."

"*Made*," I stress. "*Made* me horny because I was pressed up against you—oh my god."

I didn't just press up against him. I ground my ass against him like a cat in heat. Hayden sputters with laughter into his tiny coffee cup.

"Stop it." I put on a stern voice, fighting a smile as relief loops through me. "I'm trying to be serious."

He frowns down at his cup in a thoughtful way. "If I smell good, does this mean we're probably not distantly related?"

I burst out laughing. "No, probably not. You smell amazing."

He smiles up at me, sitting back in his chair, and warmth tumbles through my stomach.

"My body reacted. It doesn't mean anything. Nothing has changed between us."

Rule number five, the most important of all: Never get attached.

"Yeah." His smile dims, and his chin dips in a tight nod. "I know."

"I took your offer of cuddling and made it inappropriate. You're helping me and that's it."

His mouth flattens. "Yep. That's it."

And then there was the shower after. Every time he touches me, he jumps in the shower after. I try not to think too hard about that. I know I'm not his type, but to need to *shower* after touching me?

Ouch.

"Great. So we both agree it wasn't a big deal."

Hayden's smile is tight. "Already forgotten."

I paste my own smile on. This is exactly what I want, so I don't know why hearing that is so disappointing.

His phone chirps, and he pulls it out of his pocket. "Volkov's downstairs." He stands and puts the cup in the dishwasher. "Thanks for the coffee."

"Of course." The words come out too high and too chipper. "Have a great trip. I'll be watching your games."

He winks. "Bye, Darce. Stay out of trouble."

It isn't until the door closes and I hear the ping of the elevator arrive that I realize I'm really going to miss him over the next week.

"NICE T-SHIRT," Miller comments as I load my bag into the overhead bin on the plane.

"Thanks." This t-shirt is now my most prized possession. "Darcy gave it to me."

His eyebrows go up with interest as I drop into my seat. "I take it Valentine's Day went well?"

My exhale is heavy as I think about what a mess I made of things.

Miller chuckles. "That bad, huh? Alright, tell the expert what's wrong so we can fix it."

I let out a dry laugh of disbelief. "Expert? You're joking, right? Hazel hated you until, like, last week."

"Darcy didn't like the flowers?"

"She liked them." I fold my arms over my chest and stare out the window. "She liked the bracelet I got her, too."

Miller whistles. "A bracelet, too?" His grin stretches ear to ear. "Now you're thinking. What's the problem?"

"We, uh," I spare a glance at him, "cuddled."

"Cuddled?" he repeats loudly, and the guys around us look over.

"Shut the fuck up," I hiss. "Someone will hear."

"My bad. Wouldn't want someone to know you and Darcy *cuddled* out of wedlock."

"We were cuddling as friends. It didn't mean anything."

It sounds so fucking stupid out loud.

He stares at me for a long moment and bursts out laughing. "Cuddling as friends?"

"It's a thing."

It's not a thing. I needed to touch her, and it blew up in my face when she made it clear that nothing would ever come of it. That my body turned her on but nothing was ever, ever going to happen between us.

It *didn't mean anything*, she said. That's me. A pretty face and a good fuck. Even Darcy, who knows me better than anyone, can see that.

And yet, for some reason, I tucked the framed photo of us into my bag to bring on my road trip. I like torturing myself, I guess.

Or maybe I'll just miss her.

Miller looks over the seats. "Hey, Streicher, do you want to cuddle later? As friends?"

A few rows away, Streicher gives him a surly glare.

Miller turns back to me with delight shining in his eyes. "Sorry, you were saying?"

I pull the brim of my baseball hat low on my forehead and sink into my seat, the unspoken signal for *I'm taking a nap; don't bother me*, but Miller flicks my hat up.

"Owens." His smile dims a few notches as he searches my expression. "What are you doing?"

In my mind, I see Darcy's petrified expression when the engagement ring appeared on her plate at dinner. "Nothing. She's not ready for a relationship."

"So help her be ready. Show her what it could be like."

My throat knots with worry. "The last guy tried that, remember? And she freaked out."

Miller hums, thinking.

If she didn't want long term with Kit, every woman's dream guy, how's she going to feel after my shiny newness wears off?

Ward appears in the aisle and hands us each a folder. "Gentlemen."

"Coach."

He moves on, and I flip through the game packet—folders with our travel itinerary, room assignments, game schedule, and notes on each game. A Polaroid slips between the pages.

A surprised laugh bursts out of me at the picture of that stupid fucking gnome tucked into my bed, head on my pillow, wearing an eye mask.

On the back, Darcy's writing reads *Good luck! I'll be watching your games (and sleeping in your bed). - Daniel*

She must have done this when I was at practice or something. I can't stop smiling. My thoughts stray to the video I took of Darcy last night while being serenaded.

I pull my phone out. *Daniel better not jerk off in my bed while I'm gone*, I text Darcy.

Her response is immediate. *Where's he supposed to do it? He has needs.*

My grin broadens, and all the weird feelings from last night and this morning melt away. *On the patio like a normal person.*

She responds with a GIF of Jim Carrey gagging, and I beam at my phone, pop an earbud in, and pull up the video of her from last night, looking mortified while serenaded.

The morning coffees because she knows I'm useless before caffeine, the t-shirt from our favorite book series, our dumb shared jokes like the creepy gnome—my life is better when we're living together.

I always say Kit's my best friend, but he's not. It's Darcy.

I'm not dumb enough to continue denying my feelings for her, but I won't act on them and mess up the best thing that's ever happened to me.

HAYDEN APPEARS in my bedroom doorway a week later and I slam my laptop closed.

"I didn't even hear you get home."

"I know." He quirks a curious grin at me, tilting his chin at my laptop. "Are you working?"

I'm trying to figure out why the Vancouver Storm are so bad at power plays when they use all their best guys on them.

While watching Hayden's games on TV this week, something about my old analytical models called to me. It's easy to get lost in the numbers when I'm concentrating, and I've found myself working way past bedtime almost every night.

This week, one thing has become crystal clear: they'll never get to the playoffs if they can't improve their chance of scoring during power plays.

"Just some paperwork thing," I lie.

They're just for fun, though, and it's not like I'll ever show anyone. The last thing I want is Hayden telling me to back off.

We stare at each other for a long moment, and I try not to think about the cuddling. We've carefully avoided it or any mention of Valentine's Day while we texted all week.

I also try not to think about the photo I gave him as a gift, and how, when I glanced in his open bedroom doorway, I didn't see it displayed. It's not in the living room, either.

He probably tossed it in a drawer and forgot about it. I don't know what I expected.

"So, I was thinking—" I start.

"What are you—" he says at the same time.

We both let out light, awkward laughs.

"Sorry." I gesture at him. "Go ahead."

He shakes his head. "No. You."

My stomach flutters. I don't know why I'm nervous. "I've been thinking about Valentine's Day."

"Oh, yeah?" There's a weird tone to his voice, and he's watching my face closely.

"Yeah." I frown, wiggling my toes against the floor. "I was really weird about the whole engagement ring thing."

He shakes his head. "Oh, Darce. Don't worry about that."

"But I have been. Imagine if I was on a real date with a real guy. Not that you're not a real guy." I make a face. "You know what I mean."

He makes a noise of acknowledgment, mouth slanted down.

"It would be totally weird." A sliver of anger cuts through me, because even after my relationship with Kit is over, he's still coming back to haunt me, and I'm desperate to shake him off. "If you're free tonight, I'd love to take you on another practice date." I give him a tentative smile. "I promise I won't freak out if any engagement rings get put on my plate."

"Uh." He makes a hesitant face, and my stomach sinks.

"You can't," I say quickly. "You're busy. Of course you are. That's fine."

"No, um. I got invited to a party."

"Nice." I'm nodding. I feel stupid. He's the hottest guy in the NHL. Of course he got invited to a party. "Awesome."

"No, Darce." He laughs lightly. "Sorry, I'm saying this all wrong. I got invited to a cast party for *The Northern Sword*. Miller posted a picture of me wearing the t-shirt you got me on the plane, and the production studio saw it."

"I saw it, too." Who *didn't* see that picture? The online book community lost their freaking minds at the idea of Hayden Owens loving *The Northern Sword*.

"Yeah, so," he blows out a breath, "what do you think?"

"I think you should go." I force a smile. "I bet there'll be lots of women there."

Hitting on him. Laughing at his jokes. Slobbering all over him while I sit on the couch at home and try not to think about it.

He gives me an amused look of disbelief, shaking his head. "Oh my god. Andersen, I'm asking you to go with me."

I blink at him. "Shut up."

He grins. "Is that a yes?"

"Really?" My voice goes very, very high.

"*Yes*," he laughs. "Who else am I going to go with? Volkov?"

"Hayden." I run over and slap his shoulder, and he laughs again. "Shut up!"

"You don't want to go. I understand."

I make a strangled, choking noise, and he grins harder, eyes bright.

"I want to go!"

"Hmm." He inspects my face. "I don't know. You don't seem into it."

"I'm into it. I want to go. Please." I lace my fingers together and smile up at him. "Pleeease take me to the party."

"I knew I'd have to drag you out." He sighs before giving

me a quick grin and heading to his room. "Let me change, and I'll meet you in the kitchen when you're ready. We can get dinner first."

I nod eagerly and race to get ready.

CLOSED FOR A PRIVATE EVENT, the sign on the restaurant in Gastown reads when we arrive for the cast party for *The Northern Sword*.

"Name?" the guy at the door asks us, holding a clipboard.

"Hayden Owens and Darcy Andersen," Hayden says with smooth confidence, like he does this all the time, and I take a mental note. Hayden nails rule number one: act confident and chill.

The guy takes our coats and gestures us inside, and I give Hayden a funny smile. "You put my name on the list already?"

"I had a feeling you'd say yes, and I wasn't going to go without you."

Inside, I spot three cast members immediately, along with a handful of other actors who don't work on the show. And three musicians.

"There are a lot of famous people here," I murmur to Hayden, my self-consciousness rising.

He puts his hand on my lower back like he can sense my trepidation. "Don't worry," he murmurs back in my ear, his breath tickling my neck. "I'm just a regular guy."

A laugh slips out of me, and my self-consciousness eases. He dips down farther to catch my eye.

"I won't leave your side, okay?"

Gratitude expands through me. "Okay."

"Come on." He nudges me toward the bar. "Let's get a drink."

———

Sometime later, after we've met a handful of the cast, Hayden and I sit near the downstairs bar, watching the partygoers.

"There's Aurora." I subtly point to the star of the series, who's laughing with someone. She's my favorite character, the practical, hardworking maid everyone underestimated. When she unlocks her secret powers, she's unstoppable.

Nearby, the actor who plays Cadius, the Golden Prince, is surrounded by women and laughing loudly. Cadius is another of my favorite characters, but not until later in the series. That's when he really starts to remind me of Hayden. At first, Cadius is the overconfident, spoiled prince who's had everything handed to him. He has no clue how the real world works, no empathy, and no idea how privileged he is. He gets a rough wake-up call when he and Aurora go on the quest to find his kidnapped fiancée at the beginning of the first book.

He learns, though. He tries and he listens to Aurora, and he comes to care for commoners more than his ego or image. He makes sacrifices for people in his life, and he finds ways to be a better leader. He's kind and compassionate, and he'd do anything for the people he loves. When Aurora is close to breaking, he makes jokes to cheer her up and tells her she can do anything. When her power surfaced and she unleashed it, he knew she could do it all along.

The actor who plays Cadius isn't as handsome as Hayden,

though, and when I read the books, it's Hayden I picture on those fantastical adventures.

At the other bar, the actress who plays Queen Amethyst glances over at us, and an unhappy feeling twists in my stomach.

"Queen Amethyst is giving you the eyes." I try to keep my tone casual as I sip my drink.

"Is she?" Hayden glances at my lips around the straw.

"Yes." After we walked in, she asked to take a photo with him, but he dragged me into it, too. "She mentioned she hadn't seen much of Vancouver, like, four times."

He shrugs. "It's not like she's going to have time for sightseeing. They were telling me about their shooting schedules. They have zero free time."

I can't tell whether he's being deliberately obtuse or not. "Hayden, the only sightseeing she wanted to do was in your pants."

He shoots me a roguish grin. "My dick?"

"Mhm." I nod, stifling a laugh. "She wants to get to know little Hayden."

His expression turns knowing and cocky. "It's not *little*."

God, I remember. Heat races through me. "It's none of my business." I put on a disinterested expression, even though I'm very, very interested in hearing more. "And I'm not judging."

"Hey." He leans forward, getting in my face, making hard eye contact, and I start shaking with laughter. He stares at me dead-on with a mock-serious expression while his eyes sparkle. "It's not little, okay? It's huge, like a baseball bat. It's a monster. Women call it Godzilla."

I act revolted. "No one calls it that."

"They would if I asked them to," he adds, grinning. "Lots of women can vouch for it not being little."

"I'm sure." A bad taste fills my mouth. I shove my straw

between my lips and take a long sip to wash it away. "I'm sure Queen Amethyst would love to fact-check that."

He makes an unhappy noise of acknowledgment.

"She's exactly your type," I say for some reason, because I just can't shut up about this.

"What are you talking about?"

"You know. Super tall, long dark hair, big boobs." I make an hourglass shape with my hand. "Great butt. Tiny waist."

Queen Amethyst could probably crush my ribcage with her thighs while I cried for mercy.

Hayden frowns at me.

"All the women you date fit that description."

He looks away, jaw ticking like he wants to say something. "Darcy?"

I swallow. "What?"

"Shut up," he says gently, smiling, and I snort at myself.

"Right. We're on a date do-over," I say. "No trying to hook you up with other women."

"Look at you." He reaches over and puts his arm around my shoulder. "You're a quick study."

He's being touchy-feely tonight for a change, and pleasure loops through me.

"Taught by the best."

His smile dims and he takes his arm back. "How was work this week?"

"Fine." I shrug. He makes a hand gesture for me to continue, and I give him a flat look. "My job isn't conversation material for a date."

He watches me for a moment, and I can't read his expression. "You used to talk my ear off about the stuff you were working on." His eyes narrow as he looks away, thinking. "Your school project in fourth-year university. The scholarship thing?"

"The Women in STEM prediction model." I used government data to determine which girls entering university had the lowest chance of finishing based on financial hardships. "They still use it today, actually, to allocate scholarships and funding. With updated data every year, of course."

His mouth hooks into a proud smile, his warm gaze moving over me, and I grin into my drink.

"That's really fucking cool, Darce."

"It was." Using statistics to help people made that project so fun; it didn't even feel like work. "They have a Vancouver branch of the organization and a few events coming up. I might go to one."

"And you should find a job that makes you smile like that."

I snort. "Most jobs don't make people happy, and I have nothing to complain about. My job is fine. It pays the bills and I get vacation time and great benefits. They pay for my phone, which is nice. And they paid for me to ship my stuff here when I moved to the Vancouver office." I force a bright, optimistic smile. "It's not so bad."

He tilts his head, one eyebrow going up like he doesn't believe me.

"And yeah, maybe a huge part of my job is to save money for the insurance company by predicting how much patients will cost long term, and they use our data to determine premiums, ultimately making the owners richer, but that's a huge chunk of the actuarial field. And that's business." I shrug. "A lot of jobs are about money when it comes down to it."

I had a job I loved once, right out of university. And then I fucked it all up. It's better this way, with a boring job. No one gets hurt and no one gets fired.

He rubs his jaw. "I know I'm not as smart as you—"

"You are, Hayden. Don't say that." I hate when he makes comments like that, like he's some dumb jock. "There are lots of ways to be intelligent that have nothing to do with school or math. Social skills, kindness, and compassion count just as much." My expression turns wry. "And you always had good grades in school."

It's dim in here, but it almost seems like he's blushing. "I was trying to say that you deserve to have a job you get excited about, not just one you put up with. Something that doesn't feel like work."

We lock eyes for a long moment, just smiling at each other, and even in the low restaurant lighting, his eyes glitter. My gaze follows the sharp line of his jaw, his stubble, and my fingers itch to trace it.

He really is otherworldly handsome. In a different life, he'd be at this cast party as one of the actors.

That isn't why I feel lucky to be here with him, though. Hayden is one of the kindest people I know, and despite the constant attention he gets for his looks or career, or that he's essentially a celebrity in a city that loves hockey, it hasn't gone to his head. He could snap his fingers and have women fall at his feet, but he's sitting at a party with his dorky friend from university.

"This is why I don't talk about my job on dates." My smile is self-deprecating. "I'm making up a rule number six of being a player: don't talk about boring stuff on dates. Only talk about fun, sexy topics."

He grins. "Fun, sexy topics," he repeats.

"Like..." I rack my brain for something funny.

"Like..." He makes a *go on* gesture. "I can't wait to hear this."

"Like what your favorite sex position is."

CHAPTER 24

DARCY

HAYDEN BLINKS like I've grown another head. "What?"

He looks so serious and stricken that I start laughing. "Hayden, don't be so uptight. I know you have one."

His eyes flash with heat, his gaze drops to my mouth, and he swallows. "I don't know. Depends on the situation and how I'm feeling." A frisson of electricity runs up my spine at the dark look in his eyes. "Probably whatever position makes her come the hardest."

My stomach dips at the image of Hayden in bed, giving his partner his full attention as he works to make her come. My pulse begins to pound between my legs, and I sip the rest of my drink down to the ice.

"You?" he asks lightly.

My mind has gone blank, and I can't remember a single position. I'm just thinking about Hayden in bed and what it would be like. His body is ridiculous, and paired with his thoughtful, fun-loving nature, sleeping with Hayden Owens might be a life-changing experience.

No wonder he's a rumored sex god.

I get a mental image of him on top of me, pressing me into

the bed with his size and weight. I'm on my stomach, and when he pushes inside me, my eyes roll back at the intense fullness of him, the sensation of his lips on the back of my neck, and the low rumble of his groan.

My skin burns hot. "The one where I'm on my stomach, lying down?" My voice sounds thin and high. "And he's on top of me?" I clear my throat.

"That's a good one." His voice is hoarse, and he's gripping his glass so hard his knuckles go white. "Easier to give you a G-spot orgasm." He blinks. "Her. Give *her* a G-spot orgasm."

My curiosity piques. "Do most guys know how to give a girl a G-spot orgasm? It's the spot on the front wall of the—"

"I know what the G-spot is, Darcy." His eyes close briefly.

Of course he does. "I know *you* do." My face goes red as I try not to picture Hayden in my bed, fingers buried deep inside me, coaxing me closer to an orgasm. Heat coils low in my belly and I cross my legs, squeezing tight.

"What about other guys?" I peek over at him. "Is that something guys talk about in the locker room?"

"Not really."

His expression is unusually flat, totally devoid of humor or teasing, and embarrassment floods through me. Oh *god*. I just asked my wingman a horrifying question.

"You know what?" My voice is high, and I laugh to lighten the tension. "Pretend I never asked. This is mortifying. I think I'm drunk."

That makes Hayden huff with amusement, and the grin splitting across his face eases some of my humiliation. "You're not drunk."

"I'm not drunk," I confirm. "I just say dumb things sometimes. Sorry. I was going for fun, flirty conversation, and I took us straight to weird and inappropriate."

"No." He shakes his head, smiling a little. "It's fine. You can ask me anything." His gaze slides to me, curious. "Why are you asking about this?"

My face burns again. The answer is embarrassing.

"Darce," he coaxes, starting to grin.

"Because I don't think I've ever had one?" I wince. "I don't mean to put you in an awkward position. You won't tell anyone, right? I don't want people thinking Kit is, like, bad in bed or something."

He was just vanilla. A little passive and tentative. Rushed.

Boring, a voice whispers in my head. *Selfish.*

Hayden shakes his head, mouth flattening. "I won't say a word."

"Did Kit ever mention anything about that stuff to you?"

Alarm flashes in his eyes. "Sex stuff?"

I nod.

"No. Well—" He runs a hand over his hair, adopting an uneasy expression. "In December, he said something that implied you two weren't really..." His eyes meet mine. "Yeah."

"Sleeping together."

"Yep."

I'm sure Hayden has a thousand questions, but he's too polite to ask. In the last six months of our relationship, Kit and I had sex twice. I knew things weren't right, and I was talking myself in and out of breaking up with him, and sleeping together felt disingenuous. Like I was lying or giving him false hope.

He gives me a sidelong look. "You want to talk about it?"

"No." I sigh. "Yes. I don't know. Nothing was wrong. Was the sex mind-blowing and life-altering? No. It was just sex. It was comfortable and predictable and nice."

"Nice," Hayden repeats in a weird tone, looking straight ahead.

"Yes. Nice. Simple. That's how sex in a relationship is."

Another reason why I'm not eager to jump back into something long term. I want my fun hookup years.

"We were each other's first." I swallow past a knot, stirring the ice in my glass. "We didn't know what we were doing. I still don't, obviously. So I'm curious about what's out there." The idea of fooling around with some strange guy makes my muscles tense in a bad way, though. "When I'm ready."

"When you're ready," he echoes.

We're quiet for a long time, and with every second, I regret opening my big mouth.

"Have you tried a toy?" Hayden finally asks, glancing at me.

"Once," I admit. Thank god it's dark in here. My face is probably the color of a tomato. "I didn't like it. It was..." I search for the words. "Aggressive? Scary? Felt like a power sander on my lady parts?"

"Jesus," Hayden mutters.

I don't mention that Kit bought it. He was disappointed that it didn't work the way he wanted, and we never spoke of it again.

"It was loud and distracting, and I kept worrying the neighbors could hear?" A laugh slips out of me, and the corners of Hayden's mouth turn up, but his eyes are still watchful and concerned. "I didn't like it," I say again.

Another beat of silence, and my face heats even more.

"There are other toys out there." He stares at his drink. I watch his Adam's apple bob as he swallows. "Quieter ones."

"I'm sure there are, but I'm not brave enough to go into a store and ask questions." I shudder in preemptive embarrassment. "And every time I browse online, I get overwhelmed with the choices. There are literally thousands of toys online. How do I know which one is the best? Do I just order ten and try them all out?" I make a face. "And what do I do with the ones I don't like? Throw them in the garbage? What if someone sees?"

Hayden's shoulders are shaking with laughter, and I clamp my mouth shut.

"See?" I give him a look. "This is my problem. I overthink everything."

"Yeah." He smiles back at me, affection warming his eyes. "You're too in your head."

He makes a low humming noise, and I'd do anything to know what's in his head.

"I can see you thinking," I say. "Spit it out."

He hesitates. "I can help." His voice is low and a little rough, a gentle scrape that makes the back of my neck prickle, and his eyes flash with heat.

Fire races through me, and again, my mind goes to the danger zone, imagining his mouth on my neck and his hand trailing down my body, sneaking beneath my clothes, slipping into my panties, stroking over me. I picture his eyes glazed with heat and his flirty, amused smile as I writhe under him.

We shouldn't be doing this, I'd say. *I know*, he'd whisper back with a wicked smile. Desire tightens between my thighs.

"I'll ask around and find some suggestions," he continues. "For toys." His throat works. "I can ask the women I know."

Embarrassment replaces the horny thoughts, and I want to sink into the floor. He wasn't referring to helping me *like that*.

"That's okay." I wince. "I don't want everyone knowing about this."

"I'm not going to tell them it's for you." He frowns. "This stays between us. I'd never talk about your personal stuff with anyone." His jaw shifts and he folds his arms over his chest. "It's important that you get comfortable with what you like." He swallows again, meeting my eyes. "In bed."

The horny thoughts creep back into my head, but I force them out again. "You make a good point. How am I supposed to ask a guy to do something if I can't do it myself?"

His jaw flexes, and he looks like he wants to say more, but the bartender swings by, and the conversation is over.

I'M STILL THINKING about fucking Darcy in her favorite sex position when Patrick Grant, the male lead on *The Northern Sword*, who plays Prince Cadius, approaches us at the bar, and my whole body tenses.

He's Darcy's favorite character.

"Who's this cute little thing?" he asks, smiling down at her like he wants to devour her.

She grins. "I'm Darcy."

"Of course you are."

His teeth are too white, and there are too many of them. His face has that perfect, sculpted look I've seen on other Hollywood people. His British accent doesn't even sound real.

I don't like him, and I don't like the way he's looking at Darcy.

"You're not on the show, right?" He studies her with interest and arrogant confidence, like he knows he has this in the bag. "I would have remembered you."

"No," she laughs. "I'm not an actor."

Grant's eyes widen like he can't believe it, and I turn away, shaking my head. This fucking guy. He probably uses this line once a week.

"Not an actor?" he repeats, like it's the most shocking thing he's ever heard. "Well, your beauty is wasted."

"No, it isn't," I cut in with an edge to my voice.

She just laughs him off, though. "I'm an actuary."

"Brilliant." Every single overly whitened tooth is visible. "I love birds."

Darcy bites back a smile, and I drag in a calming breath, studying her reaction. She doesn't actually think his ignorance is cute, right? It's funny when *I* joke that she works with birds. With this guy, it's just annoying.

"What do you suggest I do on my evenings off in Vancouver, darling Darcy?" Grant asks, and my hand clenches at my side.

Protective feelings race through me, and I grit my teeth, because I can see exactly where this is going.

"Go see a hockey game." She gives me a private smile that makes me want to grab her hand.

"Fantastic. I love ice hockey."

"Really?" She lights up. "You're a hockey fan?"

"Huge. The biggest." He glances at me with a tight smile, like *I'm* intruding on *their* date or something. "And who's this strapping young fellow?"

Hockey fan, my ass. I give him a bold, friendly smile, gritting my teeth the entire time. "Hayden Owens."

We shake hands. I put a little extra grip into it, and he winces.

"Hayden's on the Vancouver Storm," Darcy tells him.

"Oh, yes." Grant nods and rubs his chin like he's Gandalf. "Thought I recognized you."

"I'm sure you did." I give him a tight smile, holding his gaze with challenge.

I don't like this guy. Not one fucking bit. I don't like the way he looks at Darcy, I don't like the way she laughs at his jokes, and I don't like how he moves his arm to rest on the bar behind her. His body language is clear: he's interested.

My heart jumps into my throat as he opens his mouth.

He's going to ask her out.

On instinct, I clutch her hand. "We're going to grab another drink," I call over my shoulder, hauling Darcy away. "Nice chatting with you, Peter."

He blinks at us in surprise, but I throw my arm around her, leading her to the bar upstairs.

"We could have ordered from the bar we were at," Darcy says as I pull her up the stairs.

"This one's quieter."

We reach the bar, and I order another round, keeping a hand on Darcy at all times. I shouldn't be touching her like this, but my protective instincts are in overdrive.

"He's better-looking in real life," she comments as we get our drinks. "I think they lighten his hair for the show. Also, you called him Peter. Did you realize that?"

"He's not that good-looking," I mutter. "It's dark in here. Makes everyone look hotter."

She gives me a funny smile, eyes lingering on me, and I shift under her gaze.

"What?"

She grins wider. "Why are you acting so weird?"

I take my hand off her lower back. "I'm not."

"You are."

I turn away, keeping an eye on the top of the stairs so Grant doesn't come waltzing up here after her.

"Oh my god." She smiles wider. "Are you jealous?"

I scoff. "No."

Her eyes light up. She's too smart for my bullshit. "Uh, *yes*, you are. You're jealous."

I suck in a deep breath, running my hand through my hair. "I need another drink."

"Hayden."

"Okay." I look down at her. "Yes. I'm jealous. He looked at you like—"

I cut myself off. Like he wanted to fuck her. Like he wanted to do all the things I've been dreaming and fantasizing about for years.

"Like what?"

"He looked at you like he already had it in the bag, Darce." There. That's the truth, just not the whole truth. "And I don't like the idea of some guy taking you for granted." Or taking her home. Or touching her. Or looking at her.

"Hey." Her hand lands on my arm, and she smiles up at me with a patient, amused smile. "You're still my number one."

My body relaxes, and I let out a heavy breath. "I know."

Grant appears at the top of the stairs, but he sees my hard expression and heads over to a group of castmates.

"I'm not interested in him. And if I was? Even I know not to do anything while I'm on a date with someone else." She gives me a playful nudge, and the knots loosen in my chest so I can breathe again. "I'd have to take you out again on *another* practice date. We'd be stuck doing practice dates for eternity."

Her grin is teasing, but going out on practice dates for eternity with Darcy sounds pretty damn good to me.

But that's not my job, to keep her all to myself. I'm supposed to be showing her the ropes.

"Are you ready to move on to dates with real guys?" I study her face, looking for any sign that she's done with this. "I mean, uh, real prospects?"

She wrinkles her nose and she shakes her head. "Not yet. Is that okay?"

"Good. Yes," I rush out. "Of course. You know I'm here for whatever you need."

Asshole, a voice whispers in my head.

"I know." She smiles. "So, if this were a real date," she says, bringing her drink to her lips. Without my permission, my eyes linger on her mouth pursed around her straw. "Would you say it's going well?"

"Yes." Every so often, Grant glances over here at Darcy, and my blood pressure spikes.

"Any notes?"

"Nope."

There. He looked at her again. I fold my arms over my chest, and we make eye contact. I hold his gaze, arching a brow as if to say *I fucking dare you*.

Darcy gives me an indulgent smile. "Don't go easy on me. I'm trying to learn. You must have some feedback."

I rest my arm along the top of the love seat we're sitting on. I'm not touching her, but my body language is clear.

Mine.

"You're doing great." When I look down into her eyes, all the jealous, territorial feelings melt away, and it's just me and her. The way it should be. "I'm having a really fun time with you."

We should have fucking stayed home, though. I don't know why I opened my big mouth and told her about the cast party tonight.

Because she loves the show, I remind myself. Because *she's* having fun. Because she's figuring out what she wants, and going out and making new memories is an important part of that.

"So if this was a real date and it was going really well, what would you do next?"

"What do you mean?"

"What's your next move? Do you ask her out on a second date? Do you drop hints to get her to come home with you?" Her mouth quirks up, and I want to kiss it. "Show me your moves."

"I'd make up an excuse to kiss you."

Oh, shit. I really did just say that.

Her lips part, surprise rising in her eyes. "Like what?"

My pulse picks up, and I vaguely remember vowing not to do shit like this, but *he's* over there, staring at her, and *she's* right beside me, looking so cute and pretty and sweet, and the smart part of my brain has taken a back seat.

"Like... Patrick Grant keeps staring at you and I don't want him to think he actually has a chance."

Her breath catches and her eyes dart to the bar, where Grant is indeed watching her while listening to someone else talk. "He doesn't think that."

"He does."

She gestures at herself. "Me?" She widens her eyes and glances over at him. "Him? Just bizarre."

Jesus fuck, she has no idea what she looks like or how funny and lovely she is. No fucking clue.

"Not that bizarre, Darce." I work my jaw, shifting so I'm facing her on the seat. "It would be the humane thing to do, though."

"What, kiss?"

"Yeah." I swallow, watching her expression for any sign of discomfort or hesitation. "You don't want to lead him on."

Kissing Darcy would slam the door of possibility closed on Patrick Grant, send a loud and clear message.

And more than anything, I really, really fucking want to. I've wanted to kiss her for years. My knee bounces in anticipation as I study her face.

"Right." She blows out a long breath, nodding. "I don't

want to lead him on. You know all about that." She pulls her bottom lip between her teeth as a crease forms between her eyebrows. "It's probably good to practice, too."

I raise an eyebrow at her in question.

"Kit isn't the only guy I've ever kissed," she explains. "I kissed a guy in high school, but we were sixteen and it was outside and rushed and kind of..." She mashes her palms together, and I huff a surprised laugh. "Mushy?" she says, laughing and wincing.

"Yikes." I grin. "You're a mushy kisser?"

"No," she sputters, laughing harder. "I don't think so. Kit never had any complaints."

Another stab of jealousy hits me in the gut.

"I'm happy to help you," I say, staring at her mouth.

The warning bells ringing in my head fade away, and all I can think about is how much I want her. My blood pounds in my ears as I watch her tuck her bottom lip between her teeth.

"Okay." She nods. "We should kiss, then."

I bring a hand up beneath her chin and tip her face up to mine. Our eyes lock and my heart races, and I wonder if this is a mistake before I lower my mouth to hers.

HAYDEN'S LIPS meet mine and my thoughts collapse like a house of cards.

"Holy fuck, Darce," he murmurs, angling his mouth against mine, coaxing my lips open and slipping inside.

Holy fuck, indeed.

His tongue delves between my lips, slowly stroking against mine, and I'm lost in his warmth, in the clean, masculine scent washing over me, and his taste—like mint gum and bourbon from the old-fashioned he's drinking. My awareness narrows to where we touch—his lips against mine, his thigh pressing against me, and his tongue gently exploring my mouth. The gentle grit of his stubble against my skin. My lips have never felt so sensitive, but suddenly, I can feel *everything*. Every brush and press of Hayden's mouth over mine—the same mouth that's smiled and grinned and sent flirty smirks at me for years.

Music plays nearby, but I can barely hear it. I shift closer to Hayden, electricity pulsing through my body and landing low in my belly. His hand is in my hair, and his other comes to my jaw, tilting me the way he wants me.

Kissing my best friend feels perfectly natural. I never want to stop, like it's something I've been missing, and the second it's over, I'm going to have a nagging feeling like I left something at home.

He pulls away an inch, breathing ragged as he studies me. His eyes are dark, heavy-lidded, and glazed in a way that makes my heart pound harder.

"Okay?" He sounds hoarse.

I nod hard, catching my breath and what's left of my wits. "Yep. Was it okay for you?"

He nods, and his eyes drop to my mouth. "Uh-huh."

"Not mushy?"

He lets out a tight laugh. "Definitely not mushy." He glances over my shoulder. "I don't think he saw."

"Who?" My eyebrows pull together.

"Grant."

Oh. Right. Him. Our eyes meet, and my pulse skips a beat at the intensity in his eyes.

"We should do it again," Hayden says in a low voice that sends heat to the base of my spine, "just to make sure."

"Yeah. Okay." I sound breathless. "Just to be sure he sees." I press my swollen lips together. "Any pointers for me?"

His jaw flexes and he looks at my mouth again. "You can touch me this time. If you want."

God, yes, I want to. "I wasn't sure if it was okay."

His mouth quirks up, and the long line of his throat bobs. "It's okay. It's definitely okay. We're practicing."

"Right." I almost laugh, because practicing with Hayden is so much more intense than I expected. I'm lightheaded.

I wrap a hand around the nape of his neck, pulling his mouth back to mine.

A low noise of encouragement rumbles through him, and I arch against the hard wall of his chest as he takes my mouth, more urgent this time.

Hayden's kiss turns demanding, desperate, and addictive. I sink my fingers into the soft hair at the back of his neck, and his breath catches. I gently suck on the tip of his tongue, and he groans into my mouth. A shudder rolls through him when I scrape my fingers over his scalp. The deprived, neglected data analyst inside me loves this game.

My free hand lands on his collarbone, and I slip my fingertips beneath the collar of his t-shirt to catch his warmth. I've always wanted to touch this part of him, run my fingers over the hair at the top of his chest.

I lightly nip his bottom lip, and his big hands grip my ass in a swift motion before I'm in his lap.

"God, you smell so fucking good," he says, pressing a line of kisses down my neck.

So this is what a kiss is supposed to be like, a tiny voice whispers in my head. It's not just one single kiss, it's a hundred, in a hundred different places on my body. I've had my neck kissed, but not like this.

Never like this.

It's the most intense, erotic, intimate sexual experience of my life, and we're both still wearing all our clothes.

"And you're doing so well," he says between kisses, big hand moving up and down my thigh like he's trying to touch as much of me as possible.

My breasts feel heavy and achy, desperate for his hands to cover them. He twists his hand in the back of my hair as he takes my mouth, sinking deeper, and delicious tingles run down my neck, down my back, across my skin. He's not usually so dominant. He's my goofy, sweet, fun-loving Hayden, but he's gripping the back of my hair, moving me however he wants like it's for his pleasure.

Arousal rushes through me, sharp and surprising. It's like last week's cuddle turned up to eleven. Every nerve ending in my lips is being brushed and sucked and nibbled and stroked, and when I shift, I feel the hard bar of Hayden's erection pressing between my legs.

Sparks gather behind my clit from the pressure, and my eyes go wide, unseeing. Hayden's joke earlier about not being small rings in my head, and I whimper. He catches it with his mouth, applying gentle suction to my tongue, and my brain melts.

If this is what it's like to kiss Hayden, what's he like in bed?

Flutters roll through me. We're in public, but I would be totally okay with Hayden flipping me over to my back, yanking my pants down, and taking me right here. Minutes after I admitted I'd never had a G-spot orgasm, I feel like I could probably have one if we kept at this kissing thing for a while longer.

He kisses like he's desperate for me, like he's been waiting for this for years, like he doesn't want it to end. Like he wants it to go further. The hard press of his erection against my stomach sends a flurry of flutters through my body.

The breath whooshes out of me, and he makes a low noise of approval into my mouth. I realize I just ground myself against him.

"God, Darcy," he groans against my lips. "Fucking finally."

I shiver with arousal. I want this. I want him to take this so much further, right on this couch in front of everyone.

He pulls back, and my heart pounds at the territorial look in Hayden's eyes. Something's different now, but I'm too focused on the way he's looking at me, dazed and frustrated.

He sucks in a deep breath and blinks, and the look fades from his eyes.

"That's probably enough practice," he mutters, gripping my waist with his big hands and setting me down beside him.

Every instinct in my body screams at me to climb back onto

his lap, but I just nod and smooth my hair down. My scalp still tingles from where he gripped the strands.

"Thanks," I croak, catching my breath. What the hell just happened?

He reaches for his drink and downs the rest of it, not looking at me. "Don't mention it."

WHEN WE GET HOME from the party, my heart is still pounding and I'm still painfully hard.

"How was that for a do-over?" Darcy asks with a self-deprecating grin as I open the front door.

My mind races with thoughts of our kiss. Our conversation about G-spot orgasms. The way Patrick fucking Grant looked at her. Pent-up need still rushes through me with nowhere to go, and I'm going to burst out of my skin.

This whole night has been an exercise in control, and I'm at my limit.

That kiss. That fucking kiss changed everything, and I don't know what to do.

"You did great, Darce." I pull her coat off and hang it up. "Full marks."

Her pretty mouth stretches into a pleased grin, and I'm flooded with the memory of the needy moan she made when I pulled her into my lap.

"I should go to bed." She bites her lip, toying with the bracelet I bought her. "I'm going to one of Hazel's early yoga classes." Her eyebrows lift; her mouth goes flat in a muted smile. "And you probably want to shower, right?"

I go still. "What?"

She knows. My gut hardens. Fuck. How long has she known? How much does she know? Does she know everything?

Her mouth twists and she rolls her eyes. "Every time you touch me, you race to the shower after to wash my germs off."

Is that what she thinks? That I think she's gross or something?

She takes one look at my stricken expression and laughs, but it's strained. "Hayden. It's fine." She pats my shoulder. "I'm just teasing you."

No, she's not. I can tell from the tone of her voice that she's hurt.

Fuck. Pain slices through my chest. Her feelings are hurt. My eyebrows pull together as I grapple to explain the situation without blurting out everything.

"Good night, Wingman," she says over her shoulder, walking to her bedroom.

I'm right behind her, catching up in long strides. "Wait."

She turns with a curious look. "Mm?"

My feet carry me forward until I'm a foot away, standing closer than we normally would. "There's something I want you to know."

My pulse thunders in my ears. What am I doing? I should let her go to sleep, and we can both forget this whole night ever happened.

I can't, though.

"Sex isn't supposed to be *nice*," I tell her in a low voice, watching her eyes widen as she remembers our conversation.

She blinks rapidly, lips parting, and the devil inside me wants to kiss her again.

"And it's not supposed to be predictable."

It's supposed to be like that kiss we had, but I don't know how to say that without everything falling apart.

She needs to know, though. She deserves to have everything. This phase is about her figuring out what she wants?

Well, I want her to have what she deserves.

"It's supposed to be all-consuming." My voice is a rasp, and blood rushes to my cock as I think about the way she felt sitting on my lap. "So hot you feel like you're going to catch fire. All you can think about is the person you're with, how they feel, how they taste and smell, and what their moans sound like. How to make them do it again."

Her chest rises and falls with uneven breaths, and her pupils expand, blowing wide.

"Making them come is your sole focus, and when they do? You want it all over again. You're addicted to them. Desperate to make them come *so fucking hard*."

The apartment is silent except for the sounds of our uneven breathing.

I lean a hand on the wall beside Darcy's head, towering over her, and she tips her face up, watching me with wide eyes. "And when they can't possibly come again, when they're begging you to finish inside them, your control finally breaks and you lose your mind. It's like nothing else in the world. Everything stops and it's just you and them."

Her eyelashes flutter, and I'm picturing Darcy beneath me on my bed, tensing up as we hit our peak together.

"The feeling is so intense, it can't be real. Somehow, you survive it and can't wait to do it again. You *need* to do it again." My lips hover near her ear. "Fucking them has become a craving that you can't ignore."

I've never had sex like that, but I can imagine it. I can so fucking imagine it.

Her attention on me is addictive, the way she soaks up my words, how her eyes flash with surprise and excitement. I'm fully hard, aching for her and praying she doesn't look down.

Power rushes through me. It feels good to take control like this, to stand over her while she gazes up at me with that expression of wonder. For once, it feels good not to be so considerate and *nice*.

I inhale her scent deep into my lungs, holding back a groan. "That's what sex is like, Darcy. It's sweaty, intense, and life-changing."

On the edge of control, I tip my mouth to her cheek, pressing a soft kiss there, watching her eyes widen even more.

"Good night, Darce."

"Good night," she whispers back.

I feel her gaze on me as I head to my room and close the door. Moments later, lying in bed, I relive our kiss with my hand around my cock, stroking myself closer and closer to the edge of release, until pleasure races up my spine, my balls tighten, and I spill all over my stomach with a low, pained groan that I don't even try to muffle.

Catching my breath, staring out the window, I know I can't deny my feelings for her anymore.

I like her. I've always liked her. It's not going away, no matter how hard I try.

And teaching her the things she wants to learn? It just might kill me.

THE NEXT EVENING, Miller and I sit on the bench during a game, eyes on the ice.

"How are you feeling, bud?" he asks.

I reach for my water bottle and take a long drink. "Never better," I lie.

The kiss from last night replays in my head, again and again. I woke up this morning hard as steel, thinking about the soft, breathy moan she made when I sucked on her tongue.

I'm such a fucking asshole. I'm supposed to be watching out for her, helping her, and instead, I'm jerking off while thinking of her.

Miller slants a look of amused disbelief at me. "You seem distracted."

I grit my teeth, because I know what the sports commentators are saying.

What is Tate Ward doing, moving one of his best defensemen to a new position two months before playoffs? Ward put him on the first line when he looks more like a second- or third-line player.

Since I moved positions, I've been racking up the assists, but no goals. Ward hasn't said a word, but I know I'm not playing the way he wants me to. When Volkov and I played together as a defensive pair, it worked because I became whatever he needed me to be.

"I pass to you and you pass it right back." Miller regards me for a long moment. "You're holding back. You're still playing like a defenseman."

He's right that I'm distracted. All I can hear is *do most guys know how to give a girl a G-spot orgasm? I had a toy... I didn't like it. What's your favorite sex position?*

Darcy Andersen is going to fucking kill me. I swallow hard, glancing over to where she sits with Hazel and Pippa.

"Okay." Miller nods, following the direction of my gaze with a knowing grin. "I see how it is."

The air whooshes out of my lungs in a heavy exhale. "We kissed."

He lights up. "That's great."

"It wasn't like that." My grip tightens on my stick. "It was a one-time thing. I was just—"

"Let me guess. Helping her?" He smirks. "Because you're her wingman."

My silence is enough of an answer, apparently. Miller tilts his head, narrowing his eyes at me with a growing grin.

"I have an idea."

"Miller, I don't need your dating advice."

He chuckles. "I think you do, but it's not about dating. It's about hockey." Dread gathers in the pit of my stomach at the mischief in his eyes. "Darcy's learning to be a player, right?"

My eyes cut to his, and I really don't like where this is going.

"Being a player is all about variety." He holds my gaze with challenge. "And there are a *lot* of single guys on the team who would *love* to help Darcy out. You know, with *practicing*."

Protectiveness rattles through me, and I stare back at him

with my teeth clenched so hard they might crack. He's trying to get a rise out of me and get under my skin. The rational part of my brain tells me to ignore him.

I can't, though. I love these guys like family, but the idea of them touching Darcy, of her sitting in *their* laps and stroking *their* hair while they make out, sends hot rage through my blood.

Miller grins wider at me. "That's a new look from you, Owens. You're normally so cheerful."

"I know what you're doing," I grit out.

"Great." He turns back to the ice with a pleased smile that makes me want to break something. "Score a goal tonight, or I'll make a suggestion next time we're all out at the bar. Put a little bug in Darcy's ear, you know?"

Every muscle in my body tightens. "She doesn't want that."

"Why don't you let her decide that? She's a grown woman, Owens. She can speak for herself."

She gets nervous sometimes, and she's new at the dating thing. She needs someone who will take his time with her and not rush her.

And I don't fucking want her kissing another guy.

"Gents," Ward says to Miller and me, along with the other forward, before I can tell Miller to back down. "You're up."

With my heart in my throat, we climb over the boards.

"Just one goal," Miller calls as we line up for a face-off.

I take the center-ice spot, urgency surging through me as I get into position. My pulse races in my ears as I think about one of the other players with Darcy. The ref drops the puck, and my body takes over. I claw it away and take off toward the net, blood pounding.

My instincts are different this time. As a hockey player, competition has been drilled into me since childhood, and I let it drive me. For once, instead of thinking about what my team-mates need, I think about what I want.

And I really, really want to score a goal. I really want Darcy all to myself.

I race toward the net, watching the goalie prepare. The fans are on their feet, cheering. I slap the puck toward the net. It sails past the goalie. The crowd erupts with noise, and victory rushes through me like a wildfire. Through the glass, Darcy meets my eyes with a gorgeous, proud smile, and I wink at her, grinning so hard my face hurts.

Hazel and Pippa wear their guys' jerseys, but Darcy's just in her coat, and the version of me who just shoved past everyone to score a goal wants to see her wearing my name on her back.

"There we fucking go," Miller crows, jumping on top of me to celebrate the goal, and Darcy laughs. A powerful thrill shoots through me.

At the bench, Ward gives me a pleased nod. There we fucking go, indeed.

AFTER THE GAME, I wait for Hayden at home, crouched behind the sofa in the dark apartment. The door opens, and I press my lips together so I don't start laughing.

"Darce?" I hear him flick the light switch back and forth, but the apartment stays dark—I've flipped the breaker so the lights don't work. "The fuck?" he mutters.

We kissed, and I can't stop thinking about it. We kissed, and we've been pretending it didn't happen. I need to show Hayden I'm not getting weird about it, that our friendship hasn't changed.

Even if it doesn't feel quite true.

"*Hayden,*" I rasp in a high, creepy voice.

He groans, and I clap a hand over my mouth to muffle my laughter.

"*Hayden, I've been waiting for you.*"

He's still trying the light switch. "You have some serious issues, Darcy."

"*I'm so hungry, Hayden.*"

"You're going to give me nightmares, and then I'll have to sleep in your bed every night." There's a smile in his voice. "Is that what you want?"

In the dark, behind the couch, I grin. Hayden in my bed, all warm, sleepy, and cuddly, probably only wearing boxers? I'll take it.

I turn the flashlight on, illuminating Daniel's rosy, cherub face. I stuck googly eyes on him earlier for extra drama.

"*I'm hungry for blood... your blood!*" I pull the string I attached to the base of the gnome so Daniel slides toward Hayden.

"Nope." I hear Hayden's fast footsteps down the hall to his room as I dissolve into laughter.

"Hayden, he just wants to say hi," I call, still shaking with laughter.

After I've turned the apartment lights on and hidden Daniel away in a closet, Hayden re-enters the kitchen.

"Congrats again on your goal," I tell him as he makes himself a smoothie. I replay Hayden skating hard toward the net with predatory focus and the look of relief and pride when he scored. "It seems like you're finding your footing with the new line."

He makes a noise of acknowledgment, swallowing a third of the smoothie. "Yep. I guess so."

"It felt good to score, didn't it?"

Our eyes meet, and for the millionth time, I think about our kiss and how his mouth felt on mine, how hard he got just from making out.

He's a sexual guy. He's used to having a lot of sex. It probably doesn't take much to make him hard, and it had nothing to do with me. Men are easily stimulated.

Fucking them has become a craving you can't ignore, he said about sex.

"Yeah, Darcy." His Adam's apple moves as he swallows, and his gaze drops to my mouth. "It felt really good."

Heat flares in his eyes, but his usual boyish, friendly smile appears. "Thanks for coming to my game."

"You don't have to thank me when you gave me a front row ticket. Besides, I like watching hockey."

The energy of the arena, the speed at which the game moves, and the brutal competition on the ice—there's no sport like hockey. The analytical part of my brain loves to find patterns in the way players work together, in events that repeat throughout the game, like a player favoring one side or two players who play especially well together. It's probably why I keep thinking about the hockey models on my laptop.

Seeing Hayden's ear-to-ear smile after he sank the puck into the net lit me up like a sparkler, too.

My gaze moves over the broad expanse of his chest, and I can smell his body wash or deodorant. His hair is still damp from his postgame shower, and I think about how he relaxed under my fingers as I touched it. The urge to hug him courses through me, but I don't want him to think I'm getting the wrong idea. Now that I'm single and we're spending so much time together, there's an undercurrent of tension between us that I don't want to play with too much.

Last night, I swear I heard a low groan from his room. It could have been anything, probably him reacting to something on his phone, but I heard it, and every hair on my body rose as I pictured him stroking his cock.

Was he thinking about us? Was he as turned on from that kiss as I was?

No. He seems totally normal now, like it never happened, so I should be, too.

"I should get to bed," I say quickly.

"Yeah, me, too." He gives me a quick smile. "I have practice in the morning, and you have work."

"Right. Well, good night."

"Night, Darce."

———

I'm crawling into bed twenty minutes later when my phone buzzes with an incoming call. Kit's photo flashes across the screen, and my heart jumps into my throat. We haven't spoken since we broke up.

It's late. Something must be wrong.

"Hey," I answer, immediately worried. "Are you okay? What's wrong?"

"Everything's fine." The familiarity of Kit's voice tugs at something in my chest. "I just, uh, wanted to see how you were."

My pulse slows to normal. "I'm good." The reluctance in my tone is obvious. It's not an emergency, and he's calling me this late? It's midnight in Calgary. Something feels off. "What about you?"

He exhales a heavy sigh. "Missing you. I was thinking about you on Valentine's Day."

Guilt slams into me like a freight train, because except for the engagement ring, I wasn't thinking about him on Valentine's Day at all. I was too busy having fun with Hayden. My stomach hardens into a rock.

I don't know what to say. I don't miss him; I just feel relief.

"I saw a picture of you and Hayden at some party," Kit adds.

The cast party, probably. "You know Hayden." I don't mention the t-shirt I gave him that started the whole thing. "He gets invited to a lot of parties."

"Sounds like you're having fun in Vancouver."

"I am." More unease threads through me. "I'm meeting new people and trying new things." I think about when I brought up purple hair years ago, and the way he made a face like it was a bad idea. "And I dyed my hair," I lie.

"What?"

I shouldn't be testing him like this. Maybe I feel the need to give him another chance to redeem himself, not so we can get back together but so at least I can leave my anger behind. Or maybe I want to erase that bad memory with a more pleasant one.

"I dyed my hair purple." I toy with the edge of my duvet. "It's pale purple like a mermaid and I love it."

He makes a hesitant noise. "Why? I liked your hair before."

"Because..." I scramble for the words, reeling with disappointment and irritation. It's *my* hair, but he's making it about him. "Because I wanted to. Isn't that enough?"

He doesn't answer, and a prickle of anger and hurt pokes me deep behind my sternum. It's just a hair color, but he's making it sound like I stole a car or something.

He sighs. "When are you coming home?"

The words fall out of my head. I'm stunned. I sit there, blinking at nothing, unsure of what to say. "I'm not. I'm not coming home."

"You need to get this stuff out of your system, and I'll wait until you do, but when you're ready to come back, everything's still here for you." A beat of silence. It's like he didn't even hear what I just said. "I still can't sleep on your side of the bed."

Get *this stuff* out of my system? I don't want to go back to my old life. I like going shopping with Georgia and wearing pretty dresses when I go out for dinner with Hayden and learning how to be a player. Hayden makes everything carefree and fun. I'm filled with guilt over hurting Kit, but everything inside me screams that what he's saying is wrong.

I don't love him—not the way I should—but I don't know how to say that without making this so much worse.

"Maybe it's time for you to get a new bed—" I start, but Kit cuts me off.

"You want to move to a new apartment? We'll move. You want to take a trip together after the season's over? We'll go wherever you want to go, as long as we're back for training camp. Whatever you want, Darcy, it's yours."

I suck in a sharp breath. Whatever I want, as long as it works for him and his schedule and his career. Whatever I want, as long as I'm the person he wants me to be.

"No." My nails dig into my palm as I force the words out. "I meant what I said when we broke up. We're not right for each other. I need you to understand that. Please stop waiting for me." I close my eyes. I won't cry. "I'm not ready to marry you or have kids with you."

"So we don't have to do those things right away. I'll wait," he says with frustration. "I'll wait as long as you want."

"No." My face crumples, and my eyes sting. Fuck. I hate it when he doesn't listen like this. This conversation is completely one-sided. Whatever I say, he's going to believe what he wants. "I'll never be ready, and I'll never want those things with you."

The words come out louder than intended, with more force, and he's quiet for a long time on the other end of the call.

"Wow." That one word is loaded with a bitterness that makes my throat burn. "I feel like I don't even know who you are."

That's my fault, because I coasted along with the current and faded into the background of his life. I never asked for anything and I never put myself first. I let myself be the person he wanted instead of who I am.

God, this is so fucking hard. Breaking Kit's heart all over again wasn't something I was prepared to do, but I think about the way Hayden dates with full transparency and kindness, never leading someone on.

"I'm starting to date," I tell him, forcing the words out. "And I think you should, too. It's time to move on from each other."

I hear his low, unhappy laugh. "Unbelievable. I have to go. Bye, Darcy."

He ends the call, and tears spill over, streaming down my cheeks. Sobs shudder through me. My pillow is soaked, and my face is puffy and hot.

There's a soft knock at my door. "Darce? Are you okay?"

The low, gentle tone of Hayden's voice sends another wave of tears to my eyes.

"Yep," I croak, panic shooting through me. Hayden can't see me crying. "I'm fine. Just going to bed now. Good night."

He doesn't say anything, but I can sense him waiting on the other side of the door. "I'm coming in."

WHEN HAYDEN OPENS my bedroom door and sees me curled up on my bed, crying, his expression hardens.

"Hey, hey, hey." The bed sinks as he sits beside me, hand brushing over my hair. "What's going on?"

"Kit called."

His hand stills on my hair. "What?"

I recap the conversation as tears continue to fall. While he listens, he strokes my hair, watching with concern. When I'm done, he lies down beside me and gathers me into his chest, pulling me half on top of him.

"Honey," he murmurs, mouth on my temple, breath on my cheek.

After how I've been freaking out about our practice kiss, we shouldn't be doing this, but he smells so good. His heartbeat against my ear is calming, and he's so warm. I like when he calls me *honey*, too. He probably calls tons of women that, but I don't care. I'm taking all the comfort I can get right now.

"Do you think I'm changing?" I ask quietly.

A beat passes where he doesn't say anything, but his arm tightens around my back. "Yes and no. You're learning to do new things, and you're figuring out who you are without him."

His hand lingers on the back of my hair, warm and heavy. "But you're still the same Darcy we all know and love."

"That's how I feel, too." I wipe a tear away. "I feel like the same person, just better."

His hand stroking over my hair combined with his steady, slow heartbeat under my ear lulls me into a sense of calm.

"He'll be okay," Hayden murmurs. "He just needs time. Just like you."

———

I wake the next morning to sunlight streaming into my room because I forgot to close the blinds.

Both physically and emotionally, I feel brand new and clear-headed. For the first time in a month and a half, I'm well rested and my eyes don't feel gritty and dry. I usually toss and turn throughout the night, but I don't remember waking up once. It's the best sleep I've had since I broke up with Kit.

I'm also draped over Hayden while he sleeps half-naked in my bed.

My pulse skyrockets, tripping and stumbling, and I blink, eyes wide.

We're still in the same position as last night, but the duvet covers us. Hayden's only wearing tight black boxer briefs, and while I'm still in my t-shirt, I've lost my pajama bottoms, wearing only underwear.

He's on his back, tucking me close to him with an arm around my back. My thigh is wedged between his, and I'm pressed against him, my full weight on him from head to toe. He's even caught my cold feet between his calves.

There's something about the softness to his expression, the handsome lines on his face, the tilt to his mouth, even in sleep, that makes my heart squeeze. When I start to shift off him, careful not to wake him, his arm tightens, locking me against his body.

His breathing changes, and his eyes open, bleary and adorable in the morning light. His mouth kicks up into a calm smile.

There's a shift in my body, like the clouds are clearing.

"You fell asleep." His voice is gravelly. Neatly trimmed golden-blond chest hair spans his muscled torso, trickling down his abs into his waistband. "I didn't want to wake you." He glances down at himself. "I must have pulled my clothes off in my sleep. Sorry. I get warm."

I can feel exactly how warm he is when I'm splayed out on him like this. A pathetic noise of acknowledgment slips out of me, and I nod, gaze tracing over all the lines and ridges of his perfect body.

God, he's so hot. He's so *big*. Hayden is just... so much. All broad chest, thick limbs, and muscular thighs.

I shift again, and the impressive erection that pressed into me while we practice-kissed at the cast party? It's pressing into my hip.

Our eyes meet, and my mind goes blank. Heat grows behind my clit. I have the overwhelming urge to run my palm down his chest, over his straining length. To pull the waistband of his boxers down and let his erection spring free.

I'd push him between my lips and take him all the way to the back of my mouth. A deep pressure builds between my legs when I imagine what his groan would sound like. Maybe he'd put his hand on the back of my head. Maybe he'd tell me how good it feels.

His breathing turns uneven as he looks down at my mouth. I told Hayden sex is supposed to be warm and predictable, but the hard bar of his arousal against my hip doesn't feel sweet or relaxing.

It feels like I want to fuck my best friend.

"Darce," he breathes, like a question mixed with a plea, and the hot look in his eyes crumbles my resolve. I move an inch toward his mouth—

Something starts jingling in my room, and we snap apart. A phone alarm, coming from the floor. I slide off him and he reaches over the side of the bed.

"Is that me or you?" I ask, searching for my phone.

"Me." He turns the alarm off and swings his legs to the floor so he's sitting and facing away. My eyes move over his toned back and waist before I yank my gaze elsewhere.

I'm still in my panties, too. I think I'm wet. Can he tell? God. Hayden stands, and his eyes follow as I haul the duvet over myself.

He turns away. "I should get ready for practice."

"Me, too. I mean, I should get ready for work."

His shoulders look tense as he tilts his chin to the bed. "Sorry about that."

"No." My eyebrows shoot up. "It was me. I fell asleep and you were just being a good friend."

His jaw ticks and he rubs the back of his neck. "Yeah."

A weird pause between us.

"Next time, I'll use the man chest doll you got me," I joke, but he doesn't laugh. He's probably freaking out that I'm going to get all clingy or get the wrong idea about us. "Okay, well." I give him a cheerful smile to show him I won't make this weird. "Have a great day at practice. See you tonight?"

He nods tightly, not looking at me. "I'll be late. I'm going to beer league with Miller."

"Nice." He and Rory sometimes play on a rec center hockey team with a bunch of regular guys. "That'll be fun."

"Yep. See ya."

"See ya."

He closes the bedroom door behind him, and I flop back down onto the pillows, blowing out a long breath.

Sleeping half-naked in the same bed with my roommate and wingman is dancing into dangerous territory, and I won't be doing that again, no matter how good it felt.

———

That evening after work, I've stopped at a drugstore to pick up more toothpaste when a row of colorful pots on the shelf catches my eye.

Temporary hair dye.

You would look amazing with purple hair, Georgia said.

I pause, pulling down the purple one to inspect it. That impulsive, devilish urge inside me wakes up. I feel like doing something wild.

Why? Kit asked last night with disdain, and I feel a sharp twist of resentment in my stomach. *I liked your hair before.*

Anger rises in my throat as I stare at the jar.

There's no good reason to dye my hair purple. It isn't going to get me ahead in my career, it'll probably be hard to maintain, and there's no guarantee that it'll look good.

And yet excitement trickles through me, making my stomach dip. It's like the dress Georgia found for me—I won't know until I try.

Besides, I think it'll make me happy, and maybe that's enough.

Maybe I'm not the old Darcy anymore.

THE APARTMENT'S quiet when I get home from beer league, and my eyes land on the shipping box sitting on the table beside the front door.

The sex toy I bought Darcy.

Buying it was a huge mistake, especially after the way we woke up this morning, with my dick practically drilling a hole in her thigh.

I'm not giving it to her.

I drop my bag on the floor, pull out the jersey I got her, and set it on the counter. *This* gift is appropriate for our relationship.

Whatever our relationship is now. My mind wanders to last night, to the way she looked when I opened her bedroom door and saw her crying, and pain twists in my chest.

Kit didn't know what he had with Darcy Andersen. He didn't value her. He didn't *see* her, and now he thinks she's coming back?

These thoughts I'm having about her should make me feel guilty, but they don't. He never deserved her, and the only guilt I feel is that it took me eight years to realize that.

In the kitchen, I warm up food. Then I flip through sports

highlights from the night while glancing down the hall, listening for her.

The lights are on, her sneakers are in the front hall closet, and her keys are on the table by the door, but she hasn't come out to say hi like normal.

She yanked the covers over herself this morning like she was uncomfortable.

My gut sinks.

Definitely not giving her the toy now.

"Darce?" I call, walking down the hall. Her bedroom door is open and the room is empty, but there's a sliver of light from beneath the bathroom door.

"Hi," she says from the other side of the door. I can hear her pacing around the bathroom.

Something isn't right. Is she avoiding me because of this morning? "Let's watch some TV."

"Um." The footsteps stop. "No, thanks. You go ahead."

There's a worried, distracted edge to her voice, and I frown, folding my arms over my chest. "I got you a present to say sorry about this morning."

Fucking *liar*, my brain whispers. I got her the jersey because I want to see my name on her back.

"Just leave it on the kitchen table and I'll see it in a bit."

She sounds weird, like she's stressed or anxious. "Are you sick?"

"No, I'm okay."

I grip the back of my neck. Is it her period? "There's a bottle of aspirin under the sink, and I don't mind buying tampons, Darce. Real men aren't afraid of periods." I add that last bit with a hint of teasing, trying to lighten her up.

She chuckles, and my chest eases. "Good to know, but it's not my period."

"I'm not going anywhere until you tell me what's wrong."

A long pause. "Hayden. I fucked up. Don't laugh, okay?"

"Laugh at what—"

She opens the door, and my jaw hits the floor. Her previously pale-blond hair is now bright, hideous cartoon purple. A really jarring, ugly shade.

Her eyebrows match.

We stare at each other for a long, wide-eyed moment before I press a fist to my mouth to stifle my bark of laughter.

"You said you wouldn't laugh," she cries, slapping my arm.

"I didn't agree to that," I manage, barely holding it together, almost collapsing with the relief that something isn't actually wrong.

"Hayden! I look like Grimace from McDonald's." She turns to the mirror with a mournful expression.

I howl, doubled over and leaning against the wall. She *does* look like the big purple blob, or one of the Teletubbies. "Tinky-Winky? Is that you?"

A mortified noise scrapes out of her throat, but she starts laughing. She tries to close the door but I catch it, stepping into her space. We're both gasping for air.

This is what it's supposed to be like with Darcy and me, and this is exactly why I can't fuck it up. When we're just friends, we're perfect together.

The urge to kiss her rises, though, but I shove it down.

"Holy fuck, Darce." I pull a bright purple lock between my fingers. Her hair is still soft as silk, and the bathroom smells fresh and sweet like her hair products. "What did you do?"

She cringes. "I was so mad after my call with Kit, and I felt like doing something drastic. I wanted something light and pretty, but this is way too intense. It looks like—"

"Barney the Dinosaur?"

She tries to give me a flat look but bursts out laughing again.

"Why'd you do the eyebrows?" I breathe with an incredulous expression.

"I don't know," she moans, glancing at her reflection.

"It's going to be okay." I put my arms out. "Come here."

She steps forward into my embrace, resting her head against my chest, and my chin comes to the top of her hair.

My heart jumps at the way she feels against me. "Don't worry," I murmur, "you're still beautiful."

In my arms, she tenses.

"You know, in a friend way," I add.

"I know," she says defensively.

We stand there for a long moment, and I run my hand down her back to comfort her.

"I guess Kit was right." She makes it sound like a joke, but there's an added element of vulnerability that has my eyes narrowing.

"What are you talking about?"

"I brought it up in the past, and he didn't like the idea." Her fingers tap on my chest, light and distracted. "It came up again last night. Something about his judgy tone pissed me off."

A slice of anger hits me in the gut. "You didn't tell me that."

"It's not a big deal."

"It is a big deal, Darce."

She looks up in surprise at my tone.

"You can dye your hair whatever color you want."

Her mouth tilts and amusement sparks in her eyes before she gestures at our reflection in the mirror. "Well, obviously he knew better than me."

"We'll fix it."

"I've washed my hair four times tonight. It's not coming out."

"Let's call in a professional. I'll get my friend Layla to help."

"A friend?" She arches an eyebrow with a teasing smile.

"Not *that* kind of friend." I give her a look. All the women I've dated are kind and cool, but I feel weird about Darcy meeting one of them. "She comes here to cut my hair when my schedule's packed during the season. She'll be able to fix it."

Darcy tucks her bottom lip between her teeth. "Are you sure?"

"Positive." I pull out my phone to text Layla before opening my camera app and snapping a picture of Darcy and her ridiculous hair.

Her eyes go wide as she realizes what I'm doing, and I shake with laughter.

"No!" she cries. "I don't want evidence of this." She reaches for my phone, but I'm already slipping it back into my pocket.

"*I* do." I wiggle my eyebrows at her, delight spreading through me. "I never want to forget this."

"Give that to me," she orders.

I laugh again. "No."

"Then delete it."

"Also no." I beam down at her, batting her hands away as she tries to reach for the phone again. "I love that you're half my size but think you can overpower me."

She sighs, stepping back with a determined look, but she's fighting a smile. "You're going to put it on t-shirts or something."

"Now you're thinking. I'll get one for everyone on the team."

"Hilarious." She does a dry, fake laugh before her expression turns curious. "What was this you said about a present?"

In the kitchen, Darcy pulls the jersey out of the bag and holds it up with a hopeful smile. "For me?"

I laugh. "Yeah, for you. So you can wear it to my games." Our eyes meet, and I can't read her expression. "If you want. Obviously, you can wear whatever you want."

Her gaze lingers on me. "Do *you* want me to wear it?"

I should say something cool and nonchalant, but I just nod.

Her eyes warm, and she smiles softly. God, she's so fucking pretty, even with weird hair. "I want to, then."

Still smiling, she pulls it over her head. It's a little big on her, but in a fucking adorable way that makes me want to pick her up and toss her over my shoulder in some weird caveman display.

I clear my throat, trying not to look too pleased. "Looks pretty cute."

"You think?" She looks up at me through her lashes, the apples of her cheeks popping with her smile.

"Mhm." Warm pleasure expands through my chest. "And you'll fit right in with Pippa and Hazel."

Wishful thinking, I guess, that she would fit in with them completely. That she'd be cheering for me and supporting me in the same way the Hartley sisters support their guys.

As if we were together.

I should clarify, but I just let the implication linger, testing it out.

"Thanks," she says, looking down but still smiling. "I love it."

"You are very, very welcome."

"Can I pay you back?"

"Not a chance."

She huffs a light laugh, thick lashes fluttering, and fucking hell, I want to kiss her.

"A package arrived for you earlier," she says, glancing at the box on the side table, throwing cold water all over the dumb moony feelings I'm trying to ignore.

"Yep." I clear my throat, backing up a step. "I saw it."

Her eyes linger on my expression, and I lift my eyebrows, trying to look normal and not like I'm trying to hide the sex toy I bought her.

"What is it?" She watches me with a little curve to her mouth.

"What is what?"

"What's in the box?"

"I don't know."

Her gaze sharpens, and her smile hitches higher. "Open it, then."

"I'll open it later."

"Hayden." She steps toward the box, and I lunge for it, grabbing it and tucking it behind my back. Her jaw drops and her face lights up with an accusing, knowing smile. "I knew it. You're hiding something. What is in that box?"

"It's—" My brain goes blank. "Private?"

Her grin is teasing and gorgeous. "One of those weird sex things you're definitely *not* into?" she asks, lowering her voice, wiggling her eyebrows in a suggestive way as she tries not to laugh.

"Yep." I nod. "That's it."

She stares at me for a long moment before she darts forward, but instead of reaching for the box, she digs her fingers into my ribs, just below my pec, and a gasp of laughter bursts out of me.

"Tell me what's in the box," she demands, laughing as I gasp for air. "Or I'll tickle you until you pass out."

"Darce," I groan, shaking with laughter, trying to push her hands away. "You play dirty."

"That's right, Wingman, I'm merciless." She adds a second

hand, digging into the other side of my ribs, and I accidentally drop the box in a struggle to get away from her, laughing the whole time.

"Fine," I gasp, catching my breath. "It's a sex toy."

Her hands fall to her sides. "What?"

I press my mouth into a firm line. "You, uh, said you get overwhelmed when you do research and didn't want to go into a store, so I asked a bunch of my friends, and they said this is the best one." My eyes dart to hers. "For G-spot orgasms."

Why did I say that last part?

"Oh." Is she blushing? She looks like she's blushing. "Thank you." She sounds dazed as she stares at the box.

"You don't have to use it," I rush out, reaching for the box. "It's inappropriate."

"No." She puts her hand out, and I jerk mine back so I don't accidentally touch her. "It's not inappropriate. You're my wingman." She glances between me and the box. "You're just looking out for me."

"Yeah." I nod.

"Right." She nods back and does that distracting lip-biting thing again. "It's not weird. I can't wait to use it and have all those great G-spot orgasms," she adds, starting to laugh.

I groan, closing my eyes, and she chuckles more. Fucking hell, can I picture it. Her lying on her bed, moaning and working the toy between her legs, inching closer and closer to her release while I lie in my bed on the other side of the wall.

"Yeah, well," I pick the box up and hand it to her. "Here you go. Have fun."

"Thanks." She rubs a hand over her red face before accepting it. "I'm going to bed." Her eyes widen. "Not to, like, use it or something. It's just been a long day with the hair and all."

I give her a tight nod, putting on a smile. "Alright. Good night."

"Good night."

In my room, I lie in my bed and stare at the ceiling.

Owens, what are you doing? I drag a sobering breath in, listening to her bedroom door closing and her light footsteps as she gets into her bed. *What the actual fuck are you doing?*

CHAPTER 32

DARCY

"YOUR HAIR!" Pippa lights up when I take my seat before the game the next evening. She grins ear to ear with wide eyes, wearing a Storm jersey, and I feel my face go pink.

"Do you like it?" I reach up to touch a pale-lavender lock, the intended color. Layla, the hairstylist, fixed my hair while I worked from home this morning, and she used a blow dry balm that smells incredible and makes my hair super soft.

Pippa nods with enthusiasm. "*Love* it. It's so you."

My heart squeezes with happiness. "I love it, too." I grin at Hazel, who's on the other side of her, wearing her own Storm jersey. "Hey, Hazel."

"Hello, gorgeous." She winks. "The purple is very you. Looks great with your eye color."

"Thanks, you two."

Fuck Kit for telling me it wouldn't look good. I look *amazing* with purple hair.

"And you got a jersey!" Pippa adds, beaming.

My blush deepens as I nod. "Yep. Hayden got it for me."

"Did he?" Hazel smiles like she knows something I don't. "That's nice of him."

My shoulders lift in a shrug. "Yep. That's just him, though, always buying gifts for people."

Like the sex toy he bought me that I've been thinking about all day.

"Let's take a photo in our jerseys," Pippa says, pulling out her phone. "We look cute."

I lean in and smile as Pippa snaps the picture. A moment later, the arena lights dim, the fans start to cheer, and the announcer calls players' names as they hit the ice.

"I'm so glad you're joining us for games," Pippa says in my ear over the noise of the arena.

I give her a shy smile. "Me, too."

"*Number forty-two, Hayden Owens!*" the announcer calls, and I clap and cheer.

Hayden skates past and our eyes lock. His gaze goes from my jersey to my hair before he winks, and my heart skips a beat.

When he scores a goal in the second period, I jump to my feet, whooping and cheering. Rory and Alexei skate over to him to celebrate, but he grins through the glass at me.

My good luck charm, he mouths, pointing at me.

———

After the game, Hayden enters the box reserved for players' friends and family, and his eyes find me immediately.

"Hey." His gaze flicks over my hair. "You look beautiful." He shakes his head. "Your *hair* looks beautiful," he says, correcting himself.

"You didn't even comment on my eyebrows."

His mouth twitches into a smile. Layla fixed them, and they're back to their normal color, tinted a few shades darker than my pale blond. "I liked the purple."

"*No.*" I swat at him.

His responding playful grin is so disarming.

"No one liked the purple. I don't know what I was thinking."

"Nice jersey." He tilts his chin at me. "Whoever got that for you must be a really great person." He gives me a flirty smile. "Handsome, too."

I laugh, rolling my eyes. "Yes, and very modest."

The flirtiness fades from his grin, leaving only warmth and appreciation. "I liked seeing you in it tonight."

My heart does a funny dip, and I play with the hem of the sleeves. "I liked wearing it."

Hayden deserves to have someone out there rooting for him. He deserves to have the same thing Rory and Jamie have, even if he isn't looking for a partner or commitment.

His comment on Valentine's Day about a relationship not looking so bad catches in my mind, followed by the flash of disappointment in his eyes when I urged him away from it.

The gifts, the parties, the dates. He'd make a great boyfriend, if he wanted that.

"Let's grab drinks with everyone," he suggests, eyes moving over the lines of my jersey. My gaze drops to his casual navy bomber jacket and the image on his t-shirt beneath it.

"Wait." I frown and reach for his jacket zipper, pulling it down slightly before a mortified noise slips out of me and I clap my hand over my mouth. "You're not wearing that."

He puts on a confused expression, but his eyes glitter, and the corners of his mouth tug up. "What do you mean?"

I open the sides of his jacket and stare at his t-shirt. An image of me with purple hair and purple eyebrows stares back. My lips are parted and my eyes are wide as I reach out to stop him from taking the photo.

The photo he snapped last night.

"Hayden!" My voice is strangled. "Where did you get this?"

"Oh, this?" He looks down at his t-shirt like he just realized he's wearing a freaking photo of me on his chest. "Huh. How'd that photo get on there?"

I dissolve into laughter as my hands go to the hem of his shirt and I start to pull it off. "Take it off. Right now."

"Whoa, Darcy," he teases, grabbing my wrists and grinning ear to ear. "At least wait until we get home to undress me."

Sex toy, my brain whispers to me. *Hayden's huge boner. The groan he made from the other side of the wall the other night.*

"You—are"—I'm trying to pull the shirt off, but he's laughably strong compared to me—"wearing a stupid picture of my face!"

"Oh, did I not say?" His voice is so innocent, but those blue eyes sparkle like gemstones. "I got you one, too." He pulls out his phone to show me the email confirmation of the other t-shirt he rush-ordered, time stamped last night. "It's at home. Same day shipping."

I stare at the picture with my mouth pressed into a flat line as a delirious, bubbling pressure rises up my throat. "This is a picture from that charity calendar last year."

He beams. "You remember."

Of course I remember. Good lord. A charity put together a calendar of the hottest guys in professional hockey, raising money for LGBTQIA+ youth, and Hayden was January. Kit laughed his ass off at the shirtless flexing photo of his best friend.

I always felt weird that the entire world got to see this much of his body, not to mention the flirtatious, friendly smirk on his face.

That flirty smirk is supposed to be just for me.

"You put your own picture on a t-shirt for me?" I raise my eyebrows at him. "Wow. Just wow." That fizzy, delighted pressure threatens to escape, and my face aches from holding back the smile.

From the way he grins down at me expectantly, he knows it. "You can laugh."

"I'm not laughing."

"You look like you want to."

"I don't. And if I did laugh, it would only encourage you."

"Well, I'm sorry you hate my body so much." He glances around the room. "We should get going to the bar."

"Hayden." I'm trying not to smile and failing. "Change. Now."

He gives me a pleading look. "I really want to wear my new shirt." His eyes soften, and he gives me that innocent, sad look, like Pippa and Jamie's dog, Daisy, when she wants a treat. "Please, Darce." He leans down and gives me a hug, jostling me. He's big and warm and he smells good, and my resolve melts like butter in a hot pan. "I want to wear my new t-shirt."

He's actually touching me without running to his bedroom, dry-heaving in disgust. So that's a step forward.

"Fine," I sigh. "But you're wearing the jacket zipped up."

He grins and winks down at me. "We'll see."

WE WALK into the Filthy Flamingo, and Jordan does a double take at my hair before giving me an appreciative nod. "Nice hair. Looks hot."

"Thank you." I try to suppress my smile. I'm acting deeply uncool, blushing over a few small compliments.

We sit at a big booth, and after Jordan swings by with drinks, the conversation turns to the game.

"Not hearing complaints about moving you to offence anymore, are we?" Rory asks Hayden with a proud grin, and they both eye me briefly.

Hayden shrugs and sips his beer.

"Ward wants more power play goals," Alexei adds. "Says we're dragging our feet out there."

My brain prickles, and I think about the hockey models I was playing with on my laptop at lunch today. I told myself I wouldn't keep looking at them, but I can't help myself.

Rory drags a hand through his hair, frowning. "I don't know what to do. We run the drills we practiced."

"Maybe you should switch up the power play teams," I suggest lightly, running my fingernail over a seam on the sleeve of my jersey.

The table goes quiet. Shit. I shouldn't have said that.

"What do you mean?" Rory asks. "We put our best guys on the power plays."

There's a clunk of nerves in my stomach. When I'm wrong, I'm *really* wrong, and it can have disastrous consequences, but there's a lingering feeling that I'm right about this.

"Swapping out players changes the scoring probability," I blurt out, pulse picking up. I should shut up and stop talking. I swallow hard.

Jamie leans in, watching me with focus. "How do you know this?"

"She has a statistics degree," Hayden says confidently.

I shoot him a hard look. "Um." Under everyone's watchful, curious eyes, I can't get a full breath. I'm not used to being the center of attention like this. "I build statistical hockey models."

Silence.

"For fun," I add. Oh god. They probably think I'm so weird. "Anyway—"

"Do you have the models with you?" Rory asks.

"They're on my laptop." I brought it with me to the office when I headed in late in the morning, and I came straight to the game from work.

Hayden's eyes spark with interest. "Show us, Darce."

This is getting real, so I scramble for an excuse. "I'm not going to pull my laptop out at the bar like a dork."

Hayden holds my gaze as his hand drifts toward his jacket zip, and I cough out a laugh. He grins, wiggling his eyebrows, making the message clear.

Show us the models or I'll show them the picture of you on my shirt.

"Okay," I say quickly, laughing. "I'll show you, but don't put too much stock into them. I'm just playing around."

Jamie shrugs. "It can't hurt."

It could, if I'm wrong. No one's checked my work. I'm just plugging numbers in and analyzing patterns, but they're not proven. And if I'm wrong? It could backfire on the team. The other team could score a goal. The Storm could lose the game. In professional sports, every goal counts and every game matters.

The guys huddle around my laptop as I load my power play model.

"Your power play percentage as of tonight is"—I adjust the model for the two they had during the game—"just over 20 percent. It isn't the worst in the league, but it's not great, either."

The guys sit in silence, listening.

"Your first power play line has Alexei on defense, but if you swap him out for another defenseman like Jayden, and swap Rory for one of your second-line forwards, say Dylan Lockwood," I make the changes to the model, and it spits out a new number, "your chance of scoring on the power play goes up to 27 percent. One of the highest in the league," I add, starting to feel self-conscious. "I know that seems unbelievable, and it's probably wrong because no one's verified this—"

"Are you a wizard?" Rory asks, crooking a surprised smile at me.

"No." I chuckle. "Just a dork, I guess."

"This is incredible." He leans in to read over the results on my screen again.

"Right?" Hayden nods at Rory. "She's always been good at this stuff."

My heart does a silly leap in my chest as warm, happy feelings bubble through me.

Alexei studies me with a serious expression. "Why do you think the scoring percentage goes up when I'm not on the power play team?"

"You're already on the ice so much during games." My forehead wrinkles as I think about the different iterations I did. "Players who have less ice time in that period sometimes perform better during the two minutes of a power play. It could also be that you're more of a defensive defenseman, you know? Whereas if we swap out a defenseman who plays a bit of offense, it increases the chance of getting the puck to the other end of the ice." I shrug. "I'm not sure. There's probably a great explanation, but I haven't found it yet."

The look of awe the guys give me makes my stomach dip with excitement and pride. Beside me, Hayden winks down at me, smiling, and my confidence grows.

"I did one for penalty kills, too, since that's another weak spot."

Rory gives me a wounded look, but he's smiling. "Ouch."

"Sorry." My face goes hot.

He laughs and waves me off. "Show us."

My fingers fly over the keyboard as I pull up the penalty kill model with several player configurations.

"What's this?" Hazel leans on the back of the booth to read over my shoulder.

"Darcy's showing us math magic," Rory explains.

I laugh. "It's not magic, it's just statistics. I did one for common injuries, too, predicting recovery times."

Her eyes light up, and I know I've hooked the physiotherapist side of her. "Show me."

I run through the models with them, explaining my reasoning and my data.

"Does Ward know about this?" Jamie asks.

My eyes go wide. "No. Oh my god." I make a face. "This is just for fun."

Everyone looks at me like I'm speaking another language.

"Don't tell Ward about it," I add. "It's dumb."

"It's not dumb," Hayden cuts in, frowning. "You do this for a living."

"My job is different." My face goes hot. "We work in teams, with thousands of data points, and the models go through intense verification."

There's so little responsibility and risk, it's almost laughable. My clients are corporations—if I screw up, they pay a little more or a little less, but no one gets hurt. No one misses out on insurance or care or support.

"This could really help us," Alexei adds quietly.

I feel a stab of guilt, but then I remember how devastating it was to be the reason someone else got fired, and my guilt evaporates.

"It's just me playing around with numbers. You should leave the analytics to the experts."

"Show me that power play one again." Rory reaches for my keyboard to go to the next tab but accidentally closes the window and—

An image of the hot pink toy Hayden bought me fills the screen, and my heart jolts into my throat. Beside me, Hayden stiffens.

"*Using your new* G-Spot Banger *is easy with these three steps,*" a calming woman's voice says on the video as she holds up the sex toy.

Everyone goes silent, watching.

"*Slide the Banger inside—*"

"Oh my god." I slam the laptop closed, face burning hotter than the surface of the sun while everyone stares at me in shock.

Rory lets out a howl of laughter as Alexei and Jamie stare at my screen in horror. Hazel presses her mouth tight to hide a smile. I can't look at Hayden.

"I can explain."

I *can't* explain, and it's exactly what it looks like. I was nervous about using the toy Hayden got me, so I looked up the company's website last night. I thought I closed the page.

Oh god. I was on my laptop at *work*. Even coworkers seeing that would be better than this, though.

Rory nudges me with his elbow. "Hazel has that one, too." He looks back at her with a question on his face. "Right?"

She nods, chuckling. "Yep. That's the one I told Hayden to buy."

They know that Hayden bought this for me? A horrified noise scrapes out of my throat. I want to disappear into thin air.

"No one saw anything." Hayden's voice is loud and firm, and he gives everyone a stern look. "Right, guys?"

Alexei stares straight ahead. "I didn't see anything. My contacts fell out." Our eyes meet before he looks away. "And I didn't hear anything, either." He almost looks more uncomfortable than I feel.

"Me neither." Rory wears the biggest grin while his eyes glitter. "I just saw your math magic."

Closing my eyes, I silently plead for the floor to open up and swallow me. I can never face these guys again.

"How about another round of drinks?" Rory asks, and everyone starts getting up and moving back to their seats at once.

Hayden looks down at me, eyes bright and mouth pressed into a tight line like he's trying not to laugh. "Are you okay?"

"No." I can still feel how pink my face is. "I want to die."

He snorts, eyes closing. "It's fine, Darce. That kind of thing happens to everyone."

My expression turns incredulous, but I'm starting to laugh. "Really? *That* happens to everyone?"

"Yep. All the time." He rubs his strong jaw, thinking. "But

if you want me to distract them, I can." His fingers hover over his jacket zip, and I lunge forward to catch his wrist, laughing.

"Don't you dare." His skin is warm as I tug his hand away from the zipper. "I've already shown too much weirdness. I don't want to get uninvited from the next bar night."

He lets his hand drop and gives me a knowing smile. "Over my dead body. You know you're one of us, right?"

My gaze moves around the bar, to Rory and Hazel talking with Pippa and Jamie at the next booth, to Alexei and some of the other guys chatting—I catch the words *power play percentage* in their conversation—and to Jordan mixing drinks behind the bar. She gives me a quick, quiet smile.

Back in Calgary, I didn't have a group of friends like this. Kit didn't like going out after games. Even when we were in Vancouver, Hayden and I would have to drag him out. The Calgary team wasn't close like the guys are on the Vancouver Storm.

I look around at the new life I'm creating for myself, and my heart squeezes.

Yes, I'm weird and awkward, but I get the feeling they don't care. I like it here, and I feel like I'm finally starting to find myself.

THE APARTMENT IS FREEZING when we get home that night.

"It feels like the air conditioning's on." I frown at the thermostat. It's colder than normal in here, but the heat is on like usual.

Darcy smacks a hand to her forehead. "I left my window open. Sorry, I like having fresh air in there throughout the day. I'll go close it."

She pads down the hall to her room, and I watch her walk away, my name on her back in big, bold letters.

Pride spreads through my chest and the corner of my mouth hooks up. Seeing her cheering for me, wearing that big smile after I scored a goal tonight? It almost made me forget Miller's stupid way of motivating me to be more assertive on the ice.

And the way she lit up tonight, telling everyone about her hockey models—*that's* how I want her to talk about her job. Every time I bring up her work, she rolls her eyes and changes the subject. I know it isn't making her happy.

She deserves happiness, though. She deserves all the good things.

From her bedroom, I hear a muffled noise of frustration.

"You okay?" I ask, heading to her room.

"Yep," she calls back. When I pause in the doorway, she's struggling with the window, trying to pull it closed. "It's stuck." She steps back to study it. "I think a bird flew into it and bent the screen."

I walk over and lean in to look. She's right—the screen frame is bent, and now the window won't slide on the track. Because we're so many floors up, the screens don't come out easily, otherwise I'd just pop it out. Something about building code.

"There's a maintenance number I can call." I slip my phone out of my back pocket, find the number, and dial, giving Darcy a quick smile as it rings.

"Is this an emergency?" a guy answers. The background is so noisy, he has to shout.

"Uh." I look at Darcy and she gives me an odd look. "No?"

"I'm dealing with a burst pipe on the second floor and it's flooding four apartments," the guy says. "Text me the problem and I'll get to it as soon as I'm done here."

"Got it. Thanks."

I hang up and start tapping out a text detailing the issue and our apartment number. "It might be a while."

"Oh." Darcy bites her lip, glancing at the window and then at the clock on her dresser. It's almost midnight. "I should go to bed. It's a work night. Maybe he can come fix it tomorrow morning."

I frown at her. "It's freezing in here."

"I'll close the door so it won't be cold in the rest of the apartment."

"No, Darce." Does she think I'm worried about *myself*? "I don't want *you* to be too cold."

"I'll wear a hoodie. It's totally fine."

An unhappy expression settles on my face. I don't like this. It's the middle of winter. She's going to be cold. "You can sleep in my bed."

"What?" She blinks.

My mind is already made up. "You sleep in my bed, and I'll sleep on the couch."

The force of my words surprises me, but the idea of Darcy in my bed takes root in my brain and grows, spreading like wildfire, sending heat and sparks down my spine. The caveman part of my brain likes this image.

"You don't have to do that," she says softly, gaze roaming over my face.

Is that relief or disappointment? My eyes cut to her desk and land on the sex toy I bought her before I jerk my gaze away.

"Darcy, I don't want you sleeping in an igloo all night. Worrying whether you're warm enough is going to keep me awake all night, and we have another game tomorrow." I tilt an encouraging smile at her. "And I need my rest."

"I'll sleep on the couch," she says. "Since you need your rest."

"No." I shake my head, still wearing a smile. She's so cute, especially in this jersey. I never want her to take it off. "My mind's made up. I'm a gentleman, you know."

The corners of her mouth tip higher. "I didn't say you weren't."

Her throat works, and her eyes trace over my mouth, my jaw, my neck. My mind goes to our practice kiss at the cast party and how it felt when I pulled her into my lap. How it felt when we woke up together, her head on my chest, hair spilling over my skin.

Her mouth twists like she's deliberating, and her gaze lifts to mine. "You said you need your rest."

I arch an eyebrow, and she shifts on her feet, looking away.

"It's not a big deal if we both sleep in your bed," she says, shrugging. "We're friends."

My pulse turns rapid and I drag a deep breath into my lungs.

Every time I get near her, it's almost too good to bear, and the grip on my control loosens.

The last time we woke up together, though, it was the best sleep I'd ever had. It was probably a coincidence.

What if it wasn't, though?

"I'm fine with it if you are," I say, keeping my tone casual. "Totally fine."

Tension cracks and pops in the air, and she lets out a light laugh. "I'll go get ready for bed, then."

CHAPTER 35
HAYDEN

TEN MINUTES LATER, we climb into bed, not looking at each other. My heart beats harder in my chest as she settles under the duvet beside me, sinking into the pillow and adjusting to get comfortable. When I glance over at her, my pulse does a weird leap.

It feels weirdly familiar and comfortable, climbing into bed with Darcy like this. Like we've done it a thousand times.

"Aren't you going to be too hot?" she asks, looking at my t-shirt and gym shorts.

I'm going to boil from the inside out, but I can't climb into bed beside her in just my boxers like I usually wear to sleep. "I'll be fine."

One of her eyebrows lifts. "Hayden. I know you sleep in just boxers. It's okay."

I hesitate. "Are you sure?"

She nods. "Mhm. Promise. I'll keep my hands to myself."

I chuckle, pulling my shirt over my head and tossing it onto the nearby chair.

Her eyes trail down my torso with interest before she looks away fast.

Was she... checking me out? Pride expands in my chest. I

yank my shorts off, and her eyes cut back to me, to my tight boxers, before she looks at the ceiling.

"You better not snore," I tell her.

She grins and kicks me with her cold feet.

"Your feet," I hiss, moving away. "They're like ice."

"Sorry." She wiggles her toes against my calf.

I jerk my leg away, laughing. "That's it. You're sleeping in the hall."

She laughs again, and I grin, moving onto my side to study her.

"It's like having a sleepover," she says, gaze moving over my face.

"I wouldn't know. I don't have sleepovers with women."

Her brows slide together in a puzzled expression. "I meant a sleepover, like when you were a kid, but now I have more questions." The corners of her lips tip up as she studies me. "Really? You've never slept in the same bed as a woman?"

I shake my head. "I mean, the other night, after Kit called you—"

"Right." She swallows, biting her lip. "But that was..."

"Different."

"Yeah." She nods. "Different."

A long beat of silence. "Sleepovers lead to breakfast together," I admit, "and that leads to people getting attached."

We have breakfast together all the time, my brain reminds me. She makes me coffee every morning when I'm in town. It's the best part of my day, sitting in the kitchen with her while she looks all sleepy and cute, talking about our plans for the day.

She hums, watching me. "So maybe it's *you* who snores."

I huff a laugh. "Whatever. Don't blame me when the windows start shaking because you're sawing logs."

Her smile stretches wide, and I thank that dumb bird for flying into her window and making this situation happen.

"I'm going to turn the light out," I tell her, and she nods. I reach over my shoulder and click the lamp off, darkening the room. Even with the blinds closed, a soft glow from the city lights outside sneaks through.

I listen to the sound of our breathing, but my mind wanders back to the bar tonight. How she looked so terrified at the idea of the team using her hockey models. A memory resurfaces—years ago, her talking with animated excitement about her new job.

For six months after we graduated from university, Darcy worked for the Canadian Department of Agriculture as a data analyst. I still remember the way her voice sounded when she talked about her job, full of interest and excitement.

"Hey, Darce?"

"Mmm?"

"What happened at your first job?"

She never told me why she got a new job, just that she was working somewhere else before she changed the subject. She never had that spark when she talked about work, though.

Not until tonight.

"I screwed up and got fired," she says quietly. "And I got someone else fired."

I can still make out her profile in the dim bedroom as she stares at the ceiling. "What happened?"

She exhales through her nose. "We were running a study on small-scale farms, on who could use the grant money most effectively, and my model was wrong."

Our gazes meet before she looks away, and I have the overwhelming urge to pull her against my chest and tell her it's not her fault, that it's going to be okay.

"My boss checked it, but I uploaded the wrong one. People missed out on the government grant because of it, and we only found out when we were audited." She swallows.

My chest aches at the pain in her voice. "And they let you go?"

She nods. "They let my boss go, too, though. And she was a single mom." Her expression crumples and my body tenses. "She was so nice, Hayden. She was such a good boss. She spent so much time training me and explaining things. I could tell she really loved the work, you know?"

I nod, not knowing what to say. I hate seeing her in pain like this. I hate that this has weighed on her for years and made her feel like she isn't capable.

"You were twenty-two. You were fresh out of school."

"I should have known better." She takes a deep breath and lets it out slowly. "Some of those small-scale farms had to close and sell off land. Some of them had been family farms for generations. A lot of people were hurt by my mistake."

I don't say anything for a long time. I just watch her and wonder what she'd be like if that hadn't happened. If she was still at that job and loved her career.

Christ, I want to see Darcy love her career again. I want to see her light up like she did tonight. "Everybody makes mistakes."

"Yep. Everyone makes mistakes, but sometimes they hurt people. That's why I work in insurance," she admits with a wry half smile. "No one gets hurt. Rich old men might lose a bit of money, but no one goes out of business, and no one gets fired."

She gives me a quick, reassuring smile, like she's smoothing the conversation and all her vulnerability away. But her words knot in my chest, snagging and scratching.

Her eyes close and she settles farther under my duvet. "Good night, Hayden."

I want more for her. I want her to feel on top of the world, to be excited about work and to feel like she's making a difference. I want her to take risks and see that sometimes they pay off.

"Good night, Darce."

———

I wake the next morning spooning Darcy, her body tucked against my chest, warm and soft, pretty hair all over me and her sweet scent in my nose. Intense feelings of comfort and possessiveness course through me.

She fits right against me, like we were made for each other.

In her sleep, she sighs and shifts her hips, pressing her ass back into me. Blood hurtles to my cock and my balls ache.

She lets out a low moan and does it again. My jaw clenches at how good the pressure feels against my cock, how good it feels for her to want me like this. The urge to yank her pajama bottoms down and rock against her pussy sweeps through me, but instead, I tighten my hold around her, clutching her harder against me, letting my lips fall to the exposed skin between her shoulder and neck.

I shouldn't be doing this, but I'm half asleep and not thinking clearly. Her skin is so fucking soft under my mouth, and I could spend hours like this, just teasing each other.

Her breathing changes and she stiffens before her head jerks up and our gazes meet. Her eyes go wide.

"Sorry." She moves away, and I pull my arm back, rolling onto my back.

Thankfully, between my tight boxers and the thick duvet, she can't see my straining erection and how much I enjoyed what we just did.

On the other side of the bed, she gives me a soft, slightly embarrassed smile, looking so fucking gorgeous in the morning light.

"Did you sleep okay? I wasn't, like, kicking you or mumbling about the Fibonacci sequence?"

I chuckle, shaking my head. "I slept like a rock."

The realization sinks into my gut. Not a fluke, then, that I sleep better than ever with Darcy in my bed.

We watch each other for a few moments.

"Me, too," she whispers.

Our eyes meet again and my heart thumps harder. I want to stay in this bed with her forever, just lying here talking. My mind wanders back to last night at the bar. "I like that you're playing with your hockey models again."

She rolls her eyes.

"They make you happy, though, don't they? Maybe that's enough." I reach for a lock of her light-purple hair and drape it across her upper lip like a mustache.

Beneath it, she smiles.

"It's nice to see you excited about things again."

She makes a pleased, thoughtful humming noise.

My eyes drop to her mouth, and the urge to pull her back against me and kiss her rushes through me. Our gazes meet, and something sparks in her eyes. For a moment, I think she might feel the same way.

"I should get up and get ready for work," she whispers.

"Yeah." I nod. "I'll call the maintenance guy about your window again. It'll be fixed by the time you get home tonight."

She gives me a grateful smile and leaves, closing my bedroom door behind her, and I lie there, listening to the sounds of her getting ready for work while I wrap my hand around my cock and give it slow, torturous strokes, teasing myself until I hear the front door close when she leaves.

With a few faster, rougher strokes, I come hard, white light blinding my vision and pleasure running like a hot current through my veins as I shoot all over my stomach with a groan. I can never come quietly. My breath saws in and out of my lungs as my head fills with thoughts of soft, sweet, fuckable Darcy. My Darcy.

Like always, the orgasm isn't enough. Afterward, I want her more than ever. The urge to take control rises. It's the same feeling I had on the ice the other night when I scored the goal.

Later, on my way to the kitchen, I pause in the doorway of her bedroom, eyes on the box sitting on her desk, unopened past the original shipping box.

The sex toy.

My thoughts flick to the instructional video that popped up on her laptop last night. It's not my problem, and I'm not going to get involved. No matter how badly I want to intervene, help, and make her feel safe.

Make her come.

I force myself to walk to the kitchen, clearing thoughts of her from my head as I call the maintenance guy again to get the window fixed.

Not. My. Problem.

TEN MINUTES into the game against Boston, we get our first power play. All the guys who were at the bar the night Darcy talked about her analytical models look at each other.

She doubts herself, but I don't.

"How about we switch up the power play teams?" I suggest to Ward at the bench.

He raises an eyebrow and gives me a long look. "The teams I've carefully selected and spent an entire season training with?"

I glance at Miller, whose eyes light up with curiosity, before I nod at Ward. "Yeah. I think we should try something different."

The corner of Ward's mouth ticks up. "Alright, Owens. What do you want to do?"

"Let's swap Volkov for Novotny." Jayden Novotny is the second-line defenseman Darcy suggested, who plays more offensively than Volkov. "And Miller for Lockwood."

"You want to take Miller off the ice during a power play?"

Miller and I exchange a look, and he wiggles his eyebrows, offering no help.

"Yeah." I nod at Ward. "I do."

"Miller?" Ward looks to him. "Any notes?"

"Nope." Miller grins at us. "Just excited to try it."

Ward shakes his head, a hint of a smile on his mouth. "Go get 'em, boys."

The revised team takes position for the face-off, and we nab the puck. Novotny darts and weaves around their defenseman while the noise from the stands crescendos.

He takes a shot, and Boston's goalie deflects. There's a collective *oh* of momentary disappointment before Lockwood snags the puck.

Twenty seconds left on the power play clock.

He passes to me and I take the shot. This time, the puck sails into their net. The arena roars with noise and the goal horn blows as our guys surround me. Blood pounds in my ears and I look to Darcy sitting behind the net, beaming and cheering.

See? my expression says, and she just smiles harder.

"Owens." Ward approaches in the dressing room. "Good work tonight. I like that out-of-the-box thinking on the power play." He shakes his head. "It isn't easy taking risks like that, but sometimes they pay off."

"It wasn't my idea. It was my"—I stumble over what to call her—"roommate, Darcy. She's an actuary and she plays around with analytical models for fun."

"For fun," Ward echoes, but he's smiling.

I laugh. "Yeah. She has a degree in statistics and she loves that kind of stuff."

"Is she looking for a job?"

"I don't know." Something dances around in my chest. Darcy working for the team. How fucking cool would that be? I bet she'd like it a lot more than her boring insurance job. Maybe she'd get to come on the road with us to away games. The idea of her getting excited about her work, lighting up and doing something she loves, makes hope rise inside me. "You should ask her."

Ward's expression turns thoughtful and he nods to himself. "Maybe I will."

THE NEXT WEEKEND, Georgia and I are out shopping again when she leads me into a quiet store.

It's a sea of lingerie. I clutch my shopping bags harder. I've already bought a pair of "fuck-me" heels, as Georgia calls them, and a couple of tops from her favorite consignment store.

My gaze goes to a velvet chair at the back of the store, near the dressing room. "I'll be over there. Take your time."

"Um, no. I've seen your underwear." She gives me a pitying look, referring to the time she helped me with a zipper and used the phrase *budget potato sack* with regard to my panties. "This is an intervention."

I give her a wounded look. "What's wrong with my underwear?"

She flips through a rack of gauzy thongs. "Do you want me to answer that, or do you want to feel pretty and hot?" She finds my size and hands it to me before searching through the matching bras.

"I don't need expensive underwear to feel hot." My face is warm as I think about last week, when I woke up in Hayden's bed and ground against his thick erection.

With that thing, it's no wonder he has no problem with women. I swallow.

"You don't," Georgia muses as she flips through more incredibly sexy garments that I will look like a total fool in, like a kid playing dress-up. "But it helps."

"I don't think I'm ready to start hooking up with people." I don't mention how Hayden and I kissed at the cast party or how I definitely felt ready for that.

"Lingerie doesn't have to be for other people. It's for you." Her mouth tilts in a sly smile. "There's power in having a secret. Sometimes, when the Russian is making his bitchy comments or glaring at my feet, I think *what I'm wearing under my clothes would melt your eyes out of your head*." She stares off into space for a long moment before she jerks out of it and smiles at me. "Try a few pieces on. If you don't like them, you don't have to get them."

We browse the quiet shop for a few more minutes, and nerves flutter through my stomach at the idea of wearing these items. I don't know why; it's not like anyone will see them.

Maybe because I feel like it's another way I'm leaving my old self behind.

Or maybe because every time I consider one of the lacy garments, I wonder whether Hayden would like it. I stare for a long time at a cream-colored garter belt, picturing his big hands undoing the tiny clips, and a shiver rolls down my spine.

"It must be nice having the place to yourself when the guys are away," Georgia says.

The team's been gone for five days, traveling for away games, and no, it hasn't been nice having the place to myself.

I miss Hayden.

"We slept in the same bed," I blurt out.

Her hand stills over a table before her interested eyes cut to mine and a smile forms on her mouth. "Go on."

"Because my window was jammed open."

She gives me a flat look. "Are you kidding me?"

"I'm serious," I choke out, laughing. "My window wouldn't close and it was cold and I wanted him to have a good night's sleep for the game and—" I cut myself off as Georgia smiles wider.

"Uh-huh." Her tone is loaded with disbelief, and she's grinning like a cat. "You wanted him to have a good sleep? How kind of you."

My face burns. I can make every excuse in the book, but the truth is so obvious: I *wanted* to sleep in the same bed as Hayden again. The way he smelled the next morning and the feel of his hard, broad body wrapped around mine threads through my memory, and my skin prickles.

"And, um, we woke up spooning and he had a boner and I accidentally ground against it."

I've been thinking about all of this nonstop and it's all bubbling to the surface.

"Mmm." She nods, satisfied. "That's the stuff I want to hear more about."

I still haven't used the toy he got me. If I do, I'll think about him, and I'm worried about what'll happen next. I'll like it too much.

I already like *him* too much. Maybe I have for a long time. I don't know anymore.

Our eyes meet and something in my expression causes hers to soften.

"He's my best friend and my wingman and there are a million reasons why we shouldn't get involved."

She makes a thoughtful noise that sounds like reluctant agreement.

"I'm still figuring things out." *I'm still finding myself* is what I want to say but don't know how. "I don't want to derail that."

She hums, nodding with understanding. "Can't argue with that." A tight smile pulls across her mouth. "Men ruin everything."

There's an edge to her tone. I want to know more, but she waves me over to the dressing room.

"No more stalling," she says over her shoulder.

———

Fifteen minutes later, I stare at my reflection in the dressing room.

It's the warm, flattering lighting that's making me look so good. Or the backdrop of the thick velvet curtain behind me. Or maybe it's the way the store smells fresh and comforting, like vanilla and lemon.

Or maybe this is just how I look in high-end lingerie. Delight and pride spread through me as I take a deep breath, watching my cleavage rise over the bra. The delicate purple of the embroidered flowers matches my hair and the fit is perfect. The fabric is soft and luxurious, like someone put time and effort into crafting this item. Something in my chest expands, swelling and making me stand a little taller.

I think my other bras are the wrong size, because my boobs don't normally look like this.

"Am I a genius or what?" Georgia drawls from across the curtain.

Although I can't even imagine it, I'll eventually need to take dating seriously again. *A player is always confident and chill*, the list said, and wearing something like this under my clothes would definitely give me a much-needed boost.

What I'm wearing under my clothes would melt the eyes

right out of your head, she said earlier. A thrill shoots through me at the idea of Hayden seeing me in it. Or even just wearing it around him, without him knowing.

That would never happen, but it's fun to think about.

"Yes," I call back, biting down on a smile.

———

I step out of the elevator on our floor at the same time Hayden's leaving the apartment across the hall.

"Thanks for your help, love," our elderly neighbor, Greta, says to him before she sees me and smiles with warmth. "Hayden was helping me with the upper windows I can't reach." She gives him a proud nod. "He's a good window cleaner."

Hayden and I chuckle. The guy makes millions as one of the best hockey players in the world but isn't too proud to clean his elderly neighbor's windows. My heart squeezes with warmth.

"He *is* a good window cleaner," I tell her with a grin.

"What a nice young man you have here." Her eyes crinkle with a smile. "They don't make them like this very often."

He shifts, uncomfortable with this praise, and I beam at him. "I know. He's one in a million."

"Don't let this one get away." She winks before closing the door.

In the quiet hallway, Hayden and I start laughing.

"How was your flight?" I ask, holding our door open for him. He arrived home earlier today.

"Good." He tilts his chin at my bags. "Doing some more shopping?"

"Georgia and I went after work."

He makes a pleased noise. "What did you get?"

"A few tops, a pair of shoes." And some wildly sexy lingerie that I can *never* tell him about.

He takes a seat at the kitchen island as I set the bags down. "Show me."

I nudge the bag with my lingerie aside—thankfully, the paper bag is plain white with no identifying store name—and pull out the two tops I bought. He watches with interested amusement as I flip the shoebox open, but when I lift a pale blue velvet heel, his smile drops.

"Georgia convinced me to buy them. I know they're different from what I usually wear, and they're velvet so I can wear them like, two days a year here, but—" I shrug. "They're kind of fun for spring."

And I wanted them. I felt sexy, grown up, and stylish in them.

"I think those are called fuck-me shoes." He stares hard at them, with a rough edge to his voice that makes my skin prickle.

Heat careens through me. "Are they?" My voice goes high. "I didn't know."

He swallows, blinking, and looks away. "What's in this bag?" He reaches for the white paper bag, and alarm shoots through me.

"No, don't—"

He pulls out a delicate balconette bra—cream with pretty soft-purple flowers carefully stitched onto the gauzy fabric—and I freeze at the sight of the lingerie in his strong hand.

For a long moment, he just stares at it before he drops the lacy garment back into the bag. Our eyes meet; his cheekbones turn an adorable shade of pink; my face is burning.

I shrug with an embarrassed smile. "Georgia made me buy it."

"Yeah." He rakes his hand through his hair, the long line of his throat moving as he swallows. "That's great. Lingerie is great."

"Dressing like a player and all that."

A muscle ticks near his temple and his gaze moves over me, flickering with something. Is he picturing me wearing it?

No, of course he isn't.

He rises to his feet, glancing at the lingerie bag again before he jerks his gaze away. "Have you had dinner?"

I shake my head.

His eyes spark, and he wiggles his eyebrows at my new heels. The tension dissipates, and I can breathe again.

"Let's take your new shoes out for a spin."

"THE CHERRY BLOSSOMS will be blooming soon." Darcy tips her face up to look at the trees as we walk home from dinner.

My mind slides to the lacy bra I pulled out of her bag back at the apartment. The embroidered flowers were tiny, delicate, and so pretty. I can't stop thinking about what she'd look like wearing it. What those flowers would feel like under my lips as I press soft kisses to the underside of her breasts, teasing her.

It's exactly the kind of thing I'd buy for her, if I were buying her lingerie.

Which I'm not.

But which I'm thinking about and have been thinking about all night.

What else is in that white bag in the apartment? A matching pair of panties? I get an image of her stretched out on my bed, smiling up at me, wearing the matching set as I decide where to touch first. Darcy in lingerie that she picked out, that *she* feels hot in—it's almost too much to bear. And then those shoes I've been glancing at all night.

I've never been a foot guy, but when Darcy wears sexy little fuck-me heels like that? Jesus Christ.

I need to get away from her before I do something stupid. I need to jerk off. I need to kiss her again. I need to get her out of my head, because I'm losing it.

She looks up at me expectantly, and I snap back to the present. "What?"

She laughs, green eyes lit up with the soft evening light. "I said I missed the cherry blossoms in Vancouver."

I exhale hard. "Yeah. They're... really pretty."

Her gaze lingers on me, eyebrows pinching with worry. "You're quiet tonight. Everything okay with hockey?"

"Everything's great." My grin is confident and flirty, but her eyes narrow like she sees right through me.

"Do you like playing offense?"

"I do," I admit. "I still don't feel like I'm where I need to be, though." Even with Miller's dumb trick to motivate me, something's not quite right. Discomfort lodges in my chest like a sharp kernel. At least it's gotten the media heat off me and Ward, though.

"Something changed around your game with New Jersey." Her head tilts as she looks up at me. "Your average assists went down, but you started scoring more goals."

My smile feels more genuine, because I love it when she lets her math brain out. I bet she knows the exact percentages, too, but she's holding back because she doesn't want to seem like a dork.

I like it when she's a dork, though. Darcy makes math look hot.

"Oh, yeah?" I arch a teasing eyebrow at her. "I don't think that's quite right."

Her eyes flare with determination. "Your assist rate dropped 29 percent, but your scoring average increased 32.4 percent. If you continue like this into next season, you'll be one of the top three scorers in the league."

A satisfied grin stretches across my face. "Gotcha."

She rolls her eyes, smiling. "You tricked me."

"I love it when you talk math to me, baby."

She snorts. "You're supposed to be coaching me on how to pick guys up, not scare them away."

"What are you talking about?"

"I can't talk stats with other guys," she says, like it's obvious. "It's boring and weird. I sound like a robot."

My gut hardens at the phrase *other guys*. "Talking about the things you love is hot, Darce. You should always talk about stats on dates."

The word *dates* tastes like sand in my mouth. *Only dates with me*, I'd love to add.

"You're different."

A string plucks in my chest.

She sighs. "Other guys don't want to hear about it."

"Other guys being Kit?" I ask before I can stop myself.

She shrugs, which is enough of an answer for me.

He never bragged about her having a stats degree. The few times I witnessed him introduce her to people at events, he'd call her his girlfriend, and that was it. Nothing about how she was an actuary or had a math degree or loved fantasy romance or was the reigning bowling champ among the three of us.

He didn't treat her like her own person.

"Hey." I stop walking and catch her wrist.

The sun is setting, and the golden hour light gleams off her pale-purple hair. Under my hand, the bracelet I gave her slides between us. She wears it every day. I feel a hit of possessive male pride, followed by the urge to buy her more jewelry.

"You should talk about stats on dates. If he thinks it's weird, he's an insecure loser, okay? Real men aren't threatened by a woman with a big brain who knows her way around a graphing calculator."

Her eyes close and she laughs silently. Under my fingers, her skin is so soft. "I haven't used a graphing calculator in years."

"Yeah, but you could, couldn't you?"

She grins and rolls her eyes.

"Mhm. That's what I thought. You want my advice? Hold out for a guy who wants to TI-83 you all night long."

Her chest shakes with laughter. "What does that even mean?"

"I don't know." I shake my head and blow out a heavy breath like I'm turned on. I am, a little. "But *man*, it sounds hot."

"You're so weird," she says, starting to walk again.

I let her wrist go, following at a leisurely pace. "Your recommendations worked the other night at the game."

Her gaze whips to mine, eyes widening, before she shakes her head, brushing it off. "The team got lucky."

"It's not luck. That's what you always say about these things, right? It's not luck, it's a predicted circumstance. You were right, Darce. Your math checked out."

She bites her lip, and I silently hope that she changes her mind, forgetting all about what happened in the past. *You're right, I'm an amazing genius*, she says in my daydream.

A smile lifts on her mouth. "You still haven't told me what changed."

"Miller said if I didn't score a goal, he'd set you up with one of the rookies." Even now, protective feelings spike in my gut. "Not in a creepy way. He was going to encourage them to ask you out or talk to you at the bar."

Darcy's eyes spark with amusement. "Aren't they, like, twenty years old?"

"One's eighteen."

She laughs. "Why would I ever go out with an eighteen-year-old? It would be like dating my little brother."

Relief throttles through me. "Yeah, I don't know why he thought that would work."

"I mean, it did work." She gives me a pointed look.

It seems stupid, now that I think about it. Why would Darcy be into some kid fresh out of high school? I force myself to shrug. My ears are going warm. "I didn't want you to be uncomfortable."

"Hayden." She nudges my rib with her elbow. The way she says my name makes my blood feel warm and thick like honey. "You're too sweet sometimes, you know that?"

"Don't say that." My chest feels tight, heart pumping hard.

She gives me a funny look, but when she says things like that, in that loving tone, looking up at me like I'm more than just a pretty face and a good fuck, I feel hope.

It's dangerous.

She opens her mouth to say something but winces like she's in pain, looking down to her feet.

"What? What's wrong?"

"These shoes." She leans down to tug at the strap. "They hurt. How does Georgia wear shoes like this every day? She said something about tape on my toes, but we didn't have any at home." She starts walking again, but the pained expression stays put on her face.

Concern streaks through me and I put a hand on her wrist again, stopping her. "You can't walk, Darce. You're going to get blisters."

"I already have blisters. It's fine. We're two blocks from home."

I glare at her shoes. Stupid sexy shoes, causing her pain. I could call a rideshare, but it would be faster to walk, and my instincts are yelling at me to get Darcy home so she can take the heels off.

With my back facing her, I kneel. "Jump on."

"What? No, I'm fine."

"You're not. Your feet hurt." Seeing her in pain makes my chest hurt. "We can do this the easy way or the hard way."

"What's the hard way?"

I stand and scoop her up, carrying her firefighter style down the sidewalk, and she shakes with laughter. People glance over, and an older woman smiles at us together.

"Okay, okay!" Darcy pats my chest. "I'll cooperate."

I set her on her feet and lower down, looping my hands beneath her thighs as she puts her arms around my neck. She's warm against me, and I can feel myself smiling as her hair tickles the back of my neck.

"Good girl."

A FEW MINUTES LATER, Darcy unlocks the door of our apartment and I carry her inside.

"You can put me down now," she laughs.

I carry her to her bedroom and set her on her bed before I kneel on the floor, hands going to the thin strap of her heels.

"You don't have to—" she starts, but I already have the shoe off and I'm moving to the other one.

"Do you need a bandage?" I inspect her foot, fingers wrapped around her delicate ankle. "You're not bleeding."

She shakes her head as her mouth twists into a reluctant but pleased smile, and my heart stutters. "You always take such good care of me."

I wink at her. "That's what I'm here for."

"You're here for more than that." Her eyes move over me, and my skin prickles at her intense attention. "I always love hanging out with you."

I think about the lingerie she bought—that she's going to wear for some other guy—and the urge to make a move races through me.

"Welp, good night." I rise and toss her duvet over her head.

"It's nine o'clock," she laughs from under it, shoving it aside, hair all messed up and adorable. "It's too early to sleep."

Leaning against her doorway, I linger. I should leave. My eyes move around her room and land on the box on her desk. Just a corner of it is visible beneath a stack of papers.

Every night, I lie in bed, listening for that toy, but I haven't heard it yet. I don't know what I'll do when I *do* hear it. Just the thought of her using it on the other side of the wall sends blood rushing to my groin.

"How's the toy?"

Why did I ask that?

Her gaze flares with surprise and darts to mine, then away again. "I haven't used it."

There's a long pause of silence.

"I'm intimidated by it," she rushes out, not looking at me. Her cheeks go pink in the most adorable way. "I want to. I'm just nervous, I guess. Which sounds stupid."

"No." I run a hand over my hair. "It's not stupid. You can feel however you want to feel."

Our eyes meet before we both look away. A long pause of silence. My heart beats in my ears.

"Maybe you could help," she says, and my pulse goes wild. "Like, give me some pointers." The line of her throat moves as she swallows.

My gaze slides to her top, lingering on the neckline, picturing her wearing the lingerie from before.

We shouldn't. We really, *really* shouldn't step into this territory. It's getting harder for me to pretend I'm just doing this out of the goodness of my own heart.

"Is that what you want?" I try to breathe normally.

She nods, and my blood surges with nerves and anticipation.

"I want to tell you something, though." Her eyebrows pinch

together and she looks down. The vulnerability in her expression makes me want to gather her up in my arms and hold her tight. "You're my best friend."

My heart does a hard thud in my chest. "You're my best friend, too, Darce."

"Really?" Her mouth lifts into the sweetest smile.

I can't help but chuckle. How can she not know? I spend every free moment with her. "Yeah, of course."

"Not Kit?" Her smile dims a fraction, and my chest aches.

An ugly, cold feeling weaves through me. He didn't brag about her. He didn't value her. He had her for years and he didn't build her up the way she deserved.

"After what you told me about New Year's," I admit, taking the seat beside her on the bed, "I don't want someone like that in my life."

Saying it out loud is a relief.

"At Christmas, when he went home to Ontario to visit family, and we hung out playing video games and eating chocolates?" I give her a wry smile, and her mouth curves. "I didn't miss him." My pinky shifts an inch so it's touching hers. "But I would have missed you."

I could never admit it before, could never even acknowledge it, because that would make me a fucking asshole for having those thoughts about my friend's girl.

She's not his girl anymore, though.

Surprise flares in her pretty green eyes. Her mouth tips into a small, hopeful smile. "I would have missed you, too."

Something settles in my chest, and for a long moment, we just look at each other. Tension hangs in the air, and she doesn't move her finger away from where it's touching mine.

"If we do this," she starts, biting her lip with an uncertain look, and my cock twitches, "it can't be weird after."

"Agreed." I nod hard. That's the last thing I want—a stilted, awkward turn to our friendship that ends in her moving out and us not talking anymore. My nightmare. "It won't be weird." Determination fires through me. "We won't let it."

My growing feelings for Darcy? They'll stay locked exactly where they are.

"I'm just showing you how to use the toy." My eyes linger on her mouth, plump and pretty. "We can be adults about this."

"Totally." Her throat moves and she tucks that bottom lip between her teeth.

I remember what it was like to kiss that bottom lip, to tug on it with my own teeth, and the gasp of pleasure she made. Arousal courses through me, tightening my body.

"You need to be warmed up."

"Warmed up?" She sounds dazed.

I clear my throat. "Turned on."

"Oh." Is she breathing harder than normal? "Maybe we should watch some porn or something." The corner of her mouth ticks up and our eyes meet. "You never did tell me what kind of weird stuff you're into."

The couple that looks like us? I can't show her that. She'll know. And yet I'm pulling out my phone, because why shouldn't Darcy have access to safe, healthy porn?

"There's a video you might like." I log in to my OnlyFans account. I'm only subscribed to one page, so it's easy to find. "It's a married couple." I scroll through their videos until I locate the one I'm thinking about. "She doesn't come in this video, but she enjoys it." Even talking about this with Darcy is making me hard. "It's all about her. Maybe that's a good way to start."

I take a deep breath and study her face. She's nervous, but there's a glint of fire in her eyes.

"Sounds good." She swallows and tucks her hair behind her ears.

The competitive version of me baited by Miller's stupid challenge the other week on the ice? He wakes up. She wants those fun dating experiences she missed out on? I'm going to make this the most memorable of her life.

"You don't need to come." My voice is low, and my heart pounds harder as our eyes lock. "You can just enjoy it. This is for you."

"Sure." She nods. "Great."

"You can change your mind at any time. And we'll always be friends, no matter what."

Reassured, she nods. I settle beside her on the bed, leaning against the headboard, and prop the phone up between us against a pillow.

"Ready?"

She nods, and I hit play.

ON SCREEN, she lies on the mattress while he buries his golden-blond head between her legs, dragging his tongue over her again and again. Her hand twines in his hair, her wedding ring sparkling in the late-afternoon waning sunlight.

"Don't stop," she breathes as she tugs his hair. He lets out a low, pained groan, back muscles tensing, and heat swirls low in my abdomen. She arches, and when his hand snakes up to her breast, toying with a pinched nipple, I feel the aroused tug in my own body.

I spare a glance at Hayden lying beside me, watching. They look like us. It's not just the color of the guy's hair or that he's basically a slab of chiseled muscle like Hayden, or that she's probably the same dress size as me and has hair a shade similar to mine before I dyed it.

It's that he touches her with comfortable ease, possessive but loving. It reminds me of how Hayden kissed me at the cast party, like I was his and he would take better care of me than anyone.

Hayden watches the video with focus, hands folded over his flat stomach. His breathing is uneven, but he doesn't move a muscle.

She gasps again on screen, and even as my intimate muscles clench and moisture pools between my legs, I feel a twist of envy. I want that, and I want Hayden to be the one to do it.

I know how to use the toy. The video I watched—the one that played loudly at the bar—was crystal clear. It's that I'm worried I'll think about Hayden the entire time I use it. Using it feels like a step forward into something very, very risky and messy.

Near the end of the video, instead of coming, she pulls at his arm, and he climbs up to hover over her, kissing her sweetly, softly, so lovingly. It's so tender and affectionate that my heart aches. *This* is the kind of porn Hayden's into? I thought it would be something fast, hot, and frantic.

The video ends and neither of us moves. Heat pulses through me, gathering between my legs.

"Hayden?" I breathe, unable to pull my gaze from the screen but extremely aware of the man lying on the bed beside me.

"Yeah?" His voice is hoarse.

"I think I'm good." I wet my lips. "I'm turned on now."

He nods quickly, taking a deep breath. "Good. Yeah. Okay."

We look at each other, tension in the air, and I can barely stop myself from climbing on top of him.

"Do you want me to leave?" he asks in a low voice, studying me with heavy-lidded eyes.

I shake my head. His gaze darkens.

"Do *you* want to leave?" I ask quietly.

Holding my gaze, he shakes his head. "Nope."

My pulse stumbles at the intensity in his eyes, and I wonder if, maybe, *maybe*, he wants this as much as I do. From the impressive erection straining against the front of his pants, I know he's turned on.

It's just our bodies, I tell myself. Of course we're turned on after watching porn. We can still be best friends after. I won't lose my head over him.

He stands and walks to my desk, and my heart pounds as he unboxes the toy with his back to me, muscles jumping under his t-shirt. He brings it back to the bed, and the mattress dips when he kneels on it. The pink toy in his hand is curved like a U.

"This part"—he points at one side—"sucks on your clit, and this part"—he points to the other end—"vibrates against your G-spot." His throat works. "And you can adjust the settings with these buttons."

I nod and suck in a deep breath. "You do it." Deep in my brain, the rational part of me is wide-eyed and panicking, wondering why I'm playing with matches and kerosene like this, but I ignore her. "Maybe you could use it on me," I clarify.

I also don't think he's breathing. "Are you sure?"

I nod. I want this. An ache builds behind my clit, and my panties are damp. And he smells so good and he's so hot and handsome and kind and perfect and I *want him*. I just want him. It's as simple as that.

I want Hayden to make me feel like the guy in the video made his partner feel.

Holding his eyes, I unbutton my jeans and slide them off.

"Fuck," he mutters, raking his fingers through his hair, messing it up.

His eyes go dark and drugged as his gaze slides over my legs and panties. Need shivers through me. It's that glazed, aroused look in his eyes that pushes me to pull my top off, and now I'm sitting on my bed in just my panties and bra while Hayden's lips part like I'm the hottest woman on the planet.

It's a powerful feeling, rendering Hayden Owens speechless.

"You should take your shirt and pants off, too," I whisper. "I'd feel more comfortable that way."

The side of his mouth hooks and he nods before he yanks his t-shirt over his head. I watch every muscle on his torso jump and dance with the movement, and when he undoes his belt with strong hands, another rush of arousal courses through me.

"We can stop at any time," he says, pulling his pants off.

My eyes go to the thick length distorting the front of his boxers. I can imagine the way it would feel under my palm, firm and pulsing. "I know."

"And there's no pressure to come."

I nod again, holding back a snort. From how wet my panties are and the heat coiling low in my stomach, I'm more concerned about coming the second he touches me with the toy.

He sweeps his gaze over me—lying back against the pillows, hair a mess, I'm sure—before he takes a deep breath.

"So serious," I whisper.

He huffs, a quick grin breaking across his handsome features.

It seems to spark back a bit of the Hayden I know, the teasing, friendly, fun-loving guy.

"I'm going to slip this in your panties," he says, holding my gaze and bringing the toy closer to me, and my knees fall farther apart.

I can't believe we're doing this. I can't believe this is real. He hooks a finger beneath the leg of my panties and slips the toy against me, and I instinctively arch as sensation rockets through me.

HAYDEN PAUSES with the toy barely touching my clit, the focus of all my awareness. "Talk to me, Darce."

"Good," I manage, abs and thighs tensing. My clit aches with lust. I think my toes are curling. "It's good. I'm good."

"You sure?"

"Uh-huh," I moan.

He pushes the other end of the U inside me, and my eyes close, my lips part, and I clutch the duvet as the pressure and stretch of the toy send heat rushing through me. Sparks gather low in my abdomen. The toy isn't even on, and my release is on the horizon.

"Fuck, you're so wet," he whispers with reverence, staring between my legs, his jaw tensing. I'm mostly covered by my panties, but there's a damp spot on the fabric, and his broad chest rises and falls fast as he studies it. His eyes flick to mine, and I feel another pulse of heat. "How does it feel?"

"Tight."

A desperate, pained groan slips out of him, and his eyes close for a brief moment. "I'm going to turn the suction on."

I nod, and when he hits the button, a low whirring noise

starts. I can feel it, but it isn't centered on my clit. My eyebrows slide together. "I don't think it's on the right spot."

The corner of his mouth ticks up. "I know."

He slides the suction in a slow circle around my clit, never touching the sensitive bundle of nerves where I need it. Another wave of heat rolls through me at the realization that Hayden is teasing me.

"You need to learn to be patient." He sounds hoarse.

My skin prickles. Where's my sweet, funny Hayden, and who is this version of him who tells me what to do?

"Trust me," he adds, and when our gazes meet, an electric current fires through me.

I didn't know he had this in him, but I really, really like it. He circles my clit, winding me higher and higher. I don't know whether asking him to use the toy on me was the best or worst decision of my life. The vibration part inside me isn't on yet, but I feel gentle, pleasurable nudges against my front wall. Pleasure coils in my muscles, gathering and tightening.

"You're soaking the toy," he murmurs, watching where he works it between my legs. With his other hand, he props himself up on the bed.

I feel the urge to grab it and bring it to my chest so he can touch me everywhere. "More," I gasp.

He arches an eyebrow, his cocky side surfacing in a way that's darker than I've ever seen. "Yeah?"

I press my lips tight together, squirming against the toy for more pressure. "Please."

His mouth hitches into a drugged grin. "I think you've been patient enough," he says in a low murmur, and with a slight shift of the toy, the suction lands on my clit.

My teeth clamp together at the intense pull of pleasure between my legs.

"Oh god," I breathe, arching into his touch.

"You like that, don't you?" He's still wearing that smug smile, gaze traveling between mine and the toy, lingering on everything in between—my breasts, my nipples—pinched and aching through my thin bra—my stomach, my panties.

I jerk a nod, trying to keep my eyes open. I can feel the needy, desperate expression on my face. God, this is so intense. It's never been like this—not by myself and not with Kit.

"Tell me it's good, Darcy."

"It's good." My hips tilt toward the toy, and my thoughts narrow to the warmth and pressure between my legs. "It's so good."

"Jesus Christ." There's a wet spot on the front of his boxers. The thought of making Hayden leak pre-cum from this ratchets up the pressure inside me one more notch.

I wish I could see his cock. I wish I could touch him. I wish it was his fingers inside me right now and his tongue swirling on my clit.

Hayden's eyes meet mine, bright and molten. "I'm going to turn the other part on."

Oh god, this is going to kill me. I just know it. He presses the other button and a low, intense rumbling starts against my front wall. The pressure deep in my abdomen doubles, triples, expanding and crackling, making my legs tense and shake. I can barely stand the hot, sparking thrill building around the base of my spine.

"Do you like that?" His voice is gritty as he watches me with focus, and his forehead is damp with sweat.

"I'm so close," I moan.

"What do you need?"

"Touch me," I gasp. "Need your hands on me."

He makes a low, pleased noise in his chest, and then his hand is on my thigh, sweeping over my skin in a possessive, greedy motion. He brushes up my hip, my stomach, over the fabric of my bra before his fingers pinch the stiff, needy peak of my breast. I feel the tug between my legs like a cord.

My toes curl. The hot, fascinated gleam in his eyes, the way his biceps tense and ripple, the low purr of his voice, all layer together to nudge me closer to the edge. Even the softness of the duvet beneath me is too much sensation right now.

Hayden looks down at me like this is the best moment of his life, like he can't believe this is happening. Like he's going to remember every second of this.

"You going to come on the toy I bought you, honey?"

There's no question who's in charge here, and I'm shocked at how much I like this. I nod.

"Good."

The dominant, smug tone of his voice, coupled with the pleased look in his eyes, pushes me over the edge, and I fall. My muscles clamp down on the toy, and he groans. Waves of pleasure pound through me as I arch, and when I reach my hand out, he laces his fingers into mine, squeezing.

"Hayden." My voice is thin, and a shred of my consciousness notices how warm his hand is, how good it feels to hold it like this.

"Jesus, I love hearing you moan my name like that."

I'm spinning out, holding his gaze like a lifeline as my nerves fire and urgent, delicious pulses make me shake. And when my climax finally begins to subside, he lowers the setting on the toy.

"A little longer," he urges, dropping the suction and vibration even more through the last spasms. "As long as you can take it."

I nod, clenching my eyes closed as he draws my orgasm out on the toy, and he makes a pleased noise.

"Good girl," he purrs, and warmth trickles through me. He

turns the toy off and gently slides it out of me, and I sink into the duvet with a sated sigh.

Worry clangs through me as Hayden moves off the bed to set the toy aside. But when he returns to the bed and lies down beside me, I relax.

"Come here." He gathers me against his chest, and I inhale a lungful of Hayden Owens's intoxicating, delicious scent. "Nice work," he murmurs against my temple.

I let out a light laugh. "You did all the work."

"I think our friend, the *G-Spot Banger*, is the real MVP tonight."

I grin into his firm chest and bite back the truth—that I never would have come that hard if he weren't here, teasing me, watching me, making me feel so desired and desperate.

I wouldn't want to do this with anyone but him. I can't imagine having this experience with some guy I've just met.

I lean back to meet his eyes. "Not weird, right?"

Something flashes across his expression that I can't read before he shakes his head. "No, not weird," he says quietly. His hand smooths over my hair, and even though this isn't a romantic thing and we're not *like that*, I lower my head to his chest, listening to his heartbeat.

My gaze lands on his sizeable erection, and my thoughts turn dirty and depraved. What would he feel like between my lips, and would he make more of those pained groans? Would he watch and do that jaw-clenchy thing he does sometimes?

I skim my fingers down his perfect chest and abs, and his breath catches. But the second I reach the waistband of his boxers, his hand wraps around my wrist, warm and firm.

"Not tonight." He brings my hand back up to his chest. "Tonight was about you." He swallows, gaze lingering on mine. It feels like he's holding back from saying more. Instead, he pulls the duvet out so he can cover us with it, still holding me to his chest.

"Go to sleep," he whispers against my temple, and I close my eyes.

His rejection stings, but it's for the best. If we have sex, I'll get attached. Falling for a player is a fantastic way to get my heart smashed into pieces, and the idea of messing things up with Hayden is too much of a nightmare to risk it.

CHAPTER 42
HAYDEN

AFTER DARCY'S breathing turns steady, I carefully move her off me and climb out of bed, heading to the en suite in my room. I close the bathroom door behind me and suck Darcy's orgasm off my fingers, eyes falling shut as a groan threatens up my throat.

My fucking *god*, her taste. I'm so hard it hurts. I can't think straight. I just keep thinking about the noises she made, the little pinch of agony between her eyebrows as she came, and how she moaned my name.

Turning down her offer was the hardest thing I've ever done, but accepting it without telling her how I feel—how I've been feeling for a long time—doesn't feel right.

Not weird, right? she asked.

I huff, flattening my hands against the counter to catch my breath. That experience just changed my whole fucking life, but no, it wasn't weird. Just the opposite.

It felt more right than anything. It felt like what we should have been doing for years.

I lift my head, meeting my gaze in the mirror. I'm in it now, and there's no way I'm backing out.

"You are so fucked," I whisper to my reflection.

After a quick shower and an unsatisfying orgasm that happens in record time, I head back to Darcy's room. She's still fast asleep, breathing softly with her hair spilled all over the pillow.

I should go back to my own bed, but instead, I climb in beside her. In her sleep, she sighs and curls against me, relaxing, and my heart gives a couple of heavy thuds.

The wingman-and-student relationship between Darcy and me needs to change, but I'm terrified everything will go south.

"JESUS, Owens, you're on fire tonight," Miller calls over the roar of the fans, hooking his arm around my neck and jostling me as I laugh.

With ten seconds left in the game against Washington, I've just scored my third goal of the game—a hat trick. My gaze goes straight to Darcy, who's sitting behind the net with Pippa and Hazel, and my heart jumps into my throat. She's on her feet, cheering and beaming at me.

I can't stop thinking about what we did last night.

"What's up with you tonight?" Volkov asks with a curious tilt to his mouth. "You're different."

I shrug, shaking my head. "Just feeling good, I guess."

I don't just feel good; I feel fucking *limitless*. The goals are mine for the taking. That thread of dominance I felt driving me last night? It rages in my blood, sharpening my senses.

Turns out I like being in control like this.

"Something happened again," Miller says as the game ends and we skate off the ice to the dressing rooms.

Fuck yeah, it did. My smug grin stretches ear to ear. "I don't know what you're talking about."

He studies me with a smirk. "Between you and Darcy. Something happened. I can feel it."

Another rush of that powerful, protective feeling hits me, the same one that threaded through me last night as I held her orgasm in the palm of my hand, as I guided her and coaxed her closer to it, holding off and teasing her until she could barely take it anymore.

"You're together now?" Volkov follows us into the dressing room.

My shoulders lift with my smile. "We're just having fun."

More fun than I've ever had. Living with Darcy is so much better than I expected, and I'm not about to fuck it up.

"That's bullshit."

Frustration rises in me. "You don't understand."

"I do understand." Volkov glares at me. "Make a move, or some other guy will."

This thing between Darcy and me is so fragile. I can't rush it. "She's not interested in the rookies. I told her about it and she called them *kids*."

Volkov and I stare each other down. Tension snaps in the air, and my muscles tense. His nostrils flare.

This fucking guy. He always thinks he knows best.

"What if I asked her out?" he asks in a low tone.

My chest tightens with dread. "What?"

"You said she doesn't want to date a kid." He slants me a look full of challenge, and the competitive part of me lifts its head. "I'm not a kid, and I know exactly what I'm doing."

A protective urge rattles through me. The idea of them together makes my blood boil. "Let it fucking go, Volkov."

"I don't think I will." The corner of his mouth slides up, but his smile isn't friendly; it's knowing and smug, and for the first time, I want to fucking hit him. "What, you don't trust me?"

His tone is light, almost playful, but there's something sharp in his eyes.

"She'll never go for it."

She's not interested in Volkov. She would have said something before now.

Right?

He shoots me an arrogant look. "Why don't we let her decide?"

A FEW DAYS LATER, I'm on my way to Georgia's office at the arena when I hear my name behind me.

"Hi, Darcy." Coach Tate Ward strides at a leisurely pace to catch up to me. He gives me a friendly smile, his eyes crinkling.

"Hi." I blink at him, ready for him to keep passing, but he stops and continues to give me a look I sense is meant to make me feel comfortable.

"Do you have a moment?"

I peer down the hall to where Georgia's office is. I'm a few minutes early. "Yes?"

How does he even know who I am?

"Good." He gestures for me to follow him back the way he came. "Let's chat in my office." At my hesitant expression, he grins. "It won't take long. Dr. Greene mentioned you're going for lunch, so I won't keep you."

My mind flashes to the games this week and how the power play suggestions I made are working for them. They weren't supposed to say it was *my* suggestion. Who the fuck am I? Just some random girl goofing around on her computer. And now Ward is about to put me in my place.

A cold knot of worry forms in my stomach as I follow him like I'm going to the principal's office.

It's going to be like getting fired all over again. I can't go to games and sit in the front row after this.

He holds the glass door to his office open and waves me inside. "You're an analyst for Eckhart-Foster, right?"

"Yep." I take a seat at one of the club chairs across from his desk, heart starting to pound.

"And a degree in statistics from the University of British Columbia." He sits and regards me with a thoughtful expression. On his desk, there's a framed photo of a little girl with a big smile and pigtails sticking out the sides of her head. "Dean's list."

I swallow hard. How does he know all this? Is he going to sue me or something? "You did your research."

His eyes warm. "That makes two of us. Tell me more about these analytical models."

The best policy is to be as upfront as possible, I think. "They're just for fun, and I told that to the guys. It's all public information from the league's website and data from games. Nothing proprietary. I'm not making a profit off it or selling it or sharing it with anyone else." My face burns, and I want to sink into the floor. "It was never meant to be used. It's just something I tinker with on my laptop. I like using historical data to see if I can predict the future. I never meant for anyone to find out. I told them it hasn't been checked."

Ward's silent as he waits for me to finish.

"I'm really sorry," I add, pulling my gaze to my hands in my lap.

"Why?"

"Because I'm no expert, yet I'm messing around with people's lives and I have no fucking clue what I'm doing."

He frowns with concern. "It sounds like you *do* know what you're doing. It sounds like you *are* an expert."

Is this a joke? We stare at each other, him with a strange expression I can't read, his mouth tipping up into an amused smile.

"I don't follow."

"Come work for the team."

I stare at him for a long stretch of silence. "What?" I finally ask.

He chuckles. "I would love for you to join the Vancouver Storm's analytics department."

I blink again. "Why?"

He smiles. "Because, Darcy, not only are you clearly intelligent and talented, but doing something like this for free and for fun means your heart's in it, and that's an important part of the team I'm building."

I imagine it—working for the team as an analyst and playing with my hockey models every day. Working for Ward already seems so much better than my current boss, who cares more about profits than his employees. I see why Hayden and the guys like this man so much.

And it would be fun, working with hockey stats all day, discovering new patterns in the data.

"Our analytics department consists of three retired hockey players," Ward continues. "No one with your analytical experience. You'd be a huge asset to the team." His dark eyebrows go up. "We could really use you. They're really eager to get you on board."

"I'd be the only stats analyst?"

"Yep." He lists off a generous salary number, but I barely hear it.

"So everyone would rely on my numbers?" Being the only

analyst is the exact opposite of what I want. The pressure would be tenfold.

He arches an eyebrow. "The analytics department works as a team."

"But no one could check my numbers." The pressure drops onto my chest like a weight, and it's hard to take a full breath.

Ward opens his mouth to say something, but I'm already on my feet.

"I already have a job." My shaky smile is polite but firm. "But thank you. I really appreciate it."

He studies me like I'm something curious before nodding once. "Alright. If you change your mind, you know where to find me. The door's always open."

"You bet," I tell him, knowing full well I won't be walking through *that* door again.

Before heading out for lunch, Georgia and I stop by the rink, where the guys are taking a break during practice. She talks with one of the players on the bench about something. Hayden chats with Alexei and Rory on the ice. When he spots me, he skates over wearing a tight smile.

Memories of the other night with him and the toy wash over me, and goosebumps scatter down my arms. I've never come so hard.

When I made a move to touch him after, he stopped me. Because we're not in a relationship. He was just helping me.

"Hey." He skates to a stop in front of me on the ice, eyes moving over me with curiosity.

We haven't talked about what happened, but I'm trying to act normal to show him that I'm not getting clingy.

"Georgia and I are getting lunch and she needed to drop a prescription off," I explain, glancing over at her a few feet away.

"Sure." He nods before his gaze comes back to me. "How's your day?"

"Good. You?"

He nods again, giving me a small smile. "Good."

I think about how nice it felt to wake up next to him the other morning and how well rested I was after sleeping against him all night.

I chew my bottom lip. "Ward offered me a job."

His eyes widen and a proud smile spreads across his features. "He did? That's great, Darce."

"I'm not taking it, of course."

"Why not?" He leans on the boards, focused on me, and my stomach dips. His attention is so intoxicating.

"I just..." I don't want to bring up the past again. "I don't think it's right for me."

Hayden's lips part like he wants to argue, but Alexei skates to a stop beside us.

"Darcy." He dips his chin in greeting, and I relax at the interruption.

"Hi." I give him a quick smile.

"Alright, ready to go. Thanks for waiting," Georgia says at my side before her gaze lands on Alexei. "Oh. You again."

He arches a scarred eyebrow at her. "Is there a reason I wouldn't be attending a regularly scheduled practice?"

She lifts a casual shoulder. "I figured you need more rest than the other players."

The look he shoots her is downright icy before he turns his attention to me. "I'd like to talk to Darcy in private for a moment."

At his side, Hayden's nostrils flare. I don't think I've ever seen that happen. "Why?"

Alexei holds his gaze, and there's a weird tension between them. "There's something I want to ask her."

Hayden's jaw tightens. "I don't see why you can't ask her in front of me."

The guys stare at each other for what feels like an eternity. Georgia and I exchange a bemused glance.

"Fine." Alexei turns to me, and while I wouldn't call his expression a smile, it does soften, like he's making an effort not to intimidate me. He clears his throat. "Darcy, I think we should go out."

There's a stretch of tense silence, and for the second time today, I wonder if I heard right. Georgia lets out a sharp bark of laughter while Hayden glares daggers at Alexei.

"On a date?" I repeat.

"On a date," Alexei confirms, keeping his gaze on my face.

My lips part in surprise, and I stare up at him.

I've always liked Alexei. On the ice, he's fiercely protective of his teammates, but I've never seen an ounce of that male aggression outside of hockey. His demeanor is quiet, watchful, and strong, like a giant fir tree. Beneath his towering exterior and the hard lines of his face, I know he's actually kind, quiet, and loyal to his friends.

I might have told Georgia that Alexei was hot in a scary way, but I don't have romantic feelings for him. I glance at Hayden, but his tight expression gives me nothing.

Again, I think about what we did the other night and how good it felt to wake up with him.

Never get attached, the player rules say. I think I'm starting to, but I don't want Hayden to know that.

Besides, practicing with other people is the logical next step. I can't just go on dates with my wingman forever. That'll only end badly.

"I'm not looking for anything serious," I tell Alexei, meeting his eyes.

"Neither am I."

Georgia mutters something at my side that I can't hear, and Hayden is still as a statue, watching us.

"Okay." I nod at Alexei. "Let's go on a date."

Hayden stiffens and his gaze whips to me. "You don't have to go out with him if you don't want to."

"I know." I give him a reassuring smile to show him I don't feel threatened or intimidated by Alexei. "I'm looking forward to it."

Hayden sucks in a tight breath, and something flashes in his eyes that makes my heart beat harder. It's the same dominance I saw the other night, when he teased me with the toy.

"Let's make it a double date," he says, standing taller.

"You sure you want to do that?" Alexei asks him.

"Positive," Hayden bites out. He glances to Georgia. "Georgia? You want to go on a date?"

Alexei's eyebrows snap together. "It's a conflict of interest."

"She's not *my* doctor," Hayden shoots back. The players are divided up between the two team doctors. "And she's not yours either. Right, Georgia?" Hayden asks her. "It's not a conflict of interest for you to go out, because none of us are your patients."

Everyone goes quiet, waiting for her response.

"I should say no to this drama," she mutters to me, "but I also feel like it could get interesting." She gives me a sidelong look. "What do you think?"

I don't think she has any romantic interest in Hayden, but there's still a hard little kernel in my stomach at the idea of it. He's not mine, though. "I think it'll be fun."

She smiles at me. "Great." To Hayden, she nods. "You're on, Owens."

"Great." He glances at me.

Alexei glances between us, expression unreadable. "Great."

"Great," I say, unsure of what just happened.

THE NIGHT of the double date, I lean a hand on Darcy's bedroom doorframe, watching her get ready.

She looks stunning, hair loose and pretty around her shoulders and wearing a top the shade of the roses I bought her for Valentine's Day. And it's for *him*. My nostrils flare.

This morning, I saw the lingerie she bought hanging to dry in the bathroom, but when I walked past half an hour ago, it was gone.

She's wearing it for a date with *him*. I should be supportive of her, but I just feel sick and pissed off.

"Hey." She catches sight of me. "You look nice."

"Thanks." We're going to a casual restaurant tonight, so I'm dressed in jeans, a t-shirt, and a knit sweater Darcy once said—

"That blue color makes your eyes look like the ocean." She smiles over at me.

"I know." I feel like I can't breathe. "I remember."

She hums, smiling again, turning back to the mirror as she runs her fingers through her hair. Since she dyed it, she wears it down more, like she's proud of it and wants to show it off.

My gaze drops to her outfit, and a muscle in my chest tightens. Those jeans hug her ass in all the right places. The red top she's wearing? It's snug around her waist and chest, but looser in the sleeves. My hands would fit perfectly in the curve of her waist.

I know what Volkov's doing. He asked her out to make me jealous. He doesn't have feelings for her. Any guy who sees her in this outfit, though, won't be able to keep his hands off her. And maybe tonight is the night he changes his mind.

She does a double take at my expression. "What?"

"That's what you're wearing?"

Her smile drops and her gaze swings to the mirror, flashing with uncertainty, and I hate myself. My accusing tone makes me sound like a controlling asshole.

"No, fuck. Sorry." I rub the bridge of my nose. "That came out wrong. It's just different from what you normally wear." I gesture at her top. "Red," I add, because I'm a dumbass who can't think of words.

She arches an eyebrow at her reflection. "Bad different?"

"No," I rush out. "You look beautiful. You always do."

She smiles, and something sweet aches in my chest. There's a spark to Darcy these days, something bright blooming inside her.

Our eyes meet, and there's so much I want to say. *Don't dress up for him; dress up for me*, to start. *Let's stay in so I can have you all to myself*, maybe. Or even *It's torture, teaching you how to date other guys*.

Her phone buzzes, and I look away, the unhappy feeling simmering in my gut. Volkov insisted on picking Darcy up here instead of meeting us at the restaurant.

"Hello?" she answers, shooting me a smile. "Hi. Do you want us to come down?" She listens a beat. "Okay. See you in a minute."

She buzzes him in and slips her phone into her back pocket before rifling through her makeup bag.

"Do you..." I rake a hand through my hair. "...have any questions about tonight? Want any pointers?"

She shakes her head, applying a lipstick that matches her top. I zero in on the motion, fascinated as she drags the wand over her plump lips.

"No. I feel pretty comfortable around Alexei. I'm not worried."

That tense, possessive energy weaves through me and I fold my arms over my chest to hide my clenched fists. "Comfortable. Great."

"All your lessons are really paying off." She slides a hesitant look at me. "Are you okay? You've been weird all week."

I swallow past the knots in my throat. All week, I've been restless thinking about tonight. Dreading it. Flipping between making an excuse to bail—so I don't have to watch her shine her sparkling light all over Volkov—and telling myself it'll be so much worse if I'm sitting at home, waiting and wondering.

When I wasn't thinking about the date, I was thinking about how she sounds when she comes. How she looked at me the split second before her orgasm, lips parted and eyes widening in surprise like she couldn't believe it. How she squeezed my hand with hers and it was the most intimate experience of my life.

"I'm fine." I force a reassuring smile. "Haven't been sleeping well this week."

Our eyes meet, and from the way her expression goes hazy, I wonder if she's thinking about the times we woke up together. I'm a light sleeper, but I slept like the dead with her head on my chest, my arms around her, and her scent in my nose.

There's a knock on the front door.

"That'll be one of them." She breezes past me, and I catch her perfume, warm and sweet, before I follow her.

Even before we reach the foyer, we hear them arguing.

"I'm shocked you're able to stay up this late," I hear Georgia mutter through the door.

"I'm shocked you didn't demand Owens send a Bentley to pick you up," Volkov counters, cool and disinterested. "Or have your chauffeur drop you off at the restaurant."

Darcy opens the door to them glaring at each other, Georgia somehow managing to stare down her nose at Volkov even though he's a foot taller than her.

They snap out of it, turning to us in unison. Georgia puts on an ear-to-ear smile, and Volkov's mouth curves in a polite greeting as he nods at Darcy, but they both radiate tension.

Volkov's also holding a massive bouquet of flowers.

"Hi," Darcy chirps, looking between them. "Everything okay?"

"Everything's great." Georgia walks in, sending me a friendly wink before her gaze sweeps around the apartment and she whistles. "Nice place."

Volkov hands the flowers to Darcy. "These are for you."

My stomach drops at her expression, so shocked and pleased. "For me?"

His eyes flick to me, and there's that stupid, smug look on his stupid fucking face again. "For you, Darcy."

She stares at the bouquet. "They're lovely. Thank you."

"They don't look fresh," I bite out and then immediately regret it when Georgia covers her mouth with her hand and turns away. "You should, uh, put them in water before they die."

Shut the fuck up, I think to myself, but I can't. I just stare at Volkov and pull myself up to my full height while he arches an eyebrow at me. I'm being a dick, but I don't care.

Darcy gives me a strange look. "I think they look great." She takes the flowers from him and he follows her into the kitchen.

When she can't reach the vase on the top shelf, I instinctively step forward, but fucking *Volkov* is there, helping her pull it down.

"What," Georgia murmurs, grinning, "no flowers for me?"

I give her an apologetic, embarrassed look. I've been so focused on Darcy going out with Volkov that I forgot I was also going on a date tonight. "Sorry."

She waves me off, smiling. "It's okay. We're friends, Owens. I'm just here for the entertainment." She smirks. "And you're buying dinner."

Darcy sets the flowers on the kitchen table, admiring them. "So pretty. I love getting flowers."

I'm buying her flowers every day for the rest of eternity.

"I saw them and thought of you," Volkov says to her. "They match your hair."

"They do. Good eye." Darcy leans over to smell the pale-purple flower closest to her.

"Look at you." I glare at him, my shoulder muscles tightening. "A real Casanova."

Georgia snorts, and Darcy gives me a teasing smile. "Maybe Alexei should give me dating lessons instead."

Volkov makes an amused noise in his throat and sharp jealousy stabs me in the gut.

"They look like funeral flowers," I bite out, hating myself.

I sound like an asshole. I'm *being* an asshole, but I can't stop. This is all turning into a fucking mess.

We leave the apartment, and I lock up as Darcy leads Volkov and Georgia to the elevator.

Nice, Georgia mouths behind their backs, giving me a sarcastic double thumbs-up. *Very smooth.*

My nostrils flare, and I haul a deep breath in just as the

elevator door opens and Volkov puts a hand to Darcy's lower back.

Another slice of jealous fury jolts through me.

This is going to be a long fucking night.

"YOU SHOULD WEAR RED MORE," Alexei says halfway through dinner, and beside me, Hayden tenses.

Tonight was a huge mistake. I should have checked with him before agreeing to go out with Alexei. He clearly doesn't want me dating another one of his friends in case it gets messy like it did with Kit.

But also, this is my date, and he's the one who wanted to come along.

"Thanks." I tilt my chin at Georgia. "Georgia knows all the good places to shop. And it's fun to wear something outside my comfort zone."

"The doctor is a pro at spending money." Alexei leans back, staring pointedly at her shoes.

She rolls her eyes, then turns back to me. "We'll have to go again. I need a dress for Streicher and Pippa's wedding."

Right. It's in a month, during the week between the season ending and the first round of playoffs.

Hayden and I look at each other, and his expression softens. I give him a reassuring smile to show him I'm fine, that I'm looking forward to it.

"I love weddings." Georgia wears a wistful expression. "I can't wait for theirs."

"I'll bet." Alexei sips his drink. "A hockey player and a famous singer? It'll be like a rich guy meat market for you. You'll finally catch one of your own."

"Don't be ridiculous. I'll never get married." She sends him a knowing smirk, like she knows his secrets. "Be nice to me, Russian, or I won't help you up when you throw your hip out on the dance floor."

"I'm not going. I don't do weddings. And you're the one who resigned from being my doctor."

"Unlike some doctors, I don't have a God complex. I know when my patient is a lost cause."

"Maybe you're not a very good doctor, because I feel stronger than ever."

Her gaze hardens. "Retire."

"No."

Georgia's hand flinches on the table, like she's about to reach for her knife.

The server comes by to clear plates, and the weird energy at the table dissolves. I glance at Hayden—his jaw is tight, his shoulders look tense, and his attention shifts between Alexei and me.

"Are you okay?" I whisper. My gaze catches on the dark circles under his eyes, and there's a pang of sympathy in my chest. "It's okay if you want to go home early."

"I'm not leaving." He glares at Alexei, who smirks.

"I'll make sure she gets home okay," he tells Hayden. "Eventually."

"I'm your wingman," Hayden says, focus still on Alexei. "And I'm not letting you out of my sight."

Something plucks in my chest. He's using the same tone of

voice he used the other night. *A little longer*, he said, eyes on me while I rode out the pleasure. *As long as you can take it*.

"Darcy," Alexei interrupts, leaning in, studying me. "You have something in your hair."

I bring a hand to my hair and brush through it, but Alexei catches my wrist, gentle but firm.

"I'll get it," he says.

Hayden sucks in a sharp breath.

While Alexei picks out whatever's stuck in my hair, Hayden glares at him, knee bouncing and jaw tight.

"Huh." Alexei frowns. "I thought I saw a piece of the flowers from earlier. You know, the ones I got you."

"Oh." I blink. "Okay."

"I guess I was wrong." Alexei smiles at me.

In an explosive flash, Hayden's on his feet, grabbing my hand. I open my mouth to ask what he's doing, but he's already pulling me to my feet. He whips out his wallet and drops a couple of bills on the table before hauling me out of Alexei's proximity.

Alexei just smiles after us.

"Date's over," Hayden bites out. "We're going home."

OUTSIDE, Hayden's still holding my hand as he opens the door of a waiting taxi and gestures for me to get in, wearing a thunderous expression. He rattles off our address to the driver while reaching across me to do my seat belt up.

I stare at him with my mouth hanging open. "Are you going to explain?" I ask, incredulous.

"When we get home."

I make a noise of frustration. "Hayden—"

"When. We. Get. Home."

The drive home is short, thank god, and when we step into the elevator, tense energy radiates off him in waves.

Rule number seven of being a player, I add: *Don't date your wingman's friends.*

A tiny, hopeful, stupid little shard of me wants this to be because he's wildly jealous, but Hayden doesn't get jealous. I would have seen it by now.

When we get home, he doesn't even look at me. I catch the sharp lines of his profile as he throws his coat over one of the kitchen chairs.

"I'm going to bed. Good night," he says in a low tone, kicking his shoes off and not even putting them away in the closet like he always does. Then he heads down the hallway to our bedrooms without another word.

I stand in the foyer, still wearing my jacket and shoes, listening as his bedroom door closes.

Oh, hell no. I shake my head to myself, frustration growing in the pit of my stomach.

In seconds, I'm outside his door, rapping my knuckles against it. "Hayden."

No answer.

I knock again. "*Hayden.*"

"Not now, Darce."

"Yes, now." Without thinking, I open his door. "I'm coming in," I add, when the door is already open.

Hayden stands in only his tight boxer briefs, glaring at me. Even his dark mood can't detract from how gorgeous he looks, all powerful, toned muscle and golden-blond hair.

God, he's so hot.

"Where are your clothes?" I sound outraged, like I'm not the one who threw his door open.

He puts his hands on his trim hips. "I'm going to the gym."

"Now?" He even has those V-muscles pointing into the waistband of his boxers. I didn't notice those the other day because I was too busy having the most intense orgasm of my life.

"Yes."

"I thought you were going to bed."

He exhales a rough noise, pacing across the room, agitated. "I need to do something."

"Read a book," I suggest lightly. I hate fighting with him like this. It feels all wrong. "Watch *The Northern Sword.*"

He shakes his head. "I can't sit down right now."

"Rip into me, then." I give him a pointed look. "Maybe that'll help. I've clearly pissed you off."

He folds his arms over his chest. "What are you talking about?"

A humorless laugh of complete fucking disbelief slips out of me. "Hayden. Look. I'm sorry I went out with Alexei. I've learned my lesson. But you acted like a complete asshole to both Georgia and Alexei all night. And then when I actually tried to practice these things you've been teaching me, you dragged me out of there like a teenager out past her bedtime."

His throat works, and he gives me a pained expression.

"You agree to wingman me, but then act like a territorial asshole the whole night. This isn't how friends act." The thing that's been bothering me for months rises to the forefront of my mind. "And you don't touch me anymore," I add quietly.

His eyes burn me. "What about the other night?"

My stomach dips. The toy, the way his fingers tugged at my nipples, stirring pleasure through me. The way he used the toy on me to make me come harder than ever. And how he laced his strong fingers through mine at the end.

"Not like the other night. Or the other morning." I swallow. "You don't hug me. You don't put your arm around me anymore. You don't..." It sounds so stupid. "You don't tickle me. And you move out of the way so I don't accidentally touch you."

Silence falls heavy between us for a moment. Then he laughs, but it's not his typical lighthearted, happy Hayden laugh. It's bitter, frustrated, like it hurts him.

"I don't touch you anymore." He shakes his head to himself. "Yeah, I don't touch you anymore, Darce. I can't."

His eyes sharpen, pinning me, and he takes a step forward. Then another. Until we're inches apart and I can feel his warmth.

"You want to know why?"

So I can hear him say the hurtful words out loud? "I know why."

I turn away, but his fingers come to beneath my chin, tilting my face to his. A tingle of pleasure runs through me at the dominant gesture.

"Go on, then." He stares down into my eyes, challenging me. "Say it."

"I broke Kit's heart. I hurt the person you care about."

"No." He exhales heavily, but his fingers stay beneath my chin. "You couldn't be more wrong, Darcy. I know you weren't happy with him. And after the things he did, how he proposed when he knew you didn't want it, I don't care that you broke his heart." His throat works as he drinks in the sight of me.

"You don't want me to get the wrong idea about you and me, then."

"Wrong again."

My heart pounds at the desperate, hungry look in his eyes. "Why, then?"

"You should leave." He drops his gaze, but his focus stays on mine. "Before I make a mistake."

A thrill shoots through me. "What kind of mistake?"

Heat flares in his eyes and flashes through me, curling and twisting between my legs in a delicious pressure. His attention falls to my lips like he's remembering what they felt like against his at the cast party.

God, I wish we'd kissed the other night.

"You want to know why I don't touch you?" His blue eyes grow a shade darker. "Because if I start, I won't stop."

His weird moods this week. How pissed he was when Alexei asked me out. When Alexei showed up with flowers, Hayden looked like he wanted to kill him.

He's not upset I'm moving on.

"You're—" It can't be true. It goes against everything I know about him.

"Say it."

I swallow, heart pounding, and I shake my head. Being wrong about this would humiliate me.

"Say. It."

"Jealous," I blurt out. "You're acting jealous."

Tension hangs between us, crackling and electric.

He tilts his head, breathing uneven. "Who wouldn't be, Darce?"

But he's so hot. He's the popular jock who could have anyone. I'm the weird girl who likes math, who got fired, and who was never quite right for my ex. I blink, scrambling for a way to explain this without sounding pathetic. "I just thought..."

"You just thought what?"

"I'm not your type. You're so—" I shake myself, thoughts cluttered and murky.

"I'm so what?"

My heart gallops, thundering in my ears. "You can have anyone."

"I hate hearing you say that," he says quietly. "You know why I dated women who look nothing like you?"

Speechless, I shake my head.

"Because I didn't want to be reminded of you. Because I was trying to convince myself I didn't have feelings for you." His Adam's apple slides up and down as he swallows, pupils blown wide. "It never worked, though. My thoughts always wander back to you."

My mind reels; I'm light-headed, dizzy, my thoughts racing and pinwheeling, grasping for purchase. This makes no sense. This is a hallucination. I slipped and hit my head outside the restaurant, and at any second, I'll open my eyes to Hayden,

Alexei, Georgia, and the paramedics bent over me as I lie on the sidewalk.

"You're my type," Hayden says like it hurts him. "More than anyone." His head drops to my shoulder, and he takes a deep inhale, his fist coming to the wall beside my head on his shaky exhale. "I want you, Darcy," he murmurs against my neck, and I shiver. "I want you so bad I can't stay away. If you want things to stay the way they are, you need to leave my bedroom right now."

I don't care that we're best friends. I don't care that this is going to massively complicate everything. I just need him to touch me, right now, do something with this intense pressure he's created between my legs.

I need to see what it would be like with us. Just once.

I flatten a hand on Hayden's chest, feeling the gallop of his heartbeat. His eyes burn me, helpless but dark with lust.

"I don't want things to stay the way they are," I whisper, and his mouth crashes to mine.

HAYDEN CLAIMS my mouth with an urgency that scrambles all my thoughts.

"No more double dates," he says against my lips, and I nod.

His fingers sink into my hair, and mine into his. All the frustration radiating off him is refocused into something sharper and hotter as he coaxes my lips open and strokes inside, exploring and tasting.

He presses me against the wall. I think I moan. If this is a mistake, it's the best one I ever made.

"God, yes," he groans when he gently sucks on the tip of my tongue. "No more dates at all. Understand?"

"Uh-huh."

We're not making out for practice or to send a message to some actor I'm not interested in. He's not showing me the ropes anymore or testing to see if I'm a good enough kisser.

We're doing this because we want to. Because we can't stand it anymore. Because we need to see what happens next. I'm not sure what's happening, but I'm a willing participant, allowing Hayden to take what he wants.

Which is me, from the way his thick erection presses into

my stomach. The realization thrills me and a shiver runs down my back.

"Cold?" he murmurs between kisses.

I shake my head, and he catches my bottom lip between his teeth. "Good."

This kiss is different from the first time, like a switch has flipped inside Hayden. He's lit up, focused, driven—it's the same *something different* that's been simmering under the surface for weeks now, lifting its head during games when he scores goals.

With a hand at the hem of my top, he drags a fingertip over the sliver of bare skin between it and my jeans, and my entire focus narrows to where he touches me.

"Take this off."

The command in his voice wraps another delicious coil of heat around the base of my spine. I fumble with the zipper before he lifts the garment over my head.

His throat works as he takes me in, staring at my chest, eyes moving over the pretty, delicate lace bra.

"This is what I've been thinking about for days. This"—he hooks a finger beneath the strap and lets it gently snap against my skin—"has been driving me wild since I saw it."

His fingers skim over the edges of the lace, over the tops of my breasts, over my shoulders, and goosebumps scatter across my skin.

"Who'd you put this on for tonight?" he asks in a low voice.

"You," I whisper, heart pounding. It was Hayden's reaction that I pictured as I put it on.

His mouth hooks, and I think I'm smiling back up at him as I rest my palms on his firm chest.

"That's what I like to hear," he murmurs as he lowers his mouth to mine again.

Kissing Hayden is so *delicious*. So effortless but necessary, like breathing. I never, ever want to stop, and from the way his hands roam my hips, my arms, my hair, never settling in one place, like he's trying to memorize my body by touch, I don't think he wants to stop either.

We're best friends. We're roommates. He's the life-of-the-party player who isn't interested in commitment.

He might not be that guy, though, and I might not care anymore that this could complicate things.

I just want him, and I want him to have what *he* wants.

His stubble gently scrapes my chin as his tongue strokes across mine, scattering more of my thoughts, and when the back of my knees bump something, I realize he's walked me backward to the bed.

He lowers me down, and I sink into the duvet as his scent washes over me.

"I love being in your bed," I admit as he undoes the button on my jeans.

His eyes warm. "I love you being in my bed, too."

I lift my hips to let him pull my jeans off. His eyes drag over my underwear. It's a wisp of thin lace that barely covers anything, and from the way his eyes darken as he rakes a hand through his hair, exhaling heavily, Hayden likes them.

"We're buying you more of those," he says, staring daggers at them.

He says *we* like we're a couple. It should send darts of terror through me, but it doesn't. I *like* the idea of us buying lingerie together, of his eyes flashing with heat when he sees me in it.

He climbs over me, resting on his elbows on either side of my head, gazing down at me with desire and affection before his mouth drops to mine. Our kiss is hot, fast, and desperate, all tongues and teeth and lips and gasps. We keep forgetting to breathe. His erection presses against my stomach, and I arch against it, parting my legs, making room for Hayden to settle between my hips. His weight on me is luxurious. The warmth from his skin sends a thrill through me. He threads his fingers into the back of my hair, tilting my head as he breaks our kiss and runs his mouth down my jaw and neck.

"You smell so fucking *good*," he groans, and a wave of moisture rushes between my legs. "You always do. And you taste so goddamned sweet." He nips the sensitive spot beneath my ear and a needy noise slips out of my throat. "You need more, don't you?"

I nod, barely holding back the *yes, please* blaring in my head. The corner of his mouth tips up, pleased and knowing.

His fingers find a pinched nipple, and he toys with it through the thin lace of my bra, mouth returning to mine. Each tug of his fingers pulls between my legs, warming me, ratcheting up the pressure and heat. I sink further into the sensations of his tongue against mine. My underwear is soaked, and my hips tilt against him, seeking more. Finally, his hand trails down from my breast and strokes over the front of my panties.

Pleasure sweeps through me at the contact, and we groan at the same time.

"You're so wet." He watches my face in fascination, rubbing a firm, wide circle over me, and my eyes fall closed. "Don't close your eyes," he says in a low, firm voice. There's a hint of teasing to his tone, like this is a game. "Don't you dare."

I open them, pressing my lips into a tight line to hold in the moan, and his mouth hooks up as he rubs firmer circles. Need coils low in my body, tight and hot.

"That's good, isn't it?"

I nod. He hums, smiling that dark, glazed smile, glancing between my face and where his hand works between my legs.

"What are we going to do tonight, Darce?" His tone is low

and lazy as his lips skim over my skin. "What new item are we crossing off your list?"

He pulls my bra aside, freeing my nipple, and sucks the sensitive peak. My core tightens and I gasp.

"Hmm?" He meets my gaze, lifting his hand away from me. My hips follow, demanding contact, but he just skims his fingers over the waistband of my thong, the seams over my hips, teasing me. "What's it going to be?"

He's going to make me say it. I don't know where my sweet, fun-loving Hayden went, but I love this version of him. The version who's in charge and reveling in the power.

My eyes drop to his lips. "Your mouth."

"Oh yeah?" His grin hooks. "Where do you want this mouth, Darcy?" He drops hot, nipping kisses to my shoulder, my stomach, and then my hip. I tighten up in anticipation. "Show me, honey."

Him calling me *honey* leaves me defenseless. My pulse races as my hand snakes down and rests over my panties.

"Here?" He rubs another slow, firm circle over the fabric, and I buck into his hand. "Say it, Darcy."

"Yes," I rush out, buzzing with pent-up energy. "There."

Hayden watches my face while he slips his hand beneath the fabric. At the brush of his fingers, my breath catches, and his drugged smile slides higher.

"Fucking soaked," he whispers, dragging his fingertips in circles over my clit.

My eyes roll back; He's so in tune with exactly what I need, it's like he's in my head.

"Do you trust me?"

"Of course." I know even if I can't come, Hayden won't get sulky and defensive. He'll just gather me up in his arms and kiss me.

"Good girl."

He pulls his hand away and sits on his heels, kneeling as he slides my panties off. With his hands on my inner thighs, he presses my legs open. My pulse jumps with the vulnerability, spread wide under him, unable to hide. But our eyes meet and he mutters a curse under his breath. He's so gorgeous, I don't know where to look—his handsome face, his fucked-up and messy hair, the carved chest, shoulders, and abdomen dusted with hair, or the strong thighs braced on the bed.

"I love that look on your face, so desperate for me to touch you." He pauses, watching me with an expression that looks a lot like reverence.

No one's ever looked at me like that.

He slides his hand between my legs, brushing every sensitive nerve ending with his flat palm, and my thighs tighten up as heat races through me.

"You're so pretty here." He watches his hand move over me with a glazed look on his face. "So soft and wet."

Heat gathers and throbs between my legs, and every time he brushes my clit, electricity jolts through me. His cock strains against his boxers and I feel another needy ache.

"Hayden." I reach for it, but his hand comes to my wrist and he laces his fingers with mine.

Amusement sparks beyond the hunger in his eyes. "Be patient."

I make a noise of frustration and arch against his hand, seeking more friction, but he leans forward and clamps his forearm over my hips, holding me down.

"You're going to wait," he tells me, and my blood heats at the command in his tone.

It's my teasing, funny Hayden, but with authority and dominance, and I really, really like it.

"I've waited so long for this. I don't want to rush things." He gazes between my legs with a playful, heated smirk. "And the longer I make you wait, the harder you'll come."

He brushes my clit again and I half sigh, half growl. He chuckles, drunk on power, eyes dark with lust. Higher and higher, he winds me, until my skin is so hot I could burst into flames. I can see my release on the horizon, but he holds me back, toying with me and taking his time.

"Why don't we try a different type of G-spot orgasm?" he asks in that low, seductive voice that makes me both relax and tense up in aroused anticipation. "What do you think of that?"

I wet my lips, and his eyes follow the movement. "Okay."

"It's going to feel intense, okay?"

"Uh-huh." My breathing is uneven and I'm so turned on I could burst into flames.

With his focus fixed on my face, he pushes a finger inside me. My eyes roll back in my head at the thought-scattering burn of pleasure.

"There." His low, rich voice makes me shiver. "Right there."

I nod, unable to form words. Hayden looks like a god, kneeling between my legs with that expression of power and control on his handsome face. My gaze trails over every ridge and muscle of his torso, shoulders, and arms, focusing finally on his tense forearm as he works his finger inside me.

He adds a second finger, and the aching fullness makes me see stars. He crooks his fingers forward, rubbing my front wall, and I cling to his gaze. The wet sounds of him fucking me with his hand drive me higher.

I can't believe this is happening. I can't believe we're doing this. I can't believe how good it feels. The pleasure of his thick, long fingers inside me is beyond anything I've experienced. My gaze rises to the ceiling, unfocused and heavy-lidded as he reaches parts of me I didn't know existed.

"Hey, hey, hey." His voice is low and soothing, and I pull my gaze back to him. His mouth tips into a pleased smile. "There. Good. Keep looking at me, okay?"

I nod, meeting his fascinated gaze, and another ripple of heat moves through me. This is better than the toy. A million times better. I could die and go to heaven from Hayden touching me like this.

"You're doing so good, honey."

I shudder with pleasure, clutching his hand harder as my muscles tighten around him.

His smile tilts. "You like it when I call you that?"

"Yes," I gasp.

"You're close, aren't you?"

"Uh-huh."

His thumb nudges my clit, drawing slow, firm circles, and it's enough. I tip over the edge, vision blurring and lips parting in a low moan as every nerve in my body fires at once. Just like with the toy, this orgasm is different—lower, deeper, and stronger. Warmth and pressure bubble over, melting my thoughts, and I arch and buck against his hand as he works me through the orgasm, saying things like *there we go* and *such a good girl* and *what a fucking sight you are, Darce, coming like this on my fingers*.

"Hayden," I gasp, and he groans.

Pleasure sweeps through me, and there's a sharp, delicious crackle in my blood as I cling to the reminder that *Hayden*, my best friend, the guy I've known for years, is making me feel this way. His expression is focused, his smile dark as his attention shifts between my face and where his hand is buried inside me, like my pleasure is his pleasure. With our interlaced fingers, he squeezes my hand once, and I squeeze back.

His strokes slow as I come down, and his grin slants higher.

"Breathe," he says quietly, climbing over me and kissing me. His tongue drags across mine, devouring me as both of us work to catch our breaths. His skin is so warm, and when he pulls back to smile down at me, I'm floating.

Between my legs, his erection nudges, straining against his boxers, and I get a wicked idea of my own.

BEING with Darcy like this is life-changing. I'm never going to forget her sweet, needy moan or her expression of disbelief as her body pulsed with her orgasm.

My blood beats with pride and I roll onto my back, taking her with me so she straddles my hips, mouth inches from mine and sated expression all over her pretty face.

I'm done with sitting on the sidelines, building up Darcy's confidence just to send her into the arms of some other guy. I'm done with being her wingman. I want her, and I'm going to show her.

I hold eye contact as I suck her perfect taste off my fingers, something I've been thinking about since I used the toy on her.

My mouth crooks up into a pleased smile. "I love the way you say my name."

She blinks down at me, hair a mess and face, neck, and chest flushed, and I smile harder.

"And I love the way you look right now," I admit.

She huffs. "Like I just got hit by a car?"

"Is that how you feel?" I lift a teasing eyebrow at her and smooth my hand down her lower back before cupping her ass. "I should try again."

"No," she laughs. "Not yet. I need a rest." She dips her head, burying her face in my neck, and my skin prickles. "That was the best orgasm I've ever had," she whispers against my shoulder.

An intense, possessive urge thunders through me, and I wrap my arms around her, clutching her to me. "You know exactly what to say to make me feel like the fucking man."

She chuckles, lifting her head to smile down at me.

God, she's fucking stunning. The color of her eyes, every eyelash, the slope of her nose, her Cupid's bow and the swell of her lips—every part of Darcy is perfection. Like nature gave her the best of everything, hand selected for her.

"You're an angel." I tuck her hair behind her ear. "You know that?"

Her eyes warm with amusement and those perfect lines of her mouth tip into a pretty smile.

"Sometimes," she says, before her hips tilt against my erection.

My body responds, tightening with need, and air hisses through my teeth. "Fuck." My eyelids fall halfway closed.

She watches with heated curiosity as she grinds against my cock again, and my jaw goes slack. Want fires through me. I'm so fucking close, I'm seconds from spilling in my boxers. My fingers dig into her hips to stop her.

"Darcy—"

"My turn," she whispers. Her eyelids droop, and she presses her lips in a tight line as she does it again, a sweet little frown forming between her eyebrows.

After so many years of forcing my feelings down, seeing Darcy enjoy grinding against my cock has me hurtling to the edge *fast*. Her lips part and her tits press into my chest as she drags herself up and down my aching length. We should stop before I lose control, but I can't—I'm too hooked on the way she's looking at me, like I'm hers.

"This is so good," she whispers, closing her eyes. "Why did we wait so long?"

My balls tighten, and my eyes go wide as I lose control.

"Shit, Darce—" I choke out, clutching her, bucking against her. Fire races up my spine. "I'm going to—"

She lowers her mouth to my ear and nips my earlobe, and I'm done.

White heat roars through me, rushing through my blood and tightening in my groin. My release hits, and I moan a helpless, hoarse, broken sound into her neck, teeth grazing her skin. I'm clutching her so tight to my chest she probably can't breathe, but I don't have a thought left in my head except for the overwhelming need to fuck her hard and make her mine. I'm vaguely aware of her lips on my temple, but my full attention is on her dragging her damp pussy up and down my erection and the soft, encouraging noises she whispers in my ear.

My release subsides, and I lie there, staring into her eyes, air sawing in and out of my lungs.

Jesus fuck. Embarrassment hits me and I make a face, groaning.

"What?" Darcy laughs.

"I just came in my boxers like I'm seventeen again." Way to show her I know what I'm doing.

She snickers into my neck. "It was hot." She trails her fingers through my hair and inhales, her nose buried in my neck. "I'm going to be daydreaming about that tomorrow."

I sink my hand into her hair and tilt her mouth to mine, coaxing her lips open. Our kiss is slow, deep, and intimate.

How could I ever doubt that Darcy and I were perfect for each other? This is everything. It's like nothing else exists when we're together.

After cleaning up, we lie in bed, Darcy tucked against my chest and exploring my body with light, teasing touches.

I press a kiss to her temple. "You know on Valentine's Day, when you asked what kind of porn I watched and I got weird?"

She nods.

"I didn't want to send it to you, because they look exactly like us, and it's the only porn I've watched for years." I lift my head to hold her eyes with a steady gaze. "I imagine they're us."

The corner of her mouth pulls into a tiny, adorable smile. "Oh."

"Yeah. And you mentioned that I always take a shower after we touch, like after we cuddled and after you tried flirting with me?"

She nods, eyebrows sliding together.

"It's because you turned me on so goddamn much, Darce, that I needed to come, and I can't come quietly." My mouth hooks in a lazy grin. "As you now know."

She swallows, cheeks going pink. "Oh."

"Yeah."

There's a flare of surprise in her eyes, and I know, inside her head, she's processing this info.

That's fine. I'll give her time to let it sink in.

"You're really cute when you're flustered."

She chuckles into my shoulder before glancing at the door, hesitating.

"You're not going back to your bed," I tell her.

Maybe it's my imagination, but I think she's relieved. "Bossy."

I kiss her forehead, inhaling her, stroking my hand over her back. "You want some water?"

She shakes her head, takes a deep breath, and lets it out slow, her body relaxing into mine. I listen to her soft breathing as she falls asleep, and my thoughts begin to clear.

I'm done with being her wingman, and I'll do what it takes to convince Darcy she's mine.

She'll need time to process this, and the last thing I want to do is rush her. Telling her she's it for me, that she's the only woman I've ever wanted and will ever want, will make her panic.

So I'll give her time. I'll take the pressure off.

My heart does an uneasy tug. What if I show her how good we could be together, but it's still not enough?

Just a pretty face and a good fuck.

I tighten my arm around her. In her sleep, she sighs and nestles farther into my chest, and determination floods me.

I'm racing toward a cliff with a cut brake line. My only option is to push the pedal to the floor and hope I clear it.

CHAPTER 50
DARCY

I WAKE in Hayden's bed, wrapped up tight in his arms. His sheets are softer than ever, and gentle sunlight filters into the room as his exhales tickle the back of my neck. On his bedside table sits the photo of us from university, the one I gave him for Valentine's Day. My brows slide together and I blink at it, biting back a smile. Was that there last night?

He must notice the change in my breathing, because the arm he has strewn across my chest tightens, pulling me to him.

"Morning," he mumbles against me, low voice raspy with sleep.

"Good morning."

I revel in the comfort of this moment for about four seconds before the questions start pinging around my brain.

Was that the best, dirtiest, most vivid dream of my life, or did I let my best friend and wingman give me the best orgasm of my life?

Did he enjoy it as much as he seemed to?

Is he freaking out?

Am I?

Does he regret what we did?

Do I?

I turn over so we're facing each other, and my heart skips a beat at the sleepy look on his handsome face.

"You've got bed head." I reach to smooth it down, but the thick locks spring back up, making me laugh. His smile is drowsy, happy, and adorably boyish.

"You want some breakfast?"

I shake my head. I could lie here forever with him.

Last night replays in my head—him hauling me out of the restaurant, him losing his patience and kissing me, the desperate, needy way he made me come harder than ever, and all the things he said. The porn I thought looked like us? He thought that, too. He watched it *because* he thought it looked like us.

My skin tingles as I think back to every time we've touched or smiled at each other over the past eight years, and now I'm looking at those interactions in new light. Are these feelings recent?

They must be. I'd know if they weren't.

Right?

"What happened last night?" I whisper, and worry begins to thread through me.

We've stepped so far over the line of friends, it's not even funny. But where we landed, I'm not sure.

He studies me for a beat. "I think we did something we've wanted to do for a long time." His mouth crooks. "Tell me I'm wrong."

"You're not." My pulse picks up. I say we're just friends and that he's just my wingman, but over the past few months, it's become increasingly difficult to believe it.

He's a player, though. Hayden Owens moves from woman to woman. He said it himself—he doesn't do commitment; it's easier that way.

He could change his mind. I could change *my* mind. I

thought I loved Kit and I was so wrong; what if Hayden and I get involved, and I turn out to be wrong again?

He's my best friend, and if we broke each other's hearts, there'd be no coming back from that. Our friendship would be over, and the idea of Hayden not being in my life makes me feel like crying.

I swallow past the rock in my throat, and he brushes his thumb over the crease between my eyebrows.

"What's going on in there?" he asks quietly.

"Just thinking."

He gives me a slight shake of his head, looking concerned. "Don't do that."

I break into a grin, but the hesitation remains. "I don't want to mess things up with you and me." It's so strange, lying on the pillow, talking quietly as the sun streams in. Strange and yet completely normal and natural. "There are a lot of reasons we shouldn't do this."

He pauses, wearing his own thoughtful frown. "Let's see where it goes."

I know where it'll go. Either he'll get bored in a relationship, or I'll realize that I'm exactly where I was a year ago—trapped. Hayden's so different from Kit, but maybe it's not the guy I'm with who's the problem. Maybe it's me.

Maybe I dissolve into the life of whoever I'm dating.

The thought of falling in love with Hayden but losing myself again sends terror through me. I've only started finding myself. I'm not ready to sink into someone else's life again and lose everything I've discovered about who I am.

"You need a plan, don't you?" His mouth crooks and his eyes turn warm with affection.

I huff an amused breath, because he knows me so well. I hate the cliffhanger of uncertainty. "Yes. A plan would be nice."

"Alright. Jamie and Pippa's wedding. We wait until then to make a decision. We'll go together."

We were both already planning to go to the wedding, but the idea of going together as dates makes my heart skip a beat. I think back to Pippa's words months ago—*I assumed you'd go together*.

"And until then?"

He brings my hand to his mouth and presses a series of soft, lingering kisses over my open palm. The brush of his stubble makes my breath catch.

"Until then, I keep giving you lessons. I show you everything you want to experience and learn." He swallows. "We don't have to commit to anything. We can just have fun, like you wanted."

I should feel relieved that he's taking the pressure off like this, but instead, something catches and snags behind my ribs.

Hayden Owens never settles down. Of course. I'm a novelty to him, but that'll wear off. That stuff he said last night about dating women who didn't look like me? I'm sure that's true. But it won't change who he is at his core. Even now, he's managing my expectations, emphasizing *fun* and lack of commitment while we agree to an end date.

His eyes hold mine. "Just me, though. No one else. I don't want to share you. I want you all to myself."

The determined way he says it is so different from his usual easy-going demeanor. A thrill races down my spine. I wonder what it would be like to be completely owned and cherished by Hayden Owens.

He pulls me on top of him. My legs fall to either side of his body, straddling his hips, and he grins up at me, eyes sparking with interest and mischief.

"What do you say, Darce?" The corner of his lips slides up into a flirty smile. "You want to have some fun?"

Learning to be a player has been about taking what I want. So what do I want?

I want this. He's so tempting I can hardly stand it. I want to mess around with Hayden and have the best sex of my life and wake up with him. I can have fun but stay detached. I'm exploring who I am, and maybe this is exactly what I need. It's only a month; I won't fall in love with him.

I won't.

My mouth twists to the side in a wry smile. "Alright."

My pulse picks up in excited anticipation, and a pleased smile spreads over Hayden's features as I nod.

"Good." His eyes heat. "I was hoping you'd say that."

———

When the game starts that night, something's different about Hayden. Within seconds of the puck drop, he's on a breakaway to the Philadelphia net.

Around me, the crowd starts to holler, and I'm on my feet, watching with fascination as he skates hard with two defensemen trailing him.

He shoots the puck, and when it hits the back of the net, the arena detonates with noise.

"He's an animal!" some guy behind me yells to his friend as the Vancouver players surround Hayden on the ice twenty feet away. "Owens is an animal tonight."

I grin big, watching Hayden radiate pride at his goal. He turns to find me and my stomach dips at his heated smile.

"That goal was for you," Hazel says in my ear with a teasing smile.

I roll my eyes. "No, it wasn't."

Hayden skates over, eyes dropping to my jersey, and his grin turns pleased and possessive. I think about his hands on my hips this morning, running over me like he owned me, and a pleasant shudder rolls through me.

He winks; I blush with pleasure.

My good luck charm, he mouths through the glass before skating off past the bench, bumping gloves with the rest of the team.

"Something you want to share with the class?" Hazel asks as my grin stretches even wider. Pippa smiles on, delighted and curious.

"Nope," I say, grinning ear to ear, and they grin back at me.

We're just having fun, I tell myself.

———

In the box after, he finds me the second he walks through the door. My mouth slips up into a smile as he strides toward me. He walks with that focused determination that has people moving out of his way. Someone calls his name, but his gaze doesn't leave mine.

"Hi—" I start, but his hand comes to the back of my head and he pulls me to him, mouth meeting mine in a hard, drugging, needy kiss that scatters my thoughts.

I melt against him and let him take what he wants. His hand is firm in my hair, tugging gently to tilt my mouth open more for him, and he lets out a low, pleased groan.

He pulls back to meet my eyes, and in his gaze, heat flickers with amusement at whatever my expression looks like.

He starts to smile. "Hi."

My three remaining brain cells help me blink. "Hi."

He smiles wider. "You're so fucking cute." He doesn't let me go, though. We're in the middle of the box, surrounded by the rest of the team, and my skin prickles with the weight of their gazes.

"Everyone can see us," I whisper.

"Mhm." He pulls me into a hug and presses his mouth to my temple in a sweet kiss.

On the other side of the room, Hazel, Rory, and Alexei watch us. Hazel wiggles her eyebrows, smiling, Rory's grinning broadly, and even Alexei's expression looks warmer than usual.

My mouth quirks into a teasing smile as I slide my hand down onto Hayden's butt and grab it, and he drops his head back, laughing.

"YOU SURE YOU'RE going to be okay on your own?" I ask as Darcy pulls up to the departures area at the airport.

It's our last away game stretch of the season, and I don't want to leave her.

"I promise." She gives me a quick grin. "I'm not a kid. I can take care of myself."

"I know." I like taking care of her, though, and I like making sure she has enough food in the fridge. "You can call or text anytime. Or you can call my parents if you need help with something."

She nods, resting her gaze on me, and something in my chest tugs. Things are finally on the right track for us, and leaving now feels all wrong. But I know taking things slow and giving her time to process is a good thing. The last guy rushed her, and I don't want to end up like him.

My thoughts flick to the unanswered text in my pocket. He'll be back in Vancouver for a game in a few weeks and wants to meet for a drink to catch up.

I don't want to see him. As far as I'm concerned, he's out of our lives, but a part of me wants to lay into him for what he did.

"Have a great trip." Darcy wears a small, shy smile as her

eyes move over my face. She's been doing this more in the past few days, openly looking at me, studying me.

I like having her full attention.

Heat gathers in my groin, and I lower my mouth to hers, nipping at her bottom lip. She sighs into me, hand flattening on my chest and smoothing over the front of the t-shirt she got me on Valentine's Day. My favorite t-shirt, my most prized possession.

My body's frustrated, though, and from the way her nails dig into me, she is, too. *Please?* she whispered this morning as she ground back against me. It took every ounce of my control not to sink my cock deep inside her.

Not rushing her, I remind myself while I claim her mouth. Giving her time to adjust to this new dynamic between us, a dynamic I want to be permanent. And that means no sex yet.

No matter how badly we both want it.

"You're going to miss your plane," she whispers between kisses.

"Whatever."

She chuckles. God, she's fucking gorgeous. My heart twists, and I reach for her wrist, toying with the bracelet, brushing my fingers over it, something I seem to do whenever she's in my vicinity. I kiss her again, pulling a soft, sweet moan from her.

"The back seat's big enough if you want to change your mind," she teases, sounding breathless between kisses, and I laugh. "The windows are tinted."

Fucking hell, I want to hear her come again. I pull back before I get carried away.

"I'm going to miss you," I admit, meeting her gaze. I've never said that to a woman before. It should make me uncomfortable, but it doesn't.

"I'm going to miss you, too."

She pulls her bottom lip between her teeth, and with a

curse, I kiss her again, inhaling her, threading my fingers into her soft hair.

"One more."

She laughs against my mouth, and I frame her perfect face with my hands.

"Don't do anything wild while I'm away, okay?" Under my lips, she smiles. "Save it for when I get home so we can be wild together."

"Deal," she whispers.

If I don't get out of the car now, I never will. I press one last kiss to her mouth before climbing out, just as Volkov gets out of the car behind me.

He nods at me and I suck in a deep breath. We haven't talked since the double date last week. He leans down to look in the car window and waves at Darcy.

She rolls down the window and waves back. "Hi, Alexei."

"Hi." He glances between us before raising an eyebrow at Darcy. "Want to go out again?"

She laughs, but jealousy roars through me, and my jaw clenches. I know he's fucking with me, Darcy knows he's fucking with me, but still. When it comes to Darcy and dating other guys, I can't think straight.

"No," I snap, and the corner of Volkov's mouth twitches. "She's busy." I lean down to meet her gaze and my expression relaxes. "Bye. Thanks for the ride."

She grins. "Bye."

Volkov and I watch her drive away. I'm already looking forward to coming home to her.

"You're welcome," Volkov says with a sidelong look as we head inside the airport.

My teeth grit. "For what?"

"A push in the right direction."

"Fuck you."

He laughs. The asshole actually fucking *laughs*. I stare at him in shock. I don't think I've ever seen him laugh. We flash our IDs at the entrance to the security area, and the guy waves us in.

"You know I'm right." He hoists his bag onto the conveyor to be scanned before his expression turns more serious. "It's good to see you happy."

"I'm always happy."

"Not like this."

My heart does a few hard thumps, because he's right. I've spent years telling myself I'm the type of guy women have fun with but don't settle down with.

Darcy makes me feel like more, though, and maybe I am.

———

Volkov and I settle into our seats, and a few minutes later, Miller steps onto the plane, finds me, and lets out a crow of victory.

"There's my guy." He shakes my shoulders with a big shit-eating grin all over his face. "Mr. Darcy Andersen, as I live and breathe."

I shove him off, but I'm laughing, smug pride expanding through my chest. He kneels on the seat in front of us, facing backward.

"So, what's the deal? Are you two together now?"

I shrug, trying not to smile too hard. "We're just seeing how things go."

I almost laugh at how insincere the words feel. Of course we're together. I'm not letting her go.

In the aisle, as Streicher lifts his bag into the overhead bin, he gives me an *are you fucking kidding me?* look, and I put my hands up.

"I don't want to rush her." I glance out the window, thinking about the flower deliveries I have booked for every day while I'm out of town. A pleased grin pulls up on my mouth. "We're just having fun."

Volkov and Miller exchange a look, and Miller's eyes glitter.

"I'll watch for the save the date," Miller says before turning around and taking a seat.

I grin out the window, imagining it, before I find a picture of Darcy and me from the cast party and set it to my phone background.

When the game packets are passed out, I open mine to an instant photo of that stupid gnome in my hot tub, wearing Darcy's sunglasses.

Thinking of you - xo Daniel is written in her writing.

Volkov eyes the photo. "You two are weird."

My face hurts, I smile so hard. "I know."

I wouldn't have it any other way.

I'M DOING something I absolutely should not be doing—watching game tape and gathering data—when the buzzer for the front door rings on my phone. A smile spreads over my face, and warm, elated feelings spin in my chest, because I think I know what this is.

"Hello?"

"Got a delivery for Darcy Andersen."

Knew it. "Come on up."

I buzz him in, and minutes later, the delivery guy knocks on the door.

"Third time this week." He grins between me and the enormous bouquet of flowers, and my face goes hot.

Those elated feelings join hands and spin in a huge circle before they flop over and sigh. The first bouquet was oranges and yellows, yesterday was different shades of purples, and today is soft, feminine pinks.

"Either someone screwed up big time, or he's in love."

I cough out a dry laugh as I sign for the delivery. "He's not in love."

We're just having fun. Hayden Owens doesn't fall in love.

"Whatever you say." He gives me a short wave. "See you soon, I'm sure."

I chuckle, thank him, and close the door before pulling out my phone. Hayden answers my FaceTime call on the second ring.

"Another?" I angle the camera at the giant bouquet on the kitchen counter. "What are you up to?"

"What do you mean?" He grins, lying on his bed, leaning against the headboard in the hotel room.

My fingers trail over one of the delicate petals of a pretty pink rose. "You're spoiling me."

"And?"

I blow out a breath, still smiling like a doofus. Hayden's sent me a bouquet every day since he left for away games. I can buy my own flowers, but I don't, and I have to admit, being gifted them is different—sweeter and more meaningful.

"And it's too much."

"Are you uncomfortable with me sending you flowers?" His low voice makes the back of my neck prickle.

"No," I admit.

"Are you having second thoughts about what we talked about?"

My heart lodges in my throat. "No. Definitely not."

"Good." His eyes turn soft. "Me neither."

My stomach flutters. I miss him like crazy and can't wait for him to come home so I can push him down to the floor, straddle his hips, and grind against him until his eyes do that darkened, hazy thing I find so hot.

Flowers feel serious, though. Flowers feel like a relationship. I don't want to get my heart smashed just when I'm starting to feel like myself again.

"We said we were just going to have fun," I tell him quietly.

"Buying you flowers *is* fun. I like spending money on you, Darce. Is that a problem?"

At the tone of his voice—commanding yet teasing—I bite down on a smile. "No."

"Good. What are you doing tonight?"

My attention darts to my laptop screen. I'm not taking the job with Ward, and I should leave the analytics to the professionals.

"Darce," Hayden drawls, seeing the guilt all over my expression. "What kind of trouble are you getting into?"

I huff a laugh. "Nothing." I suck in a deep breath. "Okay, I was watching the game from the other night."

"You were?"

I give him a strange look. "Of course I was. And I wore your jersey during it, obviously."

His eyes gleam with pride. "I didn't know that."

"Why are you surprised? I love watching you play. Anyway, the game the other night. Ward keeps pairing Alexei with new defensemen, and it isn't working."

I have that feeling again, the one that led me to checking the numbers for the Storm's array of power play and penalty kill configurations.

"There's this guy who plays college hockey, Luca Walker." My pulse picks up. "I think he'd play well with Alexei."

Hayden's eyebrows go up. "Oh yeah?"

"He played one game in the NHL last year, and it didn't go well, but I think it was just a one-off." I shake my head, frowning. "It was just one game, and there are a lot of reasons why a guy doesn't play well. He's young, but he has a lot of similar characteristics to you." Luca Walker is kind of sloppy, but there's talent there. "Ward has a lot of experienced guys on the team, but if I look at how teams play over, say, five years, they have more younger players that they're always developing.

There are only a few young guys on the team right now. A lot of the players are twenty-five or older."

"You think the Storm should draft this guy?"

"It's worth a try to see if Alexei plays well with him." The league's trade deadline is approaching quickly, and after that, the teams are set for the rest of the season and playoffs. The Storm are likely in the playoffs this year, but there's no guarantee. If I'm right, a change like this could make a difference. "You should say something to Ward."

He arches an eyebrow. "*You* should."

My thoughts go to the job offer in my email from yesterday morning. *In case you change your mind*, Ward wrote.

Fear holds me back, and I hate myself for that. I'm terrified that my data won't hold up and it'll lead to the Storm getting knocked out of the running for the playoffs. Careers are at stake. Someone could get hurt. The team wants to win the playoffs so badly, and I'd never forgive myself if I messed that up for them.

Hayden is a whole new element to why I can't take this job. I'd be working closely with him. I'd probably be traveling with the team. This *thing*, whatever we're doing with his sweet kisses on my neck and sleeping in the same bed every night, has an expiration date.

And then I get to watch as he moves on to other girls, showering them with his teasing smiles and pulling them into his lap.

I can't watch that. I can't take the job.

I meet Hayden's curious gaze and shake my head with a small smile.

"He's going to know who it's coming from," he says.

"Tell him you were contacted by a fortune teller."

He still grins, shaking his head. "Fine, I'll say something, but I'm sure it'll be as subtle as a bag of rocks." His gaze rests on me for a long moment. "What if you took the job, Darce?" His eyes spark. "It would be kind of fun, wouldn't it, working together? Ward always brings an analyst or two on the road. We could have sleepovers."

Against my will, I grin, picturing it. Watching movies on the plane together. Sneaking into each other's rooms late at night, tangling the sheets up and falling asleep together, exhausted.

It would be nice to love my job again, and to use my skills for something cool instead of wasting them on something I don't care about.

"Alexei's going to retire within a few years, whether he wants to or not. What if I'm the reason he never gets to the last round of playoffs?"

I'm scared, I don't say.

He studies me with a serious expression. "But what if you *are* the reason the team gets to the playoffs? What if you can help us? The risk is shared, Darce. No one's going to point fingers at you for a play we executed. There are lots of reasons plays don't work. The team's future doesn't ride on your shoulders." His mouth tips. "Besides, you know what you're doing. That mistake you made? That was years ago."

I hum, nodding and glancing away. It feels like it happened yesterday.

"I wish that shit never happened to you," he mutters, sighing. "You're brilliant, Andersen. Everyone can see it but you. And you deserve to have the life you want."

He shifts onto his side, leaning his head on his elbow and propping the phone against the pillow. As he does, I catch sight of something on the night table behind him.

"Wait." I lean in, squinting at it, and sparklers go off in my chest. "What's on the nightstand behind you?" I ask, even though I can see it perfectly well.

His expression stills, and he doesn't even glance over his shoulder. "The photo you gave me," he says with a guilty grimace, like he's done something wrong.

My heart beats harder. "You took it with you?"

He rubs his jaw, looking away. "I always take it on the road with me."

Oh god. He's so sweet. There's no relationship in my life like the one I have with Hayden. My eyes prick with emotion. If we screw up this *having fun* thing, I'd never forgive myself for losing him as a friend.

"I slept in your bed last night," I admit. And the night before. And I'll probably sleep in his bed tonight.

I'm staying detached—I *am*—but I sleep better in his bed with his scent in my nose. I'm not expecting it to last forever.

A pleased smile curls onto his mouth. "Really?"

"Mhm." My face goes warm. "Is that okay?"

"Yes." His grin broadens. "It's more than okay. I love the thought of you in my bed at home, waiting for me." His eyes fall closed as he sighs. "Fuck, I'm so horny."

A surprised laugh slips out of me. "Hayden."

"Sorry." He grins, but there's a shard of agony in his expression that makes my stomach tumble with anticipation. "I just miss you."

"I miss you, too."

There's a beat of silence where we just look at each other. God, I wish we were together right now. I wish I could sink my fingers into his hair and help him relax.

"We should go furniture shopping this weekend," he says.

I make a funny face at him. He has a whole apartment full of furniture. "We don't need anything."

"Yeah, but..." He shrugs, smiling. "It's all the furniture I had when you moved in. It should look like our place, right? I want it to look like you live there, too."

But what about after Jamie and Pippa's wedding? I want to ask. If we go back to being just friends, I can't go back to sleeping in my own bed and keeping my hands to myself like nothing happened.

"Is this because of my list?" I ask. "The player-worthy pad item?"

It feels like I made that list ages ago. The idea of inviting some strange guy into our place makes me recoil.

His jaw ticks. "No." He glances away, and the tightness in his expression clears. "I had a designer buy all that stuff, but I want something that feels like us." The corner of his mouth slides up. "I want it to look like our home."

There's a warm pull in my chest and I swallow past my warring emotions. This feels suspiciously like a girlfriend kind of thing, to pick out new furniture with him. I should be setting better boundaries, but when I picture it, I *love* the idea of a home that Hayden and I personalized together.

"I want that, too." For a long moment, we just smile at each other. "You get home on Thursday night?"

He nods, gaze resting on me while he wears a small smile.

"I'll pick you up from the airport."

"You don't have to do that. I can get a ride."

"I want to." Another girlfriend thing I shouldn't be doing. Something occurs to me, and I clap my hand to my forehead. "Wait. I can't. I have that Women in STEM event on Thursday night. The roller disco fundraiser." I sink in disappointment. Hayden does so much for me, and dropping him off at the airport earlier in the week made him so happy.

"Don't worry about it." He waves me off. "This is the seventies thing?"

I nod. "We're fundraising for the tuition fund, to send low-income girls to university. Too bad you can't make it." My mouth twists. "You'd love it."

"You could say we're trying on false teeth we found on the beach, Darce, and I'd probably have fun as long as you're there."

I gag and he laughs.

He's in love, the delivery guy said. *That goal was for you*, Hazel said. And he brings the photo of us on the road with him. My heart thumps harder in my chest.

"I bought some more lingerie," I blurt out.

His brows shoot up. "You did?" His eyes darken, and the strong line of his throat moves as he swallows. "For me?"

"For *me*," I tell him with a teasing grin. "But yes, also for you."

"Show me."

My face goes pink, but I'm delighted. "No."

He sits up on the bed, focused on the screen with fascination. "Please."

I laugh. "You'll have to wait to see it when you get home."

His head falls back and he groans. "Darce, when I get home, you're going to show me a lot more than the new lingerie."

A thrill runs through me, and I bite back my excited grin, my mind racing with dirty images. "I can't wait."

CHAPTER 53

DARCY

"HEY, DARCY?" Carmelita asks at the Vancouver Women in STEM event on Thursday.

ABBA plays over the sound system, and a disco ball hangs high above the rink while members of the organization roller skate with girls from local schools and their parents, many of them wearing ridiculous seventies costumes.

"Phoebe needs help at the front," she says. "Will you be okay here for a few minutes?"

"You bet. Go do your thing."

She squeezes my arm. "Thanks, hon."

I take in the rink and smile at Georgia, who is talking to a group of teenage girls about her job. They're watching with rapt attention, and even though I can't hear what Georgia's saying, I can see how contagious her enthusiasm for her work is.

She insisted on attending the event so she had a place to wear the knee-high white boots she bought on a whim last year, but I think it's a cover. She loves her job. So does Carmelita, who designs fuel cells for hydrogen vehicles. A lot of the women here light up when talking about work. It's the whole purpose of events like these with girls in elementary and high school, to show them options and make it possible for them to pursue a career path they love. Near the end of the event, Carmelita will hand out the scholarships, which we hope will help someone on a path to doing what they love.

A weird longing feeling sits in my chest. Everyone loves their job but me, it seems.

The Storm still hasn't signed Luca Walker. I've been bugging Hayden for daily updates, but still nothing.

His plane should be arriving around now. Excitement flutters in my stomach, and even though I'm having fun here, I can't wait to get home and climb my hot, ripped hockey player like a tree.

I mean, not *my* hockey player. Just temporarily mine, I guess.

A box arrived yesterday—a mint-green lingerie set, so delicate, soft, and beautifully made. *Love, Hayden*, the card said, which I propped up on his bedside table and smiled at as I fell asleep.

I'm wearing the lingerie now. I glance at the time again. Hopefully his flight's on time and I can see him before I fall asleep.

Who am I kidding? I'll stay up until dawn to see him. That's how much I miss him.

"Hey," a familiar deep voice says behind me. "Can I get some help lacing up my skates?"

A series of sparks and pops go off throughout my body, and I wrench around, nearly falling over at the sight of Hayden Owens in a hideous silk floral shirt, bell bottoms, and oversized orange sunglasses. He's grinning big and holding a pair of rented roller skates. He's shaved a mustache. It's not fair how hot he looks, even like this.

"Christ, it's good to see you," he murmurs, stepping into my space and leaning his palms on the railing behind me, caging me in. "You look so freaking cute. Good enough to eat." He kisses the corner of my mouth, and my pulse stumbles, drunk and disoriented.

"You're here." I blink at him in disbelief.

I sink my hands into his hair, and his eyelids fall halfway before I pull his lips to mine. He groans, and I inhale him, kissing him, showing him how much I missed him as he claims my mouth. His arms are around me, and I sink against his broad, solid warmth.

Someone whistles at us, but I don't care. I just want Hayden.

"We gotta slow down, Darce," he says against me, smiling. "These pants are already too tight, and there are kids here."

I huff a laugh and pull back to look at his outfit. "You look like Austin Powers." If Austin Powers was played by a life-sized Ken doll with perfect teeth.

He winks. "Oh, behave."

"You're supposed to be on a plane." My gaze snags behind him and I burst out laughing. "Is that Rory?"

Rory's wearing a full Elvis jumpsuit with a black wig and aviators, and he's taking a photo with a group of teenage girls.

Hayden grins. "Yep."

The entire team is here, all dressed up to some degree. Even Alexei is wearing big, sparkly sunglasses someone probably forced on him.

I feel like I'm full of hot air, like I could float. "I thought your flight didn't get in until now?"

"Darcy, you should have seen this guy at the hotel this morning," Rory says as he passes, jostling Hayden. "He was a drill sergeant, knocking on doors to get people up at the crack of dawn."

Hayden rolls his eyes. "Whatever."

Rory does a fake cough, smirking at Hayden. "I think he

needs a bit of extra attention tonight. He's sick." *Lovesick*, he mouths.

Hayden shoves him away, then smiles down at me. My face goes hot, but I can't stop beaming.

"Don't listen to him," Hayden murmurs. "He hits his head a lot."

I laugh, but my attention catches on Alexei, where he's signing a jersey with Carmelita. Hayden follows my line of sight. "We brought merch for you to auction off."

"Carmelita?" Rory calls to her, holding up his phone. "Can you send me the link for the donations? I want to post to my social media."

Hayden wraps his arms around me and I catch his scent—warm, spicy, and clean. So familiar it makes my heart ache. "Can I steal you away for a bit?"

It looks like everyone has everything handled, so I nod and take Hayden's outstretched hand. He leads me over to a bench.

"I'll do it," he says firmly when I reach for my skates. Then he kneels in front of me. He shoots me a quick wink as he tightens the laces.

On the roller rink, we skate big loops, listening to ridiculous disco music and exchanging private smiles. I'm wobbly on my skates, but he holds my hand. I know if I were to swerve or stumble, he'd be right there to catch me. A song he loves comes on, and he lights up, dancing while we skate and spreading his joyful, silly energy around the rink. Soon, everyone is dancing and goofing around, and I'm laughing at Hayden's hilarious disco dance moves.

He does a thrusting dance move and I give him a teasing look.

"Be careful with that thing," I say, glancing down at his crotch. "I know what you're working with."

"Andersen." He looks scandalized. "This is a family event."

"So I probably shouldn't do this, right?" I nudge the collar of my dress aside an inch, and Hayden's gaze lands on the delicate mint-green strap of the bra he sent me.

His eyes flash with desire before he makes a pained face and groans. "You play dirty."

I dissolve into laughter. "I'm so happy you're here," I admit.

His eyes warm with affection. "Me, too." He presses a kiss, then takes my hand and spins me.

Kit never came to events like these. If he wasn't playing hockey, he was resting or golfing. Everything revolved around him.

Hayden's so different. I don't know why it took moving in with him and doing whatever we're doing to see it. I have more fun with him than anyone. In hindsight, I realize I looked forward to hanging out with him on our trips to Vancouver more than a woman in a relationship with someone else should.

If I let myself, I could fall harder for Hayden than anyone. Roller skating with him and talking on the phone before bed and talking about stats with him? It all feels so right.

When Jamie and Pippa's wedding is over and whatever Hayden and I are doing is done, I'm going to try to remember this feeling. This is what I missed out on for years with the wrong guy.

"GOD, I FUCKING MISSED YOU." Hayden pins me against the wall in the elevator, sucking on my neck. "I thought about you constantly."

My skin flushes hot, and I arch against him like a cat as tingles run across my skin. "I used the toy in your bed."

He stills and drops his head to my shoulder with a tortured groan. I just laugh. The elevator doors open, and with a grin, he leans down and flips me over his shoulder.

Marry that man, Carmelita hissed at me after Hayden privately donated a hundred grand to the Women in STEM scholarship fund.

"This is unnecessary," I laugh, upside down, as he carries me to the front door and unlocks it. "Anyone could see."

"Let them see." Inside, he kicks his shoes off while gripping the back of my thighs to hold me steady. "They'll know we're busy for the rest of the night."

Heat coils between my legs. "You're not going to tell me to slow down?"

"No." He drops his bag and strides to his bedroom. "That was a stupid idea."

In his room, he gently sets me on my feet. In the next

instant, his mouth is back on mine. Then his hands are on the hem of my dress and lifting it over my head. When he sees the lingerie he bought me, his eyes darken, and his head falls back.

"Are you okay?" I laugh.

"No." He groans, frowning at my lingerie. "I'm so hard it hurts."

I make a low, sympathetic noise, and, holding his gaze, I bring my hand to the front of his pants, palming him. His lips part as I squeeze the hard length.

"Poor Hayden." My fingers graze up and down him, toying.

He nods, pulsing against my hand. "Yeah. Poor me."

I laugh, and he grins before unbuttoning his shirt, shoving it off, and losing the pants.

God, he's beautiful. I take a moment to just stare at him while he's smiling down at me. He winds his hand into my hair and kisses my cheek, my jaw, my neck.

"What did you think about when you were using the toy?"

"You."

"Be more specific." He sucks the skin beneath my ear and my eyes close as wetness rushes between my legs.

"Remember the video you showed me? With his, um." I press my lips together, embarrassed. I'm not used to asking for what I want, especially not in sexy situations. "Head between her legs?" My voice turns squeaky.

He chuckles against my skin. "Oh yeah. I've seen that one a few times."

"What's a few?"

"Like, a hundred."

I laugh. "Wow."

He walks me back so my knees hit the bed and pushes me to sit before climbing over me. I fall back against the pillows, mesmerized by the way he looks down at me, like he doesn't know where to start.

His gaze flicks to mine, light and teasing, while his fingers trail along the lace of my bra. "So what about that video?"

"Maybe you could... do that." I watch him explore, tracing up my lace straps. My breasts feel tight and achy, desperate for his attention.

"Go down on you."

His fingers find a pinched nipple through the fabric, and I bite my lip and nod.

He slides the bra down and watches my face as he toys with the puckered peak. Molten heat courses through me, gathering and pooling between my thighs. "Lick your pussy."

"Hayden." I blush.

He drops his head to my breast and pulls my nipple between his lips. A choked noise slips out of me at the drugging pull of his lips, the hot slide of his tongue.

"Make you come all over my face?" he murmurs against me.

I laugh, trying to focus on the conversation.

"Don't be embarrassed." He reaches around, unhooks my bra, and pulls it off. And then his mouth is back on the stiff point, his fingers on the other. "You don't know how many times I've fucked my fist thinking about going down on you."

More arousal floods my panties, and when he brushes over the front of them, he sucks in a sharp breath. "Wet already."

He draws a firm circle, and pleasure ripples through me. I'm breathing hard, watching him enjoy my body. He gives me a dark, devilish smile and slips his fingers beneath the fabric.

We groan together at the divine sensation of his fingers circling my clit.

"Did he ever make you come that way? With his mouth?"

I shake my head. Pressure builds as he drags delicious friction over the sensitive nerves. On his shoulders, my nails dig into his skin.

He slips my panties off, leaving me completely naked. Part

of me wants to feel shy and embarrassed, but the hungry look in his eyes burns away any self-consciousness.

Hayden wants me, and I want him to have me.

"Darcy?"

Right. His question. "He tried." My eyebrows pinch with the memory. "A long time ago. Back in school. It didn't work."

He makes a low, unhappy noise in his throat, gazing at my pussy as his fingers return to work, swirling, winding me higher and higher. "And then he just gave up."

I blink, unsure of what to say. Yes, that's exactly what happened. "I gave up, too."

"I'm not going to let you give up. We're going to stay right here until you're happy, whether you come or not. Just enjoy this. Okay?"

I nod.

He lowers himself between my legs, hands on my inner thighs, pushing them apart. My pulse races. This is actually happening. Hayden's about to go down on me.

When his hot tongue drags over my nerves, pleasure rockets through me. My hips arch off the bed. He turns his face to my thigh and presses a firm kiss, inhaling hard and letting it out in an agonized groan.

"Jesus Christ," he murmurs against my skin before he sweeps his tongue up my pussy again.

My toes curl. I clench the duvet. At the center of my spine, sparks start.

"You know what I did after we used the toy together, Darce?"

It's so bizarrely hot, hearing him use my abbreviated name, the one he's used so casually for years, while he laps up my arousal. Worlds collide, and I'm surprised at how well they fit.

"What?" I croak.

He explores me with leisure, dipping and sucking and tugging with his lips. I feel every. Single. Sensation.

"You got my hand all wet," he says in a low voice. He swirls a hot circle on my clit with his tongue, and my vision blurs. I've never been so attended to like this, but from the way he seems to savor me, it feels like this is more for him.

And that is very, very hot.

"I sucked you off my fingers, Darcy," he murmurs before his tongue slips inside me.

I let out a moan, and pleasure gathers inside me as I picture the image of Hayden slipping his fingers into his mouth and tasting me. "You tasted so fucking sweet. Just like you do now."

Another long, dragging lick up my seam. I heave for air, and Hayden grasps my hand and pulls it to his head.

His grin is pure sin. "Pull my hair when you come, honey."

I grasp the strands with my other hand, too, my fingers sinking into his thick locks. I try to laugh at his cockiness, but it comes out like a sigh. He lifts my thighs so they rest on his strong shoulders. The added skin contact is exactly what I didn't know I wanted. His hands linger on my thighs, squeezing and smoothing over my skin to comfort me.

At a lazy, unhurried pace, with his lips, tongue, and teeth, he explores me. Toys with me. Teases me. Winds me higher and holds me there. I don't care if I come. I could lie here forever under Hayden as he goes down on me like he needs it.

He wanders back up to my clit and pulls it between his lips, meeting my fascinated gaze and sucking hard. My eyes roll back and the air whooshes from my lungs in a choked gasp. And low in my body, my nerves begin to fracture.

I'm pretty sure I'm going to come.

He makes a pleased noise at my reaction and does it again, sucking the tight bud. I blink a thousand times in a row as sparkles burst across my vision.

"That's so good," I moan, like the smug heat in his eyes doesn't tell me he knows exactly how good it feels.

His hand moves to between my legs, and a moment later, his thick fingers push inside me.

"Hayden," I gasp. The fullness of his fingers aches in the most delicious, mind-bending way. I'm starting to spin out, nerves pulling tight and fraying. With my heels digging into his back, I tug his hair, and he groans in appreciation.

My orgasm builds low inside me.

"What's the matter, Darce?" he croons, but I pull his hair gently again, and he shuts up with a happy hum.

"This is what I wanted to do last week," he grits out against my pussy, moving his fingers, rubbing the front wall like the toy did. "This is how I *really* wanted to make you come."

He latches on to my clit and his tongue moves over it. The suction and friction combined with his fingers filling me, working me, send me over the edge.

Pleasure tightens through my body, and my hips buck against Hayden's devouring mouth as I come hard. Wave after wave of heat and sensation roll through me. My thoughts evaporate; I'm just a collection of nerves firing as he moans between my legs, guiding me through it with low, encouraging noises. My muscles spasm around his fingers, and I'm dizzy with the loss of control, the overwhelming bliss, the whoosh of blood through my veins.

Like last time, he draws it out, watching my face and slowing his movements, bringing me down softly until I'm a breathless puddle.

"Oh my god," I breathe as he climbs up beside me and gathers me against him. Blood still pounds in my ears, but a luxurious, sated, heavy feeling settles through my body.

"You're so good at that." I swallow, closing my eyes. "I didn't know it could be like that."

His lips find my temple and he presses a kiss to my hairline. His voice is low in my ear, making my skin prickle. "Trust me, the pleasure was all mine."

Against my hip, though, his erection strains. His body heat sears me through the fabric of his boxers. I'm sick of waiting. I want to make him feel the way he just made me feel.

Deep down, in the most secret part of my conscience, my heart aches at the knowledge that this will end—this easy, effortless, thrilling dynamic we've found—and I'll never find something like it again.

Which means I have to make it worth it while it lasts.

Wearing my own wicked smile, I wrap my palm around his length. His lips part in surprise and desire glazes his eyes.

It's my turn.

CHAPTER 55

HAYDEN

"DON'T SAY 'NOT TONIGHT.'" Her eyes gleam with interest and curiosity as her gaze lingers on my cock and she gives me a firm squeeze.

My balls tighten with need. "Shit."

"I want to see you." She trails her fingers up and down my length.

Just like last time, I can feel the coiling pressure around the base of my spine, the heavy ache in my balls. Fooling around with Darcy gets me there ten times faster. "I'm so fucking close already."

"Prove it."

I let out a tight laugh at her determined but playful expression. "You're going to fucking kill me, you know that?"

Her pretty mouth twists into a happy smile, and I slide my boxers off. My cock springs free, hard and dripping pre-cum, and the first brush of her fingers against my bare skin has my hips jerking off the bed.

"Wow," she breathes, staring at it with a reverence that should embarrass me but instead makes the blood beat harder through my veins. "I knew you were proportional, but..." She studies my cock, smoothing her fingertips down the underside, and I struggle to breathe, it feels so fucking good.

"But...?"

"It sounds cliché."

"Say it." I can barely get the words out.

"You're really big, and I wish you'd fuck me." Her mouth tips. "Happy?"

My cock jumps in her hand as my balls tighten. Lying here with her like this, with her making those interested eyes at me?

"Yeah, Darce, I'm happy."

She explores and plays with my erection, and I wrap an arm around her to keep her close.

"Is this okay?" she asks. "That I'm just... going slow like this?"

"It's fucking incredible," I rasp as she strokes me higher and higher into ecstasy. "Kiss me?"

She makes a sweet little pleased hum and brushes her lips over mine again. My pulse thickens at the sensations of our lazy kiss, and the unhurried, loving way she touches me melts my brain, leaving only thoughts of her and this moment.

It's so different with Darcy. A million layers of new and better. I can feel our relationship changing, and I can feel myself changing.

This. This right here—us lying tangled together and enjoying each other's pleasure is beyond anything I've experienced. And we're not going back to the way things were.

Arousal thrums through me, and I'm leaking pre-cum all over her hand as my release stirs and gathers around the base of my spine. She just keeps kissing me. The unfamiliar intimacy of this should terrify me, but it doesn't.

I sink my hand into the back of her hair, kissing her harder as she tightens her hold on my cock, and she moans into my mouth. My balls ache; my hips cant into her grip.

"Like this?" she whispers.

I nod, my heart pounding and my head spinning. I feel like I'm drunk.

"Just like that. I'm so fucking close," I mumble, voice rough and low.

"I've been thinking about what you look like when you come," she whispers between kisses, and the thought of Darcy fantasizing about me sends electricity crackling through me.

The pressure boils over at the base of my spine, and I buck my hips into her hand in jerky, uncontrolled movements.

"I'm going to come," I warn, watching her gorgeous face as my world starts to fall apart.

My heart pounds against my ribcage, my thoughts blur, and my lips part against hers. I cover her hand with mine, and we jerk me off together. A broken moan scrapes out of my throat as my balls tighten in ecstasy and I come all over our hands and my stomach.

I've been dreaming about her jerking me off like that for years, and yet it's better than I thought it could be.

"Fucking hell," I gasp as she strokes me through it. With interest and desire, her gaze swings between my face and my cock, eyes wide as I drain my release. I finish with a low moan, light-headed and exhausted.

Darcy smiles against my shoulder.

"Feeling smug about yourself, Andersen?"

She arches an eyebrow, lips curving more. "Very."

Her hand is covered in my release, and a dark, possessive urge soars through me. My gaze travels up her body, over the delicate curves of her chest, and I picture coming all over her.

Making her mine.

I lift my hand to her mouth. "Open."

Holding my eyes, she parts her lips, and her sweet pink tongue darts out against my skin, tasting my release. Her throat works as she swallows, and my thoughts go blank. Powerful, possessive urges roar through me, and blood races to my groin.

I'm getting hard again.

She bites her lip with a coy smile. I'm so fucking gone for her.

I need to get up to clean off, but my body feels weighted and more relaxed than ever.

"I don't think I can stand," I admit with an embarrassed grin, chest still heaving as I catch my breath.

She laughs. "Is that a good thing?"

"Yes, honey." I lower my lips to hers, kissing her soft and gentle. "It's a good thing."

HAYDEN and I are walking home from breakfast at a nearby greasy diner when he points at a store window.

"You would look so good in that."

I stop in my tracks. It's similar to the dress I bought last year, the tangerine one that hung in my closet with the tags on until I donated it.

The one Kit said was too loud.

The one I wish I hadn't gotten rid of. By giving it away without wearing it, I let him win.

"It's so bright," I say, as if I'm able to take my eyes off it. As if I don't feel an urgent tug in my chest toward it.

"Just try it on."

"I have nowhere to wear it." I don't know why I'm fighting this so hard. It's just a stupid dress.

It's not *just a stupid dress*, a voice insists in my head. *It's more. It's that part of you that wasn't enough for him.*

"You can wear it to Jamie and Pippa's wedding."

I *do* need a dress for their wedding. If Georgia were here, she'd already be hauling me into the store.

Hayden doesn't even know about the dress I bought and donated; that must mean *something*, right?

"Okay." I nod resolutely. "I'll try it on."

———

"You look beautiful" is the first thing Hayden says when I step out of the dressing room. He leans against the wall, gaze raking up and down my form, wearing a stunned expression.

I *feel* beautiful. Just like the dress I tried on with Georgia that time, the dress is a perfect fit, like it was designed just for me.

But it's more than that. Wearing this dress feels like victory. Like I'm a little closer to wherever I wanted to be all those months ago, when I left Calgary, lost and confused.

"It's not too"—I try not to choke on the word—"loud?"

He makes a face like I'm ridiculous. "No way. And who cares if it is? You're gorgeous. What's wrong with standing out?"

"I'm going to someone else's wedding." I study my reflection, and my stomach does an excited flop at the way the dress skims over my body. "I don't want to stand out too much and steal their thunder."

"As long as you don't get on the table and try to take it off, I think you're good. Pippa doesn't really care about the spotlight; she just cares about playing music. Besides," his eyes soften and he gives me a sweet, encouraging smile, "I like it when you wear bright colors. It feels like you're not trying to hide anymore."

When I wear this dress, I no longer feel like the girl who was never good enough for Kit or the girl who got herself and her boss and mentor fired. I feel like Darcy Andersen, the woman who loves fantasy romance, making the world better with math, and who loves to laugh with her best friend,

Hayden. The woman who has created a new life for herself here in Vancouver from nothing.

In this dress, I feel like myself.

His eyes trail down my form, his throat works, and he adjusts himself.

A grin tips up on my mouth. "Are you okay?"

"No," he laughs, looking away before his gaze swings back to my body, and his eyes spark with heat.

I step closer, walking slowly, and his eyes drag over me again. He wets his lips, and his cheekbones go pink.

I push my hair back behind my shoulders and his gaze drops to my collarbones. "Am I flustering you?"

"Yes." He grabs my waist and pulls me against him while I shake with laughter. "And if you don't stop, I'm following you back into that dressing room." He brushes his lips over the shell of my ear and I shudder with pleasure.

"Who knew you'd react like this to a dress."

"It's not the dress, Darce." His breath is warm on my neck. "It's you."

In the dressing room, I nearly choke at the price on the tag.

It's a lot. Like, two months' rent, if I were paying rent.

I'm not, though. Due to Hayden's insistence on me living there rent-free, I've saved up a bit of extra cash over the past few months. I've never spent this amount on one item of clothing before, but it's not just an item of clothing; it's something that makes me feel beautiful and special and unique. It makes me feel like myself.

"I'll take it to the front for you," Hayden says through the curtain, and I hand him the hanger.

When I head to the front, he's waiting, holding a thick paper bag with a white box inside.

"It's so weird," he says, shaking his head with a puzzled frown, but his eyes sparkle. "They gave it to us for free."

Behind him, the sales associate pretends to look busy but sneaks us glances, smiling to herself.

I sigh, smiling. "Hayden."

His hand comes to my lower back and he leads me out of the store. "They were like, please, sir, take this dress. You're doing us a favor."

"They did not say that and they definitely didn't call you *sir*. You bought it."

"And *I* said please, let me pay for it, and they insisted." He wraps his hand around mine as we walk home to the apartment.

I'm laughing. I'm trying to be stern, but I'm laughing.

"I'm paying you back. You can't let me live with you for free *and* buy overpriced dresses. It's not fair. I'm already so indebted to you."

"Hey." He stops walking and his eyebrows pinch. "Don't say that, okay? You don't owe me anything. Let me buy it for you." He gives me a patient, amused smile. "Consider it an early birthday present."

Right, it's in two weeks. Nerves twist in my stomach. I was supposed to have everything figured out by then. Between my growing worries about things with Hayden and the job offer I think about at least four times a day, nothing feels figured out. Nothing is quite right.

"You know I'm going to make your birthday special, right?" Hayden crooks an amused look at me. "We're celebrating."

"We don't need to do anything."

"I want to. I want to make it special for you." He presses a quick kiss to my temple and wraps his arm around my shoulder, tucking me against him.

My heart squeezes and I lean into him, smiling. I shouldn't be letting myself get swept up in him like this, but it's getting harder to stop.

Maybe one memorable birthday with Hayden wouldn't hurt.

I'M PACING a hole into the living room rug when Hayden gets home from practice.

"Well?"

"You look... beautiful?" His eyebrows quirk with confusion.

"Hayden." I give him an exasperated look, and he starts laughing. I'm in leggings and his old hockey hoodie, with my hair in a messy bun on top of my head.

"What?" He grasps my hips and walks me back until I'm against the wall, his lips on my neck, making me shiver. "I like when you wear my hoodie. You're so cute in it."

"I like wearing it, too." My breath catches as his teeth nip my earlobe. "It's soft, and it smells like you."

He sucks the sensitive skin beneath my ear, and my lips part in response.

Since we started hooking up, I've learned that Hayden is even more physically affectionate than I thought. I thought he was touchy-feely when we were friends? No. That was his affection on light mode. Every time we're in the same room, his hands are on me—in my hair, around my waist, on my thigh—or if we're walking, he has one interlaced with mine.

And yet, he won't let us go all the way in the bedroom. I'm

crawling out of my skin with horniness. As his lips press to my neck and his fingers sneak beneath the hem of the hoodie, toying with the waistband of my leggings, heat coils between my legs. His scent washes over me, clean and fresh from his post-practice shower, and I sigh.

Wait.

"Stop distracting me. The trade deadline is tonight. Did Ward sign Luca Walker?"

He pulls his phone out to check his email. Ward sends out team memos whenever someone joins the organization. "Still no."

I make a strangled noise of frustration. I know he's mentioned it to Ward already.

"I texted Alexei about him, too. He didn't respond." I chew at my bottom lip, insides in knots. I've been watching more of Walker's college games, and the nagging feeling that he could thrive on the Storm only grows stronger every day.

The school year's ending. Now is the time to draft him. Before someone else does.

I glance at the time. Ward's probably still at the arena. My lungs expand with a big breath before I meet Hayden's curious, entertained expression.

"I need to go to the arena," I tell him, closing my laptop and sliding it into my bag.

"Now?"

"Right now."

He beams. "Great. Let's go."

The receptionist is gone for the evening, so I'm grateful Hayden's here to buzz me into the quiet offices. He takes a seat in the private lobby outside the corporate offices and sends me a playful wink. "I'll be right here. Go get 'em, tiger."

I nod, heart in my throat. I can't believe I'm about to do this.

Ward's office door is open, and I rap a quick knock on it as I breeze inside.

"Hi," I say, louder than intended, and he looks up. I clear my throat and lower my volume to a socially acceptable level. "Sorry. Hi."

Amusement dances in his eyes. "Hi, Darcy."

He doesn't seem surprised to see me.

"You need to sign Luca Walker." I set my laptop on his desk so he can see the screen before coming around to his side. "Here's my data." I flip through the models. "I've reviewed every college game of his I could find. The same hunch I had about the Storm power plays and penalty kills? I feel that about this guy." I point at my screen with urgency, heart beating in my ears. I don't even recognize myself right now. The old Darcy would have let this go and then secretly resented Ward and myself for it for the rest of eternity, all while telling myself it was fine.

I don't know where that version of me is, but the person I am today? She knows she's right.

"You need to draft him before someone else does."

Ward studies me thoughtfully for a long moment, and I hold my breath. "I know," he finally says.

"You *know*?" I shake my head at him. "So what's the delay? Money?"

He leans back in his chair. "Come work for me."

I'm about to protest, but he shakes his head.

"I can't figure out what the hang-up is." He gestures at my laptop. "This is clearly what you're meant to be doing."

Right? something deep in my chest shrieks. My mind flits to the Women in STEM event, to Georgia, to the guys on the Storm. All these people who love their jobs.

Why can't I have that? Why don't I deserve to put the past behind me, learn, and move on? I'm so tired of letting the past hold me back.

I take a seat in the club chair across from his desk, clasping my hands together between my thighs. "It's a lot of pressure."

He nods. "Yep."

"A lot of eyes on the team." Especially this season, when they're ranking better than they have in years. Fans are getting excited.

"Definitely."

Silence stretches between us, and my thoughts yank to my boring job. The thought of staying there another twenty, thirty years gathers cold dread in the pit of my stomach.

Would I hate myself if I looked back on my life and wished I had done it differently? Would I regret not taking a job that sends an excited thrill through me?

"We're a team," Ward says quietly. "I'm never going to hang you out to dry alone. Win together, lose together."

I'm so afraid of failing again, but what about all the things I could lose out on? What if it's the best job of my life and it's exactly where I need to be? I could help people in this role.

Something occurs to me and my gaze snaps to Ward's. Something that could torch this whole thing.

"I have a conflict of interest."

His eyes narrow. "Go on."

I search for the words to explain what's happening with Hayden and me and come up empty. "Hayden Owens."

He makes a noise of acknowledgment and nods, surveying the scenery outside the office windows that overlook the city. Finally, he turns back to me and shrugs. "I'm not concerned. We have three other analysts to watch for conflicts, and I'll bring it up with the owner and legal team, but unless you're heavily into sports betting—"

"I'm not," I rush out.

Ward chuckles. "I figured." His dark brows bob, and the final question lingers in his quiet office. "Take a risk, Darcy."

———

In the lobby, Hayden stands when I come sprinting around the corner. "How'd it go?"

"I took the job."

He lets out a surprised laugh and catches me as I leap into his arms. "I took the analytics job with the team."

Hayden's proud smile is devastatingly handsome. "You did?"

"Uh-huh." I feel like I'm flying, like my heart is about to explode into a cloud of sparkles.

"That's my girl." He wraps his arms around me and I yelp in surprise as he spins me around before pinning me to the wall. His mouth crashes to mine. We're a tangle of lips and moans and teeth, my hands in his hair, my legs around his waist.

"I'm so fucking proud of you," he says between devouring kisses.

It feels so fucking good to be free, like I'm finally soaring after years in a cage.

Someone clears their throat, and we freeze. Ward stands ten feet away, eyebrows sky high, holding my laptop.

"You forgot this."

My face goes molten hot. "Thanks," I squeak.

Ward just laughs and shakes his head. The second he turns the corner, Hayden and I look at each other and burst out laughing.

"I'M GOING TO HEAD UPSTAIRS," Erik, one of the other analysts, tells me in the lower concourse at the arena. He's referring to the private box for just the owner and the analysts, a quiet space where we can watch the game tonight, run real-time data, and coordinate with the coaches on the bench.

I give him a quick smile and gesture at the hallway to the dressing room. "I'll be up in a minute."

I haven't seen Hayden since this morning when I left for work. I'm wearing his jersey, and I want him to know that going into the game. That he always has someone cheering for him.

Erik gives me a wave before he disappears.

It's been less than a week since I started as an analyst with the Storm, but I already feel at home here. The other analysts—Erik, Craig, and Jerome—unexpectedly took me for lunch my first day to celebrate my arrival on the team, and we've spent the entire week either holed up in the conference room as I showed them the models, watching old game tape, or observing practices. They're all retired players, but with how eager they are to work with me to tackle problems, I feel like we're a team. I don't feel like an outsider at all.

It's been so freaking fun. I didn't even know work could be like this.

A young player walks past in his suit, heading to the dressing room, but his gaze snags on me and he stops.

Luca Walker arrived Monday morning and has been training with Alexei all week, learning the defensive plays.

I've only seen him on the ice, practicing, usually wearing a helmet, but up close, he looks so much younger. He's tall and broad like Hayden, but with wavy dark hair and delicate, impish features. A wash of healthy pink across his cheeks and sparkling gray eyes. He reminds me of a prince from one of my fantasy romance books—boyish, cocky, and unfairly beautiful.

His eyes go to my purple hair. "Darcy Andersen?" His dark brow arches, a playful grin pulling up on his mouth.

"That's me."

"So you're who I have to thank for being here tonight."

Warmth threads through me, and I chuckle. "Let's see how you play before you thank me."

He clutches his chest like he's wounded, eyes dancing with humor. "Alright, I see how it is. I love a challenge." Something flashes through his eyes, a sliver of vulnerability, and he slips his hands into his pockets. "I mean it, though. Thank you. Whatever you saw in me, I appreciate it. After that game earlier this year, I, uh." He glances away with a tight smile. "I thought it wasn't going to happen, you know?"

If there were any doubt in my mind that this job is where I'm supposed to be, it evaporates. What I do matters, and Luca is proof of that.

The risk is worth it. "You're welcome."

Interest sparks in his gaze, and he grins higher. "What are you doing after the game? Let's go out."

I want to say I'm taken, but I doubt that's how Hayden would categorize us. "You're a little young for me."

His smile is pure seduction as he glances at my mouth. "Doesn't bother me if it doesn't bother you." He winks. "I've always had a thing for the smart girls."

He's amusing and adorable, but like a little brother would be.

"It bothers her," Hayden bites out, suddenly at my side, wearing his pregame suit. I didn't even hear him approach. Alexei's right beside him, glaring at Luca. "No hitting on the analysts."

My chest shakes with laughter. "Hi." I smile up at Hayden, who's looking deadly handsome.

"Hi." His gaze softens. "You look very cute in my jersey, Andersen."

"What did I say this morning?" Alexei snaps at Luca. "Focus on the game. Knock it off."

"Are you going to gripe at me like this for the rest of the season?" Luca asks as they head to the dressing room.

"Yes. You need a solid pregame routine that doesn't include chasing girls."

Luca sighs. "Jesus, you're obsessed with this pregame routine thing." He tilts a grin at Alexei, unfazed by his stern and abrupt demeanor. "Hey, did you realize that you're almost old enough to be my dad?"

Alexei grumbles something as they walk through the door of the dressing room, and Hayden stares after them with a tight jaw.

"Fucking cocky rookies."

"You were a cocky rookie once."

"I wasn't like that."

I cough out a laugh. "Uh, yes, you were. You were exactly like that."

A boyish grin flashes across his face. "I was better at it. More charming."

"I don't know." I sigh and gaze after Luca like I'm besotted. "He's pretty charming. And cute."

Hayden makes a noise low in his throat, and his hand comes to my back.

"Did you just growl?"

His grin is back, and we beam at each other. "Ready for tonight?"

"I think so." Nerves tumble in my stomach. "I'll be upstairs with the other analysts, watching." My nose scrunches. "I'm bummed that I can't sit in my usual spot with Hazel and Pippa."

It would never work—I need my laptop and a quiet area to concentrate so I can make real-time recommendations with the other analysts. Our data and decisions are confidential, too, so the room needs to be secure. I'd stick out like a sore thumb with my laptop in the front row.

"Don't tell me you're nervous, Darce."

"A little." It's my first game as an analyst, after all.

"Hey." He leans down until his mouth is inches from ear. "You're going to be great. Okay?" He catches my gaze, eyes bright.

When he says it like that, I believe him. "Maybe tonight you'll finally let me have my wicked way with you."

We still haven't had sex. When we fool around, he gets so hard it must hurt, but he won't let me go any further than stroking him. I should appreciate how considerate he's being, but I also really, really want to fuck Hayden.

"Your wicked way?" He bites his lip, eyes going hot. "What did you have in mind? Cake sitting? Wizard role play? Sexy tickling?"

"Sexy *tickling*?" I repeat in amused horror. "I was thinking more along the lines of pushing you onto your bed and riding your cock until we both come hard."

He stares at me, speechless, and there's a tremor of self-consciousness through me. I don't say things like this. The old Darcy didn't say things like that, at least. My nose wrinkles in hesitation as I watch Hayden's stunned reaction.

"*Fuck*." He rests his forehead against mine like he's in pain. "Please don't make me hard before I have to get changed in front of the guys."

He presses a kiss to my mouth, and I laugh, feeling lighter than air.

"Thought you said no hitting on the analysts," Luca calls from down the hall, and I dissolve into laughter against Hayden's chest. Hayden chuckles into my neck before pressing a series of quick, urgent kisses up my neck and jaw until he reaches his mouth.

"See you after," he murmurs against my lips.

"See you after."

"SHIT," I whisper as the other team scores yet another goal.

The game is a disaster, and none of the data we've provided is helping.

Their defenseman slams Hayden into the boards hard, and I'm on my feet, pressing my hands over my mouth, eyes wide. That should have been a penalty, but the ref doesn't call it. Behind the glass, fans jump to their feet, outraged and shouting at the ref. The Storm starts another play we recommended, but the other team snags the puck and scores again, and the arena deflates. Two goals in less than thirty seconds.

"So much for that play," Erik mutters, standing beside me.

The fans leave in droves, emptying the stands, and disappointment and resentment hang in the air like a thick, noxious cloud.

My lungs are so tight I can't get a full breath. It's happening again. I screwed up, and it's all my fault. From up here, I can't see Ward's face, so I flip through camera feeds on the TV until I find one of the bench. His expression gives me nothing; it's the same watchful, patient, unruffled look he always wears.

He has to be mad, though. He just hired a new analyst, and everything about this game has gone wrong.

———

When the game ends, I'm downstairs outside the Storm dressing room, waiting for Ward to finish his usual postgame debrief, nails digging into my palms.

I thought my numbers were solid, but I fucked up.

I thought this time was different, but it wasn't.

I thought I could do this, but maybe I can't.

The door swings open and Ward appears. I push off the wall, heart in my throat. "Do you have a second?"

"For you, Darcy, always." He gives me a quick smile, and my insides clench up again. "Walk with me."

We walk down the hallway, and he slows his pace so I don't have to jog to keep up with his long strides. "None of the plays worked tonight and I want to apologize. I'm going to do a full review on my own time of my data and the plays and the game to see where we went wrong. I'll get to the bottom of this before the next game."

Please just don't fire me, I beg silently.

Hesitation and worry are written all over my face, I'm sure, but I'm not ready to give it up. I just got here.

Ward lets out a heavy, frustrated exhale as we round a corner. "Volkov's injured and he didn't tell us."

My jaw drops and my eyes go wide. "What kind of injury?"

"ACL. Apparently it's been giving him trouble all week."

He had surgery on it last year. I blink about twelve times, thinking about how I'd factor this in. It changes his plays, I know that.

"The analyst team would have made different recommendations for the game," I tell Ward. "I'm not trying to sound defensive, I just—"

"I know. And Walker decided to do his own thing instead of the plays we practiced."

I missed that, but I would have caught it in my review of the game tape. Irritation singes behind my sternum. That cocky rookie.

"Don't worry, I've already torn a strip off them for that. Those two are going to figure out how to work together if it kills them." The corner of his mouth tips like he's looking forward to it, before he gives me a patient look. "You were working on bad data. It's not your fault."

It wasn't my fault. I didn't screw up. I did the best with the information I had. Relief settles through me, and my blood pressure descends to normal.

"It was a bad game, Darcy." Ward shrugs. "We learn from it and we do our best, but we're not going to let one night knock us down. That's how one game turns into a losing streak." He holds my eyes. "We fall down, but we get back up and try again tomorrow. Understood?"

Something in his words and the way he believes in not just his team, but me as well, bolsters me. "Understood."

"Good." He gestures down the hall. "I'm wanted in postgame press."

He waves goodbye and I stand there, replaying the conversation. It wasn't my fault. I did my due diligence. Losing isn't the end of the world. No one got hurt, and no one's career is over.

"Darcy."

I look up to see Alexei standing there, the hard lines of his face arranged in an expression that almost looks like remorse.

That irritation from earlier is back. "Ward said you're injured."

He grunts an acknowledgment, and the irritation doubles. He works his jaw, glancing around before he lowers his voice. "My knee. An old injury."

He probably didn't let it heal properly and now has long-term issues. The way he played during the game begins to make sense.

"I can't do my job without accurate data. I could have helped you. Why didn't you say something?"

He hesitates, blowing out a heavy breath, not meeting my eyes.

In his midthirties, he's one of the oldest defensemen in the league, and now he's being paired up with Luca, a fresh young rookie, full of energy and free of injury. Plus, all the comments about his impending retirement.

He doesn't want the coaches to know he's injured because they'll trade him, or worse, not renew his contract. For an older player like him, it's a career death sentence.

"You want to retire on your own terms. You want it to be your choice." I can relate.

"I'm sorry I didn't tell you." He gives me a tight nod before he starts to walk away, limping a little.

"Maybe I can look into it."

He stops and turns, frowning.

"I use data to find solutions." My mind whirs and spins with all the ways I could adjust the plays.

For a moment, he looks like he's about to turn me down, but his features relax. "That would be great. Thanks." He gives me a nod and lifts his arm like he's about to clap me on the shoulder. When our eyes meet, he frowns and jerks his hand back.

I hold back the laugh. "We're friends." I shrug and give him a smile. "That's what friends do."

He dips his chin. "Friends." He turns before he stops himself. "About the double date."

"I know you just asked me out to make Hayden jealous."

He gives me a guilty sidelong look. "He needed a push."

Even though I'm perfectly pleased with what happened as

a result of the double date, I roll my eyes. "The guys are right about you, you know. That you think you know best."

He makes a low noise that might be a laugh. "I do know best."

"Yeah, yeah." I grin. "Whatever."

Hayden appears at the other end of the hall, heading toward us.

"See you at the bar?" Alexei asks.

I nod. "See you there."

As he passes Hayden, Alexei claps him on the shoulder, and Hayden's expression flickers with tension.

"Hey." I lean up to give him a quick kiss. "Rough game."

He sighs. My heart aches for him because I know how hard he's trying not to let the loss get to him.

"Rough game, but we're going to the Filthy Flamingo to celebrate Walker's first night with the team. We're going to shake it off."

"Sounds good to me."

We start walking down the long concourse to the exit. I lean against his shoulder but catch the muted wince as he sucks in a sharp breath. I frown up at him. "What's wrong?"

A tight shake of his head. "Nothing."

My eyes move over him, studying the tension in his shoulders. "You're hurt." I stop walking. "That hit from the third period."

He waves me off, pulling my hand to keep walking. "I'm fine. Let's have fun."

I poke his shoulder and he stifles a groan of pain. "See? *Hayden*. You need to go home and rest."

"I'll rest later." He winks, but it feels forced. "It's Walker's first game. We need to celebrate. I can't bail. The team needs me there."

"The team needs you to take care of yourself."

He presses his mouth into a tight line, glancing down the hall where we came from as more players leave the dressing room, talking and laughing.

He's always the life of the party, ensuring other people have fun. I think about how we've fooled around up until now —always Hayden pleasing me, him putting his needs second.

"We're going home and I'm putting you to bed," I tell him, surprising myself with how firm I sound. "And I'm going to take care of you."

The strong line of his throat moves as he swallows and meets my eye, letting out a heavy breath.

"Please?" I ask.

He gives me a quick nod. "Okay."

Relief loosens the worry in my chest, and I rise up on my toes, careful not to touch his shoulder, and press a soft kiss to his cheek. His skin is warm and scratchy with stubble.

"Thank you," I whisper. "Now let's go home."

IN HIS BEDROOM, Hayden carefully pulls his t-shirt over his head before tossing it onto the chair. His hands come to his belt.

"I'll do it." I push his hands aside, and he lets out a long, heavy exhale, watching me with heat flickering behind the exhaustion in his eyes.

I unbuckle his belt, and emotion expands in my chest. My fingers slip into the waistband of his boxers. When I push them off, his erection springs free, and my mouth waters.

Hayden's cock is beautiful. It's long and thick, more than what I'm used to and a little intimidating, but the muscles between my legs clench in anticipation.

I wrap my hand around it and his breath stutters. Beneath my fingers, his length is hard like steel.

"You're so warm." My other hand comes to his balls, and he lets out a rough exhale.

"Darce." His hand covers mine, pausing my movements.

"Do you want me to stop?"

"Fuck no." Our eyes meet, a question rising in his.

He's not used to being put first. All those years supporting others, making sure others are okay and having fun.

"Let me get you off first," he says.

I shake my head. "Not tonight." I give him a soft, encouraging smile, gripping his cock a fraction harder, and his eyelids dip. "Please?"

He laughs, probably because he's learning at the same time that I am that he has no defense against me when I use that word.

"Okay. If you're sure."

"I am really"—I give him a long stroke, and his breath hitches—"really, sure."

"Can you take the jersey off?"

My mouth curves. "What's the matter, you don't like it?"

He huffs a tight laugh. "I like it. I really fucking like it, I just—" He rakes a hand through his hair, hesitating. "I like your tits more. I spent a long time picturing them before." He swallows, pupils tipping black. "Years."

My pulse throbs between my legs, and my mind spins with the high of being wanted by Hayden like this. Slowly, I pull the jersey over my head, then my sweater and t-shirt. I take my jeans off at a criminally slow rate, fizzing with delight at the tortured, desperate look on Hayden's handsome face as I stand there in a new lingerie set—a dark maroon and sheer enough for him to see the pinched, aching points of my nipples. A tiny bow is sewn between my breasts, and when his eyes land on it, I know he wants to tug it with his teeth.

"How's this?" I whisper.

He just swallows, staring at my body with a pained look. His cock twitches against his stomach, beading with moisture.

His eyes lift to mine, dark and drugged, and he swallows again. "New?"

I smile. "Yes. You bought this for me." A couple of mornings ago, he left a gift card for the lingerie store on the kitchen counter for me.

He works his jaw, tracing the lines of the lingerie over my chest and shoulders, then down to my hips and thighs. His breathing is ragged and uneven, his broad and chiseled chest rising and falling fast.

"Do you like it?" My fingers trail over the lace bra cup.

He follows my movements, nodding, and I bite my lip. I love toying with him like this.

"Do you want to come with me to the shop some time and help me pick a few things out?"

He nods again, and I try not to chuckle at the way his erection pulses. I picture us shopping for lingerie, Hayden shoving the velvet curtain of the dressing room aside and slipping his fingers inside my panties, whispering at me to be quiet so the others in the store don't overhear as he makes me come.

"Do you think you could sit nicely outside the dressing room while I tried on lacy things?"

With a helpless expression, he shakes his head. I laugh.

His mouth tilts in a boyish, playful grin. "Take it off, please."

Hayden's gaze follows my every movement as I slip my bra and thong off, until I'm standing naked in front of him, goosebumps rising on my skin under the weight of his adoring gaze.

I wish we could do this forever, but I know we can't. That isn't who he is, isn't what he wants.

I wish things were different, though.

"You are so fucking beautiful, Darcy," he says, like a curse and a prayer. "I've always thought that."

My skin flushes, and my gaze drops to the wide expanse of his chest. A red and purple bruise is already blooming under the skin on his shoulder, and worry lodges in my throat. Once he gets in bed, I'm not letting him out of it. He's going to sleep for twelve hours, minimum.

First, though, I'm going to make him come so hard he passes

out. So hard he remembers it for years, long after we're done. My knees hit the floor and he mutters an *oh, fuck*. I just smile. It's time for Hayden to get the attention he deserves.

At an unhurried pace, I brush my lips up and down his length, looking up at him through my lashes. His skin is scorching hot and velvet soft. His cock is so hard my ego gets a permanent boost. And when my tongue darts out to taste the bead of moisture at his tip, a moan tears out of him.

That look of disbelief he's wearing, like this is the best thing to happen to him? I'm drunk on it.

I take him between my lips and slide my tongue along his length. His eyelids fall heavy with his rushed exhale. I let him bump the back of my throat, and he groans, low and needy, before I add suction, keeping him there. At his sides, his hands flex and clench. I reach for one and place it on my head.

His gaze burns hotter. His other hand settles on the back of my head, and heat wavers through me. I love being in this position, kneeling before him, letting him know how much I want him and how special and important he is to me. I pull back, sucking the swollen head, and he winces like the pleasure is too much. Around his thick circumference, I smile.

He hasn't seen anything yet.

My hand wraps around his base and slowly, so freaking slowly, I suck Hayden's cock. His brow is damp with sweat. His breath saws in and out of his chest, and his fingers tense against my scalp as he struggles to keep his eyes open and on me. If it's anything like this when Hayden goes down on me, I completely understand why he said *your pleasure is my pleasure*.

"God, your mouth is heaven," he moans with tortured hunger in his eyes.

I add even more suction, dragging my flattened tongue over the sensitive underside, studying how his muscles tense.

His eyes burn me as I take him all the way to the back of my throat. His jaw clenches and the eye contact between us is like an electric current crackling through me.

His hips tilt, pushing him deeper into my mouth as I move up and down his length. Eventually, he takes over, fucking my mouth slow and steady with a tight jaw and dark eyes, making the dirtiest, neediest noises. Each moan sends moisture pooling between my legs, and if I were to reach down and run my fingers over myself, I'd come within a minute.

His fingers tighten in my hair; his breathing is uneven, and for a brief moment, he looks up at the ceiling like he's praying.

"I'm close," he begs. "So fucking close."

So I slow down.

I THINK I'm going to die.

I've never had a blow job like this, so leisurely but intense, loving, and intimate. I'm on the brink of coming, but Darcy won't let me. She holds back, keeping me right at the edge, searing every thought in my brain with the lust racing through me. At the base of my spine, pleasure gathers, hot and tight.

All I can see is her.

Darcy's gorgeous like an angel, on her knees for me, laving attention and pleasure upon me. It's never been like this. I'm never coming down from the high of this moment, never forgetting how perfect she looks, how soft and sweet she is.

Her hand works me steadily, adding to the overwhelming sensation. I gather her hair and wind it around my fist, gentle not to pull but firm enough to hold her head still while my hips speed up. I'm so fucking careful with her. Around my cock, she hums, eyes closing like she loves this, and on her arms, all the hairs stand on end.

It's all I need to stumble closer to the edge. My body seizes up, muscles tightening, pulse pounding in my ears.

"Coming," I choke out, unable to control the movement of

my hips as I hold her head. "I really want to come in your mouth," I gasp, balls tightening. "Is that okay?"

"Mhm," she murmurs around me with warmth and affection in her eyes, and the last thread of my control snaps.

Her mouth is too perfect, too warm and soft and wet, and the way her tongue swirls over the head of my cock melts my brain. My head falls back as I come, eyes clenched tight, hot pressure spiraling up my legs and squeezing the base of my spine like a tight fist. I jerk my head up just in time to see her swallowing me down, eyes on me, the hot, slick slide of her tongue rubbing the underside of my cock. It's an orgasm that lasts and lasts as she sucks me through it, drags me to the edge of sanity and back with that perfect mouth.

"God, you're so good." I can't take my eyes off her. "Such a good girl."

She hums again, slowing down as my brain puts itself back together.

My eyes prick with tears, and I don't know whether it's because of how hard I just came or because Darcy's sweet, caring attention makes me feel whole for the first time in my life.

"Come here." I pull her up to standing and into my chest, still catching my breath against her temple, inhaling her sweet scent. Can she feel my heart pounding? Can she see her name etched across it in her loopy, feminine writing? I wrap my arms tight around her, holding her to me.

"Thank you," I whisper against her hairline. It feels so inadequate, but she raises up on her toes and catches my mouth.

"It was my pleasure."

Warmth and pressure grow in my chest, demanding attention.

"That was the most effective painkiller I've ever had." I don't even feel the pain in my shoulder.

"I thought it might help." She scores her teeth over my pec with a playful grin. "Get in bed," she says gently, pressing her hands to my waist to push me back. I sit down on the mattress, hands framing her waist, pressing my lips to the curve beneath her breast in slow, snipping kisses.

She brings her hands to my hair and drags them through it, sending tingles down my spine.

"Not tonight." She steps away, out of my reach, and pulls back the duvet and gestures for me to get in. Off my alarmed, questioning look—she's not actually going to try to sleep in her bed tonight, right?—she grins again. "I'm going to get you some ice and painkillers. You'll thank me tomorrow."

My instincts protest, because I've never walked away from an intimate experience without ensuring my partner is satisfied, but she just smiles again.

"Tonight was about you," she says.

I sink against the pillows, staring at her in confusion. "Are you sure?"

"Mhm." Her eyes are warm and soft, hair spilling around her shoulders, and my heart tugs.

This is new to me, being put first like this. Not being expected to perform. For Darcy, I'm eager to make her happy, but there's a buried, broken part of me that's still terrified it's my only value.

Maybe Darcy's different, though. If anyone is, it's her.

She heads to the kitchen and I lie in bed, catching my breath, listening to my heart beat in my ears and the soft sounds of Darcy filling a glass of water, then opening and closing the freezer before she returns. She settles the ice pack, wrapped in a towel, across my shoulder and hands me the painkillers and a glass of water, supervising with a protective and worried expression as I take them.

"I'm okay," I tell her with a small smile. "I've been hit before. It's part of the job."

Her throat works, and she climbs into bed beside me, taking care not to touch me, but I pull her against me. "I know. Doesn't mean I like watching it happen, though. And doesn't mean I'm not going to take care of you."

She rests her head on the pillow and I bring her hand to my mouth, giving her fingers a kiss. When I release them, she skims them up and down the uninjured side of my chest in a calming, lazy motion that slows my thoughts.

"Is this part for me or for you?" I ask, and she chuckles.

"Be quiet," she murmurs.

I love her, I realize. I've loved her for years. Maybe since she walked into English class that first week of university, or the first conversation we had about *The Northern Sword*, or the first time I opened my blinds and screamed at the weird gnome peering into the window while she collapsed on my bed, laughing her ass off.

Or maybe I fell a little in love with her every time I saw her, every time we laughed together or texted or hugged, until I was at full capacity and head over fucking heels for her.

When she showed up in Vancouver, newly single and eager to start fresh, I never stood a chance. That I even thought I could pretend my feelings didn't exist, or that we were just friends, is fucking laughable.

She's always been the girl for me.

My mind flicks to the text from Kit. "We're playing Calgary next week." It's our last game of the season.

Her fingers still on my chest. "I know."

"Kit wants to have a drink and catch up the night before."

She lifts her head, meeting my eyes with concern. "What do you want to do?"

A long pause. "I want to set the record straight with him, and I want to tell him about us."

Her eyes linger on me with uncertainty before she nods. "Okay."

She settles her head against my chest and closes her eyes.

I've got my priorities straight now. Kit may be Darcy's past, but I'm her future.

CHAPTER 62
DARCY

ON THE MORNING of my birthday, Hayden wakes me up with slow, lazy kisses down my body before he makes me beg for release with his head between my legs.

"Do you want your present now or later?" he asks after, lounging on the bed beside me, looking like a Greek god in the morning light.

"Is it that we can finally have sex?"

He chuckles. "No. Not yet."

I groan with frustration. His tongue on my clit is heaven, but I need so much more from him. I want to feel connected in the ultimate way. A little part of me is grumpy—he's slept with every girl in town, but not me?

What's going on?

I shove the thoughts from my head. "I'd like the present now, please."

He moves closer, pressing a kiss between my breasts, nipping the sensitive skin. "Are you sure?"

I laugh, squirming away from him. "Yes, now."

"Okay, okay." He slides off the bed and I get to admire his magnificent ass as he heads into his closet. He returns a moment later with a small package.

"What could it be?" I muse, narrowing my eyes at him where he's settling against the headboard as I slide my fingernail under the tape. "It's clearly a book. *Dating for Total Losers*, maybe?"

His gaze is steady and warm. "You're not a loser."

"*How to Pick Up Guys, Bring Them Home, and Bang Their Brains Out*?"

His grin widens. "You don't have any trouble getting me into bed."

I laugh, pulling off the remaining wrapping. "Kama Sutra, maybe—oh."

My jaw drops. *The Emerald Queen* by A.R. Haddington. It's the next book in *The Northern Sword* series, due to be released later this year.

It can't be.

"How did—" I give Hayden a searching look, but he just smiles wider. "Hayden. How?"

It's impossible to get an early copy. A.R. Haddington's publisher doesn't send out early copies for fear of spoilers leaking. Tickets to the midnight release parties for her new books are sold out the day they go on sale.

"Who did you kill to get this?"

He lets out a tight laugh, and there's something in his expression that catches my attention, like he's nervous. "Is it too much?"

"No." I shake my head hard. "I love it." I flip the cover open to check the print date, and my pulse halts at the loopy signature on the title page. "Oh my god."

For Darcy, brave like The Northern Sword.
  - A.R. Haddington

. . .

I blink at it, stunned.

"Hayden." My voice sounds strange. She's notoriously reclusive. No social media, no public appearances. No one knows what she looks like, what her initials stand for, or even what country she lives in, and she definitely doesn't sign books. "Seriously. How did you get this?"

He lifts his big shoulder in a casual shrug, but a pleased smile toys at his mouth. "I pulled a couple strings."

"This is *The Devil Wears Prada* level of pulling strings. What did you do?"

"I had the Storm PR team reach out to the publisher. I told her about you."

"Who?"

He tilts his chin at the book. "A.R. Haddington."

"No."

He laughs. "Yes. I told her how we met in school and bonded over the book series, and how we've been friends for years. I told her about you finally leaving your boring insurance job for an analytics job with the Storm and how you're the only woman in the room at work but you're brave and smart and passionate about what you do." He glances away, and it feels like there's a part he isn't telling me. "I made a donation to her favorite charity, too."

"How much?"

He just shrugs, smiling.

"Hayden." I lean forward and give him a hard look, but I'm smiling. "*How much?*"

He squints. "I don't remember."

"You are such a liar," I whisper, heart beating out of my chest with affection and warmth and big, intense feelings for Hayden Owens.

I try to say words, but I have none. My heart pounds as I run my fingertip over the signature.

It's the best gift I've ever gotten. It's the best gift I could have even imagined. Only Hayden would get me something like this, something I didn't even know I wanted.

Only Hayden sees me like this.

"Thank you," I manage, and my eyes sting, sharp and sudden. "Sorry." I turn away, blinking away the tears.

Immediately, he reaches for me, turning me back to him with strong, warm hands. "Hey, hey." His voice is gentle, calming, making it so much worse. "It's okay. Come here."

He pulls me against his chest, his comforting scent and the warm planes of his torso flooding my senses. He trails slow strokes against my back while I lean into him.

"So I guess you like it?"

I huff a laugh. "Yes, Hayden. I like it. I think I like it more than anything else I own." I glance at my wrist, at the bracelet I only take off to shower. "Or just as much as the bracelet."

A low, pleased noise rumbles against my cheek. "Good."

We lie there for a long moment, looking out the window in comfortable silence.

"We're going for dinner tonight," Hayden says, "but how do you want to spend the rest of the day?"

"With you."

He makes a low noise of appreciation and presses a kiss to my forehead. "I was hoping you'd say that."

"And Daniel, of course."

"Sure, I'll find a bag of rocks and we can take him for a swim in the ocean."

We laugh, and I can feel his grin against my hairline. My lips linger on his warm stubble before I press a trail of kisses along his jaw and down his neck to his collarbones. His breathing turns ragged, and a moment later, his hand twines in my hair.

"What are you up to, Andersen?" he asks in a low, teasing voice.

I smile at him, climbing on top of him so I'm straddling his hips. His erection presses between my legs and his eyes darken. I begin my own trail of kisses down his chest and stomach, and his breathing turns ragged.

"I want to thank you properly."

"THIS IS where I wanted to take you back in university," Hayden admits that evening from across the tiny table at the cozy family-run Italian restaurant. A candle sits between us, flicking warm light all over the handsome lines of his face, and his gaze on me is steady and kind. I'm wearing a light pink dress that reminds me of the cherry blossoms we saw today.

"What do you mean?"

He smiles, but it's tight and nervous, and I tilt my head, intrigued.

"The first week of school, I wanted to ask you out. I planned to ask you out at the party that first weekend," he amends, rubbing the back of his neck.

My lips part in surprise. That first week of school, I looked forward to class and seeing Hayden, my new friend who loved *The Northern Sword*, had muscles carved from stone, and had an open, affectionate smile. Despite how handsome and popular he was—everyone already seemed to know him, probably from hockey—and knowing he was hilariously out of my league, I felt so at ease and comfortable with him from the start.

"The hockey party."

He nods.

I had hoped he would ask me out that week. I thought Kit was inviting me to the party as friends, but when I got there, he made it seem like we were more, and I went along with it. Hayden didn't seem to care; he was chatting with other girls all night, and although I was disappointed, I didn't give it too much attention.

I've thought back to that week so many times over the years, but I've always told myself I wasn't Hayden's type.

"I thought you were going to ask me out, too." I look down at the white tablecloth, remembering. "I hoped you would. I guess I could have asked you out, but you were so out of my league that it seemed like a great opportunity for rejection." My mouth twists. "And it would have made things awkward, with us being in the same class all semester."

He leans forward and takes my hand. "I was never out of your league. Just the opposite."

"I was the dorky math girl and you were the hot hockey player who could have anyone."

"That's not how I see it."

My heart lodges in my throat, and I'm swept away in the happy, floaty feelings. I love the way he looks at me, like I'm everything to him.

I want to say something like *it all worked out in the end*, but I don't know if it will. He's trying his hand at this relationship thing.

What if I'm the girl who always got away, but once he has me, he realizes the idea of me was better than the reality?

He smiles, holding my eyes, and the server swings by with my dessert. A single candle sits in the middle of the chocolate torte, dancing and flickering.

"Happy birthday, Darcy," Hayden says, watching me with a smile, brushing his thumb over the back of my hand. "Make a wish."

I close my eyes, think about the past few months with Hayden, and wish that it *will* work out in the end.

———

"Have I told you how beautiful you are?" Hayden asks as we walk home hand in hand.

I laugh. "A few times."

"Only a few?" His mouth curves but his expression turns watchful and serious. "How are you feeling about your birthday?"

Right. My goal of figuring everything out by my birthday.

"Great, surprisingly." I take a big breath and gather my thoughts. "I think I always dreaded my birthday because deep down, I knew I was on the wrong path. The wrong job, the wrong guy."

I don't have everything figured out, especially not with Hayden, but my life feels a lot better than it did this time last year.

"I wish I could go back to myself a few months ago, give her a big hug, and tell her everything would be okay." With a little smile, I nudge him. "I guess you did that."

"You didn't believe me?" His eyes glint.

"I wasn't sure. I needed to prove it to myself."

"And you did."

I hum a happy acknowledgment, taking in the man beside me, heart squeezing with something warm and intense. "Yeah. I did. I'm so lucky to have you."

He stops walking, holds my gaze, and swallows. It looks like he wants to say something, but instead, he glances behind me.

Oh. We're at the entrance to the small side street where the Filthy Flamingo is.

"Let's get a drink, birthday girl."

I nod, smiling. "Sure. Let's go say hi to Jordan."

Hayden pulls his phone out and sends a quick text, then he takes my hand again and leads me down the alley. When we reach the bar with the unmarked door, he holds it open, but it's dark inside. I hesitate in the doorway.

"I think it's closed." On a Friday night? That's weird. There are no windows in the bar, so I can't see a thing. "Did Jordan forget to lock the front door? We should call her."

"Turn the goddamned light on," someone grumbles in the dark, and I jump out of my skin. It sounds like Alexei...

The lights flick on and my jaw drops at the bar full of people and balloons.

"HAPPY BIRTHDAY!" they shout, and Hayden wraps his arms around me from behind, hugging me to him.

I stand there, blinking. The entire Vancouver Storm team and their partners fill the bar, and everyone is in costume.

"We were going to do the party next week, when everyone has time off." I sound dazed, and a little breathless.

Hayden shrugs, smiling. "Wouldn't be much of a surprise then, would it?"

Most of the women are in long, flowing medieval-looking dresses, except for Hazel, who looks like Robin Hood with a sword strapped across her back and a scar drawn down the side of her face. Pippa beams at me, her long, wavy hair sprayed white and her eyelashes coated in frost. Tiny sparrows are pinned into her hair. Georgia wears a long emerald-green cloak, her hair piled on top of her head and arranged around a diadem. In the middle of the diadem, a ruby sparkles.

Wait. I know that costume.

"This is a *Northern Sword* dress-up party?" I ask Hayden, eyes going even wider.

Georgia's dressed like Queen Amethyst, the main character in *The Emerald Queen*. Hazel is clearly Ren, the kidnapped princess. Rory's in tight black pants and a black shirt, open to mid-chest, tattoos drawn on his chest, neck, and the side of his face—Weston, Ren's laconic, arrogant rival and kidnapper, who ends up being her fated mate after she stabs him in an attempt to escape. Alexei wears a black mask over his eyes and a leather harness with prop knives in it—Piers, the warrior. Jamie's knight costume is Torsten, Ren's responsible and uptight brother. And Pippa is Magnolia, the lonely, soft-hearted ice queen.

Even Jordan behind the bar wears pointed ears someone probably wrangled her into. She's Carrot, I think, the wry, all-seeing barkeep.

"Well?" Georgia gestures at her costume, hand on her hip. "Did we nail it or what?"

My lips part and I make a strangled noise, smiling. A few people chuckle.

"I don't have a costume," I say stupidly, but Hayden just grins and reaches into a nearby duffel bag before pulling a crown out and placing it on his head.

"You're Prince Cadius." I sound dazed as I stare up at him. He looks so perfect and right with the crown on top of his slightly mussed hair.

He looks just like I envisioned the character when I read the books, before Patrick Grant was cast as him on the show. Golden blond, more handsome than I thought possible, and smiling ear to ear.

"Mhm." He wraps a red cloak around his shoulders. After rummaging back in the bag, he pulls out a slinky, silvery cape.

I stand there in awe as he drapes it around me.

"And you"—he lifts another crown, this one more delicate and spindly, with sparkling gemstones—"are Aurora." He places it on my head; it's so much lighter than I would have expected.

Aurora, the Secret Queen. The loyal, brave maid who rescues her kidnapped princess. The one everyone underestimated. Pride and delight clench in my chest at stepping into the shoes of my favorite character.

His crown, his cape, *my* cape. "These props look so real."

"I messaged the cast and they hooked me up with the wardrobe department."

"*Shut up!*" My hands fly to the crown on my head. "This is the one she actually wore on the show? Shut up."

There are rumors A.R. Haddington worked directly with the props department to design the props.

"Except for Volkov." Georgia smirks, gesturing at his leather harness. "He brought those from his personal collection."

He glares at her before turning to me. "These are also props. Happy birthday."

I roll my lips so I don't laugh. Every fan of the series hopes Queen Amethyst and Piers finally hook up in *The Emerald Queen.* "You all look amazing. Thank you so much. I—" My words break off as I choke up. "I didn't expect this."

Someone turns the music back on, and as the laughter and conversation resume, I take in all the people gathered in the bar for my birthday. I've built a life for myself here in Vancouver. I have people. Hayden kisses my cheek, grinning against my skin, and I lean back against his chest, beaming.

The door opens, and we turn.

Luca waltzes in wearing his Storm jersey and a waist-length, wavy pale-purple wig. Everyone goes silent and stares at him.

"Sorry I'm late." He shoots me a quick, boyish grin. "Girl trouble." His gaze lifts to my crown and he smiles wider. "Birthday crown. I like it. Happy birthday, Darcy."

"Thanks, Luca." I cover my mouth to stifle my laughter at his growing confusion as he notices everyone's costumes.

"What are you wearing?" Alexei demands.

Luca gestures at his wig. "I'm Darcy. Look." He turns, and his name on the back of the jersey is covered in masking tape, with the letters OWENS written in black marker.

Alexei stares at him. "Why?"

"You said we're dressing up as Darcy."

"I said we're dressing up as *Darcy's favorite TV show.*"

Georgia's laughing so hard she has to grip my arm to hold herself up. "Walker, you look like a mermaid."

Luca shoots me a quick grin, not the least embarrassed. "Sorry."

I shake my head, smiling wide and laughing. "Nothing to be sorry about, Luca. You look great."

"Right?" He bobs his head, making the wig dance. "I'm feeling this hair."

Hayden tugs me to the bar to get a drink and my gaze catches on the chalkboard with the daily specials. A pink cocktail is drawn with an umbrella and a scribbly something above it.

The Darcy - bright, sweet, bubbly, and surprisingly strong!

My heart squeezes.

"A special drink? For me?" I beam at the sign, then glance at Hayden in surprise. He just grins and winks. "Really?"

"It was Georgia's idea," Jordan says with a small smile, filling a cocktail shaker.

My heart warms with affection and I look back up at the sign. "What's the thing beside the umbrella?"

"A sparkler," she says with a defensive edge, like it's not the first time someone has asked. She tucks something on the rim of my glass, clicks a lighter, and pulls her hand back as a sphere of sparks bursts from the drink. My eyes are probably glowing.

"Like it?" Jordan asks with a wry smirk.

I lean back against Hayden, smiling so hard my cheeks hurt, as he presses a kiss to my neck. "Love it."

Later, I sit with Hayden at the bar, watching our friends enjoy the party. Between challenging people to fake sword fights, Rory keeps unbuttoning his shirt lower to make Hazel roll her eyes and laugh. Pippa's perched on Jamie's lap in the corner while he murmurs in her ear. Georgia and Alexei stay on opposite sides of the bar.

It's the best birthday I've ever had.

"I feel like I'm made of rainbows," I tell Hayden.

He shakes with laughter. "I thought you've only had two of those drinks."

"I have. I'm not drunk." I shrug and give him what's probably a very goofy smile, memorizing this moment. "I'm just happy. Thank you." I move closer so our thighs touch, then rest my hand on his.

"What makes you think I had anything to do with this?" He arches a teasing brow, and I roll my eyes, smiling wider.

With his fingers beneath my chin, he tips my mouth up to his and kisses me so soft and sweet my heart dips.

"Happy birthday, Darcy," he says against my lips.

CHAPTER 65

HAYDEN

THE NEXT NIGHT, I walk into the quiet bar near the hotel Kit's staying in, adrenaline already pounding through me. My gaze sweeps over the tables until I spot him.

He looks rough. Dark circles under his eyes and a sunken look to his face. The server drops a beer off and Kit drains half of it.

He isn't having a good season. His contract with Calgary is ending this year, and more than ever, he needs to keep his stats up, but they're down. Tonight's news won't help, I'm sure, but just remembering Darcy's devastated expression the night he called, or as she told me what he did on New Year's, sends a fresh wave of fury and protectiveness through me.

At my arrival, he straightens up. "Hey."

"Hey." I slip into the seat across from him, setting my phone on the table. He slides the menu to me and I shake my head. "I'm not staying long."

He frowns. "Thought we're getting a drink."

"Darcy and I are together now." No point in beating around the bush.

His jaw goes slack and he stares at me for a moment before

he lets out a sharp laugh. "Sorry, I thought you said you and Darcy are together."

"That's what I said. Darcy and I are dating. I'm serious about her."

My throat knots. I want forever with her.

A.R. Haddington sent me the signed advance copy because I told her I loved Darcy, that I've loved her for years. In a private note to me, she wished me luck.

Kit lets out another humorless, bitter laugh. "Well, that's going to be a fucking disaster. What, you got tired of the puck bunnies?"

Adrenaline cuts into me, coursing through my blood, and my teeth clench.

"You slept with every chick in Vancouver, so now you're messing around with Darcy?" He shakes his head, swallowing. "Is this an ego thing? Fuck my girl just to show you can?"

Shame hardens in my gut, but I remind myself I'm not that guy. He's hurt and angry, but my head pounds with all the things he did, all the ways he made her feel like she wasn't enough, and I want to hit him.

I won't, though, because just like Darce, I'm putting him in the past.

"She's not your girl anymore." My teeth grit. "And it's not like that."

"Come on." His lip curls. "Yes, it is. You'll be done with her in a week, tops."

Pain throbs behind my sternum. "Have you even stopped to wonder if this is what Darcy wants? Don't you fucking see?" I shake my head. "She's doing so much better now that you're out of her life. She actually likes her life. She's an analyst for the Storm and she actually enjoys her job."

His face twists. "You can't be serious."

Rage thunders through me. He never believed in her. "She

has the statistics background and experience for it, and she loves it. The team is lucky to have her. *I* am lucky to have her. You never felt that way, though, did you? You felt like you were doing her a favor."

Tension simmers in the air. He looks away, working his jaw.

"The difference between us," I tell him, "is that I'll do whatever it takes to make her happy."

He breaks off in a laugh of disbelief, shaking his head. "You fucking snake. You always had a thing for her. You were just waiting to swoop in. I'm surprised you didn't try this years ago."

The insult burns—I would never go after my friend's girl-friend—but he's hurt and angry and trying to get to me.

I love her. My realization from the other day rings stronger than ever, but it feels wrong telling him before Darcy.

"You had your chance, and you fucked up." My voice is low and firm. "You knew she didn't want to get engaged, and yet you popped the question in front of everyone." I lean forward, pulse picking up. "You pressured her into something she didn't want to do."

Kit's nostrils flare. "Oh yeah, her life would have been so hard." Sarcasm and bitterness drip from his tone. "Married to a professional hockey player who makes millions per year, living in a nice place, having the wedding of her dreams. Poor Darcy."

Anger rises, because even now, even after she's broken up with him several times and told him she doesn't want that life, he doesn't get it. He never will.

"I know how hard losing her must be, but it's time to move on."

A bitter smile twists onto his mouth. "I guess you think it's your turn now or something."

"No." I swallow. "It's Darcy's turn. You never saw her. You never bragged about her. You didn't know what you had."

He laughs, shaking his head. "You think this is going to work. Unbelievable."

His tone scrapes at me, and my muscles tense as I try to remember the way she tucked me into bed with an ice pack on my shoulder, lifting it off me after twenty minutes as I fell deeper into sleep, caring for me.

She cares about me. I know she does. She just needs time, and she's shown me that I'm more than the guy everyone thinks I am.

Having said what I came here to say, I get to my feet. "See you at the game tomorrow."

He doesn't answer as I walk out the door.

———

The next evening, we're winning by three goals, because Kit's more focused on letting out his frustration on me than defending the Calgary net.

He slashes his stick against my shin, but Walker shoves him out of the way. That slash should have been a penalty, but the whistle doesn't sound. A minute later, he's back. Volkov blocks him, knocking him down, and the crowd cheers.

Player targeting happens sometimes when a team wants to take the other team's star out. This isn't about me scoring goals, though.

This is personal.

"What the fuck are you doing?" one of Calgary's players asks Kit. At their bench, the coach shakes his head, frowning.

"Say the word," Volkov mutters, glaring at Kit, features tight with tension.

Volkov's the Storm's enforcer—an unofficial term given to the guy who restores balance on the team and protects players the other team is going after.

This isn't his battle to fight, though. It's mine.

"Are we going to put this fucking clown in his place or what?" Miller asks, skating over.

My gaze lifts to the box where I know Darcy and the other analysts are watching the game.

Fighting's common in hockey. It's a way to restore balance in the game when a team plays dirty or refs aren't calling penalties. My muscles tense with fury. The energy crackles; I want to end this.

It would upset her, though.

I look back to Kit, who's lost her because of his own stupidity.

I have everything, and he has nothing. I pity him. He's hurt and angry and confused, and he doesn't know how to deal with it.

"Ignore him. The ref will call a penalty eventually."

We face off again, and a minute later, as I'm scrambling for the puck, I'm slammed face-first into the boards.

Fire sears my lip. Rage vibrates through my chest, growing and gathering. I take a deep breath as I get to my feet, blood dripping from my face onto the ice. Noise erupts around me— the fans pounding their fists on the glass in outrage, my teammates shouting protests, the whistle blowing.

The arena's going wild as I meet Kit's gaze. He's surrounded by Vancouver players, refs, and linesmen, but his attention is focused on me.

His eyes flash; this isn't the guy I grew up with, my best friend from university. This is someone else.

"You're a fucking embarrassment," I spit out.

"You think she's not going to do the same thing to you?" His lip curls in an ugly sneer. "Why would she end up with you?"

With a linesman between them, Volkov tries to shove Kit. "Shut up."

Tension simmers on the ice as the refs review the play on their screens. Players circle each other. Finally, the ref skates to center ice and the arena falls quiet as he clicks his mic on.

"Five-minute major for boarding."

The arena cheers, and Kit sends me another dirty look over his shoulder as he's escorted to the penalty box.

I try to summon empathy for the guy, but I'm not going to pretend I'm the same person I was a couple of months ago.

Darcy's mine. He needs to get over that.

The game resumes, and we run a play Darcy and the other analysts recommended to Ward. Miller passes to me, I shoot the puck, and it hits the back of the net. Noise erupts in the arena, the goal horn bellows, and lights flash as Miller, Volkov, Walker, and our other forward surround me to celebrate.

"I love proving her right," I yell to Volkov over the noise, grinning ear to ear.

My gaze meets Kit's in the penalty box and his nostrils flare. I stand taller, straightening my shoulders, and level him with a challenging look.

I won, my eyes say. *You lost and you're done.*

In a shot, he's out of the box, charging at me. I hear the fans gasp. He still has forty seconds on the penalty clock.

"Are you fucking serious?" Walker crows, laughing. "This guy's got a death wish. Owens, what did you do?"

Game isn't even in play, and the ref starts blowing the whistle, but Kit's undeterred, skating hard at me. The rest of the Calgary team watches in apprehension.

Volkov mutters something to Walker—I catch *Darcy's ex* in there—and as Kit approaches and rears his fist back, the two Storm defensemen block him, shoving him down to the ice. The fans holler again, whistles blow right and left, and even the Calgary players are hauling Kit back.

"Game misconduct penalty," the ref shouts into the mic,

and the crowd cheers. The mic is turned off, and he's yelling something at Kit. The other Calgary players are pulling him off the ice as he fights them, trying to get at me, and the fans roar. The Calgary defenseman gives Kit a hard shove from the bench to the hall.

"*Driedger, you suck!*" the fans chant as he disappears to the dressing room.

"I hope this Darcy chick is worth it," Walker says, shaking his head.

She's more than worth it—she's my entire world.

Tonight? I'm going to show her.

I can't hold off anymore.

HAYDEN FUMBLES the front door open that night, never once taking his lips off mine. He yanks his jacket off, throwing it on the floor in haste.

We've been kissing since the lobby downstairs. Something about playing against Kit has Hayden unleashed. I shouldn't feel this thrill at his possessiveness over me, but I do.

What did you say to Kit to piss him off so much? I asked Hayden after the game.

The truth, he answered.

He told him we were temporary, that means. A small twist of pain hits me in the chest. It's getting harder to accept that reality, that this is just for fun and just for a few more days.

Hayden's tongue sweeps against mine, and my thoughts and worries melt. Right here, right now. That's all that matters.

I'm not going to worry about the future when I can enjoy the present with Hayden.

He shoves my jacket off, and I can barely get enough air, we're kissing so hard. I like this side of him, where he goes after what he wants, whether that's on the ice, or right now, as he's devouring me.

"Tonight?" I gasp, and we both know what I mean.

Something's changed, and it doesn't seem like Hayden's interested in waiting anymore.

He walks me back until I bump against the wall. Then he dips his head and kisses me hard. My knees go weak at the sensation of his tongue against mine. If he didn't have me pinned against the wall, I'd be sliding to the floor. He pulls back, breathing hard and resting his forehead against mine, eyes flashing with heat.

"Tonight."

The promise in that one word has arousal pooling low in my abdomen. I close my eyes and revel in the feeling of Hayden's lips all over my skin, him tugging the neckline of my top aside to nip at my shoulder. His hands stray to the hem of my jersey, lifting.

"Naked. Now."

In this household, we no longer use full sentences. I raise my arms, and he pulls the top over my head. Then I'm pulling his off, baring his broad chest and warm skin. He tugs the fabric of my bra down so his lips can wrap around the tight point of my breast, and I struggle with his belt while he fumbles with my bra clasp. The drugging pull of his lips on my nipple has my head falling back against the wall and my eyelids dropping closed. My pulse throbs between my legs.

He makes a low, frustrated noise of urgent impatience before his mouth returns to mine and his tongue delves between my lips, like even sixty seconds was too long to go between kisses.

"I love this side of you." I huff a laugh as he gets frustrated with my bra and rips the clasp apart. "Did you just tear it?"

"Probably." A quick grin appears on his face. He's flushed and breathing hard. "I'll buy you more."

He loses his pants and boxers, cock already stiff and jutting out as he pulls a condom from his wallet and rolls it on. He lowers his mouth to mine again, kissing me hard, taking my breath away.

"You didn't even stop to admire the present you bought me."

"Next time." He undoes my pants, shoving them and my panties down in haste, and I'm distracted by his scent—so fresh, clean, masculine, and familiar.

I squeak in surprise as he lifts me up like I weigh nothing, and instinctively, my legs wrap around his trim hips. I loop my arms around his neck, but his hold on me is firm, hands cupping my ass, and the length of his cock rests against my clit. At the firm press of him against my nerves, I'm overrun with need.

He takes a step so my back is pressed against the cool wall, and my eyes go wide.

"Like this?" I'm breathless, eyes darting around the foyer.

The spontaneity of having sex here in the dim apartment with just the lights of the city sparkling through the big windows makes my stomach dip with excitement.

"Like this." His mouth tilts in a dark, seductive smile that makes my intimate muscles clench in anticipation. God, this is going to be good. "That's what you wanted, isn't it? That's what you said that night at the bar, that you wanted to be fucked hard against the wall."

My thoughts blur in a rush of desire, and I nod. God, yes, I want that. "Yes, please." My gaze drops, trailing down the carved muscles of his chest, the golden-blond hair leading to his cock.

A rakish grin pulls up on his handsome face. "You don't have to say please with me, but I really, really like it."

With one hand, he holds me up, toned arm flexing in a riveting display of masculine strength. Forget the spectacular marble lines of Michelangelo's *David*. Hayden Owens is the perfect depiction of male beauty. My train of admiration derails, though, as he palms my breast. Our lips meet again, and he toys with my nipple, pulling an aching sweetness from deep inside me like there's a cord connected to my center. He shifts his hips, sliding his cock through my wetness, and I moan when his scorching hardness rubs against my clit. Molten heat swirls inside me.

"I should slow down," he says, dropping his hand to between my legs, rubbing his fingers over my arousal and watching my expression with fascination.

I shake my head, tugging on the back of his hair, and his eyes spark hotter. "Don't."

He works firm, slick circles on my center, lighting up every nerve ending in my body. My head falls back against the wall and he watches my face with determined reverence. Arousal tightens at the apex of my thighs and I'm flooded with urgency.

"Hayden," I moan. My heart's beating so hard, I'm surprised he can't hear it. "I can't wait. I need more."

The breath rushes out of him and he nods, lining himself up with my entrance. He nudges inside, and sharp pleasure sweeps through me, even as my muscles protest how thick he is. I cling to him, letting the sensations drag me under.

"Breathe," he says, gentle yet commanding.

He's a bit too big for me, and my lips part as I hold his worried gaze. Even now, he's so caring and careful with me.

"Oh my god." He rests his forehead against mine, staring into my eyes. "You're so fucking tight."

"You're so fucking big." My voice sounds thin and desperate, and I don't care that it sounds cliché. My whole focus narrows down to where my body's working hard to adjust to him. Any discomfort is washed away as electricity arcs through my blood. "Keep going."

He presses in until his hips meet mine and I'm about to lose my mind with the delicious, burning fullness of him. Already, my release stirs, waking up and coiling in my limbs.

"Okay?" he whispers.

I nod against him with a shaky breath. "You feel so good," I whisper back. "I've wanted this for so long."

His throat works. Under my hand on the back of his neck, his skin is hot and damp with exertion. A little frown of frustration and agony sits between his eyebrows. The guy looks wrecked from holding back so he doesn't hurt me. I nip his bottom lip, and the rough, pleased noise in his throat sends a ripple of warmth through me.

"I can feel you clenching me," he groans. "I've wanted this for *years*, Darcy, and somehow it's better than I thought it could be."

I wind higher, soaring from the knowledge that Hayden and I connected like this was inevitable. I was always going to figure it out and see him; it was just a matter of when.

While my body adjusts to his intimidating size, he coasts a hand over my skin like he can't get enough of me, until finally, his gaze meets mine.

"Can I move?" he begs, eyes glazed and breathing ragged.

His hair's a mess from my hands in it and his eyes are wild with desperation as he hangs on to the last shreds of his control. I nod, and he drags himself out, looking down to where our bodies meet, before he slowly pushes back into me, watching my face for any sign of discomfort.

Pleasure rolls through me; my pulse thickens.

"God," I moan.

He rocks into me again, and I feel every inch.

"You don't know how many times I thought about this." He closes his eyes, expression strained, and swallows. "I've pictured us in every position you can think of, on every surface of this apartment. Of every apartment I've ever lived in."

Heat swirls between my legs, and the pressure tightens.

He fucks me harder, and I climb higher. The painting on the wall that we bought last weekend shakes as he thrusts into me, and I'll probably have bruises tomorrow from his hand on my ass. I don't care, though. I just want more.

His hand finds my clit, and he rubs tight, firm circles.

"Hayden." My release takes shape, and I tug his hair, gazing into his eyes. I can feel the desperate expression all over my face.

He smiles, dark and dominant. "Fucking *love* when you moan my name like that, Darcy. Fucking love the way your sweet little pussy tightens around me." He presses feverish kisses against my skin as the pressure low in my belly begins to expand and my vision starts to blur. "Such a good girl, getting so wet for me, letting me fuck you hard against the wall like we both wanted."

I dig my nails into his shoulder and the corner of his mouth ticks up.

"You going to come for me, honey?"

"Mhm." I nod again and again. My nerves start to fray, and nothing else exists except us, here and now.

"Show me," he demands, clutching me as I tighten further. "Show me what it looks like when I make you feel good."

The pressure spills over, and I shatter. My toes curl. Heat courses through me as my muscles spasm around him. I'm gasping for air, moaning his name and pleading with him not to stop as my pulse races. When I think I've hit the highest peak of my orgasm, I keep soaring, keep rising, so high I think I might die. He thrusts into me again and again, holding me tight like I'm precious.

It's everything, all at once—intimate, intense, hot, desperate, hungry, and everything I've ever needed.

My release subsides, but from Hayden's clenched jaw and

tortured expression, he's close. His teeth catch his bottom lip and he groans, low and hungry. His cheekbones flush with the exertion. His hair has fallen into his eyes. God, he's so devastating like this, at the edge of his control but taking everything he wants.

"I can't hold on much longer."

"Let go." I'm eager to see Hayden lose his mind while inside me. "Come inside me."

His hand returns between my legs and with a few fast, firm circles, a second release hits me. I let out a confused and surprised sob of pleasure against his skin, shaking with the orgasm as more waves of heat radiate through me and I clamp down around his length. It's not fair how good he is at reading my body and knowing exactly what I want.

It's his undoing, though, because the raw, broken noise that grates out of his throat is pure pleasure. With strong arms, he clutches me tight to his chest. Hayden buries his face in my neck, moaning against my skin and pulsing inside me. Intense protectiveness rushes through me as he repeats my name into my skin.

My thoughts dissolve until only one remains—I wish we could do this forever. I wish Hayden wanted what I wanted.

After a moment, he pulls back with an incredulous expression. The only noise in the apartment is the pounding of my pulse in my ears and the sound of us catching our breaths.

"Are you trying to kill me?" he asks, and we both laugh.

With my fingertip, I trace the line of his bottom lip, but he dips down to catch my mouth again. "Just the opposite."

"WHAT ABOUT THIS ONE?" Darcy points at a chair in the furniture store I pulled her into after brunch.

My mind races with images of us together over the past twelve hours—the moans she made when she was close to orgasm, the peaceful way she looked before I woke her up this morning, and her low sigh of pleasure as I washed her hair in the shower. The life-altering feeling of being buried deep inside her tight, warm, wet pussy, and the way her mouth falls open in surprise and enjoyment at the first thrust.

"Hayden?"

I stare at the chair. "All I can think about is having sex with you on this chair." She'd sit on top, facing me, riding my cock while I suck on her neck and slick my fingers around that tight bud of nerves that makes her lose it.

A surprised laugh bubbles out of her and her eyes glow bright.

"Are you sore?" I ask, pulling her closer, running my lips over her temple. She smells incredible. How did I control myself for eight years? I can barely go five minutes without touching her now.

Her mouth twists. "A little."

I make a low, sympathetic noise and smooth a hand over the back of her soft hair. "I'm sorry."

"No, um." She shakes her head, cheeks going the same pink as the moments before she's about to come. "I kind of like it." She sends me a hesitant glance, biting her lip. "Is that weird?"

A breath rushes out of me, and I grin down at her, settling my arm around her shoulders. "I like it, too."

With every moment I spend with Darcy, she becomes more entwined in my DNA. She becomes a bit more mine.

God, I hope she feels the same way. It's getting more difficult not to spill my feelings all over her.

Her phone rings with a call from one of the other analysts. She mouths *one second* and heads outside.

I smile at her through the windows, where she's talking a mile a minute with bright eyes. The Storm are going to playoffs and the analysts are working overtime, but Darcy couldn't be happier about the long hours. It's everything I wanted for her— to finally love her job, for her to be excited to go to work in the morning.

Jamie and Pippa's wedding is in a couple of days, and worry knots behind my sternum. Darcy seems happier than ever, but I can't be sure. I've been wrong in the past. I never knew how unhappy she was with Kit.

"Hayden?"

At the sound of my name, I turn, and my gut drops through the floor.

"Jess." I probably look like I've seen a ghost from the way my jaw goes slack. I blink in surprise, but I recover and give her a shaky smile. "Hi. How are you doing?"

Jessica Haley, my high school girlfriend, gives me a huge, pleased grin. "Better now. Fancy running into you here. What are the odds?"

My pulse picks up and uncertainty weaves through my gut. "Yeah. Life's funny like that."

"I just moved back to Vancouver from Saskatoon," she says with a smile, attention lingering on my arms and chest. "You look amazing." Her gaze drags up and down my form, and an unwelcome, uneasy feeling settles in my stomach. "What's new?"

"You know. Hockey."

I glance to the windows where Darcy is still on the phone. I've just started to shed the player stereotype with her, and I don't want her to look over and think that the second her back is turned, I'm hitting on other women. I'm trying to show her I'm boyfriend material.

I don't even *see* other women.

Jess nods, eyes moving over me with admiration. "Yeah, I've watched you on TV with the Storm." She laughs to herself. "All my girlfriends know that I lost my virginity to *the* Hayden Owens."

Something unpleasant yanks in my stomach, and I fight a disgusted expression. "Uh. Yeah."

We're ten years older, but I feel seventeen again, trying to act cool and unaffected as she tells me she had fun with me, but that she'd rather date some other guy.

She steps into my space and lowers her voice with a secretive smile. "I forgot how big you are."

I clear my throat and involuntarily take a step backward. "Uh. Yeah. Always been tall." I rake a hand over my hair.

The tone of her voice leaves no room for interpretation—she's interested. I glance around for Darcy, who's no longer on the sidewalk.

"We should exchange numbers," Jess says with a smile.

"Look, I don't want to be rude, Jess, but—"

"Hi." Darcy's hand slips into mine and she leans against me, gazing up at me with a pretty smile.

Immediately, I relax.

She doesn't even look at Jess, she just keeps her affectionate gaze locked on me. "I missed you, baby," she says in a soft voice.

Baby? My brain starts to slur, wading through warm, sluggish feelings as I grin down at her, probably wearing a dopey, stupid expression.

"I missed you, too," I say.

What is happening? I'm not sure, and I don't really care. I just want Darcy to call me *baby* again.

Darcy turns and meets eyes with Jess. "Hi." She sticks a hand out. "I'm Darcy, Hayden's girlfriend."

Confusion rolls through me, but I'm still smiling, and when I catch the hardened edge of Darcy's faux-friendly smile, it dawns on me.

She's staking her claim. She's *jealous*. Amusement whirls through me and I smile, feeling the back of my neck go warm. I stifle the urge to laugh. Finally, she's getting a taste of how it feels to watch her get hit on. I shift her hand to my other palm and bring my arm up around her shoulder, tucking her into my chest.

"Jess." She sticks out her hand to shake Darcy's and looks between us. Her eyes bug out. "*You* have a girlfriend?" she repeats to me.

Against me, Darcy stiffens, and a sick feeling spikes inside me. This is it, the moment where Darcy turns to me like she's seeing me in a new light and goes *oh yeah, you're right, Jess. Why would I ever commit to this guy?*

Instead, she smiles at Jess, and something in her gaze feels predatory.

"We're just looking for some things for *our* apartment." She holds Jess's gaze. "Where we live. Together. And share a bed."

The knots in my chest loosen with relief. Not mad, not changing her mind about us, but territorial like I've never seen her. I *like* this side of her. My grin widens as I look down at her. What a little tiger.

"Okay," Jess says, looking weirded out, glancing between us. "I didn't think you were the girlfriend type."

"I am." I suck in a deep breath, squeezing Darcy's hand.

"I mean, I know you *thought* you were," Jess starts, laughing a little. "But a guy like you?" Her eyes move over me, eyebrow arched, and I tense. "No way. But," she shrugs, perking up, giving Darcy a bright smile, "maybe people change."

Nausea gathers in my gut and I swallow hard.

Darcy smiles up at me, innocent as a kitten, but with protective rage in her eyes. "We should get going, baby."

There's that word I like again. I swallow the weird feelings and nod. "You bet." I give Jess a tight smile. "Nice running into you."

"You, too." Jess watches us with a puzzled expression as Darcy gives her a quick wave, slips her hand into mine, and pulls me out of the store.

"Girlfriend?" I ask on the sidewalk.

She shrugs like it was nothing, but she doesn't let go of my hand. "I didn't like the way she was talking to you."

Warmth radiates through me. "Jealous," I tease.

Her eyes flick up to mine. "What if I am?"

My eyebrow goes up, along with my smile. "Thought we were just having fun, Darce."

Her cheeks go pink and she looks away, but my fingers come beneath her chin, tilting her face up so our eyes meet.

"Thank you," I tell her. "No one's ever gotten protective of me like that." I give her a smug smile. "It was nice. I could get used to it."

She studies me for a long moment, sadness rising in her

eyes. "You deserve it, Hayden." She glances at the furniture store half a block away. "Who was that? And what did she mean, she didn't think you were the girlfriend type?"

The muscles in my chest pull tight, but her hand smooths over them, and the look in her eyes is so caring and curious that my heart aches.

It's time to tell her the truth.

"JESS WAS MY HIGH SCHOOL GIRLFRIEND."

I blink, thoughts reeling. Girlfriend. Girlfriend? He's never spoken about her. Kit never mentioned her. "I didn't know you had a girlfriend in high school."

"Uh-huh." He chews his bottom lip. "Or, I thought I did. After we lost our virginity, she wasn't interested in more. Apparently, I was fun enough for her to tell her friends about, though." His expression turns wry. "I wanted to be good in bed, but I turned out to be..." He swallows. "Too good, I guess. I'm the hookup guy, not the boyfriend guy."

I stand on the sidewalk in silence, processing this and watching his face.

"That was a long time ago. You were just a teenager."

He shakes his head. "No, Darce, don't you see? I thought I could leave it behind in high school, but the reputation followed me to university."

It almost sounds like he's upset about it. Like he never wanted this reputation. "You said you cut it off before it gets serious. You always tell women upfront that you're not interested in a relationship."

"I'd rather be clear from the beginning than get my hopes up."

Oh god. The rules are for him, not for the women he dates. My heart sinks.

Fierce protectiveness floods me at the idea of those girls hurting Hayden, making him feel like he wasn't worth more than a hookup.

Hayden's spectacular. He's the whole package—kindness and humor and looks. How could they have not seen that?

"And you see me like everyone else," he says quietly.

Pain wraps around my chest, tightening, and I shake my head. "No, Hayden, I don't."

"You do," he says with more force, eyes sharp and vulnerable. "You saw it as soon as you met me. Remember that party, first week of school?"

The hockey party.

"Kit said I was the biggest player he knew and you agreed with him. You said 'I can totally see that.'" He crosses his arms and glances away.

"I remember it." My voice is soft, barely above a whisper, as the memory replays in my head. "I remember him talking about how easy you have it with women."

He was so handsome and funny and friendly, and all week, I'd been hoping he'd ask me out. I was disappointed when he didn't. When Kit said that Hayden was a player, I clung to it as a reason. It wasn't a reflection of *me*; it was just the way he was.

A few months ago, I called him "king of the players." *You're like their leader*, I said. When he tested the waters and said having a girlfriend didn't look so bad, I basically told him he wasn't cut out for it.

"I'm sorry," I whisper. "I just thought—" I shake my head. "I'm sorry."

"It's fine." His voice is tight.

It's not fine. How could I have not known? I've known Hayden for years.

I saw what I wanted to see, because it was easier that way. My mind flicks to the game against Calgary and how furious Kit was.

"What did you tell Kit?" Last time I asked this, he said he told him the truth, but we were too distracted with having sex against the wall for me to push him to elaborate.

Hayden's eyes meet mine and he sucks in a tight breath. "That I was serious about you. That I'll do whatever it takes to make you happy."

My skin is tingling. How could I have been so, so fucking wrong about Hayden? All these years, I saw what everyone else did.

I'll be turning over this information in my head all night, all week. For years, probably. I was so wrong. But right now, I need to make this situation right.

I step in front of him and set my hands flat on his chest, looking up into his ocean-blue eyes. He gives me a confused look.

"Hi." I give him a small, friendly smile. "You're Hayden, right?"

His mouth slants and his expression is confused, but he nods.

"I'm Darcy." I step closer until I'm almost pressed against his body. "I've had a crush on you from the second I saw you in class."

His mouth tips up, and something wavers in his eyes. His hands come to my elbows, holding me. "Is this how you normally introduce yourself, Darcy?"

I shake my head. "Just to you. Don't think you can fool me with your good looks, Hayden Owens."

His eyes glint with amusement. "Oh, yeah?"

"Uh-huh. You may be the hottest guy I've ever seen, but I can tell you're kind and funny, and you have a good heart. You're an incredible hockey player, not just because of how fast and strong you are, but because you care about your team and making your coach proud. And you probably like fantasy romance, don't you?"

"I do, actually." His mouth tips higher, and my chest feels so much lighter. "Incredible how you know all of this and we've just met."

I smile. "And I bet you always make sure everyone feels included at parties and stuff."

"My mom says that people always remember how you made them feel," he adds quietly, stroking a thumb over the back of my hand.

"The way people treat you is a reflection of them, not you." Emotion clogs my throat—anger that Hayden's felt like this for so long, guilt that I contributed to it, and the overwhelming need to make it better. "Would you ever tell me that I deserved how Kit treated me?"

"Never," he bites out, frowning. "That was on him, Darce. He's the asshole who didn't deserve you."

I give him a patient smile. *See?* my expression says.

Something settles in his eyes. He believes me, I think. My heart tugs, and I lean forward to kiss him.

"Maybe some people say you're a player," I whisper against his lips, "but I know the truth. You're so much more."

THAT AFTERNOON, we walk through a stretch of the park where trees line either side of the sidewalk, bursting with petals in shades of white and pink.

The park isn't too busy—a few people taking photos under the cherry blossoms, someone throwing a ball for their dog, a couple picnicking on the grass on a big plaid blanket. Some kids playing street hockey.

A breeze sweeps blossoms off the trees and they swirl around us. She stops and tips a serene smile to the sky, watching them flutter. A few fall in her hair, and I take a mental picture. I want to remember this forever.

"You're beautiful, Darcy. I ever tell you that?"

Darcy turns her smile to me, staring up into my eyes. I've never felt so connected to someone.

"Once or twice. Let's sit," she says quietly, gesturing to an empty bench, and we take a seat against the cool metal.

You're so much more, she said this morning, and my heart does a weird thump.

I can't believe I told her all that stuff, but I'm weirdly relieved that I did. An urgent, insistent rush hits me.

"I don't want this to end, Darce." Adrenaline courses

through my veins as I spill my heart to her. "I don't want to go back to being just friends after the wedding. There's no one like you, and I've never had this"—I gesture between us, swallowing thickly—"with anyone else. Have you?"

Her tongue darts out to wet her bottom lip and she shakes her head. Worry threads through her gaze.

"I'm not asking you to get married or to have kids or make any commitments you're not ready for. We'll always go at your pace. I just want you to keep living in the apartment and sleeping in my bed and letting me take you on dates." I shoot her a playful smirk, even as my heart pounds. "And I want you to keep wearing lingerie."

She chuckles.

"The choice is yours." He never gave her the choice, but I'm not him. "I will always give you the choice, Darcy. I promise."

The three words I want to say are on the tip of my tongue, but I hold them back.

And there it is, my heart placed into the palm of her hand. She could crush me. She could toss me aside and break me in half with just a few words or a facial expression. But she's worth the risk.

I'm asking her to be brave, so I need to be, too. I need to trust that my best friend and the woman I love sees me for more than a fun time, good fuck, and pretty face. That I'm not just the life of the party to Darcy; I'm the guy she wants to wake up with every day, the guy she believes when I tell her she can do anything. The guy she can't wait to talk about books with and share hockey models with.

"What if you change your mind?" She plays with her fingernails, and her voice is so small and scared that I want to scoop her up and never let her go.

The breath whooshes out of my lungs in a laugh of disbelief. "I won't. I know I won't."

She swallows, staring at her hands.

You're the one for me, I want to say, but that's too much pressure to put on her.

"Let's take the risk together," I say instead.

"Excuse me," a kid interrupts, standing in front of us with a few others, and our heads whip up. They look about nine or ten and are holding hockey sticks. "Are you Hayden Owens?"

"You bet, bud. You guys playing hockey over there?"

The kid nods and looks like he wants to say more.

"Ask him," one of the kids whispers, nudging the first boy.

"Do you maybe want to play hockey with us?" the boy asks.

My arm tightens around Darcy. Normally, I'd say yes, but with her under my arm, sitting in such a beautiful setting, I don't want to ever move.

"I don't know if I'm good enough to keep up with you guys," I tell them, glancing at Darcy.

She gives me an encouraging smile. "You should play."

One of the kids claps in excitement, unable to contain himself. "Are you sure?"

She nods, smiling wider. "I want to watch you play. I'll be cheering for you."

I sense she wants a few minutes to process what I just told her. Darcy's like that; she needs time to figure out how she feels about something.

I press a quick kiss to her cheek. "I won't be long."

"Take your time." She settles back on the bench, getting comfortable. "I'm happy to sit here and watch."

I follow the kids to where they have a net set up.

"No hitting me, okay?" I tell them, and I hear Darcy chuckle behind me. "I'm not as tough as I look."

BENEATH THE CHERRY BLOSSOMS, I sit on the park bench, watching Hayden play street hockey with a group of kids. He's so good with them, encouraging and coaching them and cheering when anyone scores.

I can see it—him having kids of his own, teaching them to play hockey, maybe coaching their teams and taking them out for ice cream after, whether they won or lost. I picture Hayden with two daughters, telling them they're smart and wonderful and that they can do anything. Then I picture him with two sons, teaching them how to be kind and inclusive of others.

The threat of not being in that picture with him makes my heart ache. I think about us not being in each other's lives like we are now, contact limited to the occasional phone call or yearly visit, and I'm flooded with bone-deep sadness.

He doesn't want this to end. There's no one like me, he said, and he's never had this with anyone else. The choice is mine.

He's not a player, I know now. He never was. He always wanted more; he just didn't think he could have it.

He could have more with me, if I let it happen.

What's the alternative? I go back to trying to be a player?

My sad attempts to date make me want to laugh. The best part of being a player was hanging out with Hayden.

I wanted to feel free and empowered. Hayden always seemed in control, and I wanted a shred of that for myself. It's because of him that I found it.

For my birthday, I wished things with Hayden would never have to end. Why can't I make my own wish come true? I've made my life into something I'm proud of. Something I've *dreamed* about.

How clueless would I be, to let a guy like Hayden slip away? I'd tell myself it was the right thing to do, that I was protecting him or myself, but one day, I'd wake up regretting that I wasn't more brave.

And my fear about losing myself in him like I did with Kit? I think back to the party thrown for me, where everyone was dressed up in dumb, hilarious costumes. That was for me, and it made me so happy.

Hayden would never let me be anyone but myself.

He passes to one of the kids, grinning and calling out encouragement, and my heart twists.

The idea of kids seems so far away, but I picture him having a kid with another woman, holding *their* baby with a besotted smile, and I want to both cry and rip this park bench out of the ground.

Maybe it doesn't need to end. After what he told me about Jess, about being shoved into a stereotype and reputation he never wanted, maybe things with us could work.

"We're going to score one for Darcy, okay?" Hayden tells the kids.

He sets up the play, and when the kid scores, he raises both palms for high fives, handing them out to each kid, shining his enthusiastic, fun light all over them and making them all feel special.

Take a risk, Ward said when I debated about taking the analyst job, and look how well that's turning out.

The stakes with Hayden are so much higher, though.

This is my pattern—I get scared, so I stand still. Hayden deserves so much more than my uncertainty and hand-wringing, though.

When the pickup game ends, Hayden signs autographs and takes photos with the kids and parents. Then he jogs back to the bench and drops down beside me.

"That was fun." He smiles down at me, cheekbones flushed and eyes bright. A few petals have fallen into his hair.

"You scored a goal for me."

He rests his arm over my shoulders, holding me against his warm, solid chest, and when he smiles down at me again, his expression softens.

"They're all for you, Darcy."

My heart twists. Maybe he won't break my heart.

His eyes drop to my hair and his mouth quirks in amusement.

"What?"

His grin widens. "You have cherry blossoms in your hair."

I laugh. "So do you."

It feels like magic, sitting here with him under the cherry blossoms and gentle sunlight. Like everything's falling into place and the timing all aligns.

I don't want to be scared anymore. I want all the good things that come with making the hard choices.

In the distance, an ice cream truck jingle plays, and I smile. Spring is finally here, and I hardly recognize myself compared to the person I was when I showed up in Vancouver this winter.

"Hayden?" Nerves rattle through me, but I swallow them.

His eyebrows snap together in concern. "What's wrong?"

My mouth goes dry, but I focus on the breathtaking myriad of blues in his eyes. "I don't want to stop doing this, either."

His eyebrows lift.

"I don't want what we're doing to end." I drag a deep breath in, meeting his gaze, and my stomach flips over at the affection in his expression. "I'm falling for you."

I've never said those words to a guy, and I wonder if he's ever heard them.

A tender smile breaks across his face. "I was hoping you'd say that."

CHAPTER 71
HAYDEN

"DARCE?" I kick my shoes off at the front door that evening, carrying a take-out bag of Thai food.

"I'm in the bath," she calls from inside the apartment, a teasing, flirty note to her voice.

Lust courses through me and I stride to the bathroom, already half-hard at the mental image of her wet, naked, and waiting for me. I yank my shirt off in the hallway and toss it aside. I can smell the sweet vanilla-orange scent of her bubble bath.

I whip the bathroom door open and make a face. "Eugh."

Daniel the Gnome is in the bathtub, surrounded by bubbles, staring at me with his beady, soulless eyes.

"*No*," I groan.

Darcy stands behind the door, fully clothed and doubled over, laughing.

"Why do you torture me like this?"

"He just wants to relax after a long day." She can hardly get the words out, she's laughing so hard, and her eyes are watering.

"You're sick, you know that?" I chuckle, shaking my head. "How long were you waiting in here?"

"About ten minutes."

I pick the stupid gnome up out of the water and set it on the floor before I turn on Darcy, smiling a wicked grin. Her eyes light up and she takes a step back.

Her words from earlier today replay in my mind. *I know the truth. You're so much more.*

Maybe she's right. Maybe I'm not the guy everyone says I am. Maybe I *am* the Streicher or the Miller, who can make his partner happy.

"You're going to get it." I scoop her up and she shrieks with laughter.

Maybe I can make Darcy happy.

God, I want to be that guy so fucking badly.

"No," she laughs as I carry her to the bath, fully clothed. "Please." She clutches at my neck, shaking with laughter while I dip her down, half an inch above the surface of the water. She's laughing so hard she can barely breathe. "Please," she begs again, and I beam down at her.

The gnome is creepy as fuck, but I love seeing her like this, happier than ever. I never want this to end.

"What do you say?"

"Sorry," she gasps, clutching me and trying to wiggle away from the water. "I'm sorry."

"And what else?"

"Daniel's sorry, too," she says, eyes sparkling, but she yelps when I dip her an inch lower, getting her ass all wet. "Hayden!"

ON SATURDAY, I walk into the main area of the suite Hayden booked at the upscale Whistler lodge, wearing my tangerine dress. He arranged for a hair and makeup artist to stop by this morning, so my hair is half-up, half-down, in loose, flowing curls, and my makeup is done in a way I could never achieve. Around my wrist, my favorite bracelet, my most prized possession, is clasped.

I feel like my best self, my most true self. Like I'm not hiding or pretending to be someone else.

Hayden's lounging in the living room, and with his handsome features, the sharp cut of the suit over his powerful form, and the backdrop of the lake, mountains, and endless blue sky through the windows behind him, the image looks like a shoot from a magazine. From a movie. Like it couldn't possibly be real.

He looks up from his phone and his mouth drops open.

"What do you think?" I give him a small smile.

He stares. "Uh."

"What?" I look down, frowning, scanning for makeup smudged on my dress.

Hayden just continues to stare at me with a dazed expression.

"You're so gorgeous, Darce." He swallows, eyes dragging up and down my form. When his gaze settles on my face, his eyes soften. "So pretty it hurts. I've always thought that."

My heart swells. *I don't want this to end,* he said. *I don't want this to end, either,* I told him.

It almost feels too good to be true, that a girl like me could end up with a guy like him. When I stand here in this dress, with this hair, with what I've achieved over the past few months, I don't feel like that awkward, dorky girl I used to be, though.

Something sweet and sparkling swells in my chest, flowing through me, and I stand an inch taller. I feel worthy of the way Hayden's looking at me right now.

He stands and reaches into his pocket. When he pulls his hand out, he's holding a pale-pink velvet box. "I got you a present."

"You're spoiling me."

His eyes warm. "My favorite activity." He cracks the box and hands it to me—a pair of sparkling earrings, pale gemstones in the same tiny clusters as my bracelet.

"They're beautiful."

Hayden just watches with a smile, standing behind me with his hands on my hips as I slip them on and admire my reflection in the foyer mirror. "You deserve the best, and buying you presents is a kink I didn't know I had."

I chuckle and kiss him on the cheek. "Thank you, baby."

He makes a low, pleased noise and runs his lips over my jaw. My breath catches.

"Love it when you call me baby," he murmurs.

I bite my lip. I love it when he uses that tone of voice with me, like he's about to pull me back into bed.

"We should get going," I whisper.

At the front door, I reach for my heels, but he takes them from me.

"I'll do it."

I sit, and Hayden kneels in front of me. He slips my foot into the shoe, wearing an adorable frown of concentration as he does the delicate strap up with his big hands. He straightens my leg, meets my eyes with a cheeky smile, and presses a kiss to my ankle. My calf. The inside of my knee. He brushes the hem of my dress higher and kisses the inside of my thigh.

"We're going to be late," I laugh, pulse stumbling.

I thought I had a good idea of Hayden's sexual appetite, but it was just another thing I had wrong about him.

Hayden doesn't just have a high sex drive. Hayden's *insatiable*. I've never come so many times per day—in bed first thing in the morning, in the shower, bent over the kitchen counter after breakfast, in the middle of the night, when he wakes me with his tongue lapping up my arousal. I didn't think my body was capable of it. Even now, need tightens between my legs and I can feel my panties getting damp.

Where Hayden's involved, maybe I'm insatiable, too.

"You're right." Against my inner thigh, he exhales a heavy breath like he's in pain. "We need to leave now or we never will."

At the door, he pauses, gaze trailing over me again, followed by the slow bob of his Adam's apple as he swallows.

"What is it?"

He lets out a light laugh, shaking his head. "Just thinking how lucky I am to have you on my arm, Darce."

"Funny." I tug his tie to pull his mouth closer. "I feel the same way about you."

WE WATCH our friends Jamie Streicher and Pippa Hartley marry, and I glance down at Darcy beside me. She looks so heartbreakingly beautiful.

She gives me a soft smile and turns back to the bride and groom, and her new earrings catch the light. Her awestruck expression, so delighted and surprised, only fed my addiction.

I'm going to marry this girl. The thought struck me eight years ago, during a conversation before class our first week of school. Embarrassed by it, I buried it as fast as it sprung up; I was eighteen, for Christ's sake.

I knew, though. A few conversations with Darcy Andersen, and I knew she was the one for me.

She glances back at me with a teasing, scolding expression and flicks her gaze to the front. *You're staring at me*, she mouths, and I grin, lifting a shoulder. *I like you*, I mouth back.

I love you, I want to say.

She rolls her eyes and I force my attention back to the reason we're here.

Pippa wears a long white dress Darcy tells me is "boho style." Streicher's in a dark gray suit, and their dog Daisy sits between them, wearing a little white bow tie on her collar. She gazes up with watchful eyes, waiting for the treats Streicher's been slipping her throughout the ceremony.

Every member of the Vancouver Storm—with the exception of Volkov—is here, including Ward. Hazel and Miller stand at the front as maid of honor and best man, exchanging private smiles throughout the ceremony, probably thinking about their own upcoming wedding.

Streicher's mom, Donna, and Pippa's parents, Ken and Maureen, sit in the front row, beaming at the couple.

When Pippa and Jamie say their vows, my eyes sting and my chest expands with warmth, not just because I'm happy for my friends to take the next step in their life and relationship, but because I want that, too, and finally, for the first time in my life, it's within reach.

Beside me, Darcy wears the orange dress, looking so beautiful and happy, it makes my heart ache.

I'm falling for you, she said on the park bench beneath the cherry blossoms.

I look around at Jamie and Pippa's loved ones, and I want this for us. I want my Darcy in the dress that makes her feel beautiful, the people who mean everything to us watching with smiles and tears in their eyes, and a big, raucous party after to celebrate.

I sniffle.

"Are you crying?" Darcy whispers, tucking her hand in mine.

"No," I whisper back.

Her mouth tips up, eyes sparkling. "It's okay if you are."

"I'm not," I insist, smiling. "And even if I were, everyone else is, too."

She smiles again, squeezes my hand, and rests her head on my shoulder for the remainder of the ceremony.

———

"Alexei didn't show?" Darcy asks in my ear when we make our way to the banquet room overlooking the lake.

I shake my head, glancing around. "I thought he might change his mind at the last minute, but—" I shrug. "Guess not."

She hums, mouth twisting with concern.

"He was engaged once," I admit, wincing. "He doesn't like to talk about it."

While we eat, the wedding party and parents make speeches.

"Upon first impression," Miller says into the microphone, "my surly, serious best friend appears to be an asshole."

He glances at Pippa for confirmation, who nods hard in agreement. Everyone laughs, and even Streicher cracks a smile.

"But everyone in his life knows he'll do anything for the ones he loves. Pippa," Miller smiles at her, "with your strength and bravery, your work ethic, and your creativity and kindness, everyone in this room can see why he loves you more than life itself. Daisy," Miller peers around the table, where Daisy is sitting at Donna's feet, getting pets, "you changed everything when you tried to follow Streicher home that day."

Daisy lets out one high bark and everyone laughs again.

Hazel narrows her eyes at Streicher during her speech. "I wasn't sure about you, Jamie, but you won me over when you encouraged Pippa, built her up to her full height, and told her she could do anything." Her expression warms. "You'd do anything for my baby sister, and I love you for that. I'm proud to call you my brother-in-law."

She looks to Pippa, and her eyes shine with love.

"I once told you I wished you knew how incredible you were, because you'd be unstoppable." Her throat works, and she blinks hard. "Now you do know, and now you *are* unstoppable. I love you. I'm so proud of everything you've accomplished and the person you are, and I thank the universe every day that we're sisters."

My eyes sting, because Hazel normally keeps her emotions locked down.

"Crying again?" Darcy whispers with a teasing grin.

"I'm *not* crying," I whisper back, blinking fast.

She smooths a hand down my thigh in a comforting motion, and I slip mine into hers, holding it tight.

"I'm crying a little," I admit.

"It's okay." She leans up and kisses my cheek. "I like that you're secretly a sappy romantic."

I huff an embarrassed laugh. I guess I am. I guess I always was.

"Jamie, you've been part of the Hartley family since that first Christmas you joined us," Ken, Pippa's dad, says with pride, chest puffing out. Maureen stands beside him at the podium, beaming. "Everyone says Jamie and Pippa are the lucky ones, but it's Maureen and me who are counting our lucky stars, and not just because we're welcoming two members of the Storm at family holidays."

Everyone chuckles. On top of being a friendly, open-hearted guy, Ken is a rabid hockey fan.

"You're a good man, Jamie. Donna did an amazing job, raising you," he tells Streicher and Donna, and Streicher leans forward, watching with his elbows on his knees. His throat works. Donna dabs at her eyes. "Pippa chose well when she chose you."

"I knew Jamie liked you," Donna says to Pippa with a smile during her turn, "when I asked if you were pretty and he wouldn't look me in the eye."

Pippa laughs and Jamie grins, shaking his head.

After dinner, Pippa plays a song she wrote for Streicher on

the guitar he bought her for their first Christmas, and when I see the look they exchange, him so proud of her and her so openly loving, I tighten my arm around Darcy's shoulders.

After, we dance to love songs, and I hold her tight, breathing in her sweet, familiar scent.

I love her, and it's getting harder to keep it in. Every day, I wonder if she's ready to hear the depth of my feelings for her.

"You want to go back to the room, Andersen?"

She holds my eyes and nods, and I take her hand, pulling her to the door.

IN THE ELEVATOR UP to our room, Hayden smiles at me, then down at our joined hands. His smile is so soft and yearning, and he's so deadly handsome in his gray suit, that I can't get a full breath.

When the elevator dings at our floor, he leads me to our room and unlocks the door and holds it open for me. We step inside the suite overlooking the lake—the room is way too big and luxurious, but when I told him this when we arrived, he backed me up into the bedroom and kissed me on the bed until I forgot how to speak.

He kneels to help me with my shoes, and I smile as I bring my hands to his shoulders for balance. He's so careful with the thin strap around my ankle, and the caring gesture tugs at my heart.

All the birthday gifts he gave me over the years. All the times he smiled at me and his gaze lingered a moment longer than other people's gazes would.

Weddings stir up emotions within people. I know this. And I know Hayden and I are new and fresh.

I watched Jamie and Pippa get married, and I thought about Hayden and me up there instead.

"Why did you agree to be my wingman?" I ask, barely above a whisper.

He sits back on his knees, regarding me, resting his warm, strong hands on the back of my calves. "Because he never gave you choices." His brow furrows like he's remembering it. "How could you possibly say no in that situation?" His throat works. "I agreed to wingman you and teach you to be a player because I wanted you to have choice and control. I wanted you to feel strong and make decisions for yourself." He huffs. "Even if it fucking killed me to watch you date other guys."

My throat tightens with emotion. For the first time, I feel truly seen. No matter what, Hayden's watching out for me. He always was.

He's so selfless. The universe used all the best ingredients when they made Hayden Owens.

He gets to his feet and takes the seat beside me. His lips press to my forehead, hands framing my jaw. "What's wrong?"

"Nothing." My heart trips. "Everything's better than ever. Too good to be true, I think."

His mouth tilts into a smile. "I know the feeling."

"I told myself you were a player and didn't want a girl-friend or commitment, because if you did want those things, you'd be perfect." My heart beats harder as he watches me, listening, absently playing with my hair. "And then I'd have no reason not to feel all the things I feel for you."

"Like what?"

My hands settle on his firm chest, toying with the seams of his shirt. "I'd realize how kind and loving you are, how you light up every room with your sense of humor and your smile. How you're so much more than a pretty face and a good fuck." My stomach twists in anger that anyone could have ever said that to him. "You care about people and you make people feel seen and special. You grew my confidence and helped me find myself when I didn't know how."

If he ever wanted those things that Jamie and Rory have—the fiancée, the settled-down life—he'd make someone deliriously happy.

Yearning yanks tight in my chest. I want that someone to be *me*.

I love him.

His mouth tips up into a gentle smile, and he tucks a lock of hair behind my ear. "Watching you become who you want to be, Darce, has been the best experience of my life."

I blink, and my pulse stumbles. Oh, god. I love Hayden. Of course I love him.

How could I not? He's wonderful. He's kind, affectionate, funny, optimistic, and hardworking. But it's more than that. It's that we love so many of the same things. That I love how he cringes when I hide that stupid gnome around our apartment. That he gets me the perfect gift I didn't know I wanted.

I take another deep breath, trying to settle my racing heart, and inhale a lungful of Hayden's scent. My skin tingles where he's touching my hair, tucking it over my ears and pushing it back behind my shoulders, and I'm flooded with impatience. I don't want to spend another moment sitting here and talking.

I'm not ready to tell him how I feel, but I can show him.

I slip my hand into his and pull him to the bedroom.

CHAPTER 75

HAYDEN

SHE LOVES ME. Darcy sees past all the ideas people have put into my head about who I am, and she loves me. She hasn't said it, but I know she feels it.

She holds my heart in the palm of her delicate hand.

In the bedroom, I press soft kisses to her neck, letting her sweet scent wash over me. She's trying to undo the buttons on my shirt, but I suck the sensitive skin beneath her ear, and her fingers fumble.

"Can't think when you do that," she murmurs, so I do it again, and she moans.

Our lips meet and I tease her tongue with mine, savoring her, coaxing her, claiming her. Darcy's mine; I tell her that with every stroke of my tongue against hers, with every brush of my fingers over her skin, with every breath we share. She nips my bottom lip, pushing me further, and my pulse thickens.

My fingers come to the side zip, and I slide it down. "I love you in this dress, but it's time for it to come off."

She laughs quietly, concentrating on undoing my shirt buttons. "I love you in this suit, but it's time for it to come off, too." A playful grin tugs at her pretty mouth, and I catch it with mine.

The dress falls to the floor around her ankles, leaving her in a strapless corset with tiny flowers on it and a wisp of a thong.

My mouth waters. "It'll never get old, seeing you wear something I bought for you that makes you feel beautiful."

She gives me a private smile. My shirt flutters to the floor, and her hands go to my belt, undoing it. Every brush of her hands against my cock has me harder, straining against my zipper, until she finally pushes my pants and boxers down, sinking to her knees.

My eyes go wide. "Wait—*oh god.*"

She takes my cock in her mouth, looking up at me with a devilish grin, and I don't have a thought in my thick head except *yes* and *Darcy* and *more.* I think I'm moaning those words out loud as she sucks me, running her tongue along the sensitive underside. Around the base of my spine, pressure builds. She hums, eyes closing like she loves this, and arousal races through me.

"Wait, baby." I pull back out of her mouth. "If you keep doing that, this is going to be over too soon." I haul her to her feet, against my chest. "Your mouth feels too good. I can't last."

She chuckles, but I unhook her corset, toss it aside, and drop to my knees, wrapping my lips around the peak of one gorgeous breast.

I grin up at her, laving attention all over her pretty tits as I kneel at her feet. "Your tits are the perfect height for this."

"Must be meant to be," she breathes, but her words catch when my finger finds the other, toying and teasing her. I suck and circle her nipple with my tongue, drawing soft gasps from her. I take her hand and put it on my head, and I groan with comfort and pleasure when she drags her fingers over my scalp.

I tease her to the edge of madness, running my lips along the top seam of her panties, pressing and brushing against her soft skin, nipping and kissing until her hips tilt toward me and I slide my fingers beneath the lace.

Between her legs, she's wet silk. My fingers swirl, and her eyelids fall halfway, gaze locked on me.

"So fucking soft." I can feel the wicked grin on my mouth. Pride beats through me at the sight of her pleasured expression. *I'm* doing that. *I'm* making her feel so good. "So fucking wet for me."

She nods, breathing hard.

I slide her panties off, baring her to me. My fingers sink into her and we both groan. I drag my fingers out, taking in the awestruck expression on her face as she watches, then lowering my gaze to that spot between her legs and sinking my fingers back into her tight, wet perfection.

"God, you're so pretty here," I tell her before I drag my tongue up her seam. The taste of her wetness has pre-cum beading on my cock and my balls aching with the need to fuck her. But this is too good, too fucking sweet. "And you taste so fucking good." An involuntary noise of enjoyment rumbles out of me as I swipe my tongue over her, back and forth.

She drops her head back in bliss, but I reach up and gently grip the back of her head, tilting her up. Her eyelids fly open. Her eyes are glazed with need, and her face is flushed in the most beautiful way.

My perfect Darcy. "Keep your eyes open, honey."

She nods, breathless, and more adrenaline drips into my blood. The high of Darcy being mine is like nothing else.

I pull a deep, sucking kiss on her clit, rubbing the sensitive ridged spot inside her in the way that drives her over the edge, and she tugs my hair so hard my eyes water.

"Hayden," she gasps.

On my shoulder, her thigh tenses. Her heel digs into my back. She clamps down on my fingers, grinding her pussy against me for more friction. Addictive, needy noises slip out of her, the kind she makes when she's about to slip over the edge.

I love when she loses her mind like this, and I love being the one to make it happen.

"I'm going to come." Her voice is thin and desperate, and I'm a man possessed. "You're going to make me come."

Sweeter words don't exist. Darcy's muscles clamp around my fingers, pulsing as she gasps and says my name over and over, and I suck the sweet bud of nerves, laving my tongue over it and soaking up every drop of her life-affirming taste. My heart races so hard as she holds on to me, shaking. I draw out her orgasm as long as I can, as long as she'll take it. Long enough to flood every inch of her body with pleasure and wipe every thought from her head except *me*.

When she relaxes, I rise, pulling her against my chest, and she tips her face to me, gazing at my mouth, asking for a kiss. I press my lips to hers instantly. I'd give her anything she wanted or needed.

She sucks my tongue, and my brain melts. Between us, my cock aches with lust. Need pounds through me, heavy and powerful.

"Fuck." I scoop her up and deposit her on the bed. Blood roars in my ears as I climb over her, kissing down her neck. "I need to be inside you, Darce. I can't wait."

SHE NODS QUICKLY and I reach to the nightstand for my wallet, but her hand settles on my arm, stopping me. There's a question in her gaze.

"What if we didn't—" She searches my eyes, and the blush across her cheeks is so fucking endearing, my heart aches.

"Didn't use a condom?" My eyebrows knit together.

She nods, and heat sears down my spine. The primal idea of coming inside Darcy floods my body with crackling electricity.

"I've never gone without one."

"Me neither," she whispers. "I'm on birth control. I started it last month."

I can't get a full breath. "Are you sure?"

She nods, biting her lip with a coy, embarrassed smile. "I want it, Hayden. I've been thinking about it."

"Jesus." I bury my head against the crook of her neck, letting out a dry laugh. She fantasized about me coming inside her? I'm not going to last more than ten seconds.

"We've had so many firsts together," she says, toying her fingers in my hair, and I smile and nod.

All the important ones have been with Darcy, and nothing before her mattered.

I notch myself at her warm, wet entrance. Her eyes are electric, and she's breathing hard. When I push inside her tight heat, I'm home.

"Oh my god," she whispers, closing her eyes. "I'm never getting used to how big you are."

Pleasure rushes up my spine, tingling and tightening. I shouldn't love hearing those words so much, but I do. I pause so she can adjust.

"Are you okay?" I grit through clenched teeth.

"Mhm." She sighs, eyes rolling back. "You feel so good." Her pussy pulses around me, and I scramble for control.

A hoarse noise scrapes out of me and I can feel the pleasure on my face. The way Darcy feels around me, gripping me, so warm and soft and wet, it flattens every thought in my head. I'm running on pure need, pure love for her.

"So fucking tight." Already, I can feel the pressure coiling around the base of my spine. "I won't last."

"Do you need me to bring up Daniel?"

I burst out laughing, collapsing with my face against her neck. "You're a sick little pervert, you know that?"

She giggles, and I lift my head to smile down at her, brushing the hair off her forehead.

"Admit it." Her lips tip into the prettiest, pleased smile. "It helps, thinking about him."

I shake with laughter. I love her. I love her so much my heart might give out.

But first, I want to make her come again. She gazes up at me with so much trust and love, and I get an idea.

"You want to try something new tonight?"

Heavy-lidded, her eyes flicker with interest. "Okay."

I slip my hand beneath her, brushing my finger down the

crease of her perfect ass until I find her back entrance. Her breath catches.

"I want to touch you here," I whisper in her ear. "I want to make you feel good."

Her teeth sink into her bottom lip, and wariness fills her gaze. "I don't want it to hurt."

My veins rattle with the need to protect her, to lavish pleasure and love upon her, and to show her everything she's never had.

"Do you trust me?"

She nods.

"We'll go slow. It won't hurt. I promise it'll feel so good. Better than you can imagine. I'll be so careful with you, Darce."

"I know." She blinks again, blows a slow breath out, and nods. "Okay."

Her trust in me is intoxicating. I catch her mouth, nipping her bottom lip, kissing her, before I suck my finger and return to her tight pucker, gently pushing inside a millimeter at a time.

"Does that feel good?" I watch her expression like a hawk.

"Yes," she gasps, blinking with wide eyes as I work my finger inside her, winding her higher. "Oh my god. Yes."

Satisfaction courses through me. "What did I say?"

Her eyes close and her lips part, then she tenses around my finger, around my cock. "You said it would be good."

"Tell me I'm right, honey."

"You're right." Her eyes roll back. She's starting to shake. "You're so right. Oh, *fuck*. Hayden?"

I grit my molars as I drag a deep breath in through my nose. "Mmm?"

Her glazed eyes spark with mischief. "Fuck me."

When she asks me that, in *that* voice, with *that* coy, loving expression, I can't say no. My control is torched. I drag my cock out of her, push back in, and groan at the way her pussy grips me, how her perfect asshole squeezes my finger. She's breathing hard, wearing a sweet little agonized frown of pleasure as I stroke in and out, eyes on her the entire time.

Electricity arcs up the back of my legs. I'm too close. I shift our angle and pull her legs up to get deeper. Her eyes widen the moment my thrusts start rubbing her clit. On my shoulders, her nails dig into me, and her eyes get that faraway look that tells me she's close.

"One more," I beg. "Please, honey. Just one more. Come for me like a good girl."

She nods and I'm overwhelmed with pride. We're both breathing hard when she tightens around me like a fist. My vision blurs—I'll never come back from this excruciating pleasure, and I don't want to.

"Harder," she manages, tense like a bow. "Go harder."

"Good girl, Darcy." Dominance grips me like a fist, and under me, she melts further. "Come around your best friend's cock."

Her lips clamp together and her eyes close as she squeezes my length so tight I can't stand it anymore. Fire races through me. I drop my head to her shoulder, chanting her name. I can't think, I can't speak, I just shatter. It's the orgasm that goes on and on, suspending us in time and space. The rest of the world disappears. Every thought, every heartbeat, every cell in my body exists for Darcy and Darcy alone.

We come down breathing hard against each other, and I press my lips to her temple, holding her tight. After we've cleaned up, I tuck her against my chest, where she belongs.

"I feel like I won something, with you," I confide to her like a secret.

She hums, smiling, trailing her fingers over my flat stomach. "I feel the same way."

I WAKE the next morning with a spectacular view of Hayden sleeping, bare-chested, golden skin, and a soft, relaxed expression on his handsome face. He sleeps soundly, broad chest rising and falling and lips parted slightly. Through the giant bedroom windows, mountains soar out of the lake, and I'm filled with an overwhelming sense of peace. I'm careful not to wake him as I slip out of bed to make coffee in the hotel suite kitchen.

Everything is perfect—until I check my phone.

On the counter behind me, the hotel room's espresso maker whirs and drips as I stare at my phone screen, rubbing the sleep out of my eyes. I'm just wearing one of Hayden's t-shirts, my hair's a mess, and I'm barefoot, but my relaxed sleepiness clears like I've been dowsed in ice water.

I have so many notifications, I don't know where to start. My pulse skyrockets. A new group chat with Georgia, Hazel, Pippa, Jamie, Rory, Alexei. Hayden's in it, too, but obviously hasn't responded. Direct texts from Georgia, Hazel, Pippa, Alexei. Texts from my parents, a bunch of old coworkers, and the other analysts. Two missed calls from Georgia, one last night and one this morning. Another missed call from Alexei. A call from Ward.

We had our phones on *do not disturb* for the wedding, and when we got back to our room, checking them was the last thing on our minds.

Don't panic, Georgia texted last night. *We're dealing with it.*

Dealing with *what*? I panic harder, pulse racing and stomach in knots. *We're going to sort this out*, Alexei messaged around midnight.

What the hell are they talking about? I scan through the group chat—they're all furious about an interview. They ask what room we're in. Kit's name appears and my eyes go wide, heart in my throat. I google *Kit Driedger*, and the first video is a press interview from yesterday, after Calgary's first playoff game.

Kit's face appears on the video with the Calgary team logo behind him.

"You and Vancouver Storm forward, Hayden Owens, are longtime friends," the interviewer says. "During last week's game against Vancouver, though, it seemed like you were targeting him. Fans are speculating that your behavior during that game is a result of Owens having his best season yet while your stats are lagging. Is there any truth to this rumor?"

Kit folds his arms over his chest, scowling. "No, there's no truth to it. I don't give a shit about him." He swallows hard. "And I bet it's a hell of a lot easier to have a good season when you're getting special treatment from the team's new data analyst, if you know what I mean." He raises his eyebrows, and his implication is clear.

There's a long pause of silence before all the reporters begin asking questions at once. I don't hear what they say after because of the blood pumping in my ears.

Something crumples in my chest.

In an instant, he cut down everything I do with the team, all my hard work and passion for my job. He slapped a big *unprofessional* sticker on me. Shame surges, coiling and sinking in my stomach, and my eyes sting.

How could I have been so wrong about someone?

"Darce?"

My head snaps up. Hayden strides toward me with a concerned frown, shirtless, just wearing his black boxers. I wish I could fully appreciate how adorable he is, all sleepy when he just wakes up, but instead, I'm reeling, spinning out, floundering.

Still speechless, I hand him my phone and hit play. His jaw grows tight as he watches the video, his muscles tense. "What the fuck?"

I stare at the screen in disbelief. "How could he do this?"

What did I do to deserve this? Is this really who I was with for eight years?

"Darce." Hayden sets the phone down and places his hands on my shoulders, turning me to face him. "I'll deal with this."

I scan through the rest of the messages, and one sticks out. *Call me*, Ward texts.

I call him, but it goes straight to his voicemail. Hayden makes his own phone call while I stare out the window. I don't think Ward would fire me for this. I've done nothing wrong, but drawing this kind of attention to the team isn't good. I've met the owner once—a nice man in his sixties with a kind smile. While he seems like the kind of patient guy I can see Ward turning into one day, I doubt he's pleased with this, either.

My mind goes to four years ago, when I sat in my boss's office as he fired me for my mistake. I was so focused on not repeating the past that I didn't even see this coming. I was looking in the wrong direction the whole time.

The pain of taking someone down with me rings sharp and clear like it was yesterday. Hayden's proven himself as an incredible forward without my help, but now that the media has gotten ahold of our relationship, he'll never get full credit for the work he's put in.

"Yep, okay," Hayden says into the phone. "I'll be there in two hours." He says goodbye and hangs up before turning to me.

"I need to talk to Ward," I tell him.

"He's already in his office." Hayden rakes a hand through his hair. "He must have driven back last night to deal with this."

While everyone else was dealing with my mess, I was wrapped up in Hayden and our own little world.

"Let's leave." I swallow and glance around at the hotel suite. We planned to spend the day in bed and drive back tomorrow, but we can't hide anymore.

I know what I need to do. This time, I'm not taking anyone down with me.

WE ARRIVE at the arena in record time. We barely spoke the whole drive, each of us consumed by our own thoughts, but outside Ward's office, I pause, touching her arm.

"Can you wait outside?" I ask her.

Her jaw is set. "No. I want to talk to Ward."

"I want to talk to him first." I swallow past the knives in my throat, barely keeping my shit together. I'm so fucking mad at Kit, but more than anything, I need to protect Darcy. "Please?"

"No." Her eyes flash with determination.

I sigh. She can be so stubborn when she wants something, which I still find cute, even if it's inconvenient. "We'll go in together."

After knocking, we hear a muted *come in*, and open the door to a tired-looking Ward behind his desk.

He waves us in. "Let's tackle this."

We take a seat, and I rest my elbows on my knees, watching him. This is my fault. I pissed off Kit. I kept my feelings for Darcy from him for years. He's retaliating against *me*, but she's getting caught in the crossfire.

I love her, and I'll protect her forever. I don't want to do this, but I don't see any other way.

"Once playoffs are over, I'd like to formally request a trade."

Trades are allowed again as soon as playoffs end. She's worked so hard for her dream, and I won't be the reason it's over. I won't compromise her happiness.

"*What*?" Darcy pitches forward to look at me, jaw dropping and eyes flashing with anger. "No."

Behind his desk, Ward's eyebrows lift in surprise.

"Yes," I tell her before turning back to Ward. "Trade me. I'll go anywhere, and I don't care if I play defense or offense."

Not the complete truth. I've come to love playing offense, and I'm good at it. My whole way of playing has changed in the past few months, my personal life mirroring it, but I'll take whatever I can get and I won't complain. This way, Darcy can stay in her dream job.

I'm not thinking about how things were so perfect until this morning. I'm not going to dwell on how things could have been. How it could have been forever.

"You can make the announcement today," I add, but Darcy's shaking her head. "Darcy can keep her job. There's no conflict of interest, and the whole thing goes away."

Every part of me revolts at the idea of moving out, leaving her, not seeing her for long stretches during the season, but I can't see another solution.

"No." I've never heard Darcy use this stern, commanding voice. She looks Ward dead-on. "Let me go."

It's my turn to look at her in shock. Ward starts to say something, but I cut him off. "*That's* your solution, Darcy? To leave the job you're perfect for, after years of hating your career?"

"I can easily find a new job in Vancouver," she tells Ward, ignoring me. "The media shitstorm goes away, and you can hire another analyst. There are plenty of us out there."

I stare at her, furious. How could she think this was an option? I'd never agree to this. "You're finally happy again."

"So are you," she shoots back.

Ward clears his throat. "Can I just—"

"That's because of you!" My voice is loaded with urgency and frustration. "I'm finally happy because we're together, and I'd do anything for you."

When our eyes meet, she looks at me with such love and care that my heart cracks in half. "You love this team. You love living here. You've finally found your spot. I'd never let you go to a new team just for me."

"I would. For you, Darcy, I'd do anything."

"I *know*." She presses her lips together and sucks in a tight breath. "And that's why I can't let you do it. I can find a job in Vancouver and we can stay together, but if you get traded"— she swallows hard, frowning down at her hands—"it's a death sentence for us."

"It's not."

"It is. It'll be so hard, Hayden. Eight months apart, with both our schedules? We'll barely talk on the phone or text, let alone see each other." She looks so fucking sad. I want to kill Kit for doing this. "You have years left in your career. How long can we really do that for?"

Within her words, I hear her actual question. All those things we saw at Streicher and Pippa's wedding, the life we want together, that's all on hold until we can be together again.

Some guys like Volkov play until their mid- to late thirties. It's rare, but it happens. I can't ask her to wait until then. To wait for me. Something in my chest wrenches with pain.

I hate both options. Both of them take something away from us.

"I don't know what to do," I admit, scrubbing a hand down my face.

Ward sighs. "Both of you be quiet for a moment," he says, not unkindly. "You've each made up your mind, but it isn't your decision." He cuts each of us a sharp look. "Either of you."

Darcy's face goes red, and I grit my teeth, sitting back in my chair.

"Neither of you are going anywhere." He folds his arms over his chest. "And if you would have let me get a word in edgewise when you barged into my office, I would have told you that." The corner of Ward's mouth tips up like he's amused.

Darcy and I glance at each other, hope rising in our eyes.

"I'm very selective and deliberate about who I hire," he continues, "and I only hire the best, including a stellar public relations department, who has been all over this since the second Driedger opened his mouth and insulted one of our own." He raises his brows at Darcy. "This job is a calling for you, isn't it? It's not just a job. It's your purpose."

She nods. "Yes. I finally feel like I'm in the right spot."

"I know." Ward reaches for a TV remote and turns on the screen on the opposite wall. Sports highlights play on mute and Ward fast-forwards until he finds what he's looking for.

"This aired twenty minutes ago." He hits play, and the sports reporter speaks.

"*Coach Tate Ward has made a statement regarding the allegations of a conflict of interest against the Storm's recent data analyst hire, Darcy Andersen. 'Darcy Andersen is an incredible statistical data analyst who approaches her role with the utmost professionalism. She is a valued member of the Storm family, and any comments to discredit her based on her relationship with Hayden Owens are sexist and degrading, a problem women in STEM face every day. On behalf of Ms. Andersen, the Vancouver Storm will be donating $100,000 to the Vancouver* *chapter of Women in STEM and making the nonprofit organization one of our official causes.'"*

The reporter turns to her colleague at the desk with raised eyebrows. *"That sure sends a message to Driedger."*

My heart is in my throat as Ward turns the TV off and leans back in his chair, regarding us.

"The team has posted on their social media in support of you. Your old colleagues from Eckhart-Foster have spoken out about your professionalism and talent as an analyst. The Women in STEM group obviously are supporting you, and Jesus, even your old university profs are weighing in." He regards Darcy. "Don't let some jerk who's bitter over something personal drag you down with him. You're not leaving." He looks to me with a stern look. *"You* aren't leaving." He looks between the two of us. "Are we clear?"

Darcy and I sit there in shock. I'm not leaving, she's not leaving, and the future we wanted together is no longer in jeopardy. We glance at each other. She starts to smile, and my mouth tips up as relief surges through me.

"We're clear," I tell Ward, smiling at Darcy.

"Crystal clear." Darcy offers her own relieved smile.

"Good. Now, please get out of my office." He nods at us. "See you Monday."

I stand and hold my hand out to Darcy. When she takes it, I pull her out of his office.

When we're finally outside the arena, walking through the park under the cherry blossoms, Darcy stops walking and turns to me with a worried expression.

"There's something I need to tell you."

"I LOVE YOU," I tell Hayden under the cherry blossom trees while the April sun shines down on us, glinting in his hair and making his eyes look more blue than the ocean. "I should have said it last night, but I froze up because I was scared. I didn't trust myself. I was scared I'd hurt you or I'd disappear into your life."

He watches with a small smile, listening patiently, and I rest my hand on his firm chest. Beneath my palm, his heart beats steadily. A breeze lifts a lock of hair that's fallen onto his forehead, and more cherry blossoms flutter from the trees.

Love blooms all around us, and I see it so clearly now.

How could I ever think I'd lose myself in this man? Wrong again, Darcy. He'd never let me. He tried to give up everything so I could keep a job I love.

"You would never let that happen," I tell him. "With you, I'm the best version of myself."

I look over my shoulder at a nearby bench, the one we sat on a couple of weeks ago. "I sat under the cherry blossoms, watching you play hockey with those kids, and realized my life was undeniably better with you in it." My breath catches with emotion as I gaze up at him.

With every fiber of my being, I hope he feels the same way.

Longing and pure affection flare in his eyes. "I love *you*, Darce. I always have. I love you more than I thought possible. You make me feel like the person I want to be." He laughs to himself. "That's why A.R. Haddington sent me the book, I think. I told her the story of us, how we bonded over her books, but I told her that I love you and that I've loved you for a long time. We know she's a romantic."

Hayden wraps his arms around me, pulling me against him, and I rest my head on his chest, listening to his heartbeat. His lips find my temple and he gives me a kiss.

"Always?" My pulse skips a beat as I lean back to look up at him, so tall and gorgeous. The man of my dreams who was right in front of me the entire time.

"Always. I never loved you like a friend, Darcy. It just took me a while to figure that out."

"Me, too," I whisper.

His hands wind into the back of my hair and he tips my face back, catching my lips with his. The kiss is soft, sweet, and gentle, but he tugs my bottom lip between his teeth and drags a finger down the back of my neck, making me shiver at the promise of more once we get home.

My head spins as he leans back to wink at me. "Come on."

As we walk home beneath the cherry blossom trees, I look up at him with a question in my eyes. "I told you the moment I fell in love with you. What about you?"

His mouth tilts into a roguish grin. "Remember that night I got hurt?"

"The big hit?"

He nods.

"Wait." I laugh. "You fell in love with me because of a blow job?"

Hayden shakes with laughter. "I've loved you always, but

that's when it hit me." He takes a deep breath, still smiling down at me, joy radiating from the depths of his eyes, from his skin, from the air around him. "No one's ever taken care of me like that, Darcy. If I wasn't in love with you then, that would have sealed the deal."

My heart aches with the sweetness in his words. "Hayden?"

"Yes, Darcy?"

"Let's go home." I wiggle my eyebrows in a mischievous way that leaves no question about what I'm going to do for him.

His eyes light up, and he reaches down before tossing me over his shoulder, and I yelp in surprise, laughing as he starts jogging down the street.

ONE MORNING IN EARLY SEPTEMBER, Hayden and I lie in bed, catching our breath after an enthusiastic round of morning sex.

"Ready for preseason?" I ask.

"Mhm." Leaning back against the headboard, he smiles to himself like he just thought of something. "I used to dread the end of summer. I think because it always meant I wouldn't get to see you as much."

I hum, resting my chin on him. "Me, too. I'd always miss you during the season."

He skims a hand up and down my bare back, toying with my hair and sending tingles down my spine.

At the end of last season, the Storm were eliminated in the second round of playoffs—further than the team has made it in years. The guys were disappointed, but Ward assured them a slow, steady incline is the way to go, and that next season, they'll be even better. He told them he was proud of how they played and he was proud to be their coach.

He looked at Hayden when he said that, and I couldn't help the proud, expanding feeling in my chest.

Along with the players, Ward gave the analyst team the

summer off, but I'm on my laptop every day, tinkering with the models, reviewing game footage, following the data and looking for patterns. Hayden pulled me away for a trip to Hawaii with Jamie, Pippa, Rory, Hazel, Alexei, and Georgia, who still won't speak to each other except for snarky comments. On weekends, we take our new boat out, meandering through the Gulf Islands, watching the sun sparkle off the water.

After the media shitstorm, rumors that Kit didn't get along with his teammates anymore were only amplified when his contract ended without renewal. He's a free agent now, but no team has picked him up. He created this mess, but I still pity him. Hayden and I have so much, and in comparison, Kit's life has gone down the toilet.

Summer being over means we're going back to real life, but with Hayden, our "real life" feels better than I could have imagined.

There's something I've been wanting to tell him for weeks. I focus hard on trailing my finger over the ridges and lines of his chest.

"I'm ready for a ring. I mean, if you want to. Or, when you're ready to give me one."

His eyes spark, but they narrow like he's confused. "What do you mean?"

"I mean..." I suck in a deep breath. "When you're ready to give me a ring and take the next step, I'm ready to say yes."

He scratches his head, making a confused face.

"That thing we talked about at the end of last season?" I widen my eyes and make a gesture between us. "The thing I was super nervous about in the past but am no longer nervous about with you because I love you and want to be with you forever?"

"You want to get a dog?"

"Ask me to marry you!" I burst out. "I've been waiting all summer!"

He doubles over, laughing, and my jaw drops in annoyance, but I can't help but laugh, too. "Hayden. You're being obtuse on purpose."

His chest shakes and the smile he gives me warms me from head to toe. "Yes, honey, I know what kind of ring you're talking about. I've had it for months."

My heart stops. "You have?"

His gaze is soft, patient, and gentle. "Mhm."

"Where?" I try to get out of bed, but he locks me against him.

"None of your business."

"Can I have it now?"

"No." He snorts. "You can wait."

"But I just said I'm ready." I make a *hurry up* motion. "Let's go."

He laughs again. "I'm not going to propose to you *here*, Darce. It has to be special. You deserve memorable and special." He runs his hand through his hair. "Besides, I wanted to check if you'd rather pick your own out. We can go to a store. You can have something designed. You can get whatever you like—"

"I want whatever you chose for me." About once a month, Hayden buys me a piece of jewelry. He's proven to have incredible taste, always selecting pieces that are special and environmentally conscious. I've told him a million times that I don't need it and that he's spoiling me rotten, but he won't be deterred.

Spoiling me rotten seems to make Hayden Owens very, very happy, actually, and watching him get what he wants makes me happy, so everyone wins.

He tugs on a lock of my hair. "You want a coffee?"

I stare at him. "How can you be so casual when we just had a monumental conversation?"

"It's not monumental to me, Darce. It's been a long time coming, and I've been ready." He slides out of bed and gives my butt a light slap.

I watch him stride out of the room, eyes on his toned ass. "You're really going to make me wait?"

"Frustrating, isn't it?" he says in the doorway, amusement in his voice. "Eight years, honey. That's how long I waited for you."

A low noise of impatience scrapes out of me and I fall back on the bed.

Hayden just laughs and shakes his head, eyes lit up. "And it was worth it."

———

At least a dozen times over the next two weeks, Hayden stops to tie his shoe—in the middle of the street, beside our table when we're out for dinner, on a little bridge over a creek, even in the shower.

"Those don't even have shoelaces," I say when he stops to inspect his slip-on sneakers.

He makes an innocent face. "I thought there was a rock."

By the end of the week, when he takes a knee in the park under the trees with their autumn leaves, I don't even stop walking. He jogs after me, laughing as I roll my eyes and hide a grin.

"Are you nervous I'll say no?" I ask one morning as he washes my hair in the shower, massaging conditioner into my scalp and melting my brain. "Is that why you're torturing me like this?"

"I don't know what you're talking about."

"I'll probably say yes."

"Probably?" Hayden grins down at me, glancing at my chest as water runs down my skin. "You're kidding, right?"

"Two can play at this game."

———

Finally, near the end of September, Hayden and I walk through our favorite park in the cool autumn sun. We approach the bench we always sit on, and his warm hand slips around mine, tugging me toward it.

"Let's sit," he says.

I plop down on the bench. Hayden doesn't sit, though. Hayden reaches into his pocket. My pulse skips, but this isn't the first time he's tried to fool me.

"Ha ha." My smile is indulgent. "Reaching into the pocket now? I see you're leveling up." I squint around the park. "Hmm. Where's the photographer hiding, huh?"

Hayden grins. "About a hundred feet away."

"Very funny."

He sinks to one knee and my confidence falters. The way he's grinning at me, it makes my breath catch.

"You're really taking this joke far today," I whisper, holding his eyes. I think mine are the size of saucers as my heart pounds and my stomach flips over with excitement.

He tilts another grin at me. "Not a joke today."

I'm smiling, nodding, sucking in a deep breath. "Is this finally happening? You're putting me out of my misery?"

He laughs. "Yep. Are you ready?"

Always giving me the choice. I hold his gaze, certain, and nod.

His expression softens and his eyes warm as he takes my

hand. "Darcy Andersen, woman of my dreams, will you marry me?"

"Yes," I say without hesitation, smiling. "I'd be lucky to."

"You haven't even seen the ring."

"I don't need to."

I memorize this moment—the way the sun feels on my skin, the sound of the birds chirping and the kids playing in the park, the breeze lifting Hayden's hair, and the way his eyes are blue like the sky. The feel of my hand in his.

"I'm sure, Hayden, and nothing can change my mind."

He arches an eyebrow and cracks the ring box open.

My jaw drops. "Holy." I stare at the sparkling gemstone, the palest pink, surrounded by a scattering of tiny white stones. It looks like something out of a fairy tale, like a prop from *The Northern Sword*.

And it's going to be mine. I'll get to look at it every single day and be reminded of Hayden.

"You like it?"

Speechless, I nod, and he smiles wider. I'm not really a jewelry girl, but Hayden's slowly changing that.

"They're all lab-grown diamonds, with recycled white gold for the band."

"It's perfect." My gaze rises to him. "You're perfect, and I can't wait to spend forever with you."

He slips the ring onto my finger, and we both smile at each other before he gets up and kisses me.

———

That evening, we open the door of the Filthy Flamingo to a chorus of cheers and applause.

"Congratulations, lovebirds," Rory says, grinning and handing us flutes of champagne.

Everyone is here—our friends, our parents, the team, and my colleagues, even Ward. There's a blown-up photo of us from the park today someone must have taken, of Hayden kneeling in front of me, holding the ring while I stare in delighted shock. From behind the bar, Jordan winks at me, mixing cocktails, and on the specials board above her, there's a new cocktail.

The Wingman—strong, sweet, and cheeky. The drink you didn't know you needed!

After everyone has congratulated us, Georgia pulls me away to inspect the ring.

"It turned out beautifully." Her smile is wistful as she tilts my hand back and forth, making the diamonds sparkle in the bar lighting. "Just beautifully."

My eyebrows lift in a teasing smile. "Did you know about this?"

She scoffs. "Of course. Everyone helped. Even the grumpy Russian." Her eyes dart down the bar. Hayden's talking with Rory, Jamie, and Alexei, who frowns in our direction, then quickly looks away.

Georgia sighs another happy sound and squeezes my hand, a smile softening her features. "I'm happy for you."

"Thanks, friend. We probably have you to thank for this whole situation. You and your obsession with lingerie."

Her mouth tilts, smug and amused. "You both just needed a little encouragement."

I shake my head, grinning. I can't even be mad. "You know who you sound like? Alexei."

She pretends to gag, taking a sip of her drink, and light glints off her hand, snagging my attention.

My eyes go wide. There's a ring on Georgia's left-hand ring finger.

"Wait." I catch her hand to look at the band. "What's this?"

She doesn't usually wear rings, and definitely not on *that* finger.

She shifts, shrugging. "Oh, that?" She clears her throat, gaze darting across the bar to something.

"Yes, *this*."

She taps her upper lip with her tongue. "I got married," she says lightly.

"*Married*?" My jaw drops. "To who? When? *Why*? I didn't even know you were seeing someone."

I will never get married, she said last year during our double date.

Her pale throat works as she swallows, and finally, she meets my gaze. "Volkov."

———

Hayden and I walk home hand in hand, buzzing from happiness and the promise of what's to come. Probably those Wingman drinks, too.

"I guess I didn't make a very good player, did I?"

He laughs. "No, you didn't, and thank fuck for that." His mouth hitches higher as he looks down at me. "I wasn't either. I was always hung up on you."

"I'm okay with that." I bump my shoulder against him. "It worked out in the end. I can't wait to marry my best friend, Hayden Owens."

Emotion flickers in his eyes. "I can't wait to marry my best friend, Darcy Andersen." He stops walking, and with his hand beneath my chin, tipping my face up, he gives me a soft kiss. "I love you."

"I love you, and even though I was terrible at it, asking you to teach me to be a player was the smartest thing I ever did."

He laughs against my lips.

I rise up on my toes to kiss him back, my heart so full of love for Hayden Owens.

* * *

- Alexei and Georgia's book is next, but in the meantime, check out Jamie and Pippa in *Behind the Net*, or Rory and Hazel in *The Fake Out*! Both books are in KU, paperback, and duet audio. Read on for an excerpt from *Behind the Net*.

- want a spicy bonus scene from Hayden's POV? Go to www.stephaniearcherauthor.com/hayden or scan the following QR code:

Pippa Hartley is standing in my living room, playing with the dog, and I can't breathe. When I opened the door, I thought I was hallucinating.

Her hair is longer. Same shy smile, same sparkling blue-gray eyes that make me forget my own name. Same soft, musical voice that I'd strain to hear back in high school while she was talking and laughing with the other band kids.

Grown up, though, she's fucking gorgeous. A knockout. Freckles over her nose and cheekbones from the summer sun and strands of gold in her caramel hair that's neither brown nor blond. Although her braces were cute back in high school, her smile today nearly stopped my heart.

I'm Pippa, she said at the door, like she didn't remember me. I don't know why that made me so disappointed.

"Do you want me to help you unpack?" she asks, playing tug-of-war with the dog. "Or I can get groceries or meal prep for you."

I watch the pretty curve of her mouth as she speaks. Her lips are soft-looking, the perfect shade of pink. They always have been.

Fuck.

"No." The word comes out harsher than I mean, but I'm rattled.

I can't fucking think around Pippa Hartley. It's always been like this.

In an instant, my mind is back in that hallway outside the school music room, listening as she sang. She had the most beautiful, captivating, spellbinding voice I'd ever heard—sweet, but when she hit certain notes, raspy. Strong, but at certain parts, soft. Always controlled. Pippa knew exactly how to use her voice. She never sang in public, though. It was always that fucking Zach guy singing, and she'd play guitar as his backup.

I wonder if she still sings.

I wonder if she's still with him, and my nostrils flare. Over the summer, I saw his stupid, punchable face on a billboard and nearly drove off the highway. *That* guy is the opener on a tour? He could barely play the guitar. His voice was average.

Not like Pippa. *She's* talented.

Eight years later, I still think about that moment in the hallway all the time. I don't know why—it doesn't matter.

The dog shakes the toy while Pippa holds on, and she laughs.

I need to get out of here.

"I have to go to practice." I snatch my keys off the counter and haul my bag over my shoulder.

"Bye," she calls as I step through the door.

———

After practice that afternoon, I'm about to open the front door when a noise in my apartment stops me with my hand on the door handle.

Singing. Fleetwood Mac plays inside my apartment. Over the tune, her voice rings out, clear, bright, and melodic. She hits all the notes, but there's something special to the way she sings it. Something uniquely Pippa.

I can't move. If I go inside, she'll stop singing.

Alarm rattles through me, because this is exactly what I

shouldn't be doing. She was supposed to leave before I got home.

I can't have Pippa around this year. It's only been a few hours, and she's already gotten inside my head.

When I open the door, my new assistant is unpacking the kitchen boxes, reaching up to set a glass on the shelf, leaning forward on the counter, giving me a clear view of her incredible ass.

Irritation tightens in my chest. This is the last thing I need.

My gaze sweeps around the apartment. Most of the boxes are unpacked. She's set up my living room, and the photo of my mom and me sits on the bookshelf. She's arranged the living room furniture differently than my apartment back in New York. The Eames chair faces the windows, overlooking the city lights in North Vancouver, across the water. The dog is sleeping on the couch, curled up in a ball.

I fold my arms over my chest, feeling a mix of relief and confusion. The apartment looks nice. It feels like a home. I was dreading unpacking, but now it's almost done.

I don't even mind that the dog is on the furniture.

Her singing stops and she glances over her shoulder. "Oh, hi." She gasps and looks at her phone on the counter before her eyes dart to mine. "Sorry. I didn't realize what time it was." She dusts her hands off and walks to the door. "How was practice?" she asks while pulling her sneakers on.

The sweet, curious way she asks makes my chest feel funny. Warm and liquid. I don't like it. I have the weird urge to tell her how nervous I am about this season.

"Fine," I say instead, and her eyes widen at my sharp tone. Fuck. See? This is why this isn't going to work. I care too much about what she thinks.

"Daisy and I went for a two-hour walk around Stanley

Park, and then I spent most of the evening training her to do tricks."

My eyebrows pull together. "Daisy?"

She shrugs, smiling over at the dog on the couch. "She needs a name." She picks her bag up. "I took her out an hour ago, so you don't need to."

I try to say something like *thanks,* but it's just a low noise of acknowledgment in my throat.

She smooths a delicate hand over her ponytail, blinks twice, and gives me that bright smile from before, the one I thought about during my entire practice.

Her cheeks are going pink and she looks embarrassed. "I'll get out of your hair." She loops the strap of her bag over her shoulder and gives me another quick, shy smile. "I'll be here tomorrow morning after you leave for practice. Good night, Jamie."

My gaze drops to her pretty lips, and I'm tongue-tied. She probably thinks I've been hit in the head with the puck too many times.

She leaves and I stand there, staring at the door.

Maybe I don't have to—

I crush the thought, like slapping a mosquito off my arm. Pippa has to go. I know from my mom and from the one relationship I attempted in my first year in the NHL that if there are too many balls in the air, I'm going to drop one. I always do.

The second she leaves, I pull my phone out and call Ward.

"Streicher," he answers.

"Coach." I rake my hand through my hair. "I need a new assistant."

Behind the Net is available in KU, paperback, and duet audio now!

ACKNOWLEDGMENTS

Thank you for reading *The Wingman*! Like all my other books, this one was written with a lot of help, guidance, and support, and I have some thank you's to hand out:

Jane Miao, thank you for telling me all the things you love about being an actuary. Your enthusiasm for your work lit my brain up like a firecracker. Thank you for not being weirded out by how obsessed I am with actuaries. Any errors in the portrayal of actuarial science are mine, not Jane's.

Becca Hensley Mysoor, thank you for your smart guidance, plot rocket fuel, and excitement for Hayden and Darcy. Working with you is so rewarding.

Chloe Friedlein, thank you for illustrating yet another mind-blowingly gorgeous cover, and thank you, Echo Grayce, for putting it all together! Big thanks to Beth at VB Edits and Brooklyn at Brazen Hearts for your excellent editing eyes.

A massive thanks to my beta readers: Esther, Marcie, Wren, Ycelsa, Jess, Brett, Nicole, and Cal. Thank you for your hilarious, insightful feedback, and for making this book so much better.

To my agents, Flavia Viotti and Meire Dias, thank you for believing in me and my books, and for your relentless support and kind guidance.

Rhea Kurien, Ellie Nightingale, and the rest of the Orion team: thank you for taking a chance on me. Working with you has been a dream come true.

Every book, the list of author friends I have to thank grows longer, and what a freaking fantastic problem to have. Thank you to the following authors for the support, love, plot voicenotes, weird gifs, book recs, and laughs: Grace Reilly, Olivia Hayle, Lily Gold, Penn Cole, Brittany Kelley, Ursa Dax, Bruce, Sophia Travers, Kyra Parsi, Samantha Leigh, Helen Camisa, and Maggie North. Becoming friends with all of you has been one of the most rewarding parts of this career.

Aimee Cox, I think about you every day, how brave, funny, smart, and special you were. I'm thankful our paths crossed, and I miss you.

To my Tim, because best friends make the best husbands. I love you so freaking much, and I can't wait to watch you be a dad. Let's be terrified together.

Lastly, thank you to my incredible readers. I really have the best, funniest, kindest readers in publishing, and I'm so grateful for you all. Thanks for letting me live out my dreams of writing romance.

Until next time,

Steph

THE VANCOUVER STORM SERIES
STEPHANIE ARCHER

He's the hot, grumpy goalie I had a crush on in high school . . . and now I'm his live-in assistant.

After my ex crushed my dreams in the music industry, I'm done with getting my heart broken. Working as an assistant for an NHL player was supposed to be a breeze, but nothing about Jamie Streicher is easy. He's intimidatingly hot, grumpy, and can't stand me. Keeping things professional will be no problem, even when he demands I move in with him.

Beneath his surliness, though, Jamie's surprisingly sweet and protective.

When he finds out my ex was terrible in bed, his competitive nature flares, and he encourages and spoils me in every way. The creative spark I used to feel about music? It's back, and I'm writing songs again. Between wearing his jersey at games, fun, rowdy parties with the team, and being brave on stage again, I'm falling for him.

He could break my heart, but maybe I'm willing to take that chance.

Behind the Net *is a grumpy-sunshine, pro hockey romance with lots of spice and an HEA. It's the first book in the Vancouver Storm series and can be read as a standalone.*

The best way to get back at my horrible ex? Fake date Rory Miller--my ex's rival, the top scorer in pro hockey, and the arrogant, flirtatious hockey player I tutored in high school.

Faking it is fun and addictive, though, and beneath the bad boy swagger, Rory's sweet, funny, and protective.

He teaches me to skate and spends way too much money on me.

He sleeps in my bed and convinces me to break my just-one-time hookup rule.

He kisses me like it's real.

And now I wonder if Rory was ever faking it to begin with.

The Fake Out *is a pro hockey fake dating romance. It is the second book in the Vancouver Storm series but can be read as a stand-alone.*

My arrogant fake fiancé? I can't stand him.

Cocky and charismatic Emmett Rhodes isn't a relationship kind
of guy, but now that he's running for mayor of our small town, his
bachelor past is hurting the campaign.

Thankfully, I'm the last woman who would *ever* fall for him.

We're total opposites—he's a golden retriever and I'm sharp
and snarky, but he'll co-sign on my restaurant loan if I play his
devoted fiancée. Between romantic dates, a prom night re-do,
and visits to a secret beach, things heat up, and the line between
real and ruse is lit on fire. I'm starting to see another side of Mr
Popular, and now I wonder if I was all wrong.

**We can't keep our hands off each other, but it's all for show . . .
right?**

*A sizzling, hilarious, enemies-to-lovers, fake-dating rom-com with
an HEA. This is the first book in the Queen's Cove series and can be
read as a standalone.*

The hot, commitment-phobe surfer is the only one I can turn to . . .

In my small town bookstore, I'm surrounded by book boyfriends, but I've never had one in real life. At almost 30, I've never been in love, and my bookstore isn't breaking even. Something needs to change, and I know exactly who's going to help me: Wyatt Rhodes, the guy everyone wants.

He agrees to be my relationship coach, but his lessons aren't what I expected.

Between surfing, mortifying dates, and revamping my store, his lessons are more about drawing me out of my shell than changing me into someone new. But when we add praise-filled 'spice lessons' to the curriculum, it's clear he wants me. He's leaving town and I'm staying to run my store, so it can't work, but that doesn't seem to matter to him.

He's supposed to find me someone to fall for but instead, we're falling for each other.

A sizzling, hilarious, small- town, friends-to-lovers romantic comedy with a guaranteed HEA. This is the second book in the Queen's Cove series but can be read as a standalone.

The deal is simple: the grumpy guy will pay off my debt if I find him a wife.

Holden Rhodes is grouchy, unfairly hot, and has hated me for years. He's the last person I'd choose to inherit an inn with. As we renovate the inn and practice his dating skills, I see a different side of him.

What if I was all wrong about Holden?

When we add 'friends with benefits' to the deal, our chemistry is so hot the sparks could burn down the inn. Holden's a secret romantic, and I'm secretly falling for him.

I'm terrible at bartending, a video of a bear stealing my toy went viral, and everyone in this small town knows my business, but Holden Rhodes is so much more than I expected.

I don't want him to find love with anyone but me.

A spicy, grumpy-sunshine, friends-with-benefits, small-town romantic comedy with an HEA. This is the third book in the Queen's Cove series but can be read as a standalone.

The guy who broke my heart is now an arrogant, too-hot fire-fighter … who's hell-bent on getting me back.

This summer, I have one goal: field work. I need it to finish my PhD. I never expected Finn Rhodes to offer help. He broke my heart twelve years ago, and now that he's back in town, I want nothing to do with him. The only problem? He insists we're meant to be together.

I'll pretend to date him, but actually? I'm trying to get him to dump me.

Between hiking the back country and cringe-worthy dates designed to turn him off, I begin to remember why we were best friends. Despite how hard I try, Finn isn't interested in dumping me … and now I'm not sure I want him to.

Finn's always been trouble, but now he's a different kind entirely. The kind that might break my heart. Again.

Finn Rhodes Forever *is a spicy, second-chance, re-verse-grumpy-sunshine rom-com. This is the fourth book in the Queen's Cove series but can be read as a standalone.*